NEON

G.S. Locke is a British crime writer whose roots lie in the Black Country. Locke is a keen amateur classical pianist.

NEON

GS LOCKE

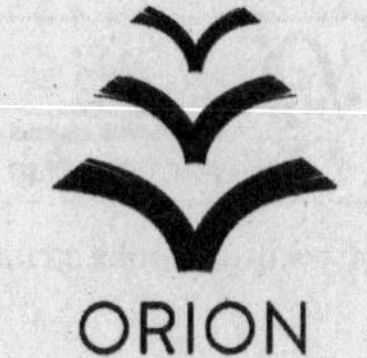

ORION

An Orion paperback

First published in Great Britain in 2020
by Orion Fiction
This paperback edition published in 2020
by Orion Fiction,
an imprint of The Orion Publishing Group Ltd.,
Carmelite House, 50 Victoria Embankment
London EC4Y 0DZ

An Hachette UK company

1 3 5 7 9 10 8 6 4 2

A CIP catalogue record for this book is available from the British Library.

ISBN (Paperback) 978 1 4091 9046 2

Typeset at The Spartan Press Ltd,
Lymington, Hants

Printed and bound in Great Britain by Clays Ltd,
Elcograf S.p.A.

www.orionbooks.co.uk

In memory of my mom and her family
who came from the Black Country.

1

He stared down at the solitary cup of coffee he'd ordered over an hour ago, still full to the brim.

A firm hand clasped his shoulder and the leather of his jacket creaked. 'You want another hot one?'

Glancing up, he met Roberto's gaze, and winced.

'Sure,' he said. 'Sorry.'

One of many things Matt Jackson had discovered since Polly's death was that he hated being an object of pity. At the funeral, only days ago, he swore police colleagues viewed him with a mixture of compassion and something akin to loathing. Especially that prick, Marcus Browne. The Detective Chief Inspector in charge of Polly's case and newly appointed SIO on the 'Neon' investigation – *his investigation* – Browne had had a hard-on for him from the get-go. Spouses shot to the top of the murder suspect list in all homicides, but the suggestion that he'd offed his own wife in a sophisticated form of copycat killing had tempted him to lure Browne down a dark alley and punch the living shit out of him.

'Double espresso, Andrea,' Roberto called over his shoulder, 'On the house.'

The pressure on his shoulder intensified.

'You doing OK, Matt?'

It wasn't a question that required a truthful answer. He played along, mumbled something neutral, his reply buried in a blast of beans grinding, milk frothing and flashing chrome. Particularly sensitive to light at the minute, he blinked.

'Early days, my friend,' Roberto said, 'You need rest. You need *sleep*.'

If only. On the rare occasions when his mind wasn't hooked on replay and he'd slept, he'd prayed Fate would step in and ensure he never woke up.

The door opened, letting in a blast of cold, wet November air, along with more customers. Clatter and bang; *Are you all rights?* and *Mornings*. Glad of the distraction, he twitched a dry smile, his way of saying, *I'm OK. Go, meet and greet*.

With a fresh coffee back on the table, he retreated once again into the shadowlands of loss and loneliness. How long could he endure? A day, maybe two – three at a stretch? Fuck it. Better get this over and done with.

Reaching into the back pocket of his jeans, he slipped out a Post-it note, on which Kenny Flavell, one of his long-time informers, had scrawled a number in smudged Biro.

Taking a breath, he punched the keys on his phone. Two rings.

'John speaking.' The voice-enhancer created the impression of a bad guy making ransom demands in a terrible nineties action movie.

Spooked, Jackson hung up, sending his phone skidding across the Formica table. The espresso slopped over the side and into the saucer. *Uncool*. He glanced around, flashed a sorry to anyone interested enough to witness his less-than-collected performance – which meant nobody.

Calm, he thought, *breathe*. It's what Polly would say and, for a moment, he pictured her sweet smile, charged with quiet confidence and steadfast belief. She had tamed him where others had failed – apart from the last six months when he'd buckled under the weight of an investigation that robbed him of sleep and reduced him to the mania of an obsessive. Days and nights he'd spent in front of a computer screen, clicking through crime-scene photos, looking for common denominators, searching for the smallest of clues. To his profound shame, he'd been unreachable and hostile to anyone who'd got in his way, and that had included his wife. Jesus Christ, that was bad enough. But what happened next haunted his every waking breath and, worse, he hadn't seen it coming.

Taking expert advice, he'd believed that serial killers adhered to certain patterns of behaviour, lived by some invented sick-and-twisted code, and selected a particular type of prey, usually vulnerable women, although not exclusively females. They favoured familiar terrain, which, in this instance, was the streets of Birmingham. The piece of shit he'd hunted got his kicks from powerful career types; the more confident, the more appealing. This guy had a genuine taste for the dramatic, the sensational, the eye-blinding; he loved the artistry, if that's what you could call it. Like some perverse Banksy, he came, he did his thing and he left. And nobody noticed. Which was almost as shocking as the manner in which he displayed his tableaux of terror. Reckless, a hybrid of planner and opportunist, 'Neon', as the Press had dubbed him, got off on very public displays of his work.

With a dry mouth and churning gut, Jackson considered Vicky Wainright, Neon's first victim. A newly-qualified solicitor from Durham, she found herself separated from friends on a hen weekend. On a night when the clocks went back, she was lured to an apartment near Mailbox, an obscenely large square edifice and shopping centre in-corporating retail, office and residential, and adjacent to the BBC building. There, and despite the area being security-patrolled, Vicky was strangled.

The high-pitched buzzing sound, a consequence of the thermal effect of gas expanding and contracting within the tube itself, was the first thing he'd noticed on entering the crime scene. A door left open to a balcony revealed a spaghetti trail of wires connecting to a transformer plugged into the mains inside the living area. The transformer powered numerous neon signs.

Vicky's fully-clothed body was arranged outside on a sun-lounger. She could almost have been sleeping, were it not for the stench. The newly dead have a distinct smell with which he was only too familiar.

Up close, there were telltale marks around her neck from the ligature used to break her hyoid bone. Petechial showers blossomed below her eyebrows and on her eyelids – a result of strangulation. He'd witnessed similar before but had never seen a body lit up in lights like a fairground attraction. The effect was the same as if the woman had been entombed in coloured glass. Comms almost went down at Lloyd House under the strain of dozens of members of the public calling it in.

A neon image depicting a grotesque red open mouth with tongue sticking out hung above her head, the UV in the fluorescent tubes strong enough to incinerate retinas and throw false shadows over her features. Somewhere in the back of his brain, he was reminded of a Stones album cover – *Sticky Fingers* – that had a similar motif.

Transfixed and bewildered, he didn't appreciate that the 'work of art' was home-grown until later. Not so, a vintage sign planted in front of the body, with the word 'End Game' beamed to anyone brave enough to view. He'd felt sick as well as sickened, yet hopeful that the reclaimed sign would provide a lead.

Investigation traced it to an outfit in London that had gone out of business a decade before. No receipts. No records. The DNA picture was confused because the apartment was let out on a regular basis, a human soup of material left behind.

Two months later, the discovery of a second victim clanged alarm bells loud and long throughout West Midlands Police. To his shame, when the call came through that the killer had struck again, dark excitement had rippled through him. He'd regarded it as a fresh opportunity. It wasn't brain surgery: the more kills, the greater the chance of nailing 'Neon'. Not that he'd shared this thought with Vanessa Booth's parents.

A pharmaceutical rep from Salisbury, Vanessa had attended a conference in the city. She, like the previous victim, was outside her comfort zone. Like Vicky, and in common with most partygoers cruising or stumbling down Birmingham's Broad Street, she'd drunk a fair bit and wasn't warmly dressed for a bitterly cold night. In other words, to a nutjob, she was fair game.

Entering through the huge cast bronze doors of the Hall of Memory in Centenary Square, only recently reopened following redevelopment of the surrounding area, Jackson had been greeted by a sight that was as searing as staring into the sun during an eclipse. Directly at the foot of a sarcophagus-shaped dais and memorial to the fallen soldiers of the World Wars, Vanessa lay naked amidst an arrangement of flickering light, as if wrapped in alternating colours of purple, lime green and sickly yellow – a stark contrast to the stained-glass window at the rear of the building. MO was the same. The emptiness in her eyes, the inertness of her skin and degree of lividity suggested that she'd been dead for several hours, which was the one major difference. The flimsy dress she'd worn lay casually draped over a bronze and glass casket that contained two books of remembrance. The senior crime scene manager had flagged it because the shrine was obscured by a free-standing sign that claimed, 'Jesus Loves,' which at that moment in time, Jackson had felt could not be further from the truth. The letters extended to three feet wide by two and a half feet tall. Smack in the face. Single finger up. *Fuck you.* What should have been a place for quiet, sombre reflection assumed the gaudiness of an amusement arcade in a seaside town at the peak of the season.

And while every contact left a trace, the killer had been tidy and sterile and savvy. *Fuck him.*

March saw the next victim, Gina Jenks, a journalist from a national tabloid. With Gina, he thought he'd caught a break.

Hoping to make a name for herself, maybe even see it in lights in the accepted sense, Gina had been investigating the 'Neon' serial killer case. She'd spent a week in the Midlands and, old story, asked too many questions in too many places. Her abandoned car was found in nearby Smethwick, but her body was discovered astride the huge seven foot three inches tall bronze bull and focal point of the Bullring in Birmingham city centre.

Dressed in a forensic suit, he'd stood, slack-jawed, trying not to recoil, and thought, *Holy Christ*.

Lights poured from every angle, refracting and bouncing off the existing illumination from shop windows of the mall. A mish-mash of free-standing retro movie signs, one flashing 'Some Like it Hot', buzzed and crackled with sound. He felt as if he were standing in the middle of a hornets' nest. Neon was odourless, but Jackson smelt something sour and rank: fear.

Dizzy, a nasty pulsing sensation building in his brain, he'd struggled to focus. His mouth felt dry and his lungs tightened in his chest. Squinting hard, cutting through the visual crap, he'd eventually found Gina. A homage to Lady Godiva, her skin was sheened in a glittering array of rainbow colours, dazzling in its vulgarity. An extension of the sculpture, designed to seem as if hanging from the bull's neck, a sign with Gina's name alight in fluorescent neon pink. If he'd had any doubts about the killer's abilities to plan, stalk and abduct, they vanished in a heartbeat.

And then there was Polly, a full six months later, with whom 'Neon' had excelled himself.

Bile filled Jackson's mouth at the memory and, with it, the desire to finish what he'd started.

The clang of a dropped milk jug made him jump, and he

picked up the phone again and hit redial. This time he stayed on the line. He felt nervous. Wary.

'I'd like to order a takeout.'

'From the set menu?' The sound of the voice-changer fizzed in his ear.

'Please.'

'And you're familiar with the terms of payment?'

'I am.'

'When would you like it?'

He coughed. 'Ten o'clock tonight.'

A heavy pause.

'Is that a problem?'

'No. Do you have an address?'

He gave the name and number of a house in King's Heath, a suburb five miles south of the city centre.

'Any particular problems with access?'

'None. It's set back from the road with a drive.'

This was met with a grunt of approval. 'What's the name?'

'Matthew Jackson.'

'Description?'

'Thirty-eight-year-old white male, six foot one-inch, eighty-three kilos, brown eyes, brown wavy hair, pale colouring, full bottom lip and scar on left cheek. I'll send a photograph now.'

Job done, he drained his cup and stood up, catching sight of his haggard reflection in the mirrored wall opposite. Staring back was a man he no longer recognised. He only hoped the hitman he'd hired to kill him wouldn't have the same problem.

2

Iris Palmer lived on a street that politicians would tell you was a triumph of multiculturalism. Iris didn't see it that way. There were posh areas in Edgbaston, but she lived in a shit bit, where ethnic groups lived in isolation and treated others with disdain or, worse, disinterest. The West Indians she'd grown up with had moved on and the Asians had moved in. The Asians disliked the Poles. The Poles disliked the Romanians. She, as a young white woman, didn't figure at all. Suited her. She wasn't looking for mates.

From the upstairs window of her flat, which sat between two houses, a condom's width apart, she had a glimpse of the cut – its dirty depths reflected off a dark and threatening sky. The letting agent, a bloke with a nasal Birmingham whine, had told her to appreciate the waterside view. Knobhead.

Grabbing her go-to 'stakeout' bag, which today contained a dog lead, clipboard, mace spray and an Ordnance Survey map that covered the target area, she slipped down the stairs on the balls of her feet, and quietly let herself out.

The cold thwacked her like an icy flannel clamped over her face. A last look back and, with a sigh, she headed off, wishing she felt better. For nights now, she'd been unable to sleep. The looseness of her clothes revealed that she'd dropped kilos. Gone right off her food, which was unusual. Weight loss she could cope with. Insomnia, she couldn't. A woman like her needed fast reactions.

Her destination that morning was a garage chucked up between Mr Mo's and Eastern European Mrs W, as opposed to Bengali Mrs W. Fuck knows how you pronounced their surnames. 'Sandwiched between things' was a hallmark of the architecture and the people in this part of the city.

A pair of boots sticking out from beneath a clapped-out Vauxhall Cavalier, circa 1993, soon announced she was at journey's end. She kicked the undersole of the nearest boot. Legs followed by torso, followed by arms and, finally, a head crowned with oily black locks emerged. Iris reckoned Keith Parish kept Brylcreem in business single-handed.

'How am ya, Iris.'

She couldn't tell whether the Black Country greeting was designed to honour her roots or whether he was taking the piss. She didn't reply, got straight to business. Her eyes alighted on a small white van parked up near the MOT section. Keith followed her gaze.

'Fuck, Iris, what will I tell the owner?'

'That he can have it back in a couple of hours.'

Keith wiped his grubby hands down his overalls, pursed his lips, as if he were giving the idea due consideration.

'Don't play the businessman. You still owe me.'

The mention of the debt had a galvanising effect. 'I'll get the keys. Need it back by dinner.'

Eight minutes later, a track from Wolf Alice banging out

from local radio, she was cruising at speed-camera-pace down the Hagley Road alongside all the other little worker bees whose pay cheques would magically land in their bank accounts at the end of each month. Not for them the cut and thrust of the independent operator.

As Alice, or whoever, sang about being bored to death, Iris's mobile vibrated against her chest. Interruptions were a constant in her line of work. Eyes flicking right and left – couldn't risk getting done for a driving offence in a 'borrowed' motor – she slipped out the phone, clocked the number. If major organs could sink, hers plummeted. She switched off the radio, pressed 'receive'.

'Iris?'

'Yes.'

'It's Mr Gudgeon.'

She knew who it was. Still couldn't get her head around why a consultant in oncology wasn't called doctor, but that's what the man insisted on. 'Hello, Mr Gudgeon.'

'Would it be possible for you to come in?'

'When?'

'Could you make it in the next half hour?'

When a senior quack wants to see you pronto, you know it's trouble.

She pulled a face. She ought to crack on. Check out the terrain. Make sure that the address, as described by the client, was exactly as he said.

'Iris, the results of the tests are back and I can't stress how important it is we talk. We've always been straight with each other. You understand, don't you?'

She understood. 'How long?'

'Pardon?'

'Be straight, like you said.'

'I'd rather we discuss this face to face.'

'I need to know.'

'Iris—'

'Now.'

Gudgeon let out a tired sigh. 'A month, two perhaps. I can't be sure. Osteosarcoma survival rates vary. Some patients can defy all expectations.'

She thought about that. Was it possible? Dared she hope? What was it she'd heard someone say: *Without your health, you can forget it – money, job, the lot.*

She looked in the rear-view mirror, indicated for the hospital.

'I'll be there in ten.'

The man in the photograph could wait.

3

Matt Jackson stepped out into St Paul's Square, rolled the collar of his jacket up and shivered. How to spend his last twelve hours? Most would spend it at home, except he no longer had one. When his house became a crime scene, he'd taken a one-bedroom apartment in the Jewellery Quarter. Somewhere temporary, to hunker down, stay warm, shelter and hide. He had no sentimental attachment to it, but it would be better there than freezing his nuts off out here. First, he would pick up a bottle of Scotch. It might warm him up and suspend the nerves he'd feel later.

At ten a.m., the pubs were still shut, apart from those that had turned themselves into twenty-four-seven eateries serving breakfast. He dropped into one favoured by the Fraud Squad. Sean, the landlord, was accustomed to his occasional requests for bottles of booze at strange times, no questions asked.

'The usual?' Sean said. A big man with hands like paddles and a serious number-one haircut, he looked more bouncer than publican.

'Make it two.' Jackson forced a smile that made his jaw hurt. 'I'm feeling . . .' What was he feeling? He wasn't feeling lucky.

'No reason needed,' Sean replied, producing two bottles of Bell's.

Jackson pulled out three twenties. 'Keep the change.' He wouldn't need it where he was going.

'Wouldn't dream of it, mate.' Sean plunged his fat fingers into a till. 'Here.' Handing back the cash, he said, 'Buy yourself a couple of ice creams.'

Jackson pitched another smile, thanked him, picked up the booze, snuck both bottles under his arm and trudged towards his temporary lodgings. He'd drink until it was time to leave. Seemed only fitting to die in the place he'd been happiest with Polly.

Histories' old businesses associated with the jewellery trade, Georgian architecture, creative workshops that had sprouted as part of an urban initiative, tourists attracted to the arty vibe that distinguished the Jewellery Quarter from the rest of the city – all of them passed him by. His sole purpose was to get drunk and, with luck, enter that perfect state of grace between oblivion and not quite being out of it.

Back in the flat, he banged up the heating, splurged on the sofa, and poured himself four fingers of booze, swallowing neat. Fire and malt and earth. Pouring more and lifting the glass to his lips for a rerun, the intercom burst into life. Jackson cursed. If he didn't answer, maybe whoever it was would go away. He took another pull of Scotch. This time, the noise was accompanied by a familiar voice.

'Matt, open the sodding door. I know you're in there. I've just seen Sean.'

Jackson let out a groan, knocked back the contents of his glass, got up, crossed the floor and pressed entry. Within seconds, Mick Cairns was standing in his kitchen-cum-living area with an expression on his thin face that told Jackson he was a disappointment. It was there in his eyes, downturned at the corners, downturned mouth too.

'What?' Jackson said, challenging. Since when had he become a lightweight? Since downing a quarter of a bottle of Scotch before eleven, he guessed.

'Getting pissed won't bring Polly back.'

'I don't need you to tell me.' The challenge morphed into full-blown boozy bellicosity.

'And it won't help you get back your . . .' Mick cleared his throat, unable to find the right word.

'Mojo, is that what you were going to say?'

'Self-esteem, as it happens, but I thought it sounded too touchy-feely.'

Cairns sat his bony frame down on the nearest chair. Matt had never considered it before, but Mick's sharp features had more than a touch of the rodent about them.

'Matt, we're worried about you.'

'Don't be. I've got it sorted. Want a drink?'

'No.'

'Mind if I have one?' His hand was already around the neck of the bottle. His brain felt clogged, mired in self-pity, but that was OK.

'It won't help you catch a killer.'

At this, Jackson had to smile. 'You seem to forget I'm off the case.'

'Only in name.' Mick reached into his jacket, pulled out a flash drive and placed it on the coffee table between them.

Jackson stared at it like it was a grenade about to detonate. He looked back up.

The lines around Mick's eyes sharpened. 'Have you any idea the risk I ran? I could lose my job, my career . . .'

'At least you won't lose the wife,' Jackson said with dry humour.

'True,' Mick agreed, softening a little. 'Did I tell you she's shacked up with an insurance salesmen?'

Jackson spun the cap back on the Scotch, leant towards his friend and, latterly, his colleague. 'What's on it?'

'Everything you need to know about Polly's murder. Post-mortem report, crime scene and case notes, interviews with witnesses, details of Marcus Bullshit's briefings. In essence, the works.'

'Jesus, Mick, what the hell am I going to do with them?' The thought of stepping back into the void, and that's what it would be, scared him more than the prospect of a bullet to his brain.

'Find out if we missed something.'

Jackson dry-swallowed, pulled the whisky bottle towards him. His hand shook. 'Unlikely. Marcus Browne is a rules merchant. Does everything by the Murder Book.'

'Not quite. He agreed with your suggestion not to release the details of Polly's death, remember?'

Which was true. The official line was that it had been a robbery gone badly wrong. His idea. This way, the press were unable to sensationalise the case and feed Neon's undoubted vanity. Jackson hoped it pissed off the killer mightily.

'Matt, we're getting nowhere.' Mick spoke quietly. Made his plea harder to resist.

'Look, Mick, I appreciate all that you've done, but, truth is, I'm too damned close to it. I lack the *necessary objectivity*.' He spat the final words.

'And how will you feel when another poor woman rocks up in the centre of the city as part of this year's Christmas decorations?'

'I'll be sad.' He wouldn't, because he wouldn't be around to see it.

'You know he isn't going to stop. He's only just getting started.'

Jackson shot him a mournful expression. Surely, Mick was wrong. Polly's murder – oh my God, he couldn't go there – indicated someone very much at home with the dark arts. Neon had peaked. At least, he hoped he had.

'It's worth one last shot, isn't it? You know the Neon investigation better than anyone. It's only due to operational reasons you're out of the loop with Polly.' Mick glanced at the table where the flash drive sat, squat and uncompromising. 'I know it's hard, mate.'

Hard? It was impossible. He felt broken. No, *was* broken.

Mick stood up. 'I'll leave it with you. If you take a look, fine. If you don't, I won't hold it against you. Just bear one thing in mind.'

'What's that?'

'Marcus Browne stands as much chance of solving this bloody investigation as I do of spending the night in the White House.'

'You want me to do this for the team?' Matt snorted.

'I *want* you to do it for Polly.'

Bastard, Jackson thought.

4

Rejection is as corrosive as guilt. It gnaws away at the soul, tainting the simplest pleasures. When he killed again, it would be their fault for ignoring his finest work and failing to show him the respect he deserved.

For weeks, he'd waited for news to break. Every time he woke up, he'd expected to see headlines, columns of newsprint, digital sound bites, radio discussion, maybe even a debate in Parliament. What had he got? Sod all. Bitches and bastards, the lot of them. This was what travelled through Gary Fairweather's mind as he entered his Colourdome.

Every whitewashed wall charted his progress from keen amateur to expert 'shaper'. (His novice stuff he'd left behind in Vegas, along with the bodies.) Prototypes for some of his more exotic creations luxuriated before him in a kaleidoscope of dazzling colour, alongside snappy little messages: 'Death Becomes Her' and 'See What You Want' glittered in hues of krypton green and yellow.

Gazing at the saturated light, he found it hard to imagine how far he'd come since those early days when it had taken him weeks to attain even a basic level of competence.

He'd suffered for his art, all right, with cuts and burns and blistered skin. But each creation had started the same way, with a humble pencil-drawn design, and finished exactly the same, with a dead woman, her name in beautiful sparkling lights. What better way to make an exit?

His mind drifted to poor old Vicky. She might have been clever but how naïve, how absolutely fucking gauche?

Arriving with huge expectations, she'd first registered surprise, confusion and then excitement and thrill. He'd more than do as an alternative, her eyes said. Of course he would, he thought, recalling her painted face framed by strawberry blonde locks, and earrings more commonly found on a fortune teller. Several sheets to the proverbial wind – 'to give me courage', she'd trilled – turned on by the risk she *thought* she was taking. Judging by her 'bunny in headlights' reaction when, too late, she registered the danger she was in, she'd clearly not drunk nearly enough.

It was a similar story with gym-fit Vanessa. Did nobody tell her that vodka cocktails are a really bad way to finish an evening? And she was a drugs rep, too. (He hadn't known it at the time, only read about that afterwards.) *Obviously*, Vanessa's drug of choice was socially acceptable, high concentrations of ethanol. Who needs heroin when you can go loco on alco?

Hers was such a peachy seduction, he remembered. Acting the Good Samaritan, he'd picked her up from the gutter into which she'd recently vomited. He'd found it hard, if not downright repugnant, to grab a part of her that wasn't bare moist flesh because, like our Vick, Vanessa was a fan of the 'I don't care if I get hypothermia' style of fashion. She had been embarrassingly grateful, right up until the last few moments before he struck and grim reality set in. Closing his eyes, he pictured her pretty heart-shaped face, the blonde bob and those wet trusting eyes.

In his experience, the lead-up to the kill never went the way so-called experts described in terms of fight or flight. It went fright and more fright. Imagining those last perfect moments, before Vanessa's light faded and she dribbled away gave him the ultimate high.

Time to map out his latest design. He got a genuine kick out of crafting an installation from scratch. Taking a 6B pencil from his extensive collection, chewed at the end (terrible habit, he knew), it was the perfect choice for the idea already fully formed in his mind. With a big sweep of his arm, he committed his first line and curve.

Several lines later, he paused, nibbling the top of the pencil. This little beauty was going to throb and pulsate and bedazzle. They wouldn't ignore him this time.

5

No blood. No bondage. No exchange of bodily fluids.

Before stepping into hell, Jackson switched on his laptop, looked at the file notes he'd illicitly kept and went back to the beginning of the investigation. Aided and abetted by two pots of strong coffee and the heating turned down to zero, he felt better, less drunk, more in control. This was his terrain and he was familiar with it. And he had nothing left to lose.

Methodically studying every millimetre of material confirmed what he already knew: that Neon had no particular physical preferences when it came to his choice of victim. Blonde, brunette, dyed red, plump or slim, short or tall, birthmark or scar, none of it factored. The only common thread: all were successful, solvent, independent thirty-somethings. Oh yeah, and they were white.

Going back over the first three crime scenes, it was clear that Neon didn't panic, took pride in his 'art' and care in removing the tools of his trade, including the ligature he used to strangle his victims. This guy was forensically aware. He chose public places because his DNA would meld in nicely with the DNA of hundreds of others.

But he'd fucked up with Polly.

Jackson warily eyed the flash drive left by Mick. *I'll look at it in a minute,* he thought. *Just need to get my head back in the game first.*

And Neon was cunning.

Birmingham was awash with CCTV, but not every road and alley was covered. When a drunk gets lost, whatever the gender, he or she tends to get very lost indeed. The massive scale of redevelopment in the city, with the ensuing chaos it created, had also aided and abetted a determined and imaginative killer. After studying acres of film, the police had tracked Vicky Wainwright so far, but then she'd vanished. With Vanessa, it was assumed that Neon had used the same tactics to snare her; so easy to slip your arms around a drunk woman, pretending to keep her away from the road and guide her to safety. A couple of witnesses had reported seeing a male figure of medium height and build, wearing a hoodie, pushing a slumped woman in a wheelchair on the night in question towards Centenary Square. It wasn't clear whether or not this was Neon or whether the woman was his second victim. Close, tantalisingly so, but nothing concrete.

And with Gina Jenks, it didn't get much more public or audacious than staging his grim light show around the iconic bull, unofficially known as 'Brummie the Bull', officially known as 'The Guardian'. This time Neon had callously taken advantage of another man's crime.

Jackson ran through the notes once more. Ten days before, Damien Lee, tanked up on Bacardi and Banks's Bitter, had vandalised the sculpture. Savvy enough to recognise that it was ringed with sophisticated CCTV, he'd pointed a handheld laser at the security network to block his activities. Like most small-time criminals, his IQ was limited; Lee failed to grasp that his ugly mug would be caught on film prior to disabling and damaging the cameras. After two previous incidents, the five-tonne bull had been taken away for repairs, but, on this occasion, work was to be carried out in situ. Large screens were erected around it – giving perfect cover for Neon to set up, arrange his tableau and power it up, care of a portable generator. The woman who turned up the next day to repair the damage to the sculpture had to be taken to the Queen Elizabeth hospital to be treated for shock. The big question had focused on how the killer had transported the body to the site.

Following Jackson's instructions, his team discovered that, in a very busy shopping area, the streets are swept up to seven times in a single day and, often, this starts in the early hours of the morning. Initially, they wondered whether Neon was one of the council workers, and thus granted access to vehicles that could help shift a body, but interviews with those employed drew blanks. The next working theory: Neon had disguised himself, no doubt wearing a high-vis jacket, easy with so much redevelopment taking place in the city, helped himself to a compact sweeper from the City Council depot and bundled Jenks inside.

Jackson took another drink of coffee, now as cold and still as the air outside the window.

In his head, Neon was a loner, a saddo, a guy who couldn't get it up. Just because he hadn't penetrated his victims didn't mean that his actions lacked sexual intent. The fact he could fade into and away from crime scenes suggested someone as colourless as the chemical element in the neon he used to display his victims. He was Mr Forgettable.

Except, Jackson would never forget. Closing his eyes, he rubbed the lids, struggling to prevent a kaleidoscope of grotesque images from taking shape.

Taking a deep breath, trying to steady his pulse rate, he returned to the facts once more. None of Neon's victims displayed defence injuries and this suggested a killer who came across as vulnerable, weak and harmless. The women never saw death coming until too late. This was the view Jackson had adopted, the one he'd believed in and pushed.

But what if he were wrong?

Serial killers were not always uniform in their actions, he'd been reliably informed. Circumstances might change, as they did with Gina Jenks, the journalist, whose stomping ground had been outside of Birmingham city centre but who Neon had found nonetheless. After spending an afternoon at the Black Country Museum, she'd visited a pub in Gornal, another in Tipton renowned for many things, including wine on tap and cash-only transactions, and the last in Oldbury. Jackson imagined that a well-dressed woman from London would have received nothing more than a sideways glance and 'Are you drinking, or not?' when she attempted to pump locals for info – that's if she could understand what they were saying in the first place. He was born in Penn near Wolverhampton and even he struggled when questioning the regular clientele in those parts. And they were protective and suspicious when it came to talking to the police even about a serial killer. If anyone knew anything, nobody was saying.

Unlike the craftsmen who worked in the lighting industry.

According to enquiries made, Neon was an accomplished 'bender' – a colloquial term used by artists in the trade. Asked how long it would take to learn the craft to a high standard, eight years was deemed average, so either Neon did it professionally or he was a uniquely talented amateur. Should have provided a lead. It didn't. Well, not one that led anywhere. The big disappointment had come early when analysis of the actual glass tubing had thrown up inconclusive results.

The other big line of enquiry focused on how Neon carted around the tools of his trade. This was a man who went about his business well equipped. Clearly, he hadn't travelled by bus. Odds on, he'd driven a van. Which wasn't great. The sheer volume of vehicles made it feel like searching for a particular pint glass in a pub. But hunt they did. CCTV footage was scoured, registrations logged in an attempt to cross-match. They didn't. By now, they were drowning in data generated from hundreds of phone calls, including those from cranks and fantasists. The more they eliminated, the more they kept on coming, like zombies from *The Walking Dead*. Pressure from the top brass, an impatient local MP, the media and a terrified public had him and his team working around the clock. *Any* connection between victims, tenuous or otherwise, in an attempt to find commonality, led nowhere. With everything against them, not least the city itself, with its bright lights and traffic, people and anonymity, morale had nose-dived.

He glanced sideways. He was stalling and knew it. Morning had drifted into afternoon. Time to get it over with. Before he lost his bottle, he picked up the flash drive and jammed it into his laptop. He was stone-cold sober. It was the right way to be, but it didn't feel good.

6

Iris felt like shit. After over an hour with Mr Gudgeon and ten minutes at the pharmacy – *Could you come back later because we're out of the drugs requested?* – she was back on the road and entering King's Heath. She'd be late getting the motor back, but, after the morning she'd had, she couldn't care less.

Not one to overthink, she looked back on her life with the sober eye of the dying. She hadn't been afraid of the lad who'd tried to abuse her at the children's home, the bloke who'd recruited her for drug running when she was a kid, the woman who'd tried (and failed) to put her on the game the second she got kicked out of the care system. Snitches, thieves, rapists and drug lords (bottom league, none of your international players) held little fear for her. She wasn't afraid of homelessness, sleeping rough, hunger or the streets. Deal with it was her motto. And deal with it she did. She prided herself on her ability to survive, but she wasn't at all sure she'd pull through the scenario painted by Mr G. She felt a first flicker of something that could be described as fear. She guessed there was an irony in that.

She dropped down a gear, the van slowing so she could have a good look. *Nice area*, she thought. Independent shops and cafes gave it a villagey feel. Shame about the charity shops.

According to the map, the house was midway between King's Heath central and Yardley Wood, and close to Billesley Common. She liked stretches of open space and wastelands. Nicely amorphous and made it dead easy to pretend to be a dog walker.

She parked the van on a wide stretch around 200 metres from the location, took out the dog lead, pulled a baseball cap down low, wrapped a scarf around her neck, partially obscuring her face, and sauntered down the road. The house was exactly as described: set back. Better still, it was up a drive, on an incline, with big tall trees on either side. Private. And private was good. Which was the only thing about this gig that pleased her.

The alarm system looked real, not some piece of fake window dressing. Technically, she could disable it, but that would take time and energy. More optimistically, if the target were in situ, then the alarm was unlikely to be primed. Not so the cameras, which were a different proposition. Her best bet was to yank out the wires first and smash the cameras later. All stuff that would slow her down, but these weren't the biggest issues.

Normally, she'd study a target, for days sometimes. She'd familiarise herself with his routines – always a 'his' and usually an arsehole – and find out whether or not relatives and friends could potentially screw up the hit, or whether the target had a big dog gagging to take lumps out of her. Never a problem, but it made sense to be as prepared as she could be, which wasn't easy without having sight of the victim in the flesh. With a ten p.m. deadline, time was not a luxury and that's how mistakes were made.

Walking past a little way, she turned on her heel as if she'd forgotten something, then returned for a second pass. This time, she stooped low to tie an imaginary shoelace so that she could have a good gawp and work out the best way to access the property. Thirties-style, three-up and maybe three-down, with a bay, it looked like a family home. Hmmm. She was getting a bad vibe. Then she remembered Mr Gudgeon. All in, including accommodation and flights, she needed around £500k and quickly.

She'd tuned out when he explained that it paid to read the small print before signing any treatment plan. When he wandered off into legalese and stuff about medical ethics, she'd almost laughed. She didn't give a shit about morality. She didn't give a monkey's about the theory behind the treatment either, or that only 'specific molecular profiles were accepted', whatever the fuck that meant. She just wanted to know if it worked. *Please.* He'd shuffled the papers on his desk, muttered something, she'd thought 'Guinea pig'. But slim hope was better than no hope if it could make the illness go away forever, and forever was a long time.

If she had enough loot.

Maybe she should put up her prices.

Secluded or not, the main entrance was a no-go, even at ten o'clock at night. With a gravelled drive to give her away, the side entrance would be risky. It left one alternative.

Iris sprung up, continued walking and turned left, straight

into a service road that ran parallel to the main house. This was more like it, she thought, a smile cracking her face.

Before her, an up-and-over garage, that was impenetrable, with a door next to it that was equally solid. How many times did people concentrate on the barrier but not on the hinges that held the barrier in place? And these were knackered. Once she was in, she'd approach the house from behind, most likely over lawn and garden. Break in. *Bang bang.*

7

Mick was damn right. When Jackson opened the folder, there were hundreds of files. To nick this level of material, he must have gained access to Marcus Browne's secure laptop, or somehow hacked into it, which was a bloody dangerous game. Either Mick's techie skills were impressive or he was a reckless fool.

Normally, Jackson would go straight to the crime-scene shots. He wasn't ready yet. Instead, he started on the file notes, Browne's mistaken thinking smeared over every single entry.

Jackson saw how Browne had made a classic error. He'd got hung up on two unassailable facts: no forced entry to the family home and an absence of defence injuries on Polly. In other words, she trusted the killer, which Browne determined was her husband. What Browne failed to recognise, Polly trusted everyone. She was that kind of woman. Kind and unassuming, always looking at the good in others, these were the qualities that had once rescued Jackson. That they'd also got her killed and catapulted him to numero uno in the suspect stakes made him flash with unexpected anger. *If only* she'd been more savvy. *If only* she'd listened to him. A hazy memory of him saying as such to Browne under caution reminded him of Browne's reply: 'So there were tensions in the marriage, Matt?' Of course, there were bloody tensions. He'd been trying to run a triple murder investigation, with several boots pressed down on his neck, and he was running out of road.

'Did you ever indulge in autoerotic or unusual sexual practices?' Jackson knew where Browne had been going with it. The nature of Polly's death had stoked that particular half-baked theory. He'd arranged his face into a picture of implacability and told Browne the truth: 'No.'

In the end, timing, a cast-iron alibi and a pathologist had saved him. When Polly was murdered, he was updating and explaining his lack of progress to several officers above his pay grade, including the new youthful and talented Assistant Police and Crime Commissioner. Had it not been so, Marcus Browne would have had him banged up, no question. Nothing like bagging one of your own. Think of the kudos.. And everyone knew what happened to coppers behind bars.

Jackson scratched his head. White noise. Ancient history. *Focus.*

Having discounted his prime suspect, Browne now leant towards a killer that was already in the system somewhere. He had him notched as a loner, not a local man but 'one who knows the area well and commutes for crime, not a man that wishes to draw attention to himself or the place he calls home.' On reading this, Jackson cracked a wolfish grin. This guy was all about attention, you dick. He wants to be admired. Everything about him shrieks 'showman'.

Jackson continued reading: 'Strong possibility Neon has an accomplice, someone to attract the attention of the intended victim and help transport the bodies.' News to him and he wasn't certain it chimed. At one stage in the investigation, Jackson had wondered whether Neon had an inside man in the road sweeping department. How else to borrow a road sweeping truck? Interviews had proved inconclusive but maybe worth another shot.

'Neon is a killer that hangs out at bookies and bars and uses prostitutes.' Jackson thought about that. There was nothing in the victims' histories to suggest a connection to prostitution, although all women had been sexually active. Another rabbit warren in which to disappear. Admittedly, while Browne's cobbled-together profile might once have resonated, Polly's death had changed all that.

Grim, Jackson clicked to witness statements, sifted through in the same way a forensic accountant goes through the figures, looking for those giveaway clues that will prove the Finance Director is fiddling the company and defrauding it of millions. So much irrelevant stuff. So much arbitrary garbage. And then . . .

A man walking his dog had reported someone hanging around near the house 'as if casing it,' he'd said, 'although it didn't register at the time.' Jackson frowned. How often did well-meaning members of the public offer observations for police officers to interpret as cast-iron evidence?

He read on. The witness mentioned a car. 'Might be black or grey. Not sure if it was a saloon. *Might* have been.' When asked for a registration, the witness was at a loss. When asked for a description, the witness replied 'a man of medium height, medium build. Couldn't really get a close look because it was dark.' *Jesus.*

Grudgingly, Jackson had to agree that Browne's situation could not be worse. House-to-house had yielded nothing. Checking out sex offenders, the same. Trawling through records, ditto. Without hard, specific information as opposed to mountains of mindless information, there was nowhere to get a foothold, and every case needed one of those from which to spring. Browne was doing the equivalent of hurtling down a run on a luge. Any time now, it would pitch him out and slam him into the side of the walled-in track at ninety miles an hour. Screw him.

Click, click, next up: the pathology report.

Jackson took a deep breath in through his nostrils and cut straight to the chase.

Unlike the other victims, Polly had been asphyxiated. According to Dr Weston, 'The ligature mark was on the right side.' Death had occurred due to 'compression of the neck'. As with the other victims, the killer had removed the ligature, 'the pattern of neck injury suggested a tendency towards the right,' therefore it was assumed the killer was right-handed. Marks and bruises indicated 'that the ligature, which could be leather, was cinched with a tourniquet'. This prolonged the process of dying, Jackson thought bleakly, and Polly would have suffered.

He dug the nails of both hands into the soft flesh of his palms. Small mercy that she had not been sexually assaulted and the knife wounds to her face were inflicted post-mortem. He noted that the blade used to carve the killer's rage into his wife's features had one sharp edge, possibly from a common or garden kitchen knife. He'd used it to coerce her, Jackson thought. Had he done it with the other women? The threat of injury would allow the killer to get up close and personal every time. With Polly, it had been very personal indeed. It would be a hell of a thing to be that close, within kissing distance, and watch someone's final struggle with death and lose.

He caught his breath, realised that he was shallow breathing. He clicked off the pathology report and switched to the crime-scene shots. Instantly, he felt that obscure fear he'd experienced when he first put his key in the lock. When calling Polly's name there was no answer. Instinct had taken over. Something bad had happened. He recalled music drifting from the music system in the living room. Polly, catholic in her tastes, would often play her favourite tracks when she got home. He hadn't recognised the cover version and, by the time he'd shot upstairs and into their bedroom, everything closed down around him, including time itself, and he was stuck fast in a tunnel of terror and screaming colour.

Mute, in shock, his eyes had flicked up to a motorised disco ball mounted with LED lights, hanging from the ceiling. It crackled and spat and taunted. On the far wall, above their king-sized bed, a huge parrot, alight in neon red and yellow, an illuminated palm tree next to it. Erected against adjacent walls, a tableau of similar birds, in tacky reds, glaring yellows and iridescent purples and blues. The illuminated disco ball delivered a strobe effect and his eyes had physically hurt with the sensory overload. He recalled squeezing them briefly shut. When he'd opened them, his gaze had travelled to their bed, where Polly lay spread-eagled upon it, long blonde hair cascading across the pillow. Her face, bathed in a blue-white glow, was twisted to one side, her brown eyes half-closed and empty, the tip of her tongue protruding through her teeth. He registered straight away that she was dead. But he had checked anyway. Felt the coldness of her skin, traced the marks to her neck, the cuts to her cheeks. A cross-hatch of wounds, he keenly remembered.

Somewhere, in the thinly functioning part of his brain, he grasped that the killer had been painstaking in his preparations. Thorough. Spending an ocean of time in the house, he'd luxuriated in every second. And he wanted Jackson to know it, the subliminal message: *This is your home and I can do whatever I like in it. I own you.*

Neon does not generate heat. It's cool to the touch. Jackson had felt as if he were in a sauna. Sweat had poured off him.

Fully clothed, Polly wore one of the dresses she kept especially for the infants' school at which she taught. It had been pulled up above her waist. She wore white knickers, but they were smeared in blood from the blade used by the killer to carve his rage into her face. Except, Jackson hadn't known it at the time. Provocative and deliberately sexually misleading, he had felt misled. Against the headboard, a sign in purple that read: 'Not So Pretty Polly.'

As he'd gaped, a primal sound of pain that he'd never heard before split the air in two. His.

8

Iris thought that Kevin Joyce's face, with its grey, deoxygenated skin and lines, looked like crazy paving.

Made redundant when the local steel factory closed – 'Too much fucking Chinese and Turkish steel,' according to Kev – he'd opened a tattoo parlour in Cradley Heath. If you walked up the high street, you'd spot a dip in the road due to subsidence, marking the exact location of Keith's commercial enterprise. Having said that, many shops and houses still stood after a hundred years.

Body art was not the only side of the business; Kev had diversified into a more lucrative trade: guns. It was the only reason she was standing in his gaff so late in the day.

'What time do you call this?' He took a fistful of keys from his jacket and hovered before a steel door at the back of the property and similar to those found in crack houses.

'Ten past eight,' Iris said, deadpan.

'Don't get fucking funny.'

Sorry wasn't a word with which Iris was familiar. Had she bothered, the consonants would have got snarled on her vocal cords.

'Had to get straight off my plane,' he grumbled with a wheezy whine.

'Donkey said.' Kev's gopher also said that Kev had been up to no good on the Costa del whatsit. Rumour had it that Kev was hooking up with a couple of ex-clients on the run. Iris thought that was bullshit. Those days were long gone and Donkey's news past its sell-by. She didn't doubt that Kev was up to something because he always was, but she had more important and pressing matters on her mind than whatever criminal enterprise Kevin Joyce was plotting. She'd already wasted time with one pointless trip to Cradley that afternoon, then another to the pharmacy that was only marginally more satisfactory. After that, it had been a dash home, quick bite to eat – never work on a rumbling stomach – and back out again. Last thing she needed now was for Kev to go all moody on her. She needed a gun. She needed it clean. And she needed it now. 'Nice holiday?'

'Shits and sangria, seeing as you asked.'

She wished she hadn't.

'Here we go,' he said with a flourish of keys, as if he were rattling a tambourine. 'Step into my lair.'

Had Iris the time, she would have had a good nose. Donkey had been busy. Racks of rifles and machine guns neatly hung on all three walls, pistols and revolvers in the type of glass compartments found in your local jewellers. Iris spotted a Ruger LC9s – small and light and a perfect conceal-and-carry weapon that would fit perfectly into a bra holster. Next to rounds of ammo, which were stacked according to calibre, two big grey units that resembled those fancy-pants American fridges. 'Winchester' was helpfully inscribed on the outside to denote the type of pump-action shotguns contained inside. Nice.

'Impressive, isn't it?' Kev's pride was mirrored in the rheumy gleam in his eyes.

Iris tipped her chin – the nearest he was going to get to a compliment. 'I need a Glock,' she said, letting her gaze drift to a compartment closest to where she stood.

'Model?'

'22, with a silencer.'

'On tick?' Kev sniffed.

'I'll pay at the end of the month, like always.'

'You've run up quite a bill.'

Something in her expression made Kevin Joyce bunch up in alarm. Good.

'Course, Iris,' he stuttered, 'you're one of my best customers. Whenever is fine by me.'

She watched as he took out a smaller key, inserted it into the locked compartment. Nervous. Deep down, Kev knew he was just a small fish rather than the big-time criminal he pretended to be, Iris observed with pleasure. Two seconds later, she had a gun in her hand.

'Ammo on the house.' He thrust a box of 9mm at her, with what could have been a smile. Hard to tell with all those lines and tattoos on his face.

'Ta,' she said, pocketing the goods. 'Won't hold you up.' She reached for her helmet.

He might have said *No problem*, *Good luck* or *Go Steady*. It was drowned out by the clang of the door shutting and a sudden surge of traffic as she made a sharp exit. Iris pulled down the visor, gunned the motorbike she normally used for personal business and drove towards the city at a steady lick.

She'd already booked a cab, private, not one of those approved by the council. Aside from scouting out the location and equipping herself with a screwdriver, a set of skeleton keys, balaclava and a wad of cash, it was the only planning she'd undertaken for the job. Not good. She had her own way of working, her own little superstitions and every one of them had flown out of a high-rise window and smashed to bits on the tarmac below.

Worse, time was tight – and not just for the job.

9

Knowing the enemy was essential as far as Gary was concerned, and he'd more than done his homework on Detective Chief Inspector Jackson. Gary knew about Jackson's dead parents – aw, sob – the place where he'd grown up – nice but dull – the school he'd attended –mixed secondary – even his fucking grades: two C's and a D, which, frankly, proved that Mr J was a massive underachiever. It probably explained why the prick had failed to find the clue he'd so conveniently left for him, a source of gnawing frustration for Gary. How he'd hoped that the DCI was smarter than that, but, then again, Jackson *was* a police officer. Dare he say it – oh yes he would – after what he'd got away with on *both* sides of the Atlantic, Gary thought that, as a profession, they were piss-poor. With his type-A personality (perfectionist, competitive, demanding and expecting the same high standards from others), he was not minded to make allowances for the dim and disappointing. Why should he? *And* they all got paid way more than him.

The question in his implied message to Detective Jackson was clear and simple: 'Wanna play?' Of course, there was an alternative scenario: maybe Jackson *had* found the clue but failed to respond which was sheer bad manners. And where the hell was his curiosity, his spirit of adventure? How else was the detective occupying his time now his darling wife had fucked off to the great primary school in the sky? Officially signed off work on compassionate leave (Gary had his sources), what did the man do all day? Did he booze his head off, eat his own body weight in fish and chips, or pies (very Midlands), *sleep*? If there was one thing Gary couldn't stand, it was whiny, self-pitying mopers.

Gary let out a pained sigh. Jeez, if only Jackson would wise up, they could have such a blast, acting out cops and robbers, for real. He'd be the badass, obviously (chicks got turned on by bad boys, didn't they?), while Jackson could man up and do what he got paid for. Gary had it all mapped out: the murders, the tastefully arranged lighting displays, the chase, *the sheer fucking drama*.

What's not to like, detective?

The anticipation of what might be almost spun him out. But first, he thought darkly, the lazy fucker needed to take the bait. In Gary's head, he'd only staged the equivalent of a home invasion into Jackson's sad and dull little life. He hadn't yet had the opportunity to mess him around before his final glorious dispatch. Just what would it take to drag Jackson, kicking and screaming, back into the game?

10

Jackson got up, went to the kitchen area, ran the tap, sluiced water over his face and poured a tumbler, drinking the contents straight off.

Returning to his laptop, he clicked to video footage recording the interior of the house. He wasn't only searching for clues. He was looking for mistakes, some slip that would give Neon away.

Serial killers often took physical evidence from the victim: hair, skin, rings and necklaces popular keepsakes. This wasn't Neon's thing, but he might have taken another form of trophy to enable him to relive those last chilling moments once more and drool over Polly's last dying breath.

Jackson shuddered, resisted the urge to throw up and glanced out of the window. Day had become evening, the fast-approaching night jewelled in lights. In just over an hour it would all be over. Carrying out this last act before his death was his way of accepting that he'd done his best and couldn't do any more.

Video footage began at the hall and moved throughout the entire downstairs section. It explored the living room, the kitchen-diner, utility and cloakroom. Jackson trailed along in the crime tech's wake. Having shipped out following the murder, Jackson hadn't been back in a while. It felt strange to see the place he'd called home through such a dispassionate lens. He tried to shake off the sensation, and focus. Intuitively, he knew that it would have to be something personal to Polly for Neon to receive the most kicks.

Like him, Polly was tidy, by nature, and a minimalist when it came to interior design. They had few paintings on the wall. One large photograph of them together he'd taken down as soon as he was given the all-clear; he could no longer bear to look at it. Neither of them were hoarders, nor did they collect ornaments and knick-knacks. Polly was not like some women when it came to trinkets. She had favourite bits and pieces but never lusted for jewellery. Anyway, Browne had already verified that nothing had been stolen during a conversation in the course of one of his interviews. Similarly, her clothes and underwear, as far as Jackson could tell, were right where she last left them. Polly's only indulgence was her books: hardbacks, paperback, the old-fashioned kind. She took a Kindle with her on holiday. Her tastes, in common with her music, were varied, although she steered right off crime. She said she got enough of that at home. His heart creased at the irony. By contrast, he only read stuff when he was on holiday, usually science fiction, an escape into another world, another reality.

Her collection of cookery books sat in the kitchen on a shelf next to the cooker. He scanned remotely. Nigella and Gordon and Jamie were there, grinning out of the shiny covers. The bookcases in the hall and living room had no gaps that he could see. Would he even notice if one went missing? Why would Neon help himself to a piece of literature in any case? This was a pretty desperate last chuck of the dice, he thought ruefully.

Upstairs, stubbornly ignoring the bed, stripped now of its sheets and mattress, Jackson noticed Polly's collection of bedtime reading, which lay undisturbed. Children's books for the children they would never have were assigned to the spare room that one day they'd hoped would be for their son or daughter. Hoped to move to a bigger house too. Hoped to grow old together. Hoped to catch a killer. A lot of hoping and every one of them a smashed dream.

Following the crime scene tech inside the spare room, he sparked with inner knowledge. Polly's pride and joy was a scarce US first-edition print of a children's book by Roald Dahl. Jackson had bought it as a special Christmas present. Might this have piqued Neon's interest?

Jackson homed straight in on the bookcase. His heart gave a lurch of disappointment at his poor lack of judgement. There it was, pride of place, unmolested.

Pissed off, pulling away from the shot, he glimpsed an unfamiliar spine. Immediately, rolling back the footage, he froze it and inclined his head to get a better view: *Las Vegas With Love* by an author with a name that sounded as if it were created from several languages.

'Las Vegas,' he repeated aloud. Home of amusement arcades, casinos, pawnshops and hotels, a paradise for call girls and con artists, gamblers, thieves, drunks and murderers. A cold thrill that only a murder detective encounters rippled right through him: Las Vegas was also the citadel of neon. It was practically born there.

The man, who had killed his wife, had taken nothing. He'd left something behind.

Deliberately, Jackson thought, reaching for his leather jacket.

With one eye on the time, the minute hand perilously close to nine-fifteen, he raced out of the apartment block and towards the car park underneath. Within minutes, he was heading out of town in his Mini Cooper. In current traffic and with a barking speed limit, it would take him thirty-five minutes. That left less than ten minutes before the deadline. His *dead* line.

11

Swallowing hard, he chucked a last look at the unfolding nightlife. Illumination from dozens of nightclubs and bars spilled out on to the pavements, laying claim to the streets. He wondered if Neon was there among them, walking and stalking and planning his next gig.

Inner city was a bottleneck. Every light was against him. With the clock ticking, he eventually floored it once he was clear, and arrived, tyres spitting dirt and gravel, at nine fifty-three.

Curtains were drawn. A memory of blue and white crime scene tape fluttered through his mind as he let himself back in. Jettisoned back to that night, with all its pain and anguish and loss, his salivary glands packed up and there was a strange thrumming sensation in the back of his head. Giving himself a mental shake, he headed straight upstairs, taking the steps two at a time. The main bedroom was now empty, all that remained the residue of a full Scenes of Crime Investigation and marks and holes in the wall from where the installations erected by Neon were taken down.

Turning right on the landing, he slid out the pair of gloves he carried like a talisman from his leather jacket and slipped them on. He had no doubt that the killer had acted with similar care.

Neon's calling card, *Las Vegas With Love*, baited him from the safety of the bookcase. With a clenched jaw, Jackson reached and pulled it out. Flicking to the inside page, written with a thin felt tip in capitals, a short dedication: *'To Detective Chief Inspector Matt Jackson. Enjoy the show. N.'*

His pulse raced hard. Sweat coated his top lip. He stared more closely and saw that faint rubbed-out pencil marks hid beneath the script, as if Neon had practised first before writing his message properly. Were there other concealed messages and clues? He wasn't sure. What was indisputable: Neon had made direct communication with him and it represented a breakthrough, something tangible he could work with, a definite lead to follow, but the one thing he didn't have was time.

Jackson glanced at his watch. Three minutes. That's all he had and he wanted longer. No, he *needed* to abort the hit.

Fumbling for his phone, he called the number for John. It rang once and diverted to 'The customer is unavailable' message, all means of communication blocked.

Running back downstairs, he shot towards the kitchen, pulled out a thin-bladed Sabatier from the knife block. Now what? From where would the hitman come? Would he ring the bell and off him the second he opened the door? Or would he sneak in through the back and slot him from behind? The guy was probably right outside.

Think.

Jackson hedged his bets, switched off the main light, flicked on a lamp, and dived behind the sofa. Best he could do. Aside from the blade, surprise was his only ally. Crouching, gripping the knife, every sense he possessed was amplified. He felt the weight of the air around him pressing in. A salt taste coated his tongue. The stench of his own fear lay heavy in his nostrils. His vision was sharper than he'd ever known it, bright and focused and, strangely, monochrome. He swore he heard music, haunting and distant, some kind of weird aural distortion. Maybe a memory.

Another check of his watch told him he had a minute to wait. He hoped his killer was punctual.

'Take it,' Iris said, shoving a couple of hundred quid towards the cab driver, a middle-aged Asian and devoted family man, if the photograph on his dashboard was anything to go by.

His eyes rolled in wonderment. 'But, mam, this is way too much, over twelve times the amount.'

'Not from someone you never saw.'

It took him a few moments to process the implication. When he did, he drew back, his face receding into the darkness inside the car. 'I want no trouble,' he stammered. 'I am a good man.'

Iris didn't agree or disagree.

'So, please, mam, just give me the correct fare and we're square.'

Iris ground her teeth. She had no time for this. Trust her to find a driver with a conscience. Already she was running later than scheduled and it spooked her. She leant forward. 'Is that your family?' Her eyes snatched to the photo.

He followed her gaze, deeply uneasy. 'It is.'

'You have a lot of children.'

He cleared his throat. 'Mam, I—'

'Then this money will come in handy.' She pushed the notes through the gap and let them flutter onto the passenger seat. He gaped at them, as if they were thirty pieces of silver, which, Iris guessed, they were.

Averting his eyes, he said in a mechanical tone, 'Mam, I have not seen you.'

A hiss of relief seeped from between his lips as she opened the cab door.

'One other thing,' she said, with menace, briefly twisting round. 'Ghosts come back to haunt anyone who speaks ill of them.'

Where the hell was he? Jackson glanced at his watch again. Had the little shit taken his money and welshed on the deal?

Frustrated, anxious and angry, he stood up, edged towards the front door and squinted through the spyhole. The drive was in darkness, the only illumination the stuttering light from a lamp post.

Straightening up, a movement caught his peripheral vision. Instinct kicked in and he lurched sideways. The bullet almost grazed his nose as it ploughed into the nearest wall. When the barrel swivelled round for a second shot, Jackson flung the knife straight at the gunman's arm. The shot went wide and a noise, like a deep-throated roar, ricocheted around the living room.

Jackson sprang, grabbing hold of his attacker's wounded arm with both hands. If he applied enough pressure, the man would drop the gun or relinquish it. Jackson didn't stop to think of consequences, or how it would look if the thing went off and he was forced to explain how he'd wound up with another corpse inside his house. He needed to survive. *Had to* because the message from Neon had, however briefly, made him regain a sense of himself. He now understood how he connected to the dystopian world that was not of his making. And with that knowledge, he would live long enough to get the job done before finally checking out.

Up close, Jackson couldn't see his attacker's face, which was concealed by a balaclava. He could feel the other man breathing and heaving, registered that he was several inches shorter and several pounds lighter. It should give him a physical and psychological advantage, but the gunman, more expert in the art of combat, knew what he was doing. The weapon stuck to his leather glove like it was soldered onto his fingers. With every twist and turn, he jabbed at Jackson with his free arm, each blow stronger than the last. Jackson failed to absorb the impact. It was like being repeatedly hit with an iron bar. His chest and chin rivered with pain and he cursed that he hadn't packed in smoking sooner.

Desperately, Jackson tightened his grip and felt warm blood ooze through his fingers. If he'd hoped the gunman would release the weapon, he was out of luck. A chair overturned as they stumbled backwards. Jackson winced as the toe of a boot scraped down his shin, followed by a fist that powered into his gut that made him retch. Gasping in shock and pain, he almost doubled over. He had the weird experience of being a spectator, as if viewing what was happening to him from a distance.

They surged towards the staircase, where his shoulder

collided painfully with one of the uprights. Another shot released, this time its destination the ceiling. Chunks of plaster exploded, showering them with debris. Jackson blinked away grit and dust, his eyeballs on fire. He thought he was weakening, and his opponent, buoyed by experience and ruthlessness, was gaining the advantage. Jackson could feel the swagger in the other man's body, the way he danced on his toes, the wiry strength in his arms. Against him, Jackson felt like the human equivalent of a skip lorry.

But if he rolled with a negative narrative, he would die too soon.

Changing up a gear, Jackson summoned all his body weight to shove his attacker, who grunted in surprise as they flew through the open doorway and into the kitchen. The gun clattered onto the tiled floor. As the attacker softened his knees to grab it, Jackson kicked the weapon away. It proved a game changer. *Now it's just him and me and fists and feet,* he thought.

Spurred on, he gave another dirty great shove, punching with both hands, right into his opponent's chest, which felt strangely soft. This time, the man that had come to kill him flailed, staggered backwards and tumbled, the back of his head glancing off a solid granite worktop. By chance or design, Jackson didn't give a flying fuck as he watched him fold in two and slide to the floor. Out cold.

He bent over, rested his sweaty palms on his thighs in an effort to stop his limbs from shaking. His mouth was dry. Nauseated, he gagged as adrenaline dumped its payload.

From where he'd slashed the attacker's arm, blood spilled onto the floor. There was a lot of it. The wound would definitely require stitches. Jackson didn't yet know whether the guy had sustained a serious head injury.

Let's have a look at you, he thought, peeling off the balaclava. His eyes shot wide as he clocked that the man was, in fact, a young woman.

12

Jackson didn't bother with niceties like the recovery position. He riffled through her clothes and fished out a screwdriver, a set of skeleton keys, a lock pick and a small hammer, a wallet containing forty-seven pounds and sixty-five pence but no debit or credit cards. Similarly, the woman didn't carry a mobile phone. It seemed she'd gone to great lengths to conceal her identity. More surprisingly, he unearthed a blister pack of pills from her jeans pocket – which he immediately recognised because one of his colleagues had been prescribed them when he'd undergone chemotherapy – but they'd been taken out of the box so there was no patient name to speak of.

He looked from the pills to her face. Eyes closed, she had pale lashes and brows. Her skin was the colour of an undercooked chip, her hair resembled soiled straw. She had thin lips, and faint lines at the corners of her eyes and along her forehead suggested that she was probably older than he'd first thought. Either that, or she'd had a particularly worrying life, which, given what she did for a living, was almost certainly the case. The rest of her features were so ordinary and unremarkable that you'd never give her a second look. Forgettable best described her – perfect for her line of work.

What the hell did he do next? What the fuck did he do with her? He had no doubt that the second she regained consciousness she'd have another crack at killing him.

He picked up the gun and stowed it, gathered shell casings and dumped them. The knife, its blade bloodied, he shoved into the utility room. He reckoned there was enough DNA on it to match her with any number of crimes. Next, he fetched a roll of duct tape, righted the overturned chair, scooped up the woman's prone body and secured her to it. The leather of her jacket was doing a poor job at staunching the flow of blood from her arm, so he grabbed a couple of tea towels and bound it. While she drooled out of the side of her mouth, head lolling, he fixed himself a stiff drink and sat on a chair opposite. He was far enough away to be out of range of a kick and, if she did decide to tip up the chair legs, like they do in the movies, and charge him, he could easily evade an advance.

Every part of his anatomy was bruised and battered. He thought he'd be stiff for days. None of it mattered. Alive for now, dead soon enough.

He turned his attention back to his captive. Right in front of him sat a ruthless and determined killer. It was sheer luck that she'd failed in her objective. Letting her go would allow her to kill again. Not good. But turning her in would be impossible without incriminating himself. And that was unthinkable. It didn't take a genius to picture the mountain of explanation, police procedure and bureaucracy that would ensue if he did.

He took a deep swallow of neat spirit. But the burn coursing down his throat had less to do with alcohol and more with avenging his wife's death. That message left specifically for him had changed everything. And despite his training, his moral code, all the values he held dear, revenge mattered more to him now than dying. And by vengeance, he didn't mean justice and a court case, or judgement and a life sentence with no chance of parole, because that still meant that Polly's killer could eat and drink, sleep and breathe, and form sick friendships with like-minded screw-ups, and reminisce and . . .

Jackson scrubbed at his face. So the really big, mind-bending question was this: if he could find the person that killed his wife, did he have the guts to kill him? Could he pull the trigger? Right here, now, and in this highly charged moment, with a glass of whisky in his hand, Jackson *thought* he could. Yet deep down he knew that anger and rage did not make for cool judgement, let alone a clean kill. And if it came to it, would he follow through, or would he lose his nerve?

Fixing his gaze on the woman sitting in front of him, he had no doubt that she could give him what he needed without a moment's hesitation. As long as there was money in it, she would do his bidding.

But was he prepared to order the hit?

Jackson took a big pull of booze. He had an especially low opinion of the scum that gave orders for contract kills, without dirtying their own hands. These were mostly drug lords prepared to mete out misery and death in pursuit of their own ends. And here he was, wondering whether to join their ranks.

Setting morality aside, there were also practical considerations. Weren't the risks too great, the stakes too high? If this went sideways, he could wind up in prison, and how could he work with a killer who, by her very nature, had double-cross and betrayal embedded in her DNA? Besides, judging from the pills she had on her, she was also sick – seriously so.

He went back and forth through the argument, drawing no conclusions, until her eyelashes finally fluttered and she opened her eyes, which were dull blue and darting. It was like watching a wild animal, sedated for surgery, regaining consciousness. At any moment, he expected her to lash out.

Wiping the corner of her mouth against her shoulder, she lifted her head upright. He had the clear impression that she was fully conscious because she stared at him as if he was within her cross hairs. The intensity was overwhelming, but he held her gaze.

Next, her eyes dipped to the floor. She was searching for the gun. Coming up empty, she scoped the room.

'What's your name?' he said.

'Screw you.'

A familiar, if unhelpful response, he continued undeterred.

'Shall we try this again?' he said.

She was having none of it. 'Who tipped you off?' she demanded.

'I did. I'm the man who hired you.'

Disbelief spread across her face, followed by an expression that said *What the fuck's wrong with you?*

'As you might have gathered, I've changed my mind.'

'I don't do refunds.'

Jackson raised his palms in surrender. 'Wouldn't expect it.'

'So why am I sitting here?'

Because I don't know what the hell to do with you, he thought.

'Either you don't know,' she continued, 'or you haven't decided yet.'

'You're right on both counts.'

'Are you tapped, or something?'

She showed no trace of fear whatsoever, he noticed. Instead, she displayed something indefinable, a willingness and acceptance for him to do whatever he wanted, coupled with a strong desire for him to stop wasting her time and get on with it. Was this connected to the pills she carried and perhaps a belief that she didn't have that long left anyway?

'While you have a little think, can you loosen these?' She wriggled against the restraints.

'Nice try,' he said, ignoring her sour expression.

Jackson tried to step into her shoes and see things from her point of view. As far as she was concerned, he'd broken their agreement and he posed a grave threat to her freedom. If he let her go, she would most likely refuse to put him out of his misery *and* take the money. Was there a chance he could use her instead? A woman with her particular skill set could, surely, help him catch a killer like Neon. So why not work the existing situation to his advantage? Frankly, what did he have to lose?

'I have a proposition for you.'

She raised her head, sniffed the air, like a lioness scenting prey.

'I need your help to find a serial killer,' he said.

Her face cracked into a smile. She had small white teeth,

he observed. Probably sharpened them. 'The roughing up has affected your brain,' she said.

He took a sip of booze, gave her a square look. 'You've heard of Neon?'

'The whole country's heard of him.' She didn't look intrigued; she looked indifferent.

'I'm going to hunt him down.'

'What are you, a cop or something?' She snorted.

'Detective Chief Inspector Matt Jackson.'

That landed, judging by the way her lips thinned. 'I don't help coppers. It's against my code.'

'I thought people like you don't have a code.'

She threw him a surly look.

'*If* we get him,' he continued, 'I want you to kill him.'

'Isn't that against *your* rules?' Her expression was cold.

It was, and the truth was he no longer cared. As for prison – something he genuinely feared – as long as she did the job, nobody was going to lock him up, even if it was discovered that he'd paid for a murder. After all, Jackson would already be dead by then.

'And afterwards,' he continued. 'I want you to go through with what we originally agreed.'

'You're not right in the head.'

'So you keep saying.'

'And I'm also saying the answer is no.'

'Are you really in a position to argue?'

At this, she sneered. 'What are you going to do about it? Turn me over to your mates and have me arrested? On what charge, exactly, DCI Jackson?'

He had to hand it to her; she recognised that she held

more power than her current physical situation suggested. He tipped the glass to his lips, took another drink.

'Are you trying to set me up?' She studied him shrewdly.

He gave her a straight look. 'No.'

She blinked slowly, thought for a moment. 'This is more than professional, isn't it?'

He waited a beat. 'He killed my wife.'

'So you want revenge?' She was cold-blooded and calculating, no emotional response at all.

Yeah, he did, but he wasn't going to tell her that. 'Rough justice.'

'Nah, you want revenge. They all do. Makes no difference to me. I don't help coppers and I don't kill them either. It attracts too much heat.'

'I'll ensure it doesn't.'

She shook her head. 'Still too high profile. And just because I do away with people doesn't make me an expert on crazies.'

'True, but you have a different perspective.'

'What?' she scoffed. 'On how to kill?'

'How to trap, snare, trick.'

'You make it sound glamorous. It isn't.'

He paused. 'So what do you suggest I do?'

'Let me go and hope to fuck that Neon falls under the nearest bus.'

Jackson didn't believe that she possessed a better nature, but if she had a streak of conscience, he was determined to appeal to it. 'You're not willing to help?'

'I'm not a fucking charity.'

'Think of all the women he's killed in the most brutal

manner,' Jackson said. 'Think of the lack of dignity in their deaths. What if it was your mum or sister, or friend?' Bearing in mind she hadn't displayed a vestige of sympathy when he'd mentioned his wife, this was a hopeless appeal, but still one he intended to make.

'What's the matter with you?' she snapped. 'Are you deaf, or something? How many more times? I'm *not* interested.' To make the point, she tilted the chair and banged the feet against the floor.

One last shot, he thought, one final crack at her. 'What if, at the end of all of this, after you've killed him, and then me, I leave everything I own to you: house, car, the money?'

At the mention of finance, her pupils dilated. He pulled out the pack of pills, held them up and watched the little colour she had in her face fade.

'You're ill – dangerously so, judging by the meds you're on. With a serious cash injection, you could afford the best treatment money can buy.'

She opened her mouth, but no words came out. He'd got her, he thought. Money, or not enough of it, was her weak spot.

'Think about it.' He got up, made a move towards her.

'You're letting me go?' she said in surprise.

'I'm a nice guy. I'll call you a cab, if you like.'

'I don't like.'

'Have it your way, but you need your arm stitched and you're most likely concussed. Q.E.'s sixteen minutes away.'

'I don't do hospitals.'

She was a mass of *don'ts* and *dislikes*, he concluded. He

wondered what floated her boat. Nothing, if her answers were anything to go by except maybe killing.

He undid the ties. 'You still need to get checked out.'

She stood up, her expression wary; as if he were about to produce a set of handcuffs and slap them on her wrists.

'You're letting me walk out of here? No catch?'

He shrugged.

'You know where to find me if you change your mind.' He liked to think that he was engendering mutual respect. 'Don't leave it too long,' he said, as he opened the front door and she stepped out into the night.

13

The guy was fucking mental, Iris thought, as she stepped onto a bus outside All Saints Church. She'd had some pretty weird experiences in her life but this topped the lot.

'Sparkhill,' she said to the driver, who frowned when he noticed her arm. She stabbed him with 'the look', one perfected through thirty-three years of rejection and hostility. Instantly, he averted his gaze, took the money for the fare. She moved along and sat next to a doddery old man who smelt of piss.

Stretching back in the seat, Iris briefly closed her eyes. Her endorphins had done a runner. Her head throbbed, her arm killed and her tits hurt from where the copper had given her a good thumping. Maybe that's why she wasn't thinking straight. Maybe that's why the money seemed too good to be true. *Maybe* that was the point: it *was* too good to be true.

And yet . . .

She'd seen that determined look in a man's eyes before and it didn't generally end well. She didn't believe his bullshit about justice. He wanted revenge all right. And vengeance was right up her street.

Like everyone else in the city, she'd read about Neon, some sick fucker who lit up his victims like Christmas trees. She didn't know he'd killed a copper's wife though. The police must really be up against it to entangle someone like her, she thought. And that told her something: this was a strictly off-the-books job. Unofficial. That also meant she was deniable should anything go south. Trust didn't feature heavily in her life – just one or two people. Period. Could she put her faith in DCI Jackson?

She sniffed, glanced out of the window and saw it was her stop. The second she stepped out, the change in air against her skin was tangible. More pungent and dense. It wasn't called the Balti Triangle for nothing. This was Migration Central. It had recently become a haven for Somalis. No pirates. Plenty of pushers and pimps though.

Her destination was a terraced house with a knackered wall, dead plants in the garden and drugs in the lounge. Even before she got down the road, she heard the sound of Punjabi rap blasting through the brickwork. Sounded like the occupants of the entire row had taken to the middle of the street to perform a bhangra.

Reaching number 83, she balled the fist on her good arm and hammered it against the front door. Someone had taken a blowtorch to the paint and given up halfway through the job.

No answer. Another attempt received a similar response. Curtains were closed, but the dirty sash window – the only nod to antiquity – was open an inch, probably to release the smell of weed and cigarettes.

Squatting down on her haunches, she got underneath the frame and hitched it up, before climbing through the gap and into the front room. There, a wall of artificial heat from an electric fire greeted her.

Three heads turned from a fifty-inch screen, including Jaspal's.

'Iris,' he said with a big smile. Nobody commented on her unusual entrance. They were too stoned.

She negotiated her way around a coffee table laden with empty fast-food cartons, bottles of pop and overflowing ashtrays.

Jaspal stood up, slipped his meaty arms around her and gave her a squeeze. Iris winced. She didn't like to be touched by anyone at the best of times, never mind when she was injured.

'Fuck's sake, Jaspal. Watch my arm.'

He drew back, dropped his dark-eyed gaze to the blood still leaking through the makeshift bandage. It produced an instantly sobering effect. 'Fighting again,' he said, with a theatrical sigh. 'Come.' He indicated that she follow him through the door and into a hall, from where he led her upstairs to a back room in which he'd been known to dig out bullets and patch up the bad and ugly. Inside was kitted out like a doctor's surgery, with a few extras. Next to a couch, a stand for saline and antibiotics, oxygen cylinders and a terrifying display of instruments that Iris didn't like to think what they could be used for. And Jaspal knew what he was about. He'd trained as a surgeon back home but hadn't made the grade as far as Border Control were concerned. Too many dodgy relatives. Not that this had prevented Jaspal from settling down and setting up shop in Birmingham.

'I took a knock to the back of my head,' she told him.

'Sit down. Let me see.'

She felt him part her hair and run his fingers over the back of her head as if he were reading Braille.

'Tender?' he asked.

'Uh-huh.'

'Skin is broken but it will heal. There's quite a lump, but, again, the swelling should go down. Better out than in. Did you lose consciousness?'

'No.' She didn't want him fussing.

'OK, I clean it up and then we look at your arm.' She nodded obediently. A stoned Jaspal was better than an official doctor who might shop her to the police.

After he'd patched up her head, she allowed him to remove the detective's emergency dressing. Next, Jaspal eased her out of her jacket. The sleeve of her jumper was in shreds.

'You need to take it off,' he said with a small delicate frown.

She did. If she had bruises blossoming on her body, Jaspal knew better than to comment or enquire. He did, however, notice her ribcage.

'You need to eat more,' he said.

Iris said nothing.

'Not sleeping? You look tired.'

'Been busy.'

With infinite care, he examined her arm. 'What was it – a machete?'

She looked up, caught his eye, saw that he was attempting to humour her. She wasn't humoured. It hurt like fuck.

'Too deep to glue,' Jaspal said.

It was long as well. Stretched from the back of her wrist to her elbow. Trust it to be her gun hand.

'I'll clean it up, but then I need to inject the wound with

anaesthetic to numb it. That's the nasty part. After that, you won't feel a thing.'

Somehow, Iris didn't share his optimism. Must have showed on her face.

'I can give you something to take with you.' With Jaspal, 'something to take with you' usually involved strong opiates.

She declined. 'Let's get this over with,' she said, as Jaspal reached for a trolley on which three syringes nestled like triplets.

Iris closed her eyes and ground her teeth. Jaspal was right. It hurt like fuck. The pain, she guessed, reminded her that she was still very much alive.

When it was done, Jaspal called one of his mates to take her home, except Iris never let anyone within a mile of where she actually lived. She waited downstairs, looked out for the flash of lights, signalling her ride.

Dropped off on the all-seeing and all-knowing Hagley Road, she walked the rest of the way on foot. Her breath made smoke circles in the cold. The city never really slept. Traffic flowed. Lights blazed. Sirens from all the emergency services punctuated the night.

It was gone three as she let herself in. Too wired to sleep, she made herself a strong brew, put a tot of whisky in the cup, added sugar and milk, downed a couple of heavy-duty painkillers and picked up her personal mobile. There were three messages. Only two people in her life regularly kept in touch. She replied to the first caller with a text, the other could wait, the last message she replied to and signed off with two kisses.

His house, his car and *his money*, she thought, as she drifted off to sleep on the sofa.

14

Gary was not a morning person and his day didn't really get going until the afternoon. He taught woodwind – principally clarinet and sax – and piano. In the past, he'd also taught accordion, although he didn't much care for it. Not a serious instrument: too fairground. When Naomi was away, which was delightfully often, he'd sometimes sleep in until lessons kicked off at three o'clock. After a long night gigging (or killing), he deserved it. Lately, he'd sworn off lie-ins because he'd been busy in town, preparing for the pinnacle of his killing career. The right opportunity had just come along. Luck had nothing to do with it. He'd taken the necessary steps and his hard work had paid off. It was all about planning meticulously in advance. But none of it would pay off if he failed to get the party started. What did DCI Jackson want? An official printed invitation?

Armed with coffee and the kind of savage rage that creates great works of art (ask any radical with a vision), he'd gone straight to his place of neon worship.

To Gary's mind, bending glass required a similar set of skills to playing sax. Every bit of you needs to be in synch.

Stripped down to the waist, with a fine hose in his mouth to modulate temperature, he coaxed glass into words and shaped ideas into images. Heat from flames shooting up from two metal burners fled over his fingers and the soft, fleshy parts of his hands, playing with fire in the most literal sense, and, though he feared it, gloves were impossible. Too cumbersome and clumsy, they didn't allow for that spiritual connection to, and interaction with, the material. Make a mistake and blow at the wrong moment and the glass would buckle and break. Every twist and curve of slender tube was bought in time and sweat and, occasionally, blood – something that the women, who played a central part in his works of art, failed to appreciate.

He blew gently into one section to make a sharp bend for the letter 'S'. White smoke swirled into the atmosphere, which he was careful not to breathe in.

Breathe. Oh, how they tried.

Gina, the journalist, had thought she was smart. She'd certainly looked it with her short, chic haircut, cool white boots, leather jacket and London swagger. Her depth of knowledge had impressed him, until he realised what her nasty little brain was thinking. Interviewing the detective's wife – *taking a human-interest angle,* as she put it – had been a very bad idea. Gary liked to think that police protocol would never have allowed it, but one could never be sure in these enlightened, touchy-feely times. Better safe than sorry – Gina had to go, (which reminded him that he still had another loose thread to snap in two). That she believed he might provide a useful lead had played right into his hands.

He took the glass back to the table and his technical

drawing, laying it against the pattern to mark and set it before making the next bend. The smoky fragrance of charred paper, pencil and wood drifted up and filled the workshop. He loved that smell.

Another little puff of air to prevent the next section of glass from blowing out – *easy does it* – and the process repeated, again and again. Any mistake and the entire tube would have to be scrapped.

Thinking back to Gina, he'd only revealed his true self once he had Gina just where he wanted: terrified and pliant. But, deep down, Gina had still thought she was clever enough, still believed she could put one over him. Right up to the beginning of the endgame, when she'd attempted to deceive him by audibly exhaling, going limp and 'playing dead'. She underestimated him. Everybody always did. As he'd throttled the life out of her, he'd explained that he knew, to within a second, how strangulation worked, that there was a tempo to each stage, that death had its own beat and that he understood its rhythm by heart.

Excitement built in the centre of his chest. Someone to be crushed, Gina had definitely been his kind of woman. Not a million miles away, in fact, from Naomi, his wife.

15

Jackson woke up late, fully dressed on the bed in the spare room. He was freezing cold. It took him a while to work out where he was, and, when he did, the events of the previous night flooded back. Christ, had he really asked a contract killer to help him? Is this what he had been reduced to? It definitely represented a variation on his usual waking thoughts – one ugly set of memories masking others. Was it possible to conceal them so deeply that they would eventually wither, rot and die? He shook his head.

Jackson went downstairs, put on the heating and headed straight to the drawer in which he'd stowed Iris's gun. The Glock was popular with the firearms unit. Jackson wondered how it had fallen into her hands. He cleared the chamber, reached for the tiny sharp-edged rectangle behind the trigger, pressed it with his thumb and released the magazine, dropping it into his free hand. Placing the magazine back in the drawer, he took the gun upstairs, stashing it in the bedside cabinet until he thought of a better place to keep it. Next, grabbing a towel from the airing cupboard, he stripped off and took a shower.

A glance in the mirror confirmed that he hadn't shaved in twenty-four hours. Polly had always admired a degree of stubble, said it made him look edgy and dangerous. He smiled sadly.

'Miss you,' he murmured.

An overwhelming sense of bleakness threatened to dismantle him. Fighting it, he told himself that, if a hereafter existed, he'd see her soon enough. Would his ending be, in fact, a beginning? Somehow he didn't think so. Death was the only certainty he had and he clung to it like a man hanging onto a piece of wreckage in the middle of a cold and choppy sea.

Most of his clothes were back at the flat in town, but he'd kept a set in the spare wardrobe: a pair of jeans, a couple of shirts and navy round-neck sweater, socks and underwear. He dressed quickly, slipped on a pair of gloves and took a more considered look at *Las Vegas with Love*.

The letters in the inscription were uniform, well-formed and precisely placed. Was Neon involved in the arts? Was he a craftsman? Or perhaps he had some connection to the printing industry. But wasn't the industry all digital and computerised these days? So maybe Neon was old-school. Jackson hoped so. A lot of serial killers recorded details of their acts to feed their drive and maintain the 'high' of a kill. In any prosecution, a diary of death would prove damning. Darkness travelled through him. If he had his way, Neon's case would never get to court.

Jackson flicked to the centre of the book and colour photographs revealing Las Vegas's showbiz history – an entire section devoted to the rise and decline of casino bands. At one time, Jackson read on a facing page, hundreds of full-time musicians in orchestras were employed. When casinos, once owned by the mob, went legit and were sold off to the highest bidder, canned music was deemed a more cost-effective alternative, and many lost their jobs. Seemed that the best musicians had trouble keeping up with the tempo of change and some went on strike. But it didn't do much good – most lost their jobs anyway.

As interesting as it was, it didn't give him any answers. Until, several pages later, his eyes fell on The Neon Museum in Las Vegas, Nevada. Historic and artistically cultural neon signs from all types of businesses stretched out over a two and a half acre site. Was this the inspiration for Neon's murderous spree? But why boast of his appreciation? Was the book designed to taunt or did it provide a clue? Either way, Neon's already sizeable ego had grown to immense proportions. Jackson wondered if he could use it to his advantage.

Slipping out his mobile, he called Mick Cairns.

'Hi Mick.'

'You OK, Matt?'

How do you answer a question like that? Jackson thought. 'Fine. Can you talk?'

'Hang on a second.'

Jackson pictured Mick getting up from his desk at Lloyd House, nodding nonchalantly towards his colleagues and making his way through the sparklingly refurbished and modern facilities.

'Yup, that's better.'

'I need you to do something for me.'

'Ask away,' Mick said, without hesitation.

'I want an item checked with forensics.'

'You found something?' Mick's voice thrilled with anticipation.

Jackson explained his discovery of the book.

'A book?' Mick sounded dubious. Clearly, it wasn't the kind of lead he had been anticipating.

'I don't expect you'll find any prints – Neon's too savvy for that – but you could check it out for latents,' Jackson said. 'The inscription might give something away.'

'OK. I see.'

Jackson sensed Mick's disappointment. 'Is there a problem?'

'Only the usual one.'

Resources, Jackson thought, and the small fact that Mick would be working off-grid. No way could Marcus Browne find out. 'I'm not back from compassionate leave for a couple of weeks and it's too important to wait. Think you can do it?'

'I'll do my best. You have it with you now?'

'Yes. I'm at the house.'

He heard Mick suck in through his teeth. 'Can't get to you right now. We've got a briefing. Would around three work?'

'I'll be here,' Jackson said, ending the call and baulking at the thought of spending any significant time in the house he'd once called home.

There was nothing to eat and no milk for tea or coffee. Unusually hungry, Jackson let himself out and walked down the road and into what locals referred to as 'the village'. He wasn't interested in organic coffee culture or vegan brunches. He needed the closest thing to a Greasy Spoon, which he found in Silver Street.

Inside the mostly empty cafe, he ordered a bacon sandwich on white bread and a mug of tea.

Waiting for his order, he thought about 'John'. Jackson had no idea whether or not she'd show up again. The extent of her illness could be a factor in any decision; maybe her prognosis was terminal. And yet, she'd fought like someone determined to live. He wondered how many people she'd killed. In recent years, gun crime, which had once taken a dip, was on the rise again. And if kids weren't shooting guns, they were stabbing each other – and, as such, the trade in illegal weapons had risen to concerning levels.

Jackson's bacon sandwich arrived. He opened it up, squirted brown sauce inside, reassembled it and took a bite. The tea was builder's brew, thick and strong. He chewed, swallowed and took a sip.

Glancing through the steamy window and onto the street, he wondered, not for the first time, if Neon had walked this way. What did he do all day? Did he spend hours in a workshop blowing glass? Had he tapped into some black-market trade in stolen illuminated signs? Neon hadn't suddenly woken up one day and decided to turn killing into a performance art. Like all serial killers, he'd sweated the small stuff, honed his skills before moving on to bigger productions. Jackson had spent oceans of time wondering where Neon lived. Maybe he should have focused on where he *had* lived while learning his craft. A stint in Las Vegas, maybe? And now he was bringing his show to the streets of Birmingham.

16

'You look different, more rested,' Mick said, striding through the hall and into the kitchen. He carried a briefcase, which Jackson presumed contained evidence bags.

'I'm off the booze,' Jackson said, though it was more of an aspirational truth. He'd decided on the walk back from the cafe that he needed to pack it in, at least for a bit. Even if it was only a very little bit. Nailing Neon was the only thing on his bucket list. After that, nothing mattered anyway. 'Want a brew?' he asked.

Mick shook his head. 'No time.' He took out a pair of latex gloves from his pocket and pulled them on. 'So, what have we got?'

Jackson showed him. 'See the message inside?' he said, opening the book.

Mick's narrow features tightened in distaste. 'I'll see if I can get this to a document examiner right away. I'll have to do it on the sly so that Browne doesn't get wind of it.'

Jackson nodded his thanks. When he'd first joined the police, document examiners were primarily used when ransom demands or written threats were issued. In a digital [illegible]asn't quite as much necessity for them, which [illegible] it could work in his favour. *Las Vegas With Love* was likely to climb up a list of priorities a lot quicker. 'Got any police contacts in Nevada?'

'Not unless you count Harry Bosch.' Mick grinned, bagging and tagging the book. Michael Connelly's fictional detective was much admired by his colleagues. 'Wait a minute,' Mick said, suddenly alive with inspiration, 'what about that woman who came over last year?'

Jackson searched his memory. Wasn't quite the way he was thinking. 'The criminologist, Krasinski or Krackowski?'

'Kozlowski.'

'That's right.' She'd spent a day at West Mids as part of her research into knife crime in the UK. She'd have been better off in the capital, Jackson had thought at the time, although since then stabbings in the West Midlands had seen a dramatic increase.

'I could *reach out* to her,' Mick said mockingly. 'See if she knows any good-tempered cops out there. What's your thinking?'

'I wondered whether Neon's interest in Las Vegas was actually more a trip down memory lane.'

'You think he *lived* there?'

'No evidence to suggest it yet, but if he'd been in Las Vegas, maybe it's where he had his first kill.'

Mick pulled a face. 'Do you have any idea how many people visit Las Vegas?'

'Assuming he's a British citizen, I still think it's worth a punt.' A couple of other ideas worth exploration were also burbling in the back of his brain. His team had talked to various people with knowledge of the neon industry. They'd turned up very little that seemed relevant. Maybe they'd been asking the wrong questions. Jackson was determined to have another crack.

Mick glanced at his watch and then at the carpet. 'Is that blood yours?'

'Cut myself.'

Mick eyed Jackson with suspicion.

'Don't you have places to be?' Jackson said pointedly.

Mick gave him an old-fashioned look, but said no more and made to leave.

Jackson walked with him to the door. 'Any news on the investigation?'

'Browne has ordered a re-interview of the guys at the rubbish collection depot.'

'Sound thinking.'

Mick cocked his head, as if he couldn't quite believe that Jackson had anything good to say about Browne.

'Anything else?'

Mick swallowed. 'It's only an idea. Not confirmed.'

'But?'

'He wants to initiate a sting operation,' Mick said. 'Use a female officer as bait.'

'Good luck with that. Had any takers?'

'Not so far.'

'Let's hope it stays that way.' Jackson thought Browne mad to endanger the life of one of his own.

They said their goodbyes and Jackson watched his friend leave. After the initial buzz of doing something useful, he felt flat and disconnected. On his way back from the shops, he'd collected basics like bread and milk and butter, but he'd not thought beyond his immediate needs. For the past few months, he'd either skipped meals or ordered in pizzas, Chinese and Indian takeaways. The odd sandwich out, like this morning, was fine. Anything else wasn't; there is nothing sadder than a lonely widower tucking into a plate of food at a restaurant on his own. A hard lump of grief formed in the back of his throat, one he quickly swallowed down before it could choke him.

Grabbing his jacket and wallet, he headed out to the Mini and drove to the nearest supermarket. Polly had taken care of all the food shopping. He hadn't catered for himself in years. Unfamiliar with the layout and without a clear objective, it took him double the time to negotiate his way around the shop. You'd think a man on Death Row would have, at least, some idea of what he fancied eating, Jackson thought. Shouldn't it concentrate his mind? Instead he found himself bewildered by the vast choice and eventually settled on a pack of minced beef, a jar of chilli sauce and a tin of red beans. Despite his assurances to Mick, he slipped in a bottle of Argentinian Malbec.

It spat with rain and sleet as he crossed the car park and felt several degrees colder than when he'd stepped outside that morning. It was dark too. It actually made him glad to return to his former home.

Pulling into the drive, his headlights picked up a figure sitting huddled on his doorstep. He searched for sight of a vehicle and noticed a motorbike – a Triumph Street Triple 675 – tucked in by the hedge.

Jackson parked the Mini, collected his shopping from the passenger seat, climbed out and locked it.

The figure stood up on his arrival.

'I'm in,' she said.

'Good to see you again, John,' he replied.

17

In a foul mood, Gary asked himself for the millionth time: *What the hell do I have to do to grab Jackson's attention* without getting caught?

Jackson didn't know it, but Gary had spotted him in a cut-price supermarket – the guy clearly had zero standards – not far from where he lived and where Gary had last killed. The memory of that glorious evening swam before his eyes in radiant colour. Feeling all warm and fuzzy inside, he took a moment to enjoy it.

Back to Jackson. The sight of his sad, pathetic face had dismayed Gary to the extent that he'd nearly given up hope. In fact, Gary thought there was a distinct possibility that the detective was about to top himself. And that would ruin every-*fucking*-thing.

He took another moment to rage; he hated it when his obsession got the better of him. Now was not the time to lose belief that things would work out fine, he told himself sternly.

18

Her skin was almost blue with cold, Jackson observed, stowing the shopping in the fridge under her watchful gaze.

'Want a drink?' He gestured at the recently bought bottle of wine.

'No.'

Of course she couldn't drink with the meds she was on, he remembered. 'Mind if I have glass?'

'Knock yourself out.'

Jackson shrugged, opened the Malbec and poured out a healthy slug. Out of the corner of his eye, he caught her studying the range cooker, the coffee machine and American-style refrigerator with its water cooler. Maybe she didn't get to see many kitchens like this.

'Would you like a glass of chilled water?'

She shook her head.

He swallowed some wine, dropped his gaze. 'How's the arm?'

'Sore.'

'Not one for conversation, are you?' It was meant to lighten the tone.

She said nothing.

'Fair enough.' He pulled out a chair from under the kitchen table, sat down and patted the seat next to him. She sat, or rather perched. 'Before we—'

'I need concrete assurances about the will, and all of the other stuff you promised.'

'I was coming to that,' he said smoothly. 'Which is why it's important we trust each other.'

Her nostrils flared. 'So how's this supposed to work and why me?'

Because I don't know any other contract killers and I need you to kill him when we find him. 'You have different contacts to mine; you move in other circles.'

'Criminal, is what you mean.'

'That's right.'

'Neon's a psycho. Doesn't mean he knows the people I know.'

'But he might and it's an avenue worth exploration.'

She slow-blinked. Jackson knew what she was thinking: that every other lead had been exhausted.

'Essentially, you work one angle and, with my access through official channels, I work another. Ours could be a terrific combination.' In every sense, Jackson thought, and mainly terrifying.

From the underwhelmed expression on her face, Jackson thought she had a very different opinion.

'So I help you,' she said. 'We get lucky. You get what you want. Then what?'

It was his turn to slow-blink.

She met his gaze with a chill expression. 'I kill Neon and you get revenge.'

Put like that, it sounded as brutal as it was. Jackson cleared his throat.

'And then, thanks very much, I take the blame.'

'If that happened, you'd kill me,' he said.

'I'm doing that anyway.'

Jackson swallowed more wine. 'True.'

'How do I know you're not lying to me, that when this is all over you won't end up leaving all your loot to some cats' home, or something?'

'How do I know you won't put a bullet in my brain the second I make the will out to you?'

She sniffed, wiped her nose with the back of her hand.

'This is what I propose,' he said. 'I'll talk to my solicitor tomorrow and get my estate signed over to you when I die.'

The light in her eyes reflected satisfaction. It was the most animated he'd seen her.

'I'll also lodge a document with a trusted colleague that, should anything of a . . . *terminal* nature happen to me before Neon is caught, the first person to get a knock at the door will be you.'

She nodded.

'But in order to leave my estate to you, I'm going to need your real name.'

Her body braced. It occurred to Jackson that, for all her streetwise and cunning nature, she knew little of how the real world worked.

'Like I said,' Jackson reiterated, 'we need to trust each other and, frankly, I feel like a twat calling you John.' He smiled, hoping that she had a sense of humour and would yield.

Seconds ticked by. He watched her eyes, which gave little away.

'My name's Iris Palmer,' she eventually said in a soft voice.

'Good to meet you, Iris,' he said. 'Call me Matt.'

19

'OK,' Jackson continued briskly, 'I'm going to run through the details of the Neon investigation from the start. Stop me if you need me to clarify a point or explain. Does that sound all right?'

Iris shrugged her narrow shoulders.

'It was my investigation until I got signed off on compassionate leave,' he explained.

'Your wife, yeah.'

Taken aback that the woman sitting at his table could be so matter-of-fact, he nearly screwed up how to continue, but continue he did, starting with the first murder. After that he was on a roll. Iris sat slight and hunched, intent and intense. He could almost see her processing the information and making deductions. Twice, she let out a sigh and gave a tiny shake of her head. He didn't know whether it signified she thought the police were crap, that Neon was running rings around them, which he was, or that she was stumped, which he prayed she wasn't. He finished with the night Marcus Browne came to his door and took him in for questioning.

'Cunt,' she said. A show of solidarity, but Jackson didn't

need her to tell him what he already felt. Then she fell briefly silent.

He drained his glass and poured himself another.

'Why did you change your mind about me topping you last night?'

Jackson told her about the book, the message it contained.

'Have you got it?'

'It's being checked out for prints.'

'In your dreams. He's fucking with you. Could I have that water now?'

'Sure.' Jackson leapt to his feet. 'No problem.'

He filled a glass and placed it before her in the same way he would nudge a chunk of meat in front of an alligator and watched her as she drank it all straight down. When she finished, she held the tumbler in one hand, ran the finger of her glove around the rim in silent contemplation.

'What kind of man is our killer?' he pressed.

'Does his homework and works by the book.'

'The book?'

'He prepares. He strikes. He clears up. He gets out. He's a pro, and he's thorough. He won't leave any digital debris behind him either.'

'You sound like a fan.'

She placed the water tumbler down on the table a little too hard.

'He's also a show-off, arrogant, manipulative and full of shit.'

Jackson suspected Iris knew a lot of men who matched that description.

'Only gets his rocks off when he can dominate women,'

she continued. 'Which tells me that, like a lot of blokes, he's a pussy underneath it all.'

'A *pussy*?' This was not a word he would readily use to describe Neon.

'Feels inferior. Not happy in his own skin. Chip-on-the-shoulder type. Thinks he's better than he is.'

'In a relationship?'

She tilted her head, appeared to give it serious consideration. 'Probably. Maybe he's the one who gets dominated. You say all his victims were strangled?'

'Yes.' Jackson tried not to flinch, unlike Iris who showed no such concern.

'What with?'

'A leather ligature.'

'And?'

'And what?' he asked.

'Thin, thick, what colour?' She drummed her fingers in irritation on the table.

'He took them with him.'

'He must have left a mark.'

Coming from anyone else, he'd have thought it a good observation. Coming from the lips of a killer, his plasma chilled to ice. What the hell was he doing entertaining this individual in his home? Had he lost his mind? Quite possibly, but then what did it matter, he'd already lost everything else.

'It's estimated the ligature was made from black cowhide, four centimetres wide. In the first three cases there was serious compression of the neck and both thyroid cartilage and hyoid bones were broken. With my wife—' Jackson's voice cracked a little, '—he used a tourniquet. Asphyxiation was slow and painful. It's a subtle but significant distinction.'

'To make a statement,' she said. '*I can do what I like. You can't catch me and I'm smarter than you*. Good move to keep the identity of her killer a secret,' she added, 'that should really wind him up.'

'You think that's the way forward? Bait him?'

She hiked a shoulder. 'Needle the fucker. Mix things up, get him off balance so he never knows where he's at.'

'Might work,' Jackson said neutrally. 'But it carries risk. Neon shut Gina Jenks up because she was snooping.'

Iris shrugged a 'so what?'.

'With both my wife and the journalist, he had motivation,' Jackson said. 'Unlike his first two victims, who were random targets.'

'Who says?'

'They were visiting the city, Iris. They weren't connected. They didn't know each other.'

'But they might have known Neon. You checked their phone records?'

He briefly wondered if she was being facetious. 'Of course.'

'No common interests?'

'Between the girls? None that came to light.'

'Then look again.' Iris stared dead ahead. Jackson tried to read her and found he couldn't.

'Neon clearly knows his way around the city,' he said. 'And with all the redevelopment and disruption, closed roads, hordes of workers, it's a gift.'

'But he still needs to slide in and out,' she pointed out. He could have interjected and told her that they'd checked all that. He decided to let her run, didn't want to break her flow. 'He won't use his own vehicle and he won't hire a cab or take the bus because he has to cart around all his kit,' she continued, 'which suggests, like you said, he has a van, either one he owns, or borrows. If he borrows—'

'Then there's someone else in on the act.' Jackson felt a sick lurch as he realised that Marcus Browne had suggested the same and he'd disparaged the idea.

'Possible, but they might not know exactly what he's up to.'

Jackson found that hard to believe and told her so. But Iris wasn't put off.

'Neon could come up with any number of excuses to scrounge from a mate, but then he has a problem because the same van with the same registration would be clocked by you lot on CCTV. Last time I checked, there were twenty-seven public-space fixed CCTV cameras and 380 separate cameras mounted on buildings and for perimeter protection, so, for my money, he has his own vehicle and switches plates after every trip. And he's smart because he operates in all the blind spots.'

Jackson felt the hairs on the back of his neck prickle. Iris spoke from experience. She, too, operated within the city's nooks, crannies and places that he'd never seen, never wanted to. 'Go on.'

'The street cleaning depot. Sites like that have CCTV. You checked the comings and goings?'

'Yes. Nothing doing.'

'You say you interviewed the workers after Gina's murder?'

'We did.'

'One of them is telling porkies. The only way Neon could pull off a stunt like that is to have an inside man. Someone drove one of those dustcarts to Neon, let him use it to deliver the body and then drove it back.'

Again, Marcus Browne seemed to be on the money, Jackson realised. But there was a hitch in Iris's thinking. 'The dustcart would be crawling with Gina's DNA. We drew a blank on those we examined.'

'Maybe you weren't thorough enough. Maybe it was switched. Sometimes you can pick up second-hand dustcarts from councils.'

'Doesn't work,' Jackson said, not wanting to pick up Iris on how she knew that or why anyone would want a second-hand dustcart. 'Neon was working on a strict time limit. He didn't know how long Gina Jenks would be in the Midlands, asking questions. He had to shut her up and quickly.'

'So he used a body bag. Stands to reason.'

Jackson scratched his head. He was a DCI for Christ's sake, and this street-urchin-cum-killer knew more about how to run an investigation than most of his colleagues did. He told her that all employees were to be re-interviewed.

'By you?'

'Sadly not.'

'Got names?'

'On file, yes. Why?'

'People who do that kind of job are one up the food chain from scaffolders.' In answer to his defensive gaze, she continued. 'Put it this way, I've known a few who have branch interests in the disposal business.'

Jackson arranged his face into a mask of calm, as if he were discussing last night's football match and not the disposing of bodies.

'Hang on a sec.' He retrieved his laptop from the next-door room, fired it up and stuck in the flash drive. Conscious of Iris looking over his shoulder, he twisted it around, out of her line of sight.

'So much for trust,' she muttered.

'I'll roll through the names,' Jackson said, ignoring her. 'Stop me if one of them rings a bell. Ahmed Khan, Dave Widdowson, Raheem Omojola, Roger King, Bo Zhang, Jordan Boswell—'

'Same height as me, thin as a whip and eyes like pickled eggs?'

'Well, now you come to mention—'

'Him,' she said. 'From up the Wrenna. Proper pikey.'

The place Iris referred to was a suburb of Dudley. Historically, it was a nexus for criminality. Seems things hadn't changed. 'Coming from traveller stock doesn't make him a criminal.'

'Jordan Boswell would sell his own kid if he thought he could make money from it. He's the weak link. Thought you said you checked phone records?'

'We trawled through *everyone's* phone records,' he insisted, flicking to a folder, clicking open the correct file. 'Two calls from a payphone were made to Jordan Boswell a couple of days before Gina's murder.'

'There you go. Did you trace the payphone?'

'We did.'

'Was it near CCTV?'

'Nope.'

Iris narrowed her eyes. 'Told you Neon's a pro.'

'You think it was from him.'

'Who else?' she said, rolling her eyes.

Jackson made a mental note to get to Jordan Boswell before Marcus Browne's team. 'Going back to Gina Jenks and the pubs where she drank,' he began.

'And asked her stupid questions.'

'And where we drew a blank,' Jackson pointed out 'because of the ridiculous code of silence adopted by people living there.'

'What did you expect? A copper walks into one of those places, it's like a Lamborghini parking its arse in the middle of a Lidl car park. Your face just don't fit.'

'You think you'd have more luck?'

'I don't *think* so. I *know* so.'

He jotted down a list on a notepad, tore out the page and handed it to her. 'Find out who she spoke to, if anyone approached her.'

She visibly braced.

'Look, I'm not giving you orders.'

She glowered. Her mouth was one tight straight line.

'Or telling you what to do, but we do need to pool resources and work together.'

After a beat, she ran her eyes down the print, scrunched up the note and slipped it into the back pocket of her jeans. 'What was Gina like?'

'Enthusiastic. Keen to make a name for herself.'

'Well, at least she got what she wanted.'

Jackson wasn't sure if this was a joke in poor taste or stating the obvious.

'Did she smoke?' Iris asked.

He appreciated the fact that she'd asked the right question. 'She did. See if she nipped outside for a fag and got talking to someone she shouldn't.'

'Do I get expenses?' Iris said.

'What?'

'Money makes people talk. You're a copper, you must know that.'

Jackson sighed. 'Fine. Whatever you spend, I'll reimburse you.'

'When?'

For God's sake, he thought. 'When we next meet.'

'OK. Getting back to Gina, where was her car abandoned?'

'Car park in Cape Hill.'

'Got a pic?'

Jackson returned to the laptop. With a few clicks, he homed in on Gina's blue Corsa parked two rows from the exit, seven spaces along, and inclined the screen towards Iris so she could have a good look.

'Have a chat with your . . . *contacts*,' he said. 'See if they've picked up anything on the grapevine.'

She gave him a stony-faced look. 'I already told you, a bloke like Neon isn't going to talk to anyone from my world.'

'Any shot, however long, is better than no shot at all.'

The expression on her face told him that he was wasting her valuable time. Time that maybe she didn't have.

'Are you OK to do this, I mean what with . . .' He petered out, coughed, reached for his glass and found he'd already drunk the contents.

Her lips twisted. She appeared to enjoy seeing him squirm.

To divert her, he got back to practicalities. 'We'll stay in touch.'

'What's your number?' she said.

'Got your phone?'

'No.'

Was she lying to him? 'I'll write mine down,' he said.

'Don't need to.'

'You'll memorise it?'

'I'm not thick,' she bridled.

Jackson didn't doubt it and he reeled off the number. 'OK, what's yours?'

'I'll let you have it when I tune in,' she said.

'Iris,' he said, a warning note in his voice. 'Don't dick me around.'

She gave him a cool look and stood up. 'Are we done?'

'Not quite.' Jackson drew himself up to his full height. 'While we work together, there's to be no more hits, no more killing.' Iris shifted her weight from one foot to the other. 'Don't think I won't come after you if you do.'

She opened her mouth to protest, but he cut her off.

'I *also* have contacts,' he said darkly. 'Now, we'll reconvene the day after tomorrow, six o'clock.' It was critical that they weren't spotted together, so he described a slick pub and restaurant just out of town. 'Unless I hear from you before,' he said sarcastically.

20

Entrapment was not a word with which Iris was familiar, but she knew what it felt like to be stitched up. She'd thought she'd got the detective right where she wanted him, which wasn't difficult because, if Jackson's investigative skills were anything to go by, he was a clown. Then, as she was about to leave, he'd had the drop on her. No more killing, or else. And she understood exactly what he meant about coming after her: he'd turn her in, she'd face the full weight of the law and a consequent loss of liberty.

She was still fuming at half past ten the next morning. *And* the twat still had her gun. She could get another but that wasn't the point and, besides, why should one come out of her pocket? The sooner she got the job done, the quicker she'd get her hands on the money, she told herself. Dreaming about that amount of cash made a pulse in her temple jive. *Keep your eye on the prize, Iris, and screw the rest.*

Pulling down the visor on her helmet, she climbed onto the classic Triumph and headed out of town towards Smethwick.

Seventeen minutes later, she was standing in the exact spot where Gina's car was found. The lot was vacant and, eight months on, she wasn't going to find anything important. She didn't doubt that the forensic mob had carried out a fingertip search, but she crouched down on her haunches anyway. A nasty little wind caught her in the small of her back where her sweater rode up above the top of her jeans. She let out a curse – nothing remained but dirt and gravel.

Straightening up, she tried to picture the play the killer had made. At some point during that ill-fated evening in March, his path had crossed with Gina's. Iris suspected Neon had promised her information on the serial killer case and suggested they meet here. She pictured Gina driving on ahead and Neon arriving separately. He'd tucked himself in somewhere, flashed his lights and Gina had climbed out of her vehicle to meet him – being the eager, nosy beaver she was, why wouldn't she?

Alternatively, Neon had walked over to where she was parked and lured her back to his vehicle. Wouldn't a woman like Gina think it too obvious and creepy? Unless he had a fancy motor and she was a petrol head, but in which case why was the woman driving a Corsa?

Iris clicked her tongue. *Stick to the facts, girl.*

So where would he have parked? she thought, tipping up on her toes, scanning the landscape. *Where would* I *wait up?*

Straight away, she zoned in on a row of sturdy recycle bins. Located along the back, they provided great cover and were far enough away from the main road.

Setting her face against the wind and plunging her hands inside her pockets, she approached the recycling area. A Micra occupied the space – in Iris's book a food mixer on wheels. As nonchalantly as she could, she squatted down, her gloved fingers sifting through the debris around and underneath the car. This close to a bin marked 'General Waste', any amount of crap could have blown out, most of which would have no connection to Neon at all. However, Iris liked to be thorough.

Having covered three sides of the vehicle and seen nothing out of the ordinary, she walked round to the boot and repeated the process.

Nothing.

A thought occurred to her then. The difference between her and Neon was that he needed to feed an ego. She only needed to satisfy her bank balance. She had no other skills. To her, killing was a dirty job. She didn't enjoy it, but loads of people hated work and somebody had to do it. She never, *ever* revisited the scene of a hit. But a serial killer often did. They couldn't help themselves; had to keep getting off on it, the dirty fuckers. After what Jackson told her about the vile message left for him, she knew they were dealing with a man who fancied his chances of evading capture as much as he fancied himself. He'd come back, all right. And most probably in the same set of wheels he'd used to entice Gina in the first place.

Satisfied, she drove down the road to Oldbury and pulled up at a car wash. Firearms officers and Border Control had raided it not long ago in a joint op to weed out illegal immigrants, but there were still people there who she knew that could provide useful information.

Like always, the place was going full tilt. She watched as three young men worked on an old Mercedes saloon.

She approached the stockiest – a man with a doughy face and eyebrows that ran in a straight line across his forehead.

'Jakub about?' Jakub was the Polish owner. With his thin, birdlike build, beady eyes and round glasses, he looked more likely to be found in a college of further education. He'd boasted to her one night after too many vodkas that he used to work as an undercover cop. A bent one, she assumed.

Dough-face jerked his chin in the direction of a clapped-out Fiesta. Iris nodded thanks and crossed the yard to where Jakub was talking to a man wearing a pork-pie trilby and thick overcoat. The moment he caught her eye, he made his apologies, shook the man's hand and moved quickly towards her. A furtive bugger, Iris thought.

Jakub danced his way through a list of pleasantries. *Nice to see you. Business has been good. You look well.* Which was a fucking lie because she knew how ill she appeared. When he ran out of steam, she asked him if he'd had any customers come in with flash cars lately.

'How do you mean?'

'Cars with tinted windows.'

Jakub spread his hands. 'I do not think so.'

'What about eight months ago?'

His face broke into an incredulous smile, but, seeing as Iris clearly wasn't joining in the fun, it soon vanished like ice in boiling water. 'I would remember, I'm sure,' he said, keen to appease her.

'Keep your eyes peeled. Any car that comes in that's particularly nice, I need you to take down its registration.'

'Particularly nice?' he repeated, frowning.

'Eye-catching, expensive, fast, interesting, exotic . . .' *Use your imagination*, she thought, with frustration.

'Ah, yes, of course. I see.' He curled a bony hand into a fist, pressed the side of it against his lips. 'And the usual terms apply?'

'I'll double it if you get a description of the driver,' Iris said.

Jakub beamed and took a little bow. 'Always good to do business with you.'

Iris turned on her heel, slung herself onto the bike, fired the engine and drove straight to The Vaults in Gornal, the first pub Gina Jenks – fresh from her visit to the Black Country Museum – visited on the night she was murdered. If Iris took it steady, she'd arrive in time for the lunchtime trade.

21

All morning, Gary had trawled the city centre, searching for inspiration. And where better to look than near one of his much-loved crime scenes, or should that be *artistic installations*?

In need of a caffeine hit, he ordered an Americano from a café close to where he'd arranged Gina Jenks's body. It was hard to overstate the satisfaction this gave him. He could almost smell her perfume before fear had kicked in and smothered it. He thrilled all over again when recollecting how he'd reeled her in and snuffed her out. If he closed his eyes, he could still picture her – dead, of course. Live women were so overrated. Gina had absolutely no idea the great care he'd taken with her body. Honestly, she would have been proud. After he'd finished with her, she'd looked positively majestic, a million miles away from the cool image she'd tried too hard to cut while she was alive. Who needs Instagram, with all its fakery, when you can have your very own personal neon artist to make you look your best for the Grim Reaper?

'Do you want hot milk with that?' the barista asked.

'What?' Gary said, pissed to have his moment of reverie interrupted.

'Hot milk,' the man snapped.

Dickhead. 'Oh, sure, whatever.'

Gary's lip curled as he watched the barista attempt to create his own blasted work of art instead of just pouring a cup of coffee. As soon as payment had been extracted, Gary took his drink outside to better eye up his intended prey.

Frustratingly, most women wore coats and thick padded jackets, scarves and hats and gloves. It wasn't what he would call stimulating. No matter, he decided to sit and drink and consider the technical aspects of his next work of art. He'd already built up a sizeable collection of signs, some frankly show-stopping pieces, with a big American theme. Christ, it was going to be good. And in a couple of days, he would pick up the keys to the venue for his big 'spectacular'. It was due to be staged right here in the middle of Birmingham, for everyone to see. How exciting was that?

Basking in the moment, he sipped his coffee. After he'd shaken the city to the core, who knew what he might achieve? He planned to lie low afterwards and, next year, he would take the summer off and go on tour with the band. Naomi wouldn't mind. According to her work schedule, she'd be busy anyway. Baz, his music mate, had already got the band's tour dates organised. Eastern Europe beckoned with gigs in Estonia, Slovakia, Slovenia and Latvia. If Gary got frustrated, he could always leave a body or two behind to cement his reputation.

But first, he needed Jackson.

A frown creased his brow. He'd hoped by now that the

detective would be back on the case, yet he'd seen precious little evidence of activity, official or otherwise. Hmm . . .

A striking woman, highly made up, shoulders back, clip-clopped by on expensive stilettoes. Gary had her down for a model or, as he liked to think of her, bait. In an instant, he knew the answer to his dilemma.

Dreamy-eyed, he watched as she walked away and disappeared among a crowd of shoppers. Pleased with himself, his gaze drifted back to the immediate scene before him. Out of the attractive and classically pretty, which lucky female would he select to have her name and death written in beautiful lights?

22

Jackson phoned the Birmingham Museum and Art Gallery and asked to speak to the curator, a man called James Bridges. According to case notes, the detective detailed to investigate had drawn a blank there. Jackson hoped he'd have better luck. Bridges listened as Jackson explained and asked if the gallery had put on any exhibitions of neon art in the last twelve months.

'No,' Bridges replied quite bluntly. 'It's regarded by some as contemporary sculpture. I come from a fine arts background,' he said in dry tones.

'Not quite your thing?' Jackson said.

'I wouldn't say that. I'm open to all expressions of art, anything that conveys the human condition. Obviously, one identifies more strongly with some forms than others.'

Jackson drew two thick lines through James Bridges's name. 'I don't suppose you'd happen to know an enthusiast, someone who might be knowledgeable on the subject?'

'Do you know the art shop and gallery in the National Indoor Arena?'

Jackson sat up. He had indeed heard of it.

'Talk to Lizzie Withers. She'll be able to help you. Oh, and another thing.'

'Yes?'

'The shop doesn't open until ten o'clock. I'd give Lizzie time to have her first cup of coffee.'

Jackson glanced at his watch and returned to the interview transcripts of the parents of Vicky Wainwright and Vanessa Booth. Neither girl was married. Vicky had recently come out of a three-year relationship, and Vanessa, according to her mother, 'had male friends, nothing serious'. At this stage, he didn't want to contact either set of relatives in the stray hope that they would reveal something of earth-shattering importance. That would be too cruel.

Both women had similar general interests: shopping, clubbing and travel. Vicky skied at Chamonix, both girls favoured exotic holidays. Like most young women, they enjoyed hanging out with friends and operated within a fairly wide circle of young, well-off professionals. Vanessa had saved enough of a deposit to buy her first house. He wished something glaring would stand out, but nothing leapt from the dense print.

Afterwards, he called David Noakes at Noakes and Standing Solicitors in Corporation Street and requested an appointment. A time was arranged for the following morning. Next, he put a call through to the manager responsible for co-ordinating street cleaning, a man called Roderick Mayo. Jackson reminded Mayo who he was and asked if it would be possible to have another chat with Jordan Boswell.

'One of your finest has already been in touch this morning,' Mayo said wearily. 'Don't you lot communicate?'

Jackson was inured to a lack of respect from the public. Many felt let down by the lack of a visible presence on the streets and, especially in Birmingham, a poor clear-up rate for burglaries. He'd lost count of the times he'd tried to manage expectations by explaining about the police cuts, the general lack of resources and low police morale – on top of all of the strains on society's less fortunate. More often than not such an approach resulted in straightforward animosity and a refusal to help.

'Sorry,' Jackson said. 'Obviously some sort of a mix-up.'

'Anyhow, you're out of luck. As I made plain to the other fellow, Jordan isn't in today.'

'It'll probably take my man until the middle of next week to get through the list, in any case,' Jackson lied with forced geniality.

'It's no wonder you haven't caught this Neon fella yet then.'

Ignoring Mayo's salty response, Jackson said, 'Think I could reach Mr Boswell at home?' The man he was looking for lived in Quinton, Jackson recalled.

'Depends.'

'On?'

'Whether or not he's there. Spends a lot of time with mates in Tividale. They're in a band, apparently.' The tone of Mayo's voice suggested that he didn't think Boswell was heading for stardom any time soon.

'What instrument does he play?'

'Tambourine and harmonica. Badly.'

Jackson thanked Mr Mayo. He pulled up Boswell's address

on file. The word 'Grove' appeared in the first line, conjuring up images of sylvan splendour. He wouldn't hold his breath.

But, first, he had a date with Lizzie Withers.

The sophisticated calm of the art gallery wrapped itself around Jackson like a duvet. Apart from the jewels of light directed over each painting, the interior was softly lit. It didn't shriek expense and culture, it whispered it.

Jackson turned to view one of the works, his gaze colliding with a figurative piece of a woman lying on a bed, her face turned towards him, eyes closed, long blonde hair cascading from the pillow onto the floor. Immediately, sweat broke across his brow and a terrible knocking sensation in his chest hammered out a warning. He reached automatically for the collar of his shirt to loosen a tie that wasn't there. Clutching at his throat, he could hardly breathe.

'Wonderful, isn't it?'

Jackson turned to meet the earnest gaze of a middle-aged man, who'd appeared, wraithlike, beside him. Jackson nodded blindly.

'Are you OK?' the man said, concern in his expression.

'Missed breakfast this morning,' Jackson muttered. 'Low blood sugar.'

The man crooked his hand underneath Jackson's elbow and guided him to a chair. Jackson let him.

'I'll fetch you a drink.'

The man crossed to the other side of the room, pushed open a door and shouted, 'Lizzie,' before disappearing from view.

Jackson blew out a long breath and drew in another, in

an attempt to calm his racing heart. *Christ*, he thought. It didn't seem to matter how hard he tried to go through the motions, to behave normally, his body was entangled in a dark conspiracy with his mind and together they'd conspired to instigate a coup.

A few minutes later, a mug of tea was pushed into his hands. 'Is tea OK? I put sugar in it.'

Jackson glanced up into the face of a mop-haired, hazel-eyed brunette with petite features. Although dressed entirely in black, she was as sparkling as the fairy on top of the Christmas tree.

'Ralph explained.' She directed her gaze towards a desk where the man who'd helped him sat, running a finger down the page of a catalogue.

'I'm sorry,' Jackson said.

'Don't be. Happens to me all the time.' She lowered her voice. 'Especially if I mainline on Pinot the night before.'

He smiled. 'Are you Lizzie Withers?'

'God, has my drunken reputation gone before me?' She didn't seem the least disturbed by the idea.

'Only in so far as you're a fan of neon artists.'

'Aha,' she said, eyes gleaming, 'is this connected to what I think it's connected?'

Jackson stood up and introduced himself.

'The Neon killer,' she said ruminatively.

'Is there somewhere we could talk in confidence?'

'Give me a moment.' Lizzie Withers approached the desk and spoke in hushed tones to Ralph. After a brief conversation, she glanced back at Jackson and pointed to the door at the far end of the room.

Jackson took another mouthful of tea and stood up, his legs still feeling like they were a little detached from the rest of him.

He followed her into a room that was small, dark and contained paintings by a British artist with whom he was unfamiliar.

'So.' She stood with her back to the wall, one knee bent, foot resting against the skirting board. 'How do you think I can help?' It was unusual for someone to be quite so at ease in front of him – most people were cautious, wary and, sometimes, suspicious in the company of the police. Not Lizzie, a woman apparently very comfortable in her own skin. In this regard, she reminded him of Polly. He did his best to ignore the sick sensation in his stomach.

'I don't know a great deal about neon art. I was hoping you could help.'

'Although viewed a bit sniffily by the art establishment, it's popular with the public and gaining traction in the art world. High-profile artists like Tracey Emin have been championing it for a while. I take it you've already spoken to a neon artist.'

'Not personally.'

'Then you should. I can put you in contact with a local guy whose work I'm planning to exhibit next year. I've got his number somewhere. Hold on a sec.'

She moved quickly and gracefully. While she was gone, Jackson pulled out a folder from his briefcase, removed several close-ups of the designs from the crime scenes and spread them out on a small table.

Lizzie returned and handed him a card, which read 'Arlo Knight, neon artist and set designer'. 'Arlo is not always the easiest person to get hold of,' she said. 'You may need to keep at it.'

'Thanks for the tip.' Close up, he noticed for the first time how pretty and dainty she was, and it terrified him to think of Neon on the loose in the same city as Lizzie Withers.

'What do we have here?' She slipped out a small magnifying glass from her pocket.

'Neon's exhibits,' Jackson explained.

He watched the concentration in the set of her jaw as she examined the photographs, the meticulousness with which she studied each picture. It was hard to detect how she rated them. Perhaps she couldn't find it in her to appreciate the work of a man who'd done such despicable things to women.

Eventually, she straightened up.

'Bear in mind I'm viewing these subjectively,' she said. 'I'm not looking at the technical aspects.'

'But?'

'They're good. Dynamic, playful – I love the parrot. Both thought-provoking and highly accomplished.'

Jackson swallowed down a rising bubble of panic. 'You'd exhibit it?'

'If I was unaware of its provenance, yes. Naturally, that's completely out of the question.'

'Anything else you can tell me?'

'Neon signs are both practical and metaphorical. The artist can have fun with conveying any message he chooses.'

Oh, he had fun, Jackson thought grimly.

'Look at the visual communication here,' she said, pointing at 'Endgame', the sign that had appeared at Vicky Wainwright's crime scene. 'Crafted from light and heat, Neon encapsulates typography, industrial and urban design. On one level, it's meaningful, elaborate and complex and, on another, superficial, garish and decadent.'

Jackson blinked. He felt as if he were listening to a high-brow arts programme on Radio 4 and failing completely to understand what the hell was being discussed. 'But what does this tell us about the person that created it? Are you saying he has a sense of humour?'

'A twisted sense of humour,' she said. 'He's also lonely, I'd imagine.'

'What makes you think that?'

'Neon artists need to have a thorough understanding of light and science. It requires many hours of patient time and effort.'

'You mean it's a solitary pursuit.'

'Similar to being a writer, I'd imagine,' she said.

Was Neon a high-functioning depressive? Jackson gave himself a mental shake. This was bollocks. Neon was a killer – end of.

'He doesn't only use neon,' Lizzie said.

'No?' Jackson took another look as if it might become clear to him. It didn't.

'Neon imparts warm tones – pinks and reds. To create turquoise, you need argon. And, judging by his colour choices, he prefers cooler hues.'

'Is it significant?'

'Only to him.'

Jackson supressed the mental image of his wife lying dead on their bed. If he gave it headspace, it would derail him. Christ, it was hot in here.

'You're probably aware that LED has superseded neon in the commercial field,' Lizzie said. 'A lot of sign makers faced extinction a few years ago. While neon has always been popular as an art form in the States, it's taken a while for it to get going here. In recent years, it's really taken off and become rather, well, cool. It has quite a dedicated following.'

'Any particular reason for the surge in interest?'

Her eyes danced with mischief. 'I suppose we all want colour in our drab little lives.'

Jackson could not imagine the woman standing in front of him living a 'drab little life', as she put it. But did Neon? He put the question to her.

'I have no idea. Maybe. It's an interesting thought.' She glanced away, as if searching for an elusive word to accurately describe what she really wanted to say. 'Maybe the thrill is as much in the risks he takes when creating his work as it is in the finished article.'

'Because of the dangers from the material?' Jackson said.

'Absolutely.'

'But not a problem for this guy,' Jackson said, gathering up the photographs.

'Oh no, he's certainly on top of his game.'

23

Two hours later, Jackson was pulling into a sink estate of flats and terraced houses, washing blowing in the light breeze, and Sky dishes displayed on every building. Jordan Boswell lived in no wooded paradise as 'The Grove' addressed suggested. The only green he could see was scrub and he bet every dog in the vicinity had crapped there. There was nowhere to park safely, or without blocking someone else in. Cars and vans, most balanced half on and half off the kerb, competed with household goods, including a fridge, a cooker, subject of a chip pan fire by the look of it, a sofa and two mattresses. Little kids, careering up and down the pavement on trikes, pointed at his car. Older kids, of school age, eyed him with open curiosity. If there were any adults around, they must have been inside watching TV.

He climbed out, locked the car, caught the cold eye of a boy of about fifteen years of age (if the bum-fluff on his face was anything to go by) and headed for number eight. With every step, and despite a bitter wind, he felt his back burn; he was an unwelcome stranger here and no surprise.

Residents on these estates had a nose for officialdom. They could spot a copper at fifty paces.

There was no gate and Jackson stepped directly onto a makeshift path of grass and cracked paving slabs. An adjoining garage was in such bad nick the roof and walls were sloped, skew-whiff. Another gust of wind and the lot might collapse, Jackson suspected.

He looked up at the property. The curtains were closed both downstairs and up, so maybe Mayo was right and Jordan Boswell was out.

About to knock on the front door, Jackson noticed that it was very slightly ajar. He knocked anyway. With no answer, he pushed it open a crack, stuck his head inside and called out, 'Anyone at home?' His voice met dead air.

Puzzled, Jackson stepped slowly into a wide corridor, with stairs off to the left, and a gap in the wall on the right exposing an alcove and general dumping ground. At the end of the corridor, Jackson opened a door to a small, square kitchen with mismatched melamine units. Hardened blobs of sauce or gravy nestled in between the gas rings of a stove. Something unidentifiable in a pan stared up at him, a bloom of mould covering its surface. From the kitchen, he crossed into a lounge, where dirty laundry covered every available surface. For a man who spent his working day sweeping and clearing roads, Boswell spectacularly failed to embrace cleanliness and order at home.

Jackson approached a sideboard, slid open drawers, checked their contents for any connection to the Neon investigation, however tenuous. A stash of paperwork on a coffee table displayed bills; most revealing that Boswell was deep in the red. Rizlas, supermarket vouchers and takeaway menus competed for space on almost every surface. But nothing more incriminating than that.

Retracing his steps, Jackson returned to the front of the house and paused at the foot of the stairs. He called Jordon's name again, this time adding that he was police, but Jackson's voice merely bounced off the walls.

With a soft tread, he made his way slowly up the stairs and onto a short landing. A box room at the end provided a view of a concrete backyard, beyond which a line of plane trees bordered a wooded area. From the window, he spied traffic flashing up and down the Quinton Expressway.

In the other two bedrooms, both double beds were unmade and unoccupied; sheets and duvet in dark colours the better to hide the various stains. If, as Iris suspected, Jordan had helped Neon, somewhere would be a stash of hush money. With this in mind, Jackson trawled through drawers, wardrobe and cupboards, but only found fifty quid. Maybe Iris had got it all wrong – maybe she wasn't as smart as she thought she was. Perhaps Boswell was like the other thousands of young men from modest beginnings: enduring a low-paid job with only the dream of a better life keeping him going.

Crossing the landing revealed an L-shaped bathroom. A half-squeezed tube of toothpaste sat in a sink rimmed with crusted limescale and flecks of what looked like cereal. Above it was a mirror, and as Jackson glanced up, he saw Jordan Boswell's face reflected in the glass and whipped round to see that, from a rope lashed around a rung inside the airing cupboard, Boswell's body hung, purple-faced and glassy-eyed.

His heart racing, Jackson approached the dead man. He could barely see the ligature because of the degree of swelling around it. In a temperature this cold, Boswell must have been dead for at least twenty-four hours. Suicide or murder, Jackson didn't know. But something told him that Neon had played a role, somewhere along the line.

Switching into police mode, he put a call through to Mick Cairns, told him the address and that a man fitting Boswell's description was inside and deceased. He went downstairs to wait.

24

Setting foot in The Vaults was like walking into your nan's living room.

Cluttered with paraphernalia and 'knick-knacks', the bar area was mostly occupied by old men and women playing dominoes and eating faggots and peas. At night, there was a different vibe. People under thirty would venture in, the big attraction being the pool table in the back room.

Caleb Mulloy broke off from drying a glass and greeted her with a 'Jesus, Iris. You all right?'

'What did I do, walk in with my pants down?'

Caleb grinned. He had swarthy features and hangdog brown eyes that apparently a lot of women found attractive. Rumour had it that there were lots of little Calebs floating around Gornal. 'If you stood sideways, I'd not see you. Are you sick?'

'I've had the flu,' Iris said. 'And you shouldn't be so fucking familiar.'

'Sorry,' he said, not particularly sounding so. 'Now, what *you* need is a nice pint of Guinness.'

'What I *need* is information.'

'Oh,' he said, switching instantly from chirpy to concern. 'Before I forget, Norman told me to send you his warmest regards.'

This was not good news. Jackson's warning not to get involved in any contract kills echoed in the back of her brain, not that she had any intention of taking his advice. 'He's here?'

Caleb jutted his chin in the direction of a closed door.

'I'll have one of those soft drinks.' She pointed at a chiller cabinet underneath the till.

'Which flavour?'

'You pick.'

'Coming up.'

'Ice?'

Iris shook her head. It was too fucking cold. While Caleb faffed about, she went straight in for the kill and asked about Gina Jenks.

'That's an odd enquiry, if I may say so.' Caleb didn't miss a beat.

Iris ignored him. 'What did Gina ask you exactly?'

'Christ knows. There's been a lot of customers in here since then. What was it, five, six months ago?'

'Nearly nine,' Iris reminded him.

'Well, whatever. I spoke to the police at the time.'

'But you didn't, did you?'

He planted the drink in front of her. 'As you well know—'

'Cut the crap, Caleb. I'm not a copper and I'm not asking for the woman's vital statistics, even though you probably clocked them. It's common knowledge she was an investigative journalist asking questions about Neon. As a barman, I bet she bent your ears.'

Caleb Mulloy threw back his head and laughed. Full and deep-throated, it made an impressive sound. Several elderly heads swivelled in their direction. 'She had as much chance of finding that sick fucker as I do of bedding the likes of you.' Iris cast him a look that said, *Be very fucking careful.* 'That was the point,' he continued. 'She knew jack shit. Already wasted a week chatting up people in the city, or so she said. And for some stupid reason, she thought a trip around the Black Country Museum and watching an episode of *Peaky Blinders* was going to magically open doors and get her onside with the locals. As if we knew anything about some psycho murdering women in the city.'

'So she came here because she'd run out of leads elsewhere?'

'That's what she told me.'

But this didn't make any sense to Iris. Gina had a very good reason, all right.

'Could have been a try-on to get me to magically produce a clue,' Caleb said. With a click of his tongue, he picked up another glass and gave it a good tweak with a tea towel. 'Mother of Mary, she was one of those overexcitable types. Very London, deeply patronising and thought everything was *cool.*' He said it in a mock-posh English accent. 'If she mentioned the word *authentic* once, to describe the bar, the beer, the bloody lighting, like I wouldn't know what the feck she meant, she said it fifty times in the space of an hour. Enough to do your head in.'

Iris sipped her drink, the bubbles tickling her nose. 'You didn't like her?'

'I didn't *know* her,' he said dismissively. 'I guess if you like that upper-class, even-featured sort of thing, then she'd do. Personally, I like my women with a few flaws, if you get my meaning.'

Iris looked straight through him.

Caleb swallowed hard. 'Look, I'm sorry the girl is dead. Really. But, Jesus Holy Christ, what was she thinking? You poke a sharp stick in certain quarters, you're likely to get your head bit off.'

Iris downed her drink and made to get out her purse, knowing that Caleb would refuse payment, which he did. She set off through an obstacle course of old tables and chairs and senior citizens.

Norman Pardoe sat at the end of a room in which natural light only just peeked through. This had nothing to do with time of year and everything to do with a shortage of windows and an illegal fog of cigarette smoke. Everyone inside looked jaundiced.

Surrounded by a coterie of hangers-on and associates, Norman raised his head. 'Here's our kid.'

As if this were a cue for all to melt away, those seated stood up to leave. Some muttered hello, others failed to register her presence.

When the last had gone and the door was shut, Iris looked into the face of the man who inspired the most fear in the entire West Midlands. Bald on top, Norman Pardoe had a long white beard and small eyes the colour of canal water. When he frowned, he looked as if he possessed the DNA of one of those old Chinese Emperors. A big man with a massive presence, some wrongly assumed he was benign. In his sixties, Pardoe had clung to power for the best part of four decades and, like many self-made men, it wasn't by being nice. Ruthlessness ran through his veins as surely as blood. He ran a haulage business, a front for transporting drugs, principally cocaine. Any number of enemies had sprung up over the years, most of them the arrogant type who believed him to be an easy target. But it always ended in tears – theirs.

Recently, Iris had played her part in keeping Pardoe safe by slotting his enemies. She stayed at the clean end of the business. He employed others to torture – either to punish or as a means to obtain information (which Iris thought a waste of time: in her experience men with blowtorches directed at their genitals will tell you any old shit).

'Rumour has it you're not well. Despite the crap light in this festering little room, it would appear to be true.'

Iris repeated what she'd told Caleb.

'So I can count on you for a big job then?'

Iris nodded agreement. What Pardoe wants, Pardoe gets if you knew what was good for you, and to hell with Jackson's request.

Satisfied, he gave his cigarette a little tap with his index finger and ash dropped onto the carpet. He studied her for a moment, a smile on his face. It wasn't a pleasant feeling. Iris felt as though his eyes were boring into her brain, messing with the wiring. She gazed back steadily.

'We're being muscled in on,' he said, breaking the silence. Blokes like Pardoe liked to use the royal 'we'. 'Originally, the cheeky beggars set up shop in Spain,' Pardoe continued.

'Tried to disrupt our trade routes, without much success I might add. Now they've moved on to our turf here. Taken two of my best lads out.'

'Got names?'

'I can do better than that.' He pulled out a couple of photographs from his coat pocket.

Iris studied the prints. She immediately summed them up as the Charmer and the Thug. The Charmer had luxuriant grey hair, twinkly eyes and louche expression. To Iris's mind, he was the more dangerous of the two. Smooth gits like him always were.

She glanced up. 'Who are they?'

'Enrik Malaj and Valon Prifti,' said Pardoe. 'Albanians.' Pardoe rested both his surprisingly small hands on his ample belly. 'Anything goes with those animals. Aside from smashing up communities, they traffick kiddies, for Christ's sake.'

Long ago, Iris had trained herself not to react to unpleasant news of degrading, disgusting acts. And while Pardoe's social concerns might be deemed admirable, Iris knew that this was not his primary interest.

'They need to be got rid of,' he said blackly.

She simply nodded as if Pardoe were asking her to pop down the shops and pick up a pint of semi-skimmed.

'They're also setting themselves up as importers and wholesalers to other organised crime groups,' he finished.

Iris understood perfectly. 'And wiping out anyone opposed to their business model,' she said.

Pardoe nodded.

'Where do I find them?' She guessed that it would be the strip club on the way into the city. It had been raided twice for operating as a brothel with girls trafficked in from Eastern Europe. But it always managed to reinvent itself. Instead, Pardoe gave her an address in a suburban avenue. 'You want both men?'

He nodded, dead-eyed.

'Normal T's and C's apply,' she said. Which meant it was going to cost him a shedload. And thank fuck for that.

'Naturally.'

'When do you want it done?'

His green eyes flickered. 'Soon as.'

'Not a problem,' Iris said.

25

'Might I ask what you're doing here?'

Marcus Browne was unfailingly polite. He didn't do anger; thought it displayed weakness and a lack of control. His words and his tone, nevertheless, were authoritative. Cairns coughed, flashed a helpless expression and walked off to speak to one of the uniforms.

Enveloped in a flurry of activity, the crime scene was now secured and Scenes of Crime officers prepared to work it. Someone had called an ambulance. A mortuary van would have been better.

'I genuinely thought it would help,' Jackson said, adopting his most contrite tone.

'I appreciate your desire to assist, DCI Jackson, but you should be at home.'

'Yes, but—'

'And I'm now the acting Senior Investigating Officer on this case,' Browne calmly pointed out. The same height as Jackson, Browne was taking the opportunity to give it to him straight, which was fair enough. But, as far as Jackson was concerned, Marcus Browne was the embodiment of a man who had spent half his adult life at university, studying psychology and criminology and then forcing his education onto the real world. Not that it was a bad idea to be in his good books. Of those that disliked him, most admitted to respecting the man, Detective Sergeant Kiran Shah especially, who stood next to Browne now and appeared to be hanging on his every word.

'This is silly,' Jackson protested. 'It's not a pissing contest, Marcus. We're all on the same side.'

'I couldn't agree more, but we need to do everything by the book. And you shouldn't be here. Simple as that.'

Jackson couldn't argue. He'd have preferred it if Browne had lost his temper, but he was too calm and reasonable for that and, somehow, this was what rankled Jackson most.

'Go home, Matt. You can do no good here.'

Jackson raised his hands. He knew when he was beaten. 'OK, I'm going.'

Shah flashed a smile of pity before following her boss into the house.

Jackson stuck both hands in his pockets and approached Cairns, who was hovering on the perimeter.

'Sorry, mate. I had no choice.'

Jackson grunted.

'How come you're here?' Cairns said.

Jackson hesitated. He could hardly confess to consorting with the killer-for-hire who'd provided the lead.

'Purely a hunch,' he said.

Cairns frowned. 'This isn't a BBC drama, Matt.'

Speculation, in common with taking advice from psychics, was disapproved of. But this was Neon. Tried-and-tested strategy wouldn't work. It had to be off-the-grid, blue-sky thinking, and all that other bollocks.

'What made you knock on this particular door, Matt?' Cairns pressed again.

'I thought Boswell was the most likely inside man.'

'Fuck me, you mean Browne is right?'

'Boswell was *not* an accomplice. He was used. There's a difference.'

Cairns shrugged. 'Could go either way.'

'I suppose it's too early to ask if you struck lucky with the Las Vegas book.'

'What do you think I am, a magician?' Cairns said with a wide grin, spreading his feet slightly apart and puffing out his narrow chest, 'But I did receive a reply to my email to Ms Kozlowski.'

'You did?'

'And Ms K was very helpful.' Cairns took out his phone and scrolled through contacts. 'There we go. The man to speak to is Axel Gonzalez, an experienced officer based at Las Vegas Metropolitan Police Department. I'll text you his direct line number.'

'Thanks, mate.'

'You're welcome.' Cairns gestured towards the house with his chin. 'Reckon this is Neon's doing?'

'One way, or another.'

Cairns didn't budge, and Jackson got the impression he was holding something back. He waited patiently to see if Cairns had more information.

Cairns sniffed the damp, bitter air and stamped his feet on the ground to get warm. He looked across to the other side of the grove. Jackson followed Cairn's gaze, saw the youth with the cold expression.

'He's a hard little case, isn't he?' Cairns said. 'Thinks he's it.'

'Didn't we all at that age?' Jackson said mildly. 'You'll keep me posted on developments?'

''Course.'

'Best you go inside before the boss sends out a search party.'

Jackson waited until Cairns was out of sight. He hoped to get to the lad before the uniforms moved in with their house-to-house enquiries, but no such luck: the space where the boy had stood was empty.

Jackson glanced at his watch. Time to move it.

Jackson drove out of the 'grove', towards Ridgeacre Road before crossing to the main road out to Rowley Regis, where Kenny Flavell ran his business. Kenny had been Jackson's snitch for the past five years. He and Kenny had an understanding that, as long as Kenny kept his nose clean, Jackson would turn a blind eye to his many past misdemeanours.

Mountains of scrap metal from every conceivable industry greeted Jackson's arrival at Kenny's yard: shells of a hundred cars waited to be disembowelled and plundered for tyres, batteries and other spare parts; pyres of aluminium cans beside fridges, freezers and random electrical equipment. Jackson parked up beside a car baler and watched as Kenny Flavell sped out of the site office and across the yard.

Jackson dropped the window on the driver's side and

Kenny crouched beside, knee bones cracking as he leant inside.

'Getting too old for this lark,' Kenny said, wincing. 'Still hanging on in there, Mr J?'

Jackson caught his breath. 'Yes, Kenny, and thanks for asking.'

'Bad business.' Kenny shook his head, looked left and right and lowered his voice. 'That number I gave you. I don't want no comebacks.'

'You have nothing to fear, Kenny.'

Kenny sighed with relief, the features in his round face relaxing.

'Family all right?' Jackson said. 'How many lads is it?'

'Three,' Kenny said. 'That's my lot. Over and out. My Mrs made me have the snip. But you didn't visit to discuss my family-planning arrangements. What brings you here?'

'The journalist abducted from your neck of the woods and murdered by Neon. Well, I've got someone stirring the pot.'

'Have you now?' A strained expression flooded over Kenny's face. Jackson understood: Neon inspired a level of fear.

'I want you to keep your ear to the ground,' Jackson continued. 'Listen to the word on the wire, see if anything breaks loose. Can you do that for me?'

Kenny scuffed the ground with the sole of his boot. 'I don't know, Mr J. This is all a bit outside my comfort zone.' He paused, obviously picked up on Jackson's disappointment. ''Course, I want to help,' he said, eager to please. 'You know I'd never let you down.'

'It's appreciated. Straight criminals are more your thing, right?'

'Yes, Mr J,' Kenny said. 'Most definitely.'

'And I have your assurance that you'll be discreet?'

'As always.'

'And you'll keep your mouth shut?'

'Cross my old heart.'

'If you hear anything about a woman called Iris Palmer, I want to hear about it.'

'Consider it done.'

'Oh, and Kenny?'

'Yeah.'

'Emergency protocol should it all go tits up.'

Kenny winked.

26

Result! And he hadn't even had to kill.

Of Gary Fairweather's personal Top Five Thrills, first place went to murder; he got genuinely excited when he held the power of life and death in his fingers. One little dexterous tweak and it was all over for the women he abducted. Sex with Naomi came a close second, but even this was about to get knocked into third place. At last, finally, and about bloody time too, DCI Jackson had stirred out of his torpor. Gary knew this because he'd seen it for himself. He'd recognised that tiny, purposeful bounce in his step. He'd witnessed him with his *knobhead* colleagues. He'd noticed that little investigative gleam in his eye. But, oh my Christ, DCI Jackson had come good. His appearance at Jordan Boswell's home – and now crime scene – had changed everything. They were in business. They were rocking and things were going to get very exciting indeed.

As his reward, and because Naomi was abroad, busy working her pretty little rear off at some big event involving the great and the good at some fuckwit, big-cheese company – boring if lucrative – he'd given himself a day off. Feet up on the pale oak coffee table – Naomi would go mad if she knew – he was online, looking at a music website. Maybe he'd visit that new club in town later on. He fancied a night out getting down with the kids in their gas masks and rubber. You never knew what sort of freaks hung out in those types of places. Or perhaps, and this might be more valuable, he'd cosy up to his new best friend, find out the lay of the land, see what the police, and more specifically Jackson, were thinking. He looked forward to discovering how the investigation was going, watching them flail, struggle and try. It put him in mind of his dear old Mum.

He drifted off for a moment. His mother's death hadn't been his fault. Not really. That was all down to fate, happenstance, 'the gods'. He supposed he could have done more to save her. Maybe, if he'd acted sooner. Truth was he'd been lost in fascination, mesmerised by the beauty of her death: all that electrical activity stimulating her brain and her unable to do a frigging thing about it.

Yeah, Gary thought, *that had been quite a sight.*

27

Happily, Jackson had no trouble getting through and securing an audience with neon artist Arlo Knight.

A chequered black and white scarf draped around Arlo Knight's neck, Palestinian style, was the first thing Jackson noticed. With his dark brown eyes, even features and warm welcome, Knight came across as easy-going, liberal, arty and warm. Jackson bet the girls really went for him. It was hard to believe that loneliness featured heavily in Knight's life, despite what Lizzie Withers had suggested about the solitary nature of the artist.

'Step into my lair,' Knight said, with an energy that Jackson had long ago lost. 'You've caught me in between projects.'

'Christ,' Jackson let out, assaulted by the glare and bling of an Aladdin's cave of neon lighting – a miasma of light and eye-bleeding colour that made him feel nauseous.

Knight chuckled. 'It's not for everyone.'

'I don't mean to be rude,' Jackson said. 'It's the sheer volume. How long have you been doing this?'

'Fourteen years, or thereabouts.'

'And you make a living from it?'

Knight crossed his arms and considered the question. 'I do now, but it took me a while to master the art. I made loads of mistakes in the beginning. Not difficult when you're working at 700 degrees centigrade. Got the scars to prove it, too,' he said, rolling up the sleeves of his hoodie.

'God,' Jackson exclaimed, taking in the buckled skin and change in pigmentation.

'Neon itself isn't hazardous. Though the make process can be. That's why it's standard practice for amateurs who attend neon workshops to sign contracts, exonerating those who run them from any responsibility. Apart from the obvious dangers of working with fire and glass, there is the explosive component of gases to consider and, of course, the big one: electricity.'

'I'd rather figured that one,' Jackson chipped in.

'The voltage may be low, but the current is what counts. The potential for electrocution is high if you don't know what you're doing. I guess you could say it's a volatile process. All part of the charm.'

'I'll take your word for it.' Jackson strode over to an impressive-looking male figure with angel's wings. Above it hung a sign that said 'SEXY' in purple, turquoise, orange and yellow. 'How long would this take you?'

'Took the best part of a month to get that one right, but it generally varies. Without including the design side, eight days is about average for less demanding pieces.'

Jackson looked around the complex machinery. Running down the centre of the space was a large layout table with rolls of paper, metal files, a pot of pencils, blades and blocks of charred wood. He picked one up. 'What's this for?'

'It's used to cool the glass when bending. At every stage a section of tubing is taken back to the table, matched to the design and marked in the places it needs to be bent. Everything is made in reverse, like a mirror image,' Knight explained, 'so that when the sign is created, the connections that need to be hidden are at the back.'

'Sounds technical.' Technical was not Jackson's strong suit.

Knight shrugged. 'Scientific, for sure.'

'Yeah?'

'The whole process got kicked off at the end of the 1890s by a Scottish and an English chemist, William Ramsay and Morris Travers. Ramsay had already discovered argon with another guy and felt sure that there was a possibility that another element must exist in the periodic table between helium and argon.'

'Right,' Jackson said, thinking that, although it was very interesting, it wasn't going to help in the investigation.

'After a lot of failed attempts,' Knight continued, 'they were proved right. Then the French got in on the act and, finally, it was introduced to the Americans a decade or so later.'

'These are yours?' Jackson glanced at one half of a wall covered in pencil drawings. He was particularly taken with a spaceship, which had the letters 'I'll Be Back' inside the design.

'They're crucial to the process. Nothing is automated because it's so intricate.'

'And you always use pencils, not marker pens?'

'Nope. A nice soft 5 or 6B pencil works best.'

'It sounds like a really tactile procedure,' Jackson said, intent on understanding as much as he could about the process.

Knight nodded in agreement. 'Literally everything is done with *these*,' he said, holding up his hands. 'And a bit of puff from me,' he added with a self-deprecating smile. 'Sounds pretentious, but I think of it as breathing life into the art.'

Jackson pondered this. Breathing life in one form to then snuff it out in another – if you were Neon anyway.

He took out his briefcase and produced the same set of photographs he'd shown Lizzie Withers. Knight picked them up, pulled a face, his lips curling in distaste.

'Oh my god,' he said. 'Are these from the actual crime scenes?'

'They are.'

Knight scanned the photographs.

'I'd like to say that they're functional and do the job. Technically sound, they're actually beautifully done. Good and varied use of colour too. The range now is more extensive than when I started out – you have the Japanese to thank for that. They're mad about neon. There's a whole substrata of Japanese trucker art. Here,' he said, grabbing an iPad, clicking to a photograph of a HGV lit up in an explosion of lurid colour that made Jackson squint.

Keen to get Knight back on track, Jackson said, 'Is it possible to tell anything about the maker from the displays?'

'You mean does he have a particular signature, like the way in which he manoeuvres light?'

'Exactly,' Jackson said.

Knight studied the photographs for a long moment and shook his head. 'Do you have the actual crime scene shots displaying the victims?'

Jackson did but he was reluctant to share them.

'It might help me to get a better understanding of what he's trying to do,' Knight explained, not without sympathy.

Jackson nodded dully and reached into the folder for pictures taken from both Vicky and Vanessa's murders. He couldn't bring himself to show Knight his wife's. He placed them down and walked off a little. The mere thought of Polly induced a physical pain so strong he suddenly understood what it was to be broken-hearted. Resting a hand against his chest, he tried to calm the knocking sensation inside his ribcage.

'He's a storyteller,' Knight said, at last. 'The women are characters in his narrative and those who discover them are his readers.'

'I thought you might say that.' Jackson failed to disguise the cynicism in his voice.

Knight didn't take offence. 'I'm just comparing it with other pieces of work. Some artists like to send witty, challenging or disturbing messages.'

'And these aren't disturbing?' Jackson said doubtfully.

'Well, yeah, there's a murdered woman in the middle of the display, but the actual signs reveal nothing particularly unique. Neither does he play around with the contrast between the physical and perceptual, like some artists.'

Lost, Jackson scratched his head. 'So what's Neon's story?'

'I'm no psychotherapist. Maybe women – or a woman – represent a threat, but also something to be desired. In this guy's head, he wants to show them at their best, give them a fitting send off. He loves them as much as he hates them.'

They were both silent a moment.

'If I have a criticism,' Knight said, tapping one of the images, 'it's that they're too dynamic and vibrant – for my taste anyway. But I guess that's the point. How big do the letters measure?' he asked, indicating one of the signs used in the murder of Vicky Wainwright.

'Six inches.'

'Giving it a viewing range of around 200 feet. Did you know one tube letter may contain as many as seven or eight bends?'

Jackson remembered Lizzie Withers' comment about Neon's patience.

'Interesting choice of colour too,' Knight said. 'Red is the most readable. When it comes to clarifying, or getting rid of impurities, it's necessary to first insert extra tubing between the letters.'

'Giving it that spaghetti-like appearance?' Jackson asked.

'That's right. And see here: to ensure each character stands out he's blacked out the superfluous bits with a coat of acrylic-based black paint. It's a clever trick of the eye and professionally done.'

'You mentioned getting rid of impurities.'

'It's called bombarding. Here,' he said, showing Jackson over to the industrial side of the workshop.

Jackson clocked an impressive array of gas burners, torches and lengths of four-feet-long straight sticks of hollow glass.

Knight stopped by a piece of machinery. It had a yellow metal fascia of dials with a panel in the middle of it and a set of numbers ranging from 0 to 1000. 'First the tube is evacuated of air and then a high current, around 20,000 volts, forces any debris to dissipate. I liken it to putting a beating heart in Frankenstein. Once the tube is cooled, which must be done slowly, gas is inserted under low pressure.'

'Where do you buy all the kit?'

Knight gave a wry smile. 'Where do I buy, or where does someone with evil intent buy?'

'Someone like Neon.'

'It depends how long he's been doing it and, viewing his work, I'd say he's been at it a while. A lot of commercial manufacturers of neon went to the wall after the advances in LED lightning. Maybe he bought up a job lot. You can also purchase quite a lot of stuff off the internet. Transformers for powering the signs are easy to get hold of.' Knight offered Jackson a sympathetic smile. 'That's not what you want to hear, is it?'

Jackson let out a weary sigh in response.

'You didn't pick up anything off the actual tubes?' Knight asked. 'Can't you swab them or something?'

Jackson shook his head. 'Every piece was washed with an ammonia solution that contaminated results.'

Knight nodded. 'It's generally used for cleaning old signs.'

'What about the way in which the electrodes are attached?' Jackson enquired. 'Anything strike you as unusual?'

Knight took a good look. 'Nope. He certainly hasn't rushed it. If he had, you'd see the line where the glass aligns with the electrode. He's a patient individual.'

Patient and deadly, Jackson thought.

28

The Black Swan pub in Tipton, known as the 'Dirty Duck' by locals, was closed and boarded up, with a 'For Sale by public auction' notice pinned on the front door. According to an old woman, who was pushing a shopping basket on wheels with a small white terrier perched inside, it had gone out of business the previous month.

Iris stroked the dog's head and let it lick her hand. She liked animals. You knew where you were with them. 'What's her name?'

'Mitzi. Six years old and as pretty as the day I picked her up. She's a rescue dog.' The woman's face crinkled into a proud smile.

Iris wished someone had rescued her at six years of age. She patted Mitzi and thanked the woman again for the information and headed off to The Old Nag's Head in Oldbury. Someone was soft in the head when they dreamt that one up, Iris thought. A nag by definition *was* old.

On the drive over, Iris thought about Norman Pardoe's Albanian job. It sounded desperate and rushed, not his usual style. Not hers either. A perennial client who'd provided her with steady work for years, either surveillance or disposal, Norman wasn't a man you put objections to. 'No' and its variations wasn't in his vocabulary. And Norman had seen her right, often when she'd been skint. Work for Norman, it had to be said, had paid her bills. But now she needed a lot more than that, which was where the Jackson job came in. It offered an opportunity of a lifetime. She'd never have that kind of cash, not in a hundred jobs. She wasn't stupid – she couldn't do this line of work forever. Killing men – she'd not yet done a woman because she'd never been asked to – was a youngster's game. More critically, she was fast running out of time. How much had she actually got?

As a freelancer, she long ago recognised the sound business sense of taking on anything that came her way. Becoming dependent on one source of income was for idiots. With a little fancy manoeuvring, she'd ride both Jackson's and Norman's horses and bring each over the finish line. She'd have to be clever – there was no way either Jackson or Pardoe could know about the other. That was the problem with clients: each thought they were the most important.

The 'Old Nag' was only ancient by name. The landlord had redecorated a couple of years ago, unfortunately by ripping everything of character out and painting it toilet pink. Originally a cosy public bar with a separate lounge, it was now a single, homogenised space. At one end, local teenagers played darts and drank pints of lager; the other end was reserved for a bingo session that was in full swing.

Dodging an A-frame sign announcing a 'Pie night', Iris bumped straight into Davey Jelf, a kid on the make, who she really didn't like and who cropped up more often than he should. Wherever she went, he was a couple of paces behind, like a malignant shadow.

With his seemingly lidless eyes, Jelf had a face like a jaundiced dogfish that had been left out on a supermarket slab for too long. An assortment of metal studded his ears, nose and chin. He often hung around Norman in an attempt to muscle in on the bigger gigs. *Dream on*, Iris thought. Short-fused, hostility and aggression leaking out of his pores, he didn't have the right temperament for her line of work.

'How's Orchid?' she asked in lieu of any pleasantries. Surprised to overhear that he'd rescued a greyhound from the knacker's yard, she had been less shocked to discover him giving the creature a good kicking. Davey had wound up with two black eyes and a broken nose, and the threat that she'd come back and kill him if he pulled a stunt like that again.

'Stupid skinny bitch.'

She wasn't certain whether the jibe was aimed at her or the dog, but she didn't care. 'Didn't see you at The Vaults this morning. Weren't you invited?'

'Fuck off. I was busy.' He jutted out his chin. A flash of gold moved with it. She wasn't fooled – Davey hated to miss out. She hoped it ate away at him.

'Well, I'm pretty busy myself. See ya.' She stalked off, grateful that Jelf didn't follow, and hung around the bar while Linda Gardner, the landlord's wife, finished pulling a pint.

'Hello, stranger,' Linda said. 'How are you keeping?'

Braced for the inevitable observation about her pale skin and weight loss, Iris said she was well.

Linda, an *always look on the sunny side* woman by nature, breezed on, 'What you having then?'

Iris ordered a Britvic orange. Linda said it was good to have five fruits a day.

Several customers came and ordered food. Iris watched and waited until the late dinner rush dissipated and only the two of them were left at the bar.

'Wayne not in?' Iris asked.

'Gone to the cash and carry. I won't see him for days,' Linda replied, with affection.

God knew what she saw in her husband, Iris thought, a miserable man of few words and fit to burst with unspecified resentments. Iris had heard he was handy with his fists too.

'We've started doing karaoke on Thursdays, if you're interested,' Linda said, obviously keen to oil the flow of conversation, the precise reason why Iris had targeted her.

'I'm tone deaf.'

'So are most of the punters,' Linda retorted with a giggle. ''Course, we still have live music every Saturday. Here,' she said, leaning across the counter, 'we held a séance last night. Well, not *we*, a friend of a friend of Wayne's from Blackheath. Went down a treat. We had all sorts come in for it. Packed to the ceiling, we were.'

Iris thanked the stars that Linda was a good gossip.

'Don't suppose anyone summoned up the spirit of Gina Jenks?' Iris said.

'Gina . . . oh,' Linda said, lowering her voice. '*That* Gina, the journalist who . . .'

'That's the one. Just after she'd been here, isn't that right?'

Linda gave Iris a conspiratorial look. 'Wayne said she'd been asking questions about that mad, murdering bugger who turns women into light shows.'

'Did she talk to anyone in particular?'

'You know,' Linda said, with another eye roll, 'I asked exactly the same question.'

'And?' Iris sipped her drink.

'Everyone gave her the cold shoulder, apparently. You know what people are like round here. She might as well have come from Mars. To tell you the truth,' Linda said, 'it always goes a bit quiet after a big do.'

'In March?' Iris thought it unlikely.

'Battle of the Bands, wasn't it? Kids and musos everywhere. We were mobbed.'

'When was this?'

'A couple of nights before . . . *you know*,' Linda said.

Had Gina Jenks been in the crowd? Iris wondered. 'How many bands did you have?'

'Seven, maybe eight. Loud, for sure. I was glad to be out of it.'

'You weren't here?' Iris muzzled her disappointment.

'At my mom's, in Spain.' Linda's face clouded. 'Wayne said I'd left him in the lurch and I had to stay and help next time, or else.'

Iris had a fair idea of what 'or else' meant.

'Do you know if Gina Jenks was there that night?'

'Iris Palmer,' Linda said with a shrill laugh, 'you sound like a copper.'

And everyone knew you don't talk to coppers. Iris forced

a grin that made her cheeks hurt. 'She didn't go out for a cigarette, or leave with a bloke?'

Whether it was the tone, or edge in her voice, Iris couldn't say, but Linda's voice betrayed a sudden nervous ring. 'All Wayne told me was that Gina Jenks really liked music.'

29

It was nine o'clock in the morning in Las Vegas when Jackson spoke to Axel Gonzalez, a man who exuded American 'can do' and warmth.

'No pun intended, but any light you could throw on it, I'd be grateful,' Jackson said.

'So, what you got?'

Jackson ran through the details of the investigation. Gonzalez's only interjection occurred when Jackson described how he'd been accused of the copycat killing of his wife. 'That sucks,' he said. Jackson continued by revealing the inscription and personal message in the book.

'Las Vegas, huh?' Gonzalez replied.

'I think our killer has been there.'

'Along with over thirty million other tourists every year. As likely, the killer saw the book and bought it off Amazon.'

'Where else would he learn his craft? We've checked every possibility on this side of the Atlantic.'

'You can learn how to build a bomb on the internet. Maybe he practised at home.'

'You're not buying my theory?'

'I'm not convinced, is all. You got the book analysed?'

'It's being examined as we speak.' Jackson explained about the erased pencil marks beneath the message.

'Seems like this guy is tossing you a challenge. Saying come and get me.'

'He *wants* to be caught?'

'Subconsciously, maybe, but not necessarily. Cocksucker wants you to play his game.'

Or read his story, according to Arlo Knight.

'What if I don't?'

'Some killers go cold and run to ground,' Gonzalez said.

Jackson pulled a face. Allowing Neon to slide away wasn't an option. Increasingly, he didn't think it would appeal to Neon either.

'Or he'll kill again to grab your attention,' Gonzalez continued.

Was that what Boswell's death was about? Jackson reminded himself that the post-mortem reports weren't in yet, but it was hard to remain open-minded when Neon dominated his every waking thought.

'Sounds like a lose-lose then.'

'Tell me about the ligatures,' Gonzalez coaxed. 'You said they were leather?'

'According to the pathologist.'

'Leather is a natural product. Often a hide will have individual markings. My dad worked in Texas. Cattle-farming country,' Gonzalez said, as if to explain his specialist knowledge. 'I'm guessing there were no identifiable imprints on the victims.'

'None, other than we believe he's right-handed.'

'One thing's for certain.'

'What's that?'

'He carried out practice runs somewhere. He wouldn't want you seeing his early work.'

An interesting observation. 'Like an artist only putting his best work on display?'

'Something like that,' Gonzalez remarked. 'You need to find his worst stuff, the attempted murders, the shit that didn't quite come off.'

'Which brings me back to Las Vegas.'

'You really think this son of a bitch got started out here?'

'It's possible, isn't it?'

'Possible is not the same as factual,' Gonzalez said. 'Any idea of his age?'

Previously, Jackson had estimated anything between twenty-five and forty-five. After talking to Withers and Knight, he'd been forced to revise it to nearer his own age. 'Mid to late thirties. Could you go back over the past fifteen or twenty years and look at previous unsolved murders, or attempted murders in which the attacker tried to strangle his victims?'

The line fell silent. He pictured Gonzalez blowing out his cheeks, scratching his ear, shaking his head. Advice was one thing. Poring through stats for a case he wasn't involved in was another. 'Is this an official request?'

Jackson hesitated.

'Unofficial,' he said.

Silence.

'I really think I could be onto something,' Jackson suggested.

A pause that seemed to last forever told Jackson that, though he'd done his best, he'd better not waste any more of this man's time.

'Say I do take a look,' Gonzalez said. 'It won't be too thorough. But let's see if anything shakes out.'

It was more than Jackson dared to hope for.

The glare from the 24-hour petrol station's forecourt lights illuminated the house as brilliantly as anything Neon could knock up.

Iris still couldn't quite believe where she was – standing beneath a plane tree in what should be a quiet cul-de-sac – or what she was doing – watching the comings and goings of several men from a thirties-style house, not dissimilar to the detective's. It was bloody obvious it was a brothel and she didn't understand how or why the neighbours put up with it.

Until she remembered who was running the show.

If you don't want the flesh flayed from your body and your dismembered limbs to be strewn across the nearest motorway, or dumped in a canal, you don't fuck with the Albanians.

Standing in the shadows, freezing to death, she glanced at her watch. She'd been there almost four hours and it was past two a.m. Men like Malaj and Prifti lived like vampires. It could be a few hours yet before either emerged. The flask of tea she'd brought with her for the stakeout was finished over an hour ago. She was getting colder by the second and, worse, she really needed a piss.

Taking a chance, she moved off down the hill and used the toilet facilities adjoining the garage, before entering the shop. Disguised enough to form an indistinct image on any

CCTV cameras, she didn't raise a ripple of interest from the tired-looking Asian man at the till. She picked up two chocolate bars and made use of the drinks machine: coffee, white, with two sugars.

Behind her, the door clanged open. A gust of Arctic air billowed in, followed by two voices speaking in a language she didn't recognise. The shop assistant dropped his phone, stood up, hunched his shoulders and pressed both his palms together, clearly terrified. Iris remained still.

Both men wore tight-fitting leather jackets and jeans. The boots on their feet – in Prifti's case a size twelve, she estimated – looked as though they were designed for stamping. On the back of Prifti's neck, beneath his close-cut hair, a tattooed cross with angel's wings sprouting from each side. Obviously, had a twisted sense of humour, Iris thought.

Enrik Malaj ordered two packs of cigarettes. To Iris's ears, he sounded like he'd gone to one of those posh schools – didn't sound foreign at all. Meanwhile, Prifti cruised an aisle for snacks. Malaj turned to him and said something in Albanian. Prifti stopped and dropped the several packs of crisps and nuts, cradled in his arms, to the floor.

'Is there some place we can eat, have proper food?' Malaj tipped his head, which gave Iris a perfect view of his profile. He had high slanting cheekbones and his nose was a straight line; grey flecked a neatly clipped sideburn. Nothing like the unkempt Prifti.

'The only place I know closed an hour ago,' answered the clearly worried shop assistant.

Malaj's smile was slow. It spread over his handsome

features like a bloodstain on white wool carpet. 'Nowhere? We like Indian food.'

The shop assistant swallowed hard. 'My uncle has a restaurant not far away.'

'Then call him. If we like his food, we'll give him a review on TripAdvisor.'

If it was a joke, the man behind the till wasn't laughing. He picked up his mobile, punched in a number and spoke in Urdu. Iris didn't speak the language, but she recognised the tone, which went quickly from pleading to fear and, finally, to frustration and anger. Maybe his uncle wasn't playing ball. Finally, the shop assistant fell quiet, said something else and hung up.

'My uncle will be pleased to welcome you to the Spice Rooms,' he said finally, in a *please don't hurt me if you hate the food* tone. 'It is just across the road, next to the launderette. Very convenient.' Somehow, Iris suspected Malaj already knew this. A man like him left little to chance.

She remained absolutely still until the two men left. She replaced the chocolate bars on the shelf and took the coffee to the till to pay. Perspiration coated the Asian's top lip and his expression was a mixture of relief, gratitude and fear. It seemed to say that they'd both had a very close brush with death. Iris handed over a tenner and collected the change without a word.

30

The city by night was sleek and dangerous and glossy, a mask for the terror beneath. Give her the honest-to-God, downtrodden streets of her youth any day.

Unable to sleep, Iris spent the early hours cruising through Birmingham on her bike, under a moonlit sky that bathed everything in green and orange.

She dropped into Len's on the Northfield Road. A wheelchair-bound pimp, Len had a reputation for keeping his ear to the ground, soon to be officially undeserved.

'Neon? Me?' Len said. 'Are you fucking joking?'

From there, she moved on and spoke to Dougie, a homeless man who slept in the city's underpasses, when the police weren't moving him on, and asked if he'd noticed a man with a fascination for illuminated signage and a taste in stalking and trapping professional young women. He shook his head and she asked him to keep a lookout.

About to climb onto her bike, Dougie called after her.

'Try that club near Snow Hill Station.'

'Which club?'

'Dunno what it's called, where they dress all funny.'

Dougie's brain had rotted years ago due to a concentrated diet of White Lightning and hard spirits, so Iris wasn't hopeful of a more detailed answer.

He puffed out his hollow cheeks and ran the dirty fingers of one hand through a tangled beard. 'They dress in black.'

'Like Goths?'

'Yeah,' he said, giving the idea considerable thought. ''Cept they ain't like Goths.'

This was going nowhere, Iris thought, ticking with frustration.

'They like a splash of colour, see?' Dougie said.

'Like neon, is that what you mean?'

'That's it,' Dougie replied with a wide smile. 'Pinks and reds and that.'

'What time does the club shut?'

'About four. I know 'cos some of them come this way afterwards.'

Iris looked at her watch. She had a little over an hour left. It wouldn't take her long to zip across the city at that time. A club near Snow Hill station wasn't much to go on, but it was all she had.

As it turned out, she found the place easily enough care of a group of party-goers, dressed just as Dougie described, emerging blearily onto the street. The entrance to the club was down a flight of steps and along an underground tunnel. Iris wondered whether it had been created from an old WWII air raid shelter. She'd heard that there were quite a few across the city, most lying dormant and undisturbed.

Turning a corner, she collided with a guy wearing a black

PVC trench coat that crackled as they made contact. Beneath a shock of dark hair, he had bright green eyes, ringed with black eyeshadow – the rest of his face concealed beneath a leather mask. She'd put money on it that he wore coloured lenses – she sometimes did the same for the more exotic jobs. He studied her for longer than she was comfortable with. *What's your hurry?* she thought, staring back. He muttered an apology and strode away.

Electronic music provided a tribal beat. The closer Iris got to the guts of the building, the louder the noise. On entering what looked like a cavern of neon and strobe lighting, she experienced a total mind-drain. Dozens of young men and women with brightly-coloured hair and fake extensions writhed and twisted to a pounding, hypnotic, synthesised sound. It was confined and it was sweaty, and Iris reckoned that, if she spent too much time there, she'd slip into a visually-induced coma.

Edging her way through a wall of human flesh, she headed for a packed bar. Giving up on getting a drink any time soon, she stood with her back against a pillar and watched. Dressed in black, the girls accessorised with bright fishnets and platform boots. Most had multiple piercings. A lot of guys wore tight rubber and shiny PVC and, some, goggles and gas masks. Iris didn't scare, but the sinister sight would terrify plenty. Designed to shock, they shocked.

An idea she couldn't quite grab scratched the back of her mind. Casting around, eyes straining at the volume of reflective material in bright yellows and greens, her mind travelled back to the guy in the corridor. His manner, the way he stared and studied her made her think something was off about him. Then again, they were all the same down here – weird. Standing out from the crowd and knowing her face didn't fit, she figured it was time to get out.

31

'You at home?'

'Yup.'

'Let me in,' Cairns said.

Jackson peered out of the landing window and saw Mick Cairns looking up. He had a broad grin on his face.

'I bring glad tidings.'

'I'll be right down.'

Jackson opened the door and Cairns bowled in. 'Christ, it's parky out there.'

'Coffee?'

'Great. Black, no sugar.'

'Must be hot news for you to rock up at . . .' Jackson broke off from putting the kettle on, glanced at his watch, 'just gone eight.'

'Early bird and all that,' Cairns said. 'Before I forget, Browne fast-tracked the results on the rope. Initial findings suggest that Jordan Boswell was either a contortionist or murdered.'

'Thought so.'

'We're going with murder because the direction of movement of the knots suggests that a) whoever did it was right-handed, and Boswell was a leftie, and b) Boswell couldn't have tied them easily if his hands were up behind his head. He also had a sodding great bruise on his temple, suggesting that he was jumped by an attacker.'

'Any DNA on the rope?' Jackson asked, pouring out coffee and passing a mug to Cairns.

Cairns took it and shook his head.

'Straight out of the Neon playlist,' Jackson murmured. Cairns, he noticed, avoided his eye. 'What?'

'Browne doesn't believe there's a connection.'

'You're joking.'

'No lights, no camera, no action.'

Jackson stared at Cairns open-mouthed. Was he losing the plot? Was his desire to find Neon blinding him from more obvious and logical deductions? He recalled his conversation with Gonzalez and how the officer had questioned his theory about Neon spending time in Vegas.

'And Boswell had a colourful personal life, when he wasn't sweeping streets,' Cairns continued. 'Could have pissed off any number of lowlifes.'

'This is bollocks. It was Neon, for Chrissakes.'

Cairns flinched at Jackson's loss of volume control. 'I'm only the messenger, mate.'

Jackson apologised, annoyed at his brief absence of self-restraint. Mick was the last person deserving of his frustration.

'Don't worry about it,' Cairns said amiably. He sipped his coffee.

'Anything else?' Jackson asked more in hope than belief.

'Haven't heard a squeak from the document examiner.

Seeing as she's doing me a favour, I don't like to poke.' Cairns drained his mug. 'I'd best be getting back to the bear pit.'

'Before you do, I have something for you.' Jackson plucked a sealed envelope from the window ledge.

'Looks official, what is it?'

'Instructions on what to do if something happens to me.'

Startled, Cairns looked him in the eye.

'You're the only person I trust.'

Cairns shook his head, held the envelope between his thumb and forefinger as if it were a piece of evidence to be properly secured. 'Look, Matt, it was me who came to you. I thought it would help get you through, to be honest, give you a focus, but this is daft. It wasn't supposed to make your life dangerous.'

Jackson ignored him. 'It's all in there. Keep it safe. Don't open it unless you have to.'

Cairns grudgingly slipped the envelope inside his coat pocket. 'I'm not happy about this.'

'Promise not to open it?'

'Sure.'

'Say it.'

'You. Have. My. Word.'

Jackson thanked him and saw him out.

Due at his solicitors in an hour, Jackson intended to make a small but very important purchase afterwards, from a shop specialising in the latest technological gizmos for vehicles. He was washing up when his mobile rang from a number he didn't recognise.

'Hello,' he said.

'Is that Detective Chief Inspector Jackson?'

'Who wants to know?'

'My name's Andy Fenner, I'm the—'

'Crime correspondent, at the *Post*,' Jackson chipped in.

'We're about to run a story on the Neon investigation.'

'I'm no longer on the case,' Jackson said.

'That's what I want to talk to you about. I understand that your wife was Neon's last victim.'

'You what?' A burst of anger exploded inside him.

'It isn't true then?' Fenner said, surprised.

'Who the hell told you?'

'It came straight from the press office.'

'Well, it shouldn't have done,' Jackson barked, unable to contain his irritation.

'I'm sorry if this has come as a shock, but now's your opportunity to tell your side of the story.'

'No comment.' Jackson hung up. It was more polite than fuck off.

32

By design or, due to her subconscious working overtime, Iris found herself riding to the detective's house the next morning, despite the fact that she was supposed to meet him in the evening. The truth was, she'd didn't fancy the pub and restaurant he'd named. It was a meat rack, full of young professionals with fake tans. Miles out of her comfort zone, places like that made her uncomfortable. From a strategic point of view, it was dangerous. Someone like her stood out. Heads might turn and, if they did, her own might roll. She'd give Jackson what she knew now, they'd pool information and then they could move on to the next stage.

Nearing Jackson's house, she pulled over, removed her helmet and called his mobile. It went straight to a messaging service. Undeterred, she drove the rest of the way and headed up the drive. It looked empty because it was empty. Huddled under the porch, she punched in another number.

'Everything all right?' she said.

The voice that answered was as familiar to her as the skin on her back. She and her only friend went way back. Iris admired her for her strength, calm and resourcefulness. Only, today, she didn't sound composed.

'Have you considered the doctor's advice?' her friend asked.

Iris had thought of nothing else. How could she not? 'I have.'

'And?'

Iris felt time itself slide through her fingers. Without hard cash, it would, one day, run out. In her case, there was a strong chance of that being sooner than later.

'I'm working on it.'

'Iris, I really think—'

'Is everything OK is all I wanted to know.'

'It is but – '

'I can't stop. I'll check in again later.'

Iris cut the call and rested her back against Matt Jackson's front door and wished to hell that she felt more optimistic about the future.

Tracking back down the drive on the Triumph, she headed for home. There, she'd catch up some on sleep, fuel up on carbs and caffeine and, later on, stake out the Albanians. She hoped they'd make the curry they'd had the night before a regular treat. Routines were the death of every victim she'd ever known.

'You cunt.'

Jackson stood in front of Browne and didn't care if the entire police force heard him. Out of the corner of his eye, he noticed Kiran Shah, an anxious and protective expression on her face. He doubted it was for him.

'You tipped off the press.'

Not a man who enjoyed public scenes, Browne's expression was pained. 'Let's go somewhere we can talk privately, DCI Jackson.'

'Here is fine.' Jackson glanced around. They all looked completely exhausted. Not many met his eye. You'd think he was standing in the middle of the room with an assault rifle in his hand.

Shah crept closer, backing off when Browne shook his head discreetly.

'Come on, Matt.' Browne indicated an empty interview room. Jackson followed. He'd made his point. Inside, Browne sat, but Jackson remained standing. 'I understand you're upset.' Marcus Browne's reasonable response only served to fuel Jackson's fury.

'Andy Fenner from the *Birmingham Post* phoned me at ten o'clock this morning to run some facts past me before they go to print, and the phone hasn't stopped ringing since.'

Browne looked genuinely apologetic. 'That must have been a shock.'

Almost more shocking was Browne's complete composure. 'You didn't even have the common decency to warn me.'

Browne's brown eyes darkened a shade. Jackson had seen dog shit of a similar hue. 'Matt, I'm truly sorry. Clearly, the press office is at fault.'

'Is that all you have to say?'

'Other than I can assure you that the decision to inform the media about Neon's latest victim was taken by the highest authority.'

'The commissioner?' Jackson ran his fingers along his jaw. He was outgunned.

'Why don't you sit down?' Browne said.

And, drained now of all energy, Jackson did.

'A choice had to be made. You, of all people, recognise the strain on budgets, resources and time.'

He did – except, from a personal perspective, Jackson had enough of all three. If it took him until the day when Iris finally pulled the trigger on him, he would not give up until Neon was caught and Iris had done her worst.

Browne's voice, scraping through the stuffy interior of his office, punctured his thoughts.

'Matt, may I speak to you as a friend, and not a detective?'

Jackson stayed quiet. Marcus Browne was and never would be a mate, yet he didn't doubt that the man had integrity, as hard as that was to admit. He'd have preferred him vindictive and arch.

'I'm not a married man and I can't possibly conceive of what you're going through, but truly I am not unsympathetic to your situation. You're under enormous pressure, resulting in a state of cognitive dissonance.'

Cognitive what? 'Care to explain in plain English?'

'It's when emotions and prejudices come into play instead of facts. Frankly, any detective working a case as complicated as this, and for such a long time, is bound to cling to a fixed set of ideas.'

'That's—'

'How long have you worked for the police?'

A damn sight longer than you, he thought. 'Almost eighteen years.'

'Your thinking is institutionalised.'

'If being institutionalised means seeing what's right before your eyes, I'm happy to plead guilty.'

'Ah, you mean Boswell. Cairns mentioned your concerns.'

'Neon killed Boswell,' Jackson insisted. He knew that he sounded like a track caught on repeat.

'It doesn't have his signature and Neon only kills and displays females.'

'With Boswell, Neon's motivation was purely based on shutting him up, which he did very successfully,' Jackson said. 'Neon intended to make a news item, not a bloody movie.'

'There you go again,' Browne declared. 'Fixed thinking coupled with dramatic, emotive language.'

Jackson opened his mouth to protest, but Browne carried on talking.

'Matt, I understand how upsetting this must be. I'm actually trying to help, if only you'll let me.'

I'm way beyond help, Jackson thought. He longed to escape, itched for a drink, anything to get out of this room with a man whose 'do it by the book' philosophy was driving him crazy. And yes, he hated the way he felt: out of control. Worse, he knew that what Marcus Browne said contained more than a grain of truth.

'While emotional outbursts are entirely understandable in the circumstances, they have no place in the modern police service,' Browne opined, his voice assuming authority. 'For this reason, for your own good and the good of the investigation, it's been decided to suspend you.'

Jackson's face drained cold at the prospect. 'That's not necessary.'

'You'll be on full pay.'

'I don't care about the money. I care about the case.'

'Of course you do, and you'll be pleased to hear that there is a strategy in play.'

'Using female police officers to bait Neon? Are you out of your mind?' Jackson's voice briefly soared with anger.

'That's an entirely confidential piece of information.' Browne pushed the bridge of his glasses back up his nose. 'I suggest you use the time to take a holiday. Leave us to get on with things.'

'Don't do this.'

'I'm afraid the decision is out of my hands,' Browne said, although Jackson very much doubted it. He wondered how many cosy conversations Browne had shared with the Chief Super.

'I'd appreciate it if you give me your warrant card.'

'I have to work,' Jackson said, regretting the desperate note he now struck. 'I need it.'

Browne held out his hand, palm up. Coursing with alarm, Jackson fumbled for his wallet, took out his card, handed it over.

'Thank you.'

'Are we done?' Jackson was unable to contain his despair, let alone his belligerence.

'Not quite.'

Another jive of alarm attacked him. Jackson kept his mouth shut.

'An associate of yours, Kenny Flavell, was arrested this morning on a drugs charge.'

Jackson almost passed out.

'Let's be clear,' Browne continued seamlessly, 'I know that DS Cairns hacked into my computer and provided you with information that you were not entitled to.'

'I asked him to do it,' Jackson said, bullish.

'I'm sure you did, but if you'd wanted to know anything about the investigation with regard to your wife, you could have spoken to your FLO or, indeed, me.'

'What Cairns did was wrong,' Jackson said, furiously recalibrating his approach to Browne, 'but it was simply as a result of misplaced loyalty to an old friend.'

'Which is why this is a matter that stays between the three of us and Cairns remains in post.'

'Thank you,' Jackson said, feeling awkward now.

'Please don't make me put you forward for a disciplinary and force me to review DS Cairns's situation.'

'But—'

'I advise you to sever all connections to DS Cairns until the Neon investigation is brought to its natural conclusion. Are we clear?'

'Yes,' Jackson replied, feeling further away from catching Neon than ever.

33

Gary had decided to broaden his reach and sphere of operation. To date (he didn't count tying up that pesky loose end in the suburbs), he'd only displayed his talent in a city environment. It was high time to shake things up. It could even be a blast. If nothing else, it would attract the right kind of attention. *Come on, detective, prick and all-round fuckwit, what are you waiting for?*

While Gary loathed the idea of close contact with the countryside, from a kill-and-display perspective it had its advantages. Firstly, it offered the opportunity to spring that unique element of surprise, or should that be *shock*? Yes, definitely shock. *And* awe. Secondly, it would take the police an age to get into gear and add it to their extensive list of investigations, muddling them up even more. (And they were so easy to confuse.) Thirdly, the press would go nuts.

On the downside, a city dweller like him would need to take steps *not* to stand out from the rural crowd. He wasn't for one second planning to up sticks and move his enterprise to the wilds of Wales or the West Country. *No, no, no*. He had far too much invested on his current home turf. He was thinking more in terms of dipping into a nice piece of countryside, somewhere that connected and glanced off the boundaries of the urban environment. Not a million miles away from Jackson's childhood home, in fact. And if his location hunt today delivered, if he chose exactly the right place, drew the equivalent of a fucking big 'X marks the spot' as a lure, it could reap deeply satisfying rewards.

Gary already knew the visual effect he wanted to create, the kind of emotional punch he wanted to pack. If that didn't fetch the law running with their jaws jacked open, nothing would. And that would royally piss him off.

But, hey, let's not get negative, he thought. *Negative is for losers.*

To offset any potential domestic difficulties, it was important to time the kill accurately. Naomi wasn't due back for a couple of weeks. According to her work diary – something in which he took a keen interest – she was scheduled to start her next project soon after a brief touchdown. In other words, he didn't need to rush things, or skimp on covering all the logistical bases. He hadn't got this far to have some random event fuck it up now.

34

Browne had Jackson's balls in a vice.

With the speed of a man pursued by a gang of thugs in fast cars, Jackson sped up the road. Free of the city and, to his mind, the sanctimonious stench that hung around Marcus Browne, he did not breathe easy. The pulse in his neck continued to hammer an early warning.

A low-lying winter sun turned the sky to burnished copper, as blinding as anything Neon could create. Jackson flipped down the visor, reached for his shades and squinted hard against the light.

He drove to Quinton. If Marcus Browne wanted hard evidence of a connection between Neon and Boswell, he would unearth it.

Jackson pulled into the road where Jordan Boswell had lived. It was bin day and he had to compete with stuffed rubbish bins as well as vehicles to find somewhere to park. In the end, he gave up, turned the car around and pulled up in a neighbouring street that was less run-down. It was odd how the social fabric of a residential area could alter so radically within the space of a few feet.

He was assailed by the smell of rotting food and bonfire. Freshly spent Roman Candles and rockets littered the ground, evidence that Guy Fawkes celebrations had extended beyond the fifth of November. Jackson imagined the close had sounded like a war zone during last night's belated and impromptu festivities.

There was no sign of the cold-faced teenager he'd spotted a few days back. Instead, a kid, about nine years of age, riding a bike that was too small for him, pulled up, examining Jackson.

'Shouldn't you be at school?' Jackson said.

The kid flicked him the finger and rode off, furiously pedalling towards a house with an open front door, and beyond which Jackson could hear an argument in full swing. A brief dip in volume as the kid no doubt announced that the 'social' were in town, before it picked up right where it left off.

A crime scene tent still masked the exterior of Boswell's home. Curtains were drawn in the semi next to it. On the other side, the occupants had clearly moved out – a satellite dish half hanging off was all that remained.

Jackson started working his way down the opposite side of the road. Most people were out. Some were in and not inclined to answer the door. Of those who did, nobody was either able or willing to help.

At last, he approached a bungalow with a skip outside piled high with plaster, a dismantled wardrobe and shelving. A chair with the stuffing leaking out perched precariously on top.

Jackson glanced through a window. The TV was on, an elderly woman parked in front of it. When he knocked at the door, she didn't stir. He knocked again. Louder. It swung open. The youth who had stared him out on his previous visit stood before him. He didn't utter a word. Up close, Jackson caught a whiff of cigarettes on the boy's breath.

'I'd like a word.'

'You police?'

Jackson hesitated. 'Yes.'

'Spoke to them yesterday.'

'I have some follow-up enquiries.'

'Nothing to follow. Didn't know the bloke. Didn't see anything. Don't know nothing.' The youth yawned and Jackson was given an intimate view of his numerous fillings.

'You seem like a bright boy. I bet you don't miss much.' Jackson reached into his jacket, extracted his wallet. 'What's your name?'

The boy maintained the same disinterested pose, except his eyes tracked Jackson's hand to the wallet. 'Tommy,' he said.

'What did you see, Tommy?'

'It was dark.'

'So it happened at night then?' Jackson slid out three twenty-pound notes.

Tommy took a step forward. Automatically, Jackson stepped back.

Looking from side to side, checking the coast was clear and satisfied it was, Tommy invited Jackson in. 'Not doing this on the doorstep,' he added.

Jackson followed him down a narrow hall to a kitchen that was sparse but clean.

'Just you and your gran, is it?' Jackson said.

Tommy eyeballed him. 'How much have you got?'

To the point and on the hook, which was exactly where Jackson wanted him.

'I didn't invite you in because I'm looking for a mate,' Tommy added.

'I'll get on with it then.' Jackson handed over the cash. It disappeared into the pocket of a hoodie with the lightning speed of a magician.

'Got any more?'

'That depends. Tell me what you saw.'

'A bloke hanging around outside Jordan's door.'

'When?'

'Three nights ago.'

'That's very specific.'

'I'm a very pacific person.'

'Not the night before Boswell was found then?'

'Are you deaf, or something, granddad?'

Jackson flicked an apologetic smile. 'What time would this be?'

'Dunno. Eleven, maybe later?'

'What car did this bloke drive?'

'Didn't see one.' Which made sense. Neon wouldn't want his registration clocked. What didn't make sense: why would Neon make such an elementary mistake and allow himself to be seen and, therefore, compromised?

'Did you get a look at him?'

Tommy scratched his head. 'Not really.'

'Was the man tall, short, fat, white, black?'

Tommy crossed his arms, parked his narrow hips against a Formica-topped kitchen table.

Jackson took out two more twenties. Again, it was spirited

away. He wished he'd sent Iris round – she'd no doubt have got the information quickly, and he'd be a hundred pounds better off.

'About your height,' the youth said.

'Similar build?'

'Stockier.'

'What about his face?'

'Didn't see it.' Again Tommy scratched his head. His tell, Jackson thought.

'Full moon, wasn't it?'

Tommy hiked a shoulder. 'Had his back to me. He didn't walk like a black guy.'

Jackson wasn't certain that this was a very culturally accurate observation, still less a politically correct one. 'What was he wearing?'

'Jeans and a jacket.'

'Like this?' Jackson indicated to his leather.

'Maybe. Longer.'

'Did he wear gloves?'

'Yeah.'

'Did he go inside?'

'Dunno.'

'And you have no idea whether Jordan knew him or not?'

'How should I know? The bloke might have been trying to flog double glazing or something.'

Jackson thrust him an *is that likely* expression. 'Did you notice anything else?'

Tommy plunged his hands into the pockets of his hoodie. 'He had dreads.'

*

Jackson left and returned to where his car was parked next to an electrician's van. He scanned up and down. All the houses were set back from the road, up an incline, and nearly every one of them had driveways, some big enough for two vehicles. At eleven o'clock at night, residents would be indoors, curtains closed, and some would be asleep. Would anyone notice a stray vehicle? The odds weren't good.

Officers would already have carried out house-to-house, but their timeline wouldn't necessarily match events described by the boy. Jackson bet uniforms didn't know that Boswell's late-night caller had dreads either. If they'd unearthed those nuggets of information and reported them back, Browne could not have resisted the opportunity to rub his face in it. Jackson was forced to reluctantly admit that it was also entirely possible that Boswell's visitor was innocent and simply someone to be eliminated from enquiries.

Jackson trawled up and down the row. Claiming he was a police officer following an active investigation, he asked several householders if anyone had spotted a car parked up three nights ago. Responses ranged from 'Sorry' and a shake of the head to 'Thought you lot were supposed to do the detecting,' followed by a swift closing of the door. The word 'tragic' came up twice. Four householders were out. Jackson made a mental note to come back.

Climbing into his car, he spotted a middle-aged woman in a shadow black Ford Fiesta returning home. *One last go,* he thought.

He reached her as she leant over to remove shopping from the boot. 'Want a hand with those?'

She turned. Her carefully made-up face creased in

suspicion and deep grooves appeared at the corners of her mouth. 'Haven't you seen the notice?' She gestured towards the window: 'NO COLD CALLERS'.

He applied his most reassuring and winsome smile. 'I'm police.'

'Oh,' she said, like he'd winded her. She glanced at the carrier bags then back at him. 'Mind if we go inside? It's chilly.' She went to pick up her groceries.

Jackson stepped smartly forward. 'Here, let me take those.'

Inside, they stood in a living room decorated in cool greys and creams.

'Apologies for the brisk welcome,' she said, peeling off her coat. Jackson noticed highly polished nails. Liver spots on her hands suggested that she was older than she'd first appeared.

He asked for her name and if anyone else lived in the house.

'Divorced,' she said.

'Going back to three nights ago,' he prompted, eager to cut to the chase.

'I came back late after visiting my son in the West Country. I noticed a car outside number 29. Chrissie and Jim were at home and had plenty of room on their drive for visitors, so I assumed it was someone visiting a resident in the grove. Terrible place,' she said confidentially.

'Did you recognise the make and model?'

She placed a manicured hand against her chest and gave a light laugh. 'I'm afraid I'm not very good at that sort of thing.'

'Saloon, hatchback, estate, sports car?'

She thought for a second. 'Sporty-looking. Lower to the ground than my Fiesta.'

It wasn't much of a steer. 'Do you recall the registration?'

'Goodness, no.'

'Which way was the vehicle facing?' Jackson said.

'Towards me.'

'Pointing towards the main road?'

'That's right,' she said.

'You said you noticed it. Why was that?'

'It was unusual.'

'In what way?'

'The colour,' she said.

'Which was?'

'Brilliant yellow. Blinding. Almost neon.'

Jackson waited patiently at the out-of-town restaurant and bar. The excitement and confidence he had felt at catching a break dissipated when, at seven-thirty, he realised that Iris wasn't coming. The terrible low that inexorably follows a high plunged him deeper. What the hell was he doing? He had a death wish and she had a death sentence. What was the point of any investigation?

Phoning her 'hitman' number had elicited a similar unobtainable tone to the one he'd received on the night of the aborted hit. Cloaked in disappointment, he decided to give it another half-hour and then call it a day. He was mightily fed up with drinking tonic water.

Scoping the bar for any male with dreadlocks, he found himself watching the beautiful and the in-crowd at play, working the room.

He didn't count himself handsome, but a brunette in the corner had been eyeing him from the moment he sat down.

He inadvertently caught her eye and she smiled, whispered something to her friend. Jackson picked up his glass with his left hand and very deliberately displayed his wedding ring.

In the weeks after Polly's death, he'd barely been able to function. The happiness they'd shared was still too painful to remember. Grief had corroded every joyful memory, but he wasn't about to salve his wounds with a cheap lay.

It was now clear that Iris wasn't coming, so he got up and walked out into a night stuttering with stars. The car park was rammed. No bright yellow vehicles, sports or otherwise.

About to climb into his Mini, he had the definite sensation that he was being watched. Stock-still, he turned around slowly through one hundred and eighty degrees, convinced that someone in the shadows was watching.

Lamps illuminated the walkways. Headlights from passing cars spilled onto his face, the strobe effect triggering a vision of another night, terrible in its savagery: the glitter ball sparkled with malice, the sight of Polly's disfigured face – what Neon had done to her – burrowed into his brain. Jackson couldn't move. He was paralysed, pinned to the spot, blinded. The tip of his tongue travelled across lips that felt cracked and dry and he listened hard for anyone driving away at speed. Any noise was drowned out by strange music in his head, the familiar melody he'd blanked out until now. A cover version of an old song, a man's deep voice shattered the dark. Terrifyingly, he sang about his vision stabbed by neon light.

Jackson let out a low moan. Tearing open the car door, he clambered into the Mini, switched on the radio and jacked up the volume. Anything to obliterate 'The Sound of Silence'.

35

Iris valued the importance of cul-de-sacs. One way in and one way out, they were designed for a quick extraction if she got made. Not that she intended to.

In the early hours, she'd set up camp in the front garden of an empty house with a 'To Let' sign outside. Facing downhill and towards the main road, she'd parked her bike close to the porch and next to the garage. There were no security lights. If a brothel could operate right under their noses, nosy residents were hardly going to give two shits about her. On the off-chance one might, she'd inform them that she was simply doing her civic duty and keeping an eye on the property opposite. 'Haven't you noticed the strange goings-on?' she'd say, calmly.

The Albanians finally drove up the avenue in a Nissan truck with bull bars – an *I've got massive bollocks* machine – around four a.m. They entered the house and never came out.

She wore a thick padded jacket over two sweaters, leggings and jeans and still she was cold to her bones. Her teeth felt chilled and brittle and she wondered if they might shatter the second she had her first hot cup of tea. Right now, that's all she could dream of. Tired and bog-eyed, she felt ill, as if she'd aged a decade.

At around seven o'clock in the morning, the avenue woke up. Steam escaped from central heating systems and collided with the cold morning air. Lights came on. Curtains were drawn. Doors opened for dogs to be let out and cats let in. There was a general thrum of activity as families rose for the day, and parents gave kids their breakfasts and got them off to school and themselves off to work. Time to hop it before she was seen.

Pulling her helmet on, she swung her leg over the bike, rocked it back and forth, until the centre stand popped off and the toes of her boots touched the ground. About to fire it up, Iris spotted Enrik Malaj step out of the house alone, climb into the Nissan, reverse out of the drive and speed towards the roundabout at the end of the road.

Iris followed.

Indicating right, then left, Malaj headed for the city. Morning traffic was building up. Like every other motorist, Malaj was going nowhere fast. Keen not to give her position away, Iris dropped back, crawled along at snail's pace, past the People's Dispensary for Sick Animals on the left and, finally, The Amber Tavern on the right. Approaching the top of the hill and the King's Arms, the truck indicated right towards Harborne.

Iris sped up, rolling down the outside lane, eager to catch the traffic lights at the top before they turned red. Over they went, the Nissan gathering speed, and Iris keeping up, a vehicle's length behind. She followed to the next roundabout, where it turned off, tracking along the main street and into an outside car park. Malaj drove into an empty lot, climbed out and fed coins into a pay-and-display meter. Iris followed and parked up a few spaces away.

Caught in a blast of winter sunshine, Malaj cut an imposing and formidable figure. Wearing his trademark long leather coat, his grey hair looked recently washed and shiny.

Iris bent over the bike, pretending to adjust a wing mirror, and Malaj walked straight past as if she was invisible. Close up, she noticed a scar parted his left eyebrow, and the flat, high planes of his cheeks gave him an almost aristocratic appearance. The cruel twist of his mouth suggested a man that would enjoy someone else's pain and laugh long and loud when describing his agony and death to others.

She set off after him in the direction of Lordswood Road. For a big man, Malaj moved lightly on his feet, purposefully, a swagger in his step.

The landscape became more urban, glossy and respectable. When he slowed, so did she. Familiar territory, she thought, as he walked towards a cafe with a bleached wood frontage and tables outside, every one of them occupied by men with worldly-wise faces and women who favoured black lip liner. Smoke from a dozen cigarettes formed a heavy cloud over the street.

Iris hung back and crossed to the other side of the road, watched as Malaj was greeted like a rock star, with much slapping of backs, bear hugs and fist bumps. A chair was immediately vacated and Malaj sat on it. The others gathered around him.

In less than a minute, a barista had walked outside, deposited an Americano in front of the crime boss – she'd observed the separate jug of hot milk. Malaj politely thanked the guy, slipped out a pack of cigarettes from his pocket and lit up. He nodded, then laughed at a bloke with a shaved head and lips the colour of a freshly squashed fly. Iris wondered whether the others had noticed that Malaj's mind was elsewhere.

He pulled out a smartphone, scrolled and texted. Modern communications had made it easier for blokes like the Albanians to move people, weapons and drugs. Using secret communications, he would always be two steps ahead of the cops. Norman Pardoe could learn a thing or two from his main competitor. His problem: he was too ancient and old-school to adapt. He didn't get that benefits for staying under the digital radar only counted for a woman in her profession. She reckoned Neon was cut from the same cloth as her.

From the way in which Malaj intermittently broke off from what he was doing, scanning the street both ways, he was waiting for someone. His hangers-on seemed oblivious to their boss's mood. Too busy trying to impress.

Iris crossed over and, squeezing through the crush of bodies, entered the bleached wood interior and ordered a mug of tea, a toasted teacake and a glass of water. If she didn't wash down a couple of painkillers soon, she'd keel over.

A table for two sat empty in the corner. Iris made a beeline for it. From there she had a perfect view of Malaj and any accomplice he planned to meet.

Her order arrived and she gulped down her medication. The tea was exactly as she wanted it, hot and strong.

Malaj brought the cup to his lips, swallowed and said something to the others, who immediately got up and walked away, leaving their coffee behind and untouched. Now alone, Malaj leant back, rearranged himself so that his boots were square on the pavement. His coat, which trailed the ground, fell slightly open. Iris thought it a statement, as if Malaj intended the man who was now approaching to glimpse his weapon. She'd witnessed a similar move countless times before. Establishing who was boss, Malaj did not get up and the man did not sit down until invited.

Iris could not tell the difference between an Albanian or a Latvian, an Estonian and a Lithuanian, a Slovakian and a Pole. But she could definitely identify a Brit when she saw one. The man that approached was British, a Midlander to be precise.

He wore grey jogging pants, white trainers that blinded and a white hoodie that didn't. She wasn't interested in his godawful clothing. A bottom feeder with Norman Pardoe, his first name was Bryce and his middle name was 'Rat', which was more than apt in the circumstances. How else could Malaj wipe out two of Pardoe's finest? All of it came back to the inside man, which in this case was Bryce Butler.

Clearly, Bryce's Albanian was as bad as hers. The good news was he spoke in English. The bad news: laminated glass and noise from traffic meant that Iris had to strain to hear. Butler, from what she could make out, was babbling about Pardoe's business associates. Some of his information was misinformed or out of date. Not all, and worryingly, she overheard Bryce reveal the entire hierarchy at Pardoe PLC. Iris loathed Davey Jelf, but she wouldn't see him taken out by an outsider and, at this rate, Pardoe and his crew would be rolled up in weeks. When Malaj spoke in English, he mentioned an industrial unit near Brierley Hill.

Finishing her tea, waiting for Bryce to leave and then waiting some more, she finally exited the cafe. She'd go back to collect the bike soon. First, she had to find a payphone. It would provide greater anonymity than her mobile.

36

Jackson's mood was bleak. Unable to excise the song from his brain, he'd sunk one whisky too many when he got home the night before. Like the aura that lingers in the wake of a blistering headache, a dull echo of the melody remained. Had Polly been playing Disturbed's cover version of the classic song, or was it Neon's idea of theatre?

He finally went through the motions of getting up, washing and dressing. Downstairs, with a mug of tea in his hand, the nagging light on his answering machine reminded him that it was jammed. He'd been too messed up to deal with it until now. Apart from a call from BT trying to flog him a mobile package, the rest of the voice messages were from journalists slavering for a story. He deleted the lot, switched it off and disconnected the phone.

When a group of hacks turned up with entreaties through his letter box, his mind was made up. He collected Iris's gun and the ammo, a multitool and threw them into a bag with his laptop. He drew the curtains, grabbed his keys and left the house, bowling through a scrum of press with a 'No Comment.'

Two idiots – both promising exclusives – clung to his car

as he made his exit. A hand held flat against the horn had the desired effect and he spun out of the drive and headed to the flat in town. Several of the more determined of them followed, but by taking a circuitous route, he soon got rid of them. It had been a mistake to return. He should never have gone back. On top of everything else, the home he'd shared with Polly signified coupledom. He'd always feel adrift there and that was without the added visuals he experienced every time he walked past their former bedroom.

The flat felt a good deal safer on every level, and so he set to work. First, he loaded the Glock, then removed a tea towel from a kitchen drawer, wrapping the weapon in it. Next, he took out the multitool and selected the screwdriver attachment, walked into the bathroom and removed the ventilation cover from the wall. He placed the gun inside the cavity next to the ducting, put the plate back on and screwed the grille back up.

Satisfied, he picked up a beanie hat, drew it down close over his ears and face and went on foot into town.

It took him thirteen minutes to reach Centenary Square, home to the Hall of Memory – and Neon's second victim. It remained a massive construction site, despite the Hall reopening recently.

From there, he skirted the Birmingham Repertory Theatre and Birmingham City Library. New buildings and new skylines had changed the entire urban landscape. Whichever way you looked, there were cranes and scaffolding and construction workers. The effect was disorientating and bewildering.

How to spot a killer from the hundreds of workers and shoppers and commuters? Would he ever find him? Jackson thought in despair. Neon could easily pass himself off, with a hard hat and high-vis jacket, as just another worker. And where was the CCTV – how much of it was fully functioning?

Jackson entered a rat run, boards on either side preventing people from entering the Paradise Development site.

Ejected out the other side, close to the Museum, Jackson heard an accordionist playing 'Autumn Leaves'. He walked through Chamberlain Square to Victoria Square and down towards Grand Central. In all likelihood, Neon had walked this way, past the glitz and glamour of a city gearing up for Christmas. Had he admired all of the LED decorations of golden snowflakes, trees and red berries?

Veering left to the Bullring, Jackson caught a sickly smell of waffles that made him gag and, bowled along by a crush of shoppers, he entered an overpass, encased by glass, from which he had a view of Grand Central Station, all futuristic architecture, in polished aluminium, without form or definition. *Blade Runner* meets *Terminator*. An ad flashed on: 'Join The Rebellion.' Ironically, the font chosen for the street signs, including one for the Bullring and Link Street, was neon. Everywhere he looked, the killer seemed to be there, embroidered into the fabric of the city, and yet Jackson could not see him.

Down to the next floor and out in the open, Jackson found himself stuck in a human traffic jam until, finally, the crowd thinned and he approached the statue of the bull – Gina Jenks's last resting place – at the entrance to the Bullring. Jackson felt a stab of rage at the sprawling city that had, inadvertently, concealed the activities of a ruthless killer. Just half an hour spent in the city centre made Jackson realise that he was no closer to finding Neon at all.

*

Back at the flat, Jackson made a pot of coffee strong enough to keep him fired for the rest of the day and sat down with his laptop. He created a file and folder and tapped in:

Dreads

narcissistic

manipulative

highly intelligent

storyteller

Neon went to Las Vegas to practise his art?

With a jolt, he wondered how many dummy runs Iris had performed. He also considered her reasons for failing to show the night before. Had fear made her run? He didn't believe it. From what he'd seen, nothing scared Iris. Did she have a more pressing appointment? Was her cancer worsening? He genuinely hoped not.

He checked his phone to see if she'd left any messages, but there were none.

Frustrated, he returned to the keyboard.

Geography of deaths fall within a Golden Triangle.

He'd walked the area many times. Minutes apart and covering less than a mile in distance, the nexus of Neon's crimes occurred after midnight, possibly from the same starting point. Afterwards, Neon had fled before substantial police activity got underway. Yes, he wanted his art to be seen, but he also ensured he got the hell out in time. And that indicated a man close to home. Jackson had concluded early on that Neon did not operate from outside the area, a view that directly contradicted Browne's.

Jackson tapped out another note.

Inside man dead.

Neon slips up – been clocked.

So has a vehicle: neon yellow, sporty. His?

Jackson thought about this. Why would a guy who was target aware and forensically savvy make such a stupid and fundamental mistake? Killers did, of course, but in Neon's case, Jackson was inclined to think it a deliberate ploy. He remembered Gonzalez's remark about Neon's subconscious desire to be caught. It tallied with Neon's thirst to engage.

An idea brewing in his mind, Jackson picked up his phone. Before he could make a call out, he had an incoming.

'Jackson,' he said to a recorded voice that told him that he had a reverse charge call. Iris, he thought. He clicked a yes to proceed.

'I need my gun,' she said without any introduction.

'Really?'

'I want it back.'

No way, he thought. 'Like to explain what happened last night?'

'I had things to do.'

'Good, then we need to pool information.'

'I tried to do that yesterday,' she said. 'You weren't in.'

Jackson thought back. He'd been taking a pop at Marcus Browne. 'Sorry, I also had stuff to do. Where are you now? I can come to you.'

'Only if you bring my gun.'

'I don't have it.'

'Then get it.'

'Iris, we've already discussed this.'

'You're a fucking thief.'

'Iris, listen to me. The press are all over the story. My boss tipped the media off about Polly's murder. He told them Neon was responsible and every journalist on the planet is after me.'

'Then I'm out.'

'The focus is on me, not you.'

'And that's the way it's going to stay. Have you any idea what could happen if I'm seen within spitting distance of a police officer?'

He ran a hand underneath his jaw. He had to keep Iris in play. She might have information that could prove vital. As importantly, he needed her to kill Neon. 'Without me, you won't collect.'

'Without me,' she countered, 'you rot in your miserable world, and so does Neon.'

Jackson's insides lurched at the prospect. If he didn't do something, she'd walk away. Somehow he had to make her see sense. He had to play to her one weakness.

'I've seen my solicitor. The will's all good to go.'

'I don't believe you.'

'My entire estate is left to you after I'm gone. I can prove it, Iris.'

'Yeah, yeah.'

'As a sign of good faith, I'll advance you 25k from an inheritance left when my mother died.' It was the last card he had to play. If she refused, he'd be flying solo. No job, no wife, perhaps no chance of ever unmasking Neon and avenging Polly's death. He held his breath. Silence ticked for several seconds.

'Tell me where to find you,' she said.

'I'm in a flat in the Jewellery Quarter.' He described the location, hung up, and heaved a sigh of relief.

37

Jackson was more pleased to see Iris than he let on. He took care of their financial business straightaway, wiring funds directly to a designated account that she'd promised was untraceable. 'So don't bother with any funny stuff,' she added threateningly. In fact, Iris's whole disposition was edgy and grim. She shot him a venomous look and sat down.

'I want my gun.'

'I already told you. I don't—'

'What have you done with it?'

He cleared his throat. 'I chucked it in the canal.'

She stood up, slapped her thighs, raised her fists, in attack mode.

'You had no right.'

'I'm sorry but we had an agreement.'

'*We* didn't.' She plunged her hands into her pockets and paced up and down.

'It's for your own good. Possession of a gun and ammo carries a minimum ten-year sentence. I did it to protect you, Iris.'

She clearly took a different point of view.

Suddenly, a phone went off and it wasn't his. Iris gave a start, reached into her pocket, took it out and cut the call.

'What did you find out?' He spoke softly, determined to get the conversation back on track.

About to answer, her phone went off once more. She grimaced.

'Shouldn't you get that?'

She cut the call again and glowered at him. 'Got any tea?'

'Sure. No milk though.'

'I can't drink tea without milk.'

God, she was hard work.

'Stay here,' he said. 'I'll get my coat.' He disappeared into the bedroom and got what he needed. On his return, she was busy texting. She seemed agitated and he wondered what she was up to. He waited for her to finish and took out his own phone. 'What's your number?'

She blinked; quite reluctant, it seemed, to give it.

Jackson stood his ground. 'The sooner you let me have it, the sooner you'll get your cuppa.'

She rattled off a number, which he inserted into his contacts.

'Don't touch anything,' he warned. 'Have a nap. You look as if you could use one.'

He hurried to the Express shop, bought a pint of milk and hurried back. Glancing up to his flat, he took a breath and headed down to the underground car park. Iris's Triumph was tucked away in a bay behind a pillar. Slipping out his phone and the tracking device he'd bought the day before, he activated the SIM, then took out his multitool, unscrewed the tail section and removed the seat. He worked quickly, disconnecting wires, snuggling the tracker inside, feeding through the connections before reconnecting and screwing the seat back down. The process took him a little over an hour – a very long time to buy some milk from the local shop. At any moment, he expected to see her angry face. Creating a password, he synched the device with his phone and returned upstairs where, to his relief, Iris was out for the count on his sofa. The years appeared to drop away from her. In repose, she looked peaceful and benign, a far cry from the woman she appeared to be.

Jackson peeled off his coat and made them both drinks. She stirred as he put two mugs on the coffee table.

Iris's hollow cheeks puffed out as she blew on her tea and took a tentative sip. 'You shouldn't have let me sleep that long,' she complained. The brief rest had not improved her mood.

He asked again what she'd found out.

'Gina Jenks made a nuisance of herself for well over a week before she fell into Neon's clutches. She'd already spent days prodding and poking in town.'

'Nothing we don't already know.'

'I'm describing the situation,' Iris said, tight-lipped.

Jackson put both palms up in apology.

'The pub where she was last seen—'

'The Old Nag's Head.'

'She'd gone there a couple of nights before she was murdered.' Iris explained about the Battle of the Bands night and Gina Jenks's interest in music.

With a throbbing pulse, Jackson tamped down the unwanted musical memory from the previous night. But what was it Mayo had said about Boswell? *He played tambourine and harmonica badly.*

'Gina could have run into Neon on the music night,' Iris continued. 'There were hordes of people. One woman talking to a bloke, or being chatted up, nobody would notice.'

'Wasn't a random encounter,' Jackson remarked. 'Neon doesn't do anything by chance.'

'Agreed,' she said.

'If he got wind of her poking her nose in, he'd have stalked her.'

'Any decent killer researches his victim,' Iris said with terrifying self-possession.

Was there such a thing as a 'decent' killer, Jackson wondered, baulking at the thought. 'Was she on to something, do you think?'

'Definitely,' Iris said.

'Could music be the connection?'

'What did you have in mind, a murdering DJ?' Iris scoffed. 'I suppose he'll have an interest in Country and Western too.'

Despite her mocking, Jackson made a mental note to check out DJs in the area, and find out whether Neon's first victims had any particular interest in music.

'The pub must have had flyers publicising the evening,' Jackson said. 'Maybe posters too. That would tell us exactly which bands were playing.'

Iris didn't look sold.

'I'm serious,' he said.

'You want me to go back and ask?'

'I can do it. Got plenty of time on my hands now I've been suspended.'

Her eyes widened. 'Then how the fuck is this supposed to work? I thought I was supposed to be your contact on the ground while you had *access through all the official channels,*' she said, quoting him directly.

'I still have professional contacts.' Except would Cairns still play ball? He had a mortgage and a divorce to pay for, after all.

Iris took another sip of tea, unimpressed. 'Did you check out Boswell?'

'Haven't you heard?'

She stared blank-eyed.

'He's dead.'

'Neon killed him?'

'Not according to Marcus Browne.' Jackson explained Browne's thinking and told her about his own enquiries and what he'd unearthed.

'A bloke with dreads and a yellow car. Not exactly a smoking gun, is it?'

'Who needs a smoking gun when I can smoke him out?'

Iris elevated an eyebrow so pale Jackson only noticed because of the crease in her forehead.

'Thanks to Marcus Browne, Neon is basking in the limelight. To his warped little mind, his accomplishments are celebrated on every media outlet. Polly is the pinnacle of his murderous career and, finally, he gets the credit for it.'

Iris stuck the heel of her hand under her chin and glowered.

'We give him time to enjoy his rewards and satisfy his ego,' Jackson continued.

'The opposite of what we agreed.'

'Temporarily,' Jackson said.

'What are you going to do?' she asked warily.

'The press are snapping at my heels for an exclusive. I'm going to use the media to speak directly to Neon. I'm going to tell him how he cocked up. I'm going to warn him that we're on to him and closing in.'

38

He's cracked, she thought. Iris knew a lot of lunatics and Matt Jackson was right up there with the rest of them. It's why she'd decided to keep quiet about her collision with a stranger in a club for weirdos.

After Jackson gave her a load of old rubbish about how he appreciated her help, she agreed to go to the pub. Not one for chat, Wayne was a stickler for keeping records. He'd have the information. All she had to do was prise it out of him. Afterwards, she'd visit the industrial unit in Brierley Hill and find out what Malaj and his mates were up to.

When she arrived at The Old Nags Head, Wayne was outside. His arms were crossed and he was eyeing up the roof with a concerned eye. She drew alongside and gazed up to a dark patch beneath the guttering.

'See where that slate's come loose?' Wayne said. 'It's let in the damp. And damp means dear.'

Iris hadn't the time or inclination to commiserate. 'Is Linda inside?'

He muttered a 'yes'. Wayne, she reckoned, would be a while yet.

Putting out salt and pepper and vinegar on tables, Linda gave Iris a wary look.

'It's like a morgue in here,' Linda muttered, glancing around the empty bar.

Iris glanced too, on the lookout for a crackpot with dreads. She didn't care what Jackson said. For all she knew, Neon could be watching her now, preparing to make his move. *Come and get me.* Win-win, if he did.

Iris came straight out with it, no messing. 'Got any flyers or posters left from the Battle of the Bands night?'

'Might have.' Linda was a lot less sharp than Wayne, but she wasn't stupid.

Iris could have affected a pained sigh and come up with some excuse, but she didn't have the time. 'I want one,' she said.

Linda looked at Iris as if she might be joking. Iris thrust her a look that convinced her she wasn't.

'Mind the bar for a tick then, would you?' Linda said. 'Help yourself to a drink,' she called over her shoulder, always eager to please, and scurried off into a back room.

Iris walked through to the other side and took up a position in front of the optics. She twisted to reach a glass and heard a creak behind her. Spinning round, she was brought up short by the sight of Davey Jelf's miserable face and his equally miserable dog.

'Boss wants to see you.' Jelf was trembling, either with crystal meth or excitement. But why would Pardoe send a creep like Jelf? 'Now.' He gave a vicious yank on the lead. The greyhound yelped.

'I warned you.' Iris smacked open the trapdoor in the counter and advanced on Jelf.

'Not sure you're in a position to threaten.' He locked eyes with hers.

Iris swung her arm back, prepared to drill a fist into Jelf's bony face—

'There you go,' Linda said, depositing dozens of posters and flyers. 'Hello, Davey,' she said with false brightness. Iris let her arm go slack.

'Hello, Lind,' Jelf said. 'We're not stopping, are we, Iris? Mr Pardoe isn't a patient man.'

At the mention of Norman Pardoe, Linda's skin turned pale. She looked from Jelf to Iris, and back to Jelf again.

Furious, Iris grabbed a poster, folded it and stuck it inside her jacket, and walked outside into an unforgivably cold afternoon.

Jelf slipped out a packet of cigarettes, lit up and stayed right where he was. 'Over there,' he said, gesturing with his chin.

Across the pub car park was parked Pardoe's BMW X5, engine running. Pardoe was in the back. He had his usual driver with him, a bloke called Fred Staines. Nobody was sitting in the passenger side, which Iris interpreted as a good sign.

She plunged her hands in her pockets and walked smartly over. With Pardoe she knew it was best never to display unease.

Staines got out and opened a rear door, indicating for Iris to get in. A haze of cigarette smoke enveloped her, making her eyes sting. The door closed shut behind and she heard the locks click tight.

Pardoe loomed like a thundercloud. The leather seats creaked and she found herself inched into the corner. The tip of Pardoe's beard grazed her face.

She stayed silent and heard Staines climbing back into the driver's seat.

'How long have we known each other, Iris?' Pardoe asked.

'Six years.'

'Give or take a couple of months,' he said with a nasty little smile.

'If you say so.'

'Have I always been fair?'

'Yes.'

'I've always been straight with you?'

'You have.'

His green eyes narrowed. 'Then why the fuck are you talking to the police?'

'I'm not.'

'Our kid,' he said, quietly menacing, 'You were *seen*.'

She let out a breath. This is exactly what she'd warned Jackson about.

'What would he want with you?' Pardoe said. 'Cocked up, have you? Got sloppy?'

Iris flared inwardly that a shit like Pardoe should question her professionalism. If Jelf had tailed her, she would have made him. Someone had talked or, more like, Jackson had. The best thing was to ignore the barb. She could make up a fairy tale, but too often she'd witnessed the results of what happened to people who lied to Pardoe. As bad as her situation was, she had to tell him the truth. 'He wants me to carry out a hit.'

'Fuck me,' she heard Staines say.

Pardoe couldn't have looked more surprised if she'd announced she was about to marry and settle down. He eased away and Iris straightened up.

She didn't have long to recover. Pardoe pushed his face in front of hers again. He had the bearing of a rattlesnake about to strike.

'He doesn't work for the police any more,' Iris said, which was sort of true.

Pardoe looked towards his driver. 'Well, that's all right then,' he said with heavy sarcasm, to which Staines snig-gered.

'Mr Pardoe, he has no interest in you or your affairs.'

'That might be the case, but how are you supposed to do a job for me if you're also working for him. Split priorities, Iris.' What Pardoe really meant was split loyalties. And he couldn't abide those.

'But I'm making progress with the Albanians. I know what's going down.'

'Go on.'

She ran through what she knew.

When she told Pardoe how Bryce Butler was snitching on him, his slitted eyes almost disappeared into his face. 'The little fucker.'

'What do you want me to do?'

'A bullet's too good for him. Leave that one with me.' He tapped Staines on the shoulder. Staines looked straight ahead and nodded. Iris knew what that meant. 'How close are you to a strike?' Pardoe said.

She told him about the cafe, a lousy place for a hit, and the industrial unit at Brierley Hill, which might be a go. 'I can scope it out this afternoon.'

He patted her knee with a paw of a hand. 'You do that, Iris. Let me know how you get on.'

The locks clicked open.

'Will that be all, Mr Pardoe?'

'All's well that ends well,' he said amiably. 'You've done good work, Iris. Proud of you.'

Iris climbed out and walked slowly across the car park.

Jelf was still standing by the entrance to the pub, twitching like a junkie, a spiteful look on his face.

'Enjoy your chat?' He lobbed the cigarette he was smoking onto the tarmac.

Iris walked straight up to him, raised her leg and took immense pleasure in connecting her knee to his groin. While Jelf yowled and doubled over, she climbed on her bike and drove off to Brierley Hill.

The industrial unit lay on an abandoned site on Thorns Road. Brick-built, with a weatherboarded top storey, the office area seemed in relatively good condition. Consisting of eight triple windows upstairs and four below, the layout could house a sizeable workforce – certainly enough space for Malaj and his crew. At one end, there was a covered area, like a massive carport. Recessed at the back was a door. She wondered what was inside, concluded that if there were drugs, the place would be guarded. There were no cars and no signs of human activity, but Iris went over to check. Predictably, it was locked.

Conscious she was on a timeline, Iris crossed a substantial yard to three warehouses, each with metal up-and-over doors. She tried to roll up the first two, but neither budged. The third came away from the floor easily, and she walked inside the huge space. Skylights ran the length of the roof, illuminating a pile of metal girders lying haphazardly on the concrete floor.

She covered the distance between the exit and the end of the building in seconds. Ahead, an overturned chair, a cylinder of gas and a blowtorch. Knives littered the ground.

She stopped short of a large pool of congealed blood. Above, a man hung from a hook attached to a rafter. His face was remarkably unscathed, in contrast to his ruined body. Nobody did business with the Albanians unless they were Albanians, something Bryce Butler was too dim to understand, and he'd paid the ultimate price for his mistake.

Iris walked swiftly out of the building, pulled out her phone and called Norman Pardoe to deliver the news.

39

As the silvery tones of Debussy's 'Arabesque Number 1' came to an end, Gary burst into a spontaneous round of applause.

'Bloody well done, Olivia. I can see how hard you've worked.'

Olivia beamed, the porcelain skin on her sixteen-year-old cheeks flooding the same colour as her hair. 'I only got the timing right after you leant me that CD.'

'Credit's all yours, honey.'

Olivia beamed with delight, stood up from the piano stool and packed away her music.

'Hey, before you go, I've got a wicked idea. Do you know Jasmine Kendrick?'

'She's at my school. Plays the clarinet. Does lots of competitions.'

'How would you like to accompany her?'

'Me?' She blushed again.

Cute, Gary thought. 'Why not? Might be fun.'

An eight-drawer storage unit sat along one wall and Gary slid open the second from the top, rummaged through and pulled out the sheet music for Saint-Saen's Sonata for piano and clarinet 1st movement. He handed it to her.

'Give it a go. See what you think. We could run through it next time.'

'That would be so fun,' she said. 'See you next week, Gary.'

'Looking forward to it already, hun.'

Gary watched the girl leave. Kids that age didn't walk. They bounced. Oh, to be a teenager again, he thought, wondering if he had time to make a cup of coffee before his next pupil arrived. Aidan, a sullen kid, who had no interest in learning the piano, or anything else, had the misfortune to be foisted with a pushy set of competitive and totally deluded parents. In their heads, Aidan played Rachmaninoff's 'Piano Concerto no.2'. In reality, he'd barely risen above 'Chopsticks'. Consequently, an hour of both their lives was wasted each week in stultifying boredom. He guessed he should take a pragmatic view. If Mum and Dad were happy to keep chucking money in his direction, then he should be happy pocketing it. It's what Naomi would say. Naomi said a lot of things, which, to be scrupulously fair, was her right. Her favourite phrase was 'Bring home the bacon.' And he could not complain. Naomi was a global events manager, and a walking gold mine. Every man should have one.

Not that he was lazy. He scraped by teaching piano and woodwind and gigged with a couple of outfits in town. He also shopped, cooked, cleaned, vacuumed, laundered and ironed. If asked how he felt about this, usually by disbelieving males, he replied that he was a domestic project manager, and where was the problem in that? Droning on about equal opportunities and gender equality only appeared to work one way, it seemed. Gary knew a couple of guys who were in a similar boat, but they had kids, which elevated them to a respectable and socially acceptable stratum. Out in company – and they ate out a lot on Naomi's substantial salary – he told people that he was a music teacher. End of. Didn't matter if business was sporadic and he went months without earning a dime. Kids were more interested in becoming singers these days because it was an easier gig. He blamed it on *X Factor* and other similar reality shows. Frankly, not many had the talent or commitment to master a musical instrument.

Gary wandered into the kitchen, spooned three helpings of finest freshly ground Colombian coffee into a cafetière and waited for the kettle to boil. The kitchen had bifold doors that led out to the garden. Given his way, he'd have the lot concreted. Gardening represented another addition in his skill set because Naomi liked flowers, roses in particular – thorny little bastards.

At the sound of a key in the lock, Gary crossed a wide hall of elegant Georgian proportions (there were some advantages to having a wife with taste and money). He stepped back as Naomi blazed in. *Shit*, he thought, this was unexpected. He took care to arrange his face into a picture of delight.

With her lustrous hair, and colouring that spoke of a Middle Eastern gene somewhere along the line, Naomi was, by any standards, a looker. At 5 ft 9 inches in towering heels, she went in and out in all the right places and represented the whole package. It pleased him that other men lusted after her when they were out together. Took the spotlight off him and his lack of 'bring home the bacon' credentials.

'You're home early.' He loathed surprises of any description and took every measure to ensure they didn't happen. In the current circumstances, it was a fucking disaster. Nonetheless, he put on his 'normal face' and smiled. What else could he do? Naomi was his meal ticket to an interesting life.

'We wrapped things up way sooner than expected and I caught an earlier flight.' She dumped her bags and flung her arms around him, enveloping him in Yves Saint Laurent perfume and clothes by Reiss. Only the best for his girl. 'Oh, I've missed you,' she said, squeezing him tight.

'Me, too.' His hands slid down to her firm little rear and he gave her a long, slow, lingering kiss on her Bobbi Brown lips.

'That's better,' she said, pulling away a little. 'I'm *so* sorry I didn't keep in touch as often as I should have done. It was just *so* manic.' 'So' was one of Naomi's favourite words. If she removed it from her vocabulary, it would reduce all conversation by fifty per cent, Gary reckoned.

'No worries, babe.'

'So how have you been?'

'Good. Work's been steady. Bookings are getting firmed up for Christmas, which is ace.'

'Told you they would. You only needed to be patient.'

If they were giving out awards for patience, he'd take the top prize. Naomi had no frigging idea.

'Is this with RocknRoller?'

'Amazingly so.'

Naomi pulled a face. It didn't alter her stupendous good looks. 'I take it Phil is still banging on about Spaghetti Junction?'

'When he's not banging someone else's wife; Phil must

have slept with more married women than you've filed tax returns.'

Naomi's laugh was high, tinkly and bright. She liked all his jokes. Didn't matter how lame they were.

'Why he's got into his head that he wants to manage a bunch of spotty teenagers, with average guitar skills, eludes me.' Phil had let them christen the band, hence the shit-awful name. When Gary had picked him up on it, Phil claimed he was being democratic. As their manager, Phil should have been a dictator. 'They've eaten so much of his time lately, we hardly ever get to gig any more.'

'Oh, poor honey.' She dropped a soft kiss on his mouth. 'Thought you preferred playing with the Jazz Outfit anyway.'

True. Stripped-back arrangements of classic numbers, in which his skills as a saxophonist and clarinettist could shine, were definitely his melodic bag. Audiences were more select, sophisticated and appreciative too. If he were honest, Phil only wanted him for his musical muscle. Raucous and raunchy had its place, but he tired of it. The only nod to a calmer tone was 'Baker Street', which Phil insisted on to close a set. Gary had loved Gerry Rafferty's iconic saxophone solo the first time. After the millionth, he could cheerfully strangle Mr R; except the Mighty Rearranger had beaten him to it – Gerry had already gone to the great recording studio in the sky.

'Which is why,' he said, with a flourish, 'we're going on a European tour next summer. Baz has sorted it.'

'Next year?' Her arms dropped to her side. She didn't look as pleased as he thought she would. In fact, her bottom lip trembled and there was genuine dismay in her eyes.

'Have I said something wrong? I mean, I know the house still needs looking after, but it would only be for a few months. Send the laundry away. Get someone in, a cleaner, or whatever.' Get a cook, for Chrissakes. Maybe Naomi would get used to hired help and give him a break.

'Yeah,' she said absently. Like she'd lost her car keys and was feverishly running through the places she saw them last.

'What is it?' Gary probed.

She flashed a mega-kilowatt smile. He deduced that, metaphorically, she'd found them. 'Nothing to worry about. We'll discuss it later.'

Discuss what? He tingled with alarm. Maybe she'd planned to cart him off to Bali or Hawaii. Naomi loved her holidays, which was deeply strange for a woman who spent three-quarters of her life in foreign climes.

'God, I need a bath.'

Pushing away the nagging thought that she was about to ruin not only his musical ambitions but his life, he reverted to nice, thoughtful and, very importantly, *natural*. 'Go up, slip out of your things and I'll bring you a cup of freshly made coffee.'

'Sounds divine.' She gave him a dreamy smile. 'Join me?' Her voice was husky with desire. Seriously, the offer was tempting. They had chem and Naomi was an enthusiastic and adventurous lover. Five years of marriage had done nothing to take the shine off the physical side of their relationship, thank God. If anything, it had got better and better. He put it down to the fact that she travelled a lot for work. No time to settle into routine and sameness. He couldn't cope if she were there all the time. *Obvs.*

'Can't, babe. Got a lesson in . . .' He glanced at his watch, a TAG Heuer and birthday present from his wife, 'less than two minutes.' However horny he felt, he didn't think a quickie was going to satisfy his wife.

Naomi pouted her lips, a perfect rosebud. 'Later then.'

'You can count on it.'

He watched her glide upstairs, the nether part of him clearly wishing to follow. Giving himself a mental shake, he headed for the kitchen.

The doorbell rang and, thinking his next lesson had arrived, Gary suppressed a groan, stopped what he was doing and answered.

He stood there for a full five seconds.

'Are you going to let me in, or am I going to freeze to death?'

'Phil,' Gary said, collecting himself. 'Almost didn't recognise you. What the hell happened to your hair?'

40

Jackson had visited a shop selling DJ equipment at the Custard Factory in Gibb Street. Officially the creative quarter of the city, it got its name from being located on the site of the famous Bird's Custard Factory. His talk with the staff revealed little, apart from recommendations for other music shops in town selling instruments, and three selling vinyls. Most were closed. In the only one open, the owner, a large guy with a ponytail that only accentuated his fleshy features, told him, 'A lot of musos come in here, browse and then buy their instruments online. Cheaper that way.' When Jackson had enquired about any guys coming in with dreads, he'd given Jackson a funny look. Iris was right. They were running on fumes.

He tried Cairns again. The first time, after Iris left, the call rang out and then disconnected. The second, it didn't connect at all. Jackson got it. He was persona non grata. He hoped Cairns hadn't forgotten about the document examiner. She must have found something by now.

Disconsolate and out of sorts, he drove back to the Jewellery Quarter, walked upstairs to his flat and found what resembled a leaflet poking out of the letter box. Easing it out, he saw that Iris had come good.

41

'Hold up,' Gary said, 'I have to take this call.'

Phil sprawled out on an armchair in the kitchen, both arms extended, like he was crucified. In his hand, he held a newspaper. Maybe they'd received a decent review, Gary thought.

He listened, digested the news, thanked the caller, punched the air and let out a jubilant cry.

'Did someone invite you to play at Ronnie Scott's or something?' Phil said.

'My next lesson just cancelled.'

Phil raised an amused eyebrow. 'That bad?'

'You have no idea.'

'Got time for a catch-up then.' Phil hoisted his right leg and rested the heel of his cowboy-style boot against his left knee. Phil didn't so much as sit as plant himself, Gary thought. The other thing about good old Phil: he was a Yankee under his skin.

'Be with you in a second. Read your newspaper or something.' Gary re-boiled the water in the kettle. Naomi wouldn't like it. Hopefully, she was too knackered to spot the difference. Seeing as Phil wasn't going anywhere soon, he offered him a drink too.

'Sure,' Phil said, slipping out the hand cleanser he perpetually carried. According to Phil, it annihilated ninety-nine per cent of household germs. Consequently, his hands were always red and occasionally raw, not a great look for a rhythm guitarist. It was the only blip in Phil's laid-back persona. Everyone was entitled to one or two, Gary believed. Maybe it explained why Phil had diversified into management of under-talented teenies.

While Phil sprayed his paws with gel, Gary trotted upstairs to where Naomi was flat out on the bed fully-clothed and gently sleeping. Clearly, she'd been too exhausted to make it into the bath. He placed her coffee quietly on the bedside table, leant over, kissed her forehead and drew up the covers and returned downstairs.

Mugs apiece, they decanted to the lounge – Naomi called it a sitting room. Never let it be said that his woman lacked social aspirations. 'When did you get back?'

'Late last night. Tana wanted to stay for longer but—'

'Don't tell me, her husband found out.'

'Not quite.'

'Close shave?'

'You could say.' Phil lowered his gaze.

'One day you'll get caught.'

'Managed to evade capture so far.'

'I've warned you a million times. You're playing with fire.'

'That's rather the point,' Phil said with a louche grin. 'And Tana is beautiful, talented and solvent. Take a look.' Phil handed him the newspaper. 'Check out the business section.'

'Local Beautician Wins Business Award.' Gary didn't read the guff. His eyes were hooked on the statuesque redhead, winner of awards and winner of life. He glanced up at Phil. '*That's* Tana?' *How does this OCD hygiene conscious freak pull them?*

'Told you she was gorgeous,' Phil said smugly.

Gary's mind was working all kinds of angles. About to hand the *Post* back, his eyes snagged on the first page: Police Officer's Wife Revealed as Neon's Latest Victim. *Oh, how fucking sweet.*

'Give it back then,' Phil said, a bit testy, Gary thought. Phil might have got the band and the bird, but there was no need to get narky. Meekly, Gary did as he was told. He'd read it online later. What a delicious prospect.

A prickly silence descended and Gary wasn't going to be the first to break. He'd already tuned out, disappeared into Planet Gary. His was a bright and shiny, wondrous universe.

Phil gabbed on about Spaghetti Junction, how well the band were doing after their win at the Battle of the Bands, the places they were going. To Gary's ears, it was all white noise and yadda yadda. He was in the zone, thinking and plotting and planning.

'All right if I leave the car around the back as usual?'

Gary started out of his reverie and nodded.

'I'll leave the keys with you.'

'Sure thing.'

Phil got up, and Gary followed suit. 'Gotta bust a groove. Good to see you, dude,' Phil said. Gary tried not to flinch. Phil was approaching forty. The muso patois he insisted on spouting was as out of date as flared trousers. Getting down with the kids didn't require you to make a twat of yourself. At least, Phil didn't do hugs, thank Christ. It might invite too many germs. 'Seeing as I've got a lot on with the band,' Phil continued, 'shall I keep the van at mine for now?'

'If you like.'

'Best decision we ever made to pool resources.'

'It's certainly come in handy,' Gary said, deadpan.

'I'll get Tana to run me back to collect the motor. You and Naomi could meet her.'

'Grand plan.'

Gary went outside with Phil and opened the double gates that led to the parking area at the rear. He stood back as Phil drove past in a beast of a vehicle, a yellow left-hand-drive Mustang, bright enough to make your eyes bleed.

42

The recording studio that had sponsored the Battle of the Bands opened at ten o'clock, according to their website. Jackson phoned. The line rang and rang, until a messaging service kicked in. He announced that he was a police officer, required a chat and left a number for someone to call.

Next, he headed to Steelhouse Lane to one of the music shops that had been closed the day before.

'Are you familiar with these?' Jackson spread out the poster. A young guy, about seventeen years of age, studied the print. He had an impressive hole in his left ear lobe. Jackson could see right through it to a display of accordions on the opposite wall.

'Pop,' he said in the same way he'd say *fuck*. 'Not my thing. I'm more a grindcore kind of guy.'

Jackson didn't have a clue what he was on about.

The boy stuck a piece of chewing gum in his mouth, offered Jackson a piece, which he took.

'The only thing I can tell you,' he said, tapping the poster with his finger. 'Is that the recording studio on there went out of business a month ago. Too much competition.'

'Great,' Jackson muttered.

'You a cop or something?' The lad furiously worked his mouth around the gum.

Or something, Jackson thought. 'I'm working the Neon investigation.'

The lad's eyebrows shot up almost to his hairline. 'Cool.'

Jackson didn't dwell on that reaction. 'It's possible he had connections to the music industry.'

'Good luck with that. It's ma*hoosive*. I can give you a list of other recording studios, if that might help.'

'Appreciated,' Jackson responded, poised to feed in the information to his iPhone. Afterwards, he handed the youth a card. 'If you hear anything, however insignificant, give me a call.' He didn't mention dreads and bright yellow cars and a possible interest in US music. A description like that was on a par with a lousy photofit.

He ran through the same routine at a couple of other shops. It ate a shedload of time and delivered nothing of value.

Back at the flat, he got on the phone to Wayne Gardner. Wayne reacted the way Jackson expected him to.

'I'm a publican, not Simon sodding Cowell.'

'What about the recording studio that promoted the event, who did you deal with?'

'I don't remember.'

'Find a name and call me back, or I'll find you.' He cut the call. Why did he have the feeling that he was being led along a road to nowhere? To drill down every music lead would take a staggering amount of man hours and, without access to Lloyd House, he could no longer make use of their resources. Time to initiate plan B.

Googling the number for BBC Birmingham, Jackson contacted Reception and requested to be put through to the Newsroom. Neon's first victim was discovered in an apartment block adjacent to the building. It was only fitting that he should give his first and only interview to the TV crew inside.

'Jack Andrew, news editor,' a voice came back, the taut tone suggesting a man under pressure.

The second Jackson gave his name, the mood music changed. Andrew invited him in straight away, offered to meet him any time, any place and anywhere. He would have offered him a fee, Jackson was sure, if he'd pushed for it. Finally, Andrew ran out of words. Very quietly, Jackson explained when he wanted the interview to go out and the angle he wished to take. He'd expected objections and comments about creative input and integrity. Instead, Andrew asked if Jackson could arrive an hour before they went on air and said he looked forward to meeting him.

Jackson's mobile rang a couple of minutes later. 'Mick,' he said in surprise. 'I thought you were lying low.'

'I am. Look, I don't have long. The document came back.'

A vein pulsed in Jackson's temple in anticipation.

'You were right about the pencil marks. They're significant.'

'How so?'

'When musicians score music, they write in pencil first then go over it in pen. It's called engraving. The final copy is often written with a thin felt tip and, obviously, the pencil marks are erased. The idea is to keep all the finished marks as consistent and symmetrical as possible.' Cairns broke off. 'Hello? You're not saying much.'

It all dovetailed, Jackson knew. He brought Cairns up to date and asked if he was prepared to carry out the legwork of contacting recording studios, approaching bands and putting the squeeze on Wayne Gardner.

'I've got a couple of rookies working with me. I can put them onto it.'

'Can they be trusted to keep quiet?'

'DCs Tonks and Mander don't care for Browne any more than you or I do. Obviously, this will run parallel to the official investigation.'

Jackson wrote down both names. 'If I thought Browne would run with it, I'd gladly share the information.'

'But he won't. Can I ask what you'll be doing?'

'Tune into the news tomorrow night and you'll find out.'

After the call, he switched to a social networking site and checked if Iris was in the vicinity. The co-ordinates revealed that she was in Cradley Heath. What was she doing there? Who was she speaking to?

As if thoughts could translate into actions, his phone dinged and a cryptic text appeared. He texted back, waited a beat. Clocking the time and location, Jackson picked up his coat.

'I want the same again,' she said. 'And the Ruger. I'll pay cash.'

Kevin Joyce slipped on a pair of gloves and removed each gun from their respective cabinets. 'Ammo?'

Iris muttered a reply. A creature of instinct, she had a bad feeling. Pardoe, unsurprisingly, wanted to press the button, as he put it, on cutting the Albanian connection. The problem was she was nowhere near ready. He'd picked up on her reluctance and had, consequently, ordered they meet later. 'After we shut up shop,' he'd said, 'the usual place.' Iris didn't like *usual* places for all the same reasons she disliked routines.

'Business must be brisk,' Joyce said, handing her a brown paper bag, containing a box of 9mm ammunition.

'What about you? Had many customers lately?'

Joyce thrust her a wary look. 'What you after, Iris?'

It was a good question. *Fuck knows*, she thought. 'Got any clients who are keen on music? Could be a bloke with dreads.'

Joyce's mouth tipped open. A cigarette clung perilously to his teeth. 'Have you any idea how fucking stupid that sounds? It could be half the population of—'

'This guy's white.'

'In that case, the answer's no.'

'I thought that might be the case.'

She looked at her watch. Timing was all. She'd go back home, have a wash and force down a meal. She had a feeling that she'd be killing later tonight.

43

Gary served up a killer smile and watched as Naomi tucked into her favourite dinner of seafood pasta. He'd risen early that morning and gone to the market specially, to make sure that the scallops were fresh. After a stimulating drive down memory lane, he'd stopped off for two expensive bottles of Macon, with which he'd liberally plied her, and a box of chocolates from a new emporium to have for afters. Paul Desmond provided a soothing, smooth sax background. As charm offensives went, he didn't think he could do much better. Nothing more had been said about the 'thing to be discussed'. Part of him felt relief, the other a sense of foreboding.

Naomi gleamed with radiance and contentment. She really did look very beautiful. He preferred her without make-up and dressed down because it made her seem more vulnerable. Candlelight enhanced her dark sultry features. It was like having a Middle Eastern princess at his table. 'What would I do without you, my gorgeous man?' she purred.

What would *he* do without *her*?

Inside, he glowed with pleasure. He'd read online, and in

detail, that Neon had murdered Polly Jackson, the detective's wife. Everything was moving in the right direction. Everything was going his way. The deeply satisfied look on his face Naomi clearly thought was meant for her. *Not so fast, baby.*

'Now I've got you all to myself,' she said, wide-eyed and luminous. 'I want to tell you about my fabulous idea.'

Gary took a decent swallow of wine. For some reason it tasted a little sharp. 'Intriguing. Shoot away, babe.'

The tip of her tongue poked out between her perfectly formed teeth and lips. 'You know how hard I work, Gary. Long hours. Trips abroad. Not enough time for *us*.'

He didn't like the emphasis and wondered where she was going with it. 'It kind of works though, doesn't it?'

'It's been great.' She glanced down, ran a manicured nail around the rim of her glass.

Been. How can one word strike such a bum note? Was she telling him that she wanted a divorce, to move on, that they were over? A tremor of panic shivered through him. 'Sorry, babe, I don't quite follow.'

'What do you say to us selling up and moving to the country?'

A sharp intake of breath made a direct hit on his lungs. It was as if he'd inhaled liquid mercury. Jesus Christ, he couldn't breathe. He was choking.

'We'd make a killing from selling this place,' she prattled on, oblivious, 'and, if we move far enough away, somewhere quaint and rural, we could buy a really lovely home with the proceeds.'

'We already have a lovely home.' He squashed the anxious ring in his voice.

'And we'll have another. Just think about it, Gary.'

He *was* thinking about it. Mud and vegetation and animal shit and crucifying boredom. In one conversation, Naomi had smashed his entire reason for being. Images of his other life, his creations, the women, the sport, the visits to the club where he could be like other people shattered into a gazillion pieces.

'But we've spent so much time and money on this place.' His time and her loot. 'The concrete polished floor, the cornices, restoring the casement windows.' And the other thing, of which she knew nothing.

'We can do it again,' she enthused.

No, we could not, he thought. Time to get practical. 'What would we do for money?'

'We'll have a simpler life, grow our own vegetables, keep some chickens – pigs maybe.'

Pigs? Fuck's sake. He gave a nervous laugh, doing his utmost not to place his hands around her neck, squeeze, listen for and feel that uniquely satisfying crunch. 'You're not serious. We're city people, Naomi. You're from round here and I'm from London. We wouldn't last five minutes out in the sticks.'

'How do you know?' she said, bright-eyed. 'You can still teach.'

Who exactly? he thought. To him, rural meant people on horseback, red-faced farmers, stay-at-home mothers with tribes of snotty-nosed kids, in a place, someone once told him, where ducks fly backwards. 'What about the bands?'

'Put together your own.'

'I don't dig folk music.' It was a stupid thing to say but he didn't care. Over his dead body would he give up all he'd strived for, all he'd built.

'Don't look like that, Gary. It could be the greatest adventure of our lives.'

That he very much doubted. Somehow, he had to talk her out of it. 'Look, I get it. You're tired. The last big promotion wasn't the easiest. A little break and you'll be good as new and ready to do a fantastic job on your next project.'

Naomi sat back in the chair with a thump and took an unhealthy interest in her empty plate. Her pretty mouth poked down at the edges. He knew that expression. Mutinous.

He leant across, took her cool, slightly resistant, hand in his. 'Babe, we have a great life together. Here. In Birmingham. It would be such a pity to rock the boat.'

Underneath those dark dark lashes, she flashed him a look that was as challenging as any his mother had ever thrown at him. And look how that had turned out?

'I want to have babies.'

Her words felt like a sucker punch. She'd never talked this way before. He never even knew kids were on her agenda. It was as if his wife had had a personality transplant. He opened his mouth, closed it again. Pure, overwhelming terror swept through him. If this was what shock felt like, he was in it.

Naomi's eyes sparkled with tears. 'Don't you want children?'

No, he bloody didn't. Christ on a crutch, they wailed and squealed half the night, every night. He was as nocturnal as a bat, but he wasn't sharing it with an infant. Night was *his* playground, *his* moment to shine.

'Of course I want children,' he lied, 'but not right now. Let's face it,' he said, with a level expression, 'babies are incompatible with the life of a muso. It wouldn't be fair.'

'*Fair?*' Her face contorted in fury. 'My biological clock won't keep ticking forever.' At that moment he wished it would spectacularly break down and stay broken.

Tell her what she wants to hear. He forced a sympathetic smile. 'I understand, babe. I do. Let me think about it, yeah?'

She reached across, planted a kiss on his mouth, the offer of hope enough to placate her – for now. 'I should have mentioned it before, rather than dumping it on you in one go,' she said, softening.

Damn right, he thought, his brain scrabbling for mental footholds. 'It's OK. I'll give it some thought. Lots to get my head around,' he said, tossing her his warmest, most reassuring smile.

44

Iris stopped off at the betting shop – or, as Pardoe liked to describe it, the 'bookmakers' – in Dudley, as arranged. Staines opened the door and ushered her in. Pardoe was out the back with a couple of his cronies, drinking whisky and eating pork scratchings.

'Good to see you, Iris,' he said. 'Need a stiffener?' He knew she didn't drink, so it was a stupid question.

Iris politely replied, 'No thank you, Mr Pardoe.'

'Tooled up?'

She nodded, kept her eyes on Pardoe and ignored the other creeps.

'Word on the wire says our friends from Albania are at their premises right now.'

Iris had no idea how Pardoe had come by the news, or which grapevine had yielded the information.

'Which means tonight's the night,' Pardoe continued. 'If you can't get both, get one.' His small, green eyes danced with mischief and anticipation. Blokes that never pulled the trigger always got the biggest kick out of killing, she thought drily.

'That might be dangerous.'

'You're in the danger business, our kid.'

'I meant for you, Mr Pardoe.' True, but it was also riskier for her. Pardoe might have information on Malaj and his man, but Malaj was no fool. He'd also have information on Pardoe, which was why it was vital that she slotted the pair together. She did not wish to wind up in the same state as Bryce Butler's monstrously tortured body.

Pardoe briefly shifted his gaze to Staines, who'd been standing quietly by the door, on lookout. 'Not your concern, Iris,' Pardoe said. 'Off you go, then. When the job's done, we'll reconvene later at the lock-up.'

Which was a safer idea than returning to the betting shop. She was almost out of the door when he called her back.

'No leads to me, Iris.'

As if, she thought.

It was a thirteen-minute ride to the Albanian's warehouse. There was no way she was walking straight onto the site – she might as well paint a bullseye on her back.

She parked the bike half a mile away in a church graveyard and eight minutes later she was at the industrial unit.

She hung back in the shadows and watched. It seemed quiet, like a place that was not yet up and running. She imagined the boss inside plotting how he was going to wipe out the opposition and further his business plans.

Security lights illuminated Malaj's truck over two hundred yards away. He was in the warehouse somewhere. Hopefully, his sidekick, Prifti, was with him. A two-in-one hit and she'd get Pardoe off her back and then she could fully concentrate on Neon, the money and the way out.

Her biggest problem was ignorance. She had no idea how many men were inside, ready and willing to kill her. Direct entry into the building was, therefore, out of the question. Her best bet was to wait until Malaj drove out through the entrance and onto the main road. In the split second he paused to check the traffic both ways, she'd pump a couple of bullets through the driver's side window, take out Malaj first, then do Prifti. And then run.

Cursing the way she'd been rushed into a job for which she hadn't properly prepared, she pulled her baseball cap down over her face, gritted her teeth and settled in for a long night.

Two miles north of Wolverhampton city centre, Jackson parked up on the concrete forecourt of a disused petrol station and dipped his headlights.

A text from Kenny Flavell's eldest son, Aston (named after Kenny's favourite football club, Aston Villa), could only mean one thing: bad news about Iris. He sensed it would explain her irritability earlier.

A hooded figure approached on a skateboard. Jackson flashed his lights. The figure bent down, jumped and flipped the board over, landing smack down, and glided effortlessly towards the car. It was a technically flawless and impressive display, yet Jackson considered it a strange activity for a man pushing thirty.

He reached across, opened the passenger door, switched off the headlamps and clicked on the interior light. Aston clambered in, dragging the skateboard with him. He rested it against his knees and crossed his arms. Not happy sitting next to the policeman who'd failed to protect his father, Jackson deduced. He asked after Kenny.

'My dad's all right, considering.'

Jackson could apologise. He could try to explain. He could say that he'd see Kenny all right. But he did none of these things. His world was far darker and more complicated, and he had no time to waste on things that could not be changed.

'What you got?' Jackson said.

'Dad says your woman does wet work.'

Jackson already knew this.

'For Norman Pardoe,' Aston added.

Pardoe was one of those villains who, quite literally, got away with murder. Connected to any number of crimes, Pardoe had evaded justice for decades. The public failed to understand that it was one thing to know a man was guilty; it was something else entirely to prove it. So far, the police had never been able to definitively tie Pardoe down, not even with a recent spate of killings attributed to him.

And now Jackson knew why.

'Pardoe's got problems,' Aston continued. 'The Albanians are moving in on his turf.'

'So he's using the woman to deal with it?'

'That's what Dad thought, but rumour has it that Pardoe's fallen out with her. Big time.'

Jackson snatched a look, hoping that Aston could provide him with more detail. Was Iris's life in danger? In response, Aston shrugged his shoulders, giving the impression that it was outside his box.

'Is there anything else?'

'That's it,' Aston said, reaching for the door.

'Thank your dad for me,' Jackson called, but Aston was already back on his board and skating away.

Jackson scrolled through the contacts on his phone and called Iris to warn her that she'd pissed off Norman Pardoe big time. Waiting for the call to connect, he drummed his fingers on the steering wheel.

'Sorry,' a recorded voice informed him, *'the number you have called is unrecognisable.'*

'Shit,' Jackson cursed. Iris had duped him. Thank Christ he'd put a tracker on her bike.

Movement. Iris could hardly believe her luck. She'd barely got into the mental zone when a figure stepped out bathed in a blanket of light. Prifti. Her heart banged inside her chest. She peered through the darkness, praying that Malaj would emerge and follow him.

He didn't.

Prifti climbed into the Nissan, gunned the engine and drove at speed across the forecourt. Iris prepared to strike. Her senses went into shutdown. She zeroed in and raised her weapon. Everything surrounding her receded and she did not hear the thundering noise from the main road that signalled the immediate approach of an artic lorry. Only Prifti saw it. He stopped, letting the engine idle, allowing the truck to pass.

Iris took a breath, released it a little, holding the rest. Her finger primed, she lined up the Glock with the target, squeezing off two shots, hitting Prifti in the temple. At short range he stood no chance and his body slumped against the steering wheel, head twisted towards her, open-eyed and blood trickling from his mouth. The Nissan jerked forward at speed, slewed across the road, straight into a brick wall on the other side. In the quiet, it sounded like a bomb exploding.

Iris didn't wait for reaction or reprisal. She took to her heels, ran and didn't stop. With a thudding heart and pounding head, she reached the graveyard and the bike, climbed on and rode as if she had Neon giving chase behind her.

45

Jackson tracked Iris's route.

Locating her at a churchyard in Brierley Hill, she was suddenly travelling at speed towards Dudley. He put a call through to Cairns.

'Jesus, Matt, no I haven't—'

'Anything going down in Brierley Hill tonight?

'Nope.'

'You sure?'

'Matt, I'm knackered and I'm about to go off shift.'

'Sorry, mate. Could you check?'

Cairns let out a sigh. Jackson heard him clicking away on a computer and asking around. Silence on the line and then, 'Fuck. You psychic, or something?'

Jackson ground his jaw.

'Report of shots fired. Hold up,' Cairns said. 'There's also an RTA.'

What have you done, Iris? 'Any fatalities?'

'Too soon to tell. Like to tell me what's going on?'

'Best you don't know.'

'Matt, this is really getting—'

'I'll call you later.' Jackson pressed his foot on the accelerator, changing up the gears. Iris was still moving. He had to stop her.

Iris hurtled towards Dudley. She halted briefly to lob the Glock into the slimy depths of a canal before continuing, via a circuitous route to avoid tails, to the lock-up.

Parking a few streets away in an area that seemed prosperous, she walked directly into an area that was anything but. The urban landscape could change from OK to shit in the space of a few houses.

Pardoe's lock-up was one of ten, right at the end of a row of up-and-over white metal doors. A single lamp, from a neighbouring street, shone a gauzy yellow light, offering little in the way of illumination. Its absence made her immediately think of Neon. He would hate it here. Or would he? Did he have a lock-up in which he practised his craft? She'd mention it to Matt after she'd got things sorted with Pardoe.

There was no breeze. The air felt damp. Not a dog barked nor cat yowled; no sound of urban foxes riffling through dustbins. Too quiet. It felt instantly wrong. Was Pardoe's information meant to mislead? Was Prifti a decoy to draw attention away from Pardoe? Had Malaj struck while she'd been slotting his second-in-command?

Stomach clenched, Iris narrowed her eyes for sight of Pardoe's motor, but all she saw was unending darkness. She bitterly regretted getting rid of her gun and leaving the Ruger at home. Glancing backwards into a no man's land of

November night, she saw nothing and nobody and yet she felt as though there was someone there. Waiting. Stalking. Ready to pounce.

Jackson parked in front of Iris's bike. No lights shone from the houses in the street. In his gut, he felt she had to be somewhere nearby. But which way should he go?

He stood by the Triumph. The engine was still warm – she couldn't have gone far. He looked up and down, listened. Saw nothing, heard nothing. Ahead, there was a narrow side street, which he took, for no other reason than he couldn't think of a better idea.

He passed a corner shop, long since closed; a row of houses that became more squalid the further he travelled. He felt strangely alone and wondered if this is how it would roll with Neon, the two of them slugging it out in some back-street of Birmingham. Without Iris, Jackson didn't think it would play out at all. He had to find her.

Emerging into another street, he saw the remnants of a metal fence glinting in the moonlight and, beyond, open ground. He crossed over and discovered a row of broken-down-looking garages and lock-ups.

He heard footsteps ahead, and froze. So did the footsteps. However much he strained, he could not see through the wall of darkness.

Suddenly, a light from an upstairs window doused the land in front of him. Caught in its glare, two figures, adjacent to each other. The smaller one in front turned as the one behind raised its arm. Jackson didn't think. He hammered his hand against the nearest metal door and ran.

*

Alerted by the noise, Iris twisted round, her mouth frozen when she saw Davey Jelf, a gun in his hand. He briefly ducked, as if he'd been shot, then recovered and fired. Instinctively, she leapt aside, out of the ring of light now shining from several houses, and hit the ground. The bullet's trajectory from muzzle to sky made a fresh parting in her hair and scorched her scalp. Dirt grazed her chin. Rolling away, she crouched beside a pile of fly-tipped rubbish, from where she saw Jackson grab Davey from behind. He had his hands around Davey's neck.

Matt just saved her life, she realised.

But how the hell had he found her?

Another shot ripped into the sky and, this time, several more lights went on, illuminating the yard. The man arched his body and threw back his head. Lightning pain exploded in the middle of Jackson's face. Anger swelling, blood spurting from both nostrils, tears ejecting from his eyes, he clung on and pressed the back of his forearm against the throat of the struggling man. Clasping hold of his right hand with his left, he applied as much pressure as he could.

'I'm a police officer. Drop the gun,' Jackson yelled. Instantly, several lights went off.

The man gurgled and thrashed. Jackson continued his hold, dragged him backwards and lifted him off his feet. He could feel him weaken but the attacker still had the gun. As long as he held it, Jackson knew his life was in danger. The muscles in his arms juddered and his face felt on fire.

A movement from near the bins caught his eye. Iris had

crawled out of her hiding place. Alarmingly, she looked about to break cover and draw attention away. If she did, the man would summon every last atom of energy to break loose and Jackson didn't think he could hold on, didn't think he could stop him.

Taking a deep breath in, he relaxed his grip with his left hand, swung back his arm and powered a fist into the man's temple. A direct hit and the gun flew from the man's hand. Next, his legs buckled.

Jackson's arms suddenly went limp and light. Gasping for breath, he stood over the prone figure and, to be certain, drew his boot back and powered it into the man's jaw.

46

He was on top and in deep and reading her naked body like a piece of music. First the *andante* and then the *allegro* and then *subito*. Approaching a crescendo, he curled his index finger and placed it at the base of her throat, pushing up and slowly back, lightly at first.

Submissive, Naomi gasped and shivered with pleasure beneath him. Turned on, he stepped up the intensity. Two blinks signalled for him to take it to another level, to dominate, to control, to create pain. Unable to speak, she was vulnerable. She was his.

'Don't move,' he commanded.

She obeyed. Her body was tight, like a tuning fork, her nipples rock hard.

He slipped both hands down and around her throat. Danger was part of the deal and this was the risky part. Too much pressure and he'd kill her. To play her, while thrusting away, took a similar skill to creating his neon designs. But he was a maestro and her body was his orchestra.

Slick with sweat, he watched her face, saw her eyes roll,

losing herself as her brain leaked oxygen and flooded with a dopamine rush as powerful as heroin. In spasm, her body shuddered then went slack and, with savage joy, he came.

47

'Iris, no, for Christ's sake.'

She had her attacker's revolver in her gloved hand. Her blank expression told Jackson she was intent on pulling the trigger.

'He tried to kill me.' Her voice wasn't raised. It was calm and rational and chilling. It meant business.

'Don't waste the bullet.'

She didn't move. The gun didn't move either.

'Iris, I have perfect grounds to arrest him for possession of a firearm.'

'Except he doesn't have it, I do.'

'You can't kill him in cold blood. Not like this.'

Why not? her eyes said. Having a conversation with Iris was like talking with a blade held to your throat.

The guy was unconscious. Jackson didn't think he'd be out for long. Already, he'd seen his eyelids flicker. If he could persuade Iris to hold off, it would buy him time to do things the right way. 'Don't you want to know why he tried to shoot you?'

'Davey Jelf wants my job.'

'You know him?' Jackson said in surprise.

'He's my fucking shadow. Gagging to work for one of my clients.'

'Maybe he already is.'

Her eyes narrowed, her lips drew back in a snarl. 'How did you know I was here?'

'Lucky guess.'

Her blank expression told him she wasn't buying it.

'If we wait for Jelf to come around,' he continued briskly, 'we can question him. Now give me the gun.' He held out his hand.

'No.'

'Iris,' he warned, dropping his arm to his side, 'you can't carry a weapon.'

'You had mine and now I've got his. We're even.' She slid the revolver inside her jacket

Jackson didn't ask again.

Jelf stirred and opened his eyes. Startled, and desperately calculating the amount of shit he was in, he struggled to get up. Iris's boot on his chest pressed him back down into the dirt. To emphasise the point, she withdrew the gun and aimed it at his head. Jelf let out a garbled plea.

'Please, no, Iris. It wasn't my fault. Please.' He was snivelling and crying – begging. Appealing to Jackson now, he implored, 'Don't let her do it. You're a copper. You wouldn't let an innocent man die.'

'Innocent?' Jackson said. 'That's an interesting interpretation.'

Taking Jackson's comment as a green light, Iris tightened her stance.

'You kill him,' Jackson said gravely. 'You'll have to kill me next.'

Iris wavered.

'You wouldn't want that,' Jelf said, snivelling. 'Think about poor old Orchid.'

'Shut up, Davey.' Iris stamped her boot on his bony sternum.

'Ow,' Jelf spluttered.

'Who's Orchid?' Jackson asked.

'The dog he beats.'

'No, I—'

'Shut it,' she said.

'Please, Iris.' Jelf squirmed 'I was only following orders. Norman sent me. It was his idea.'

Anger pinched at the muscles in Iris's face, neck and jaw. Jackson could virtually read her processing the information, working out what had brought her to this. 'Did Pardoe pay you?' she asked Jelf.

He nodded. 'Half upfront, half afterwards.'

This was good, Jackson thought. It provided a neat link in the evidential chain; follow the money trail straight to the man.

'Where did you get the revolver?' Nothing in her tone indicated that she'd changed her mind about shooting Jelf dead.

'Norman gave it to me. It's a Smith & Wesson—'

'Six-chambered .357 Magnum revolver,' Iris interrupted. 'I know what it is.'

To Jackson's surprise, she put away the revolver and

removed her boot from Jelf's narrow chest. He let out a gasp of relief.

'The Albanians got hit tonight,' Iris said, darkness in her voice. 'I'm going to put it about you did it.'

Jelf's bruised jaw fell open. 'Iris, for fuck's sake. On my mum's—'

'Best make the most of your freedom, Davey.'

'Fuck, no. Please Iris,' Jelf pleaded. 'Please, I'm begging you.'

Jackson had to admire her cunning, although he had a better idea. He put a call through to Cairns.

'What?' Cairns snapped, after several rings. Jackson surmised that Cairns had stayed on after the report of the RTA and shots fired rather than going off shift.

'Want an opportunity to get back into Browne's good books?'

'The reckless part of me doesn't give a flying fuck, the sensible part wouldn't say no.'

'How would you like to bring down Norman Pardoe?'

Iris's lips very slightly parted. She glared at him.

'I'm listening,' Cairns said, sounding eager.

'I have a young man here willing to work with you.' Jackson ignored the film of fury in Iris's eyes and the shock in Jelf's. He gave the details and Cairns said that he'd be with Jackson inside the hour.

'You shouldn't have done that,' Iris said, tight-lipped.

'I never said I was working with the police,' Jelf whined. 'I knew she was a grass,' he muttered, before shrinking under Iris's dead-eyed expression.

The temptation to beat him into unconsciousness again

made Jackson's hand itch. Dealing with this was time wasted in his pursuit of Neon.

Iris rounded on him. 'Do you realise what you've done? You've hung me out to dry with Enrik Malaj and cut off a primary source of income.'

'Here's the thing, Iris. Why work for a man who wants you dead? It doesn't make good business sense.'

She stared at him as if he were three years old.

'Because it's *my* choice, not yours, how I run my life. Because in *my* world bosses stitch people up all the time. Because *I* could have won Pardoe round.' Her eyes sparkled with rage. She turned on her heel and walked away.

Jackson's throat tightened. 'Iris, don't go.'

'I'm not sticking around for your pal, Cairns. Good luck with Neon,' she said. 'Best play it dirty, or you won't stand a fucking chance.'

Jackson needed Iris and she needed him. He'd saved her life, for God's sake. She was stubborn as hell, but once she realised her limited options, she was bound to come back, he told himself. Inside, he was less certain. In Iris's black-and-white mind, he'd meddled in her universe, wrenched control from her nail-bitten fingers and betrayed her. All three were hanging offences in her book.

The wait for Cairns was interminable. As thick as he was repellent, Jelf fizzed with nervous energy and didn't stop talking. Fortunately, Jackson sussed that Jelf's survival instinct was strong. Animal cunning would tell him that a botched job for Pardoe would result in instant termination, and it wouldn't be simply of his employment contract.

Jelf's best bet was to co-operate with the police and take his chances with the law.

'Do I get to go on one of those witness-protection things?' Jelf whined.

Jackson kept his mouth shut.

'I'm not talking to no one unless it's guaranteed.'

What the hell was he doing here? Jackson thought. While he was babysitting, Neon could be lining up his next victim.

'And I want a flat, car, money.' Since Jelf had picked himself up off the deck, he'd become absurdly cocky to the point of delusional.

Jackson stared blankly into the distance. It amazed him how many snitches thought 'helping the police' would result in instant wealth.

'And I want a—'

'Something we should get clear,' Jackson warned. 'One mention of Iris Palmer to the police and I'll make good on her threat to give you up to the Albanians.'

Jackson took rare pleasure in seeing a line of sweat form on Jelf's brow. It glinted in the light of the moon.

'We clear?' he said.

'As crystal meth,' Jelf mumbled.

'Good, now walk.'

They returned to Jackson's car, where Iris's bike had gone. The remains of the tracking and its assorted wires had been dumped in the road. Shit, now he couldn't even find her.

'Got any tunes?' Jelf said as they sat inside with the heater on full blast. Jackson ignored him, his thoughts with Neon once more.

At last, Cairns drew up, got out and slipped into the back seat of the Mini, where Jackson explained Jelf's situation.

'Does it have any connection to a hit tonight?' Cairns asked.

'I didn't do it,' Jelf darted in.

'Is he a comedian, or what?' Cairns said. 'It takes more than a streak of piss like you to match Enrik Malaj and his crew.'

'Any idea who carried it out, Mick?' The edge in Jackson's voice was strictly for Jelf's benefit.

'The Albanians have made a lot of inroads since they moved in. They've also made a lot of enemies. Pardoe isn't exactly the only drug lord pissed with them.'

'It's important you close down Malaj before it turns nasty.'

'I think, my friend, that particular horse has already bolted.'

Jackson didn't reply.

48

A tidal wave of anxiety washed over Jackson as he lay in bed the next morning. The prospect of going on prime-time television that evening and talking to God knew how many people in some half-baked attempt to challenge Neon now seemed ridiculous. That's what Iris would say if he'd asked for an opinion, he knew.

After getting washed and dressed, he checked out Spaghetti Junction – the winning band mentioned on the flyer – on the internet. Their website was slick and professional. Marketing had taken four fresh-faced teenaged boys and ascribed to each the same look duplicated in groups the length and breadth of the UK. The lead singer had gone for *sexy*, the drummer for *mad*, the bassist *moody* and the guitarist apparently provided the comedy element. Spots lined up for the following year at prestigious music venues in Bristol and Camden indicated the boys had a decent agent. In the lead-up to Christmas, the band was primarily booked to play in the city. The next date was for the following evening.

Jackson flicked to a YouTube video of the band in action. Ten seconds later, he'd clicked off. A load of baby Ed Sheerans crammed onto a stage was not his thing. Interestingly, he noted that the website, label, booking agent, press officer and tour manager were all registered to the same domain – to a man named Phil Canto, 'musician and recording producer', according to the blurb. He lived in Clent, not far from the pub where Jackson had arranged to meet Iris and she had failed to show.

Jackson clicked for more information. Instantly, a photograph popped up. Zeroing in on a white male, with blonde dreadlocks, his mouth dried. Canto fitted the description of the man who'd visited Jordan Boswell. Jackson gave himself a mental shake. *Don't run ahead of the evidence.*

Returning to his digital trawl, it became quickly evident that Canto led a rock and roll lifestyle, with a clear eye for good-looking women. According to one online piece, some years previously, Canto had been associated with a married doctor. The relationship floundered and it was rumoured that she was not the first married lady to succumb to Canto's muso charm. If there were any future illicit relationships, Canto had managed to maintain his privacy and keep any adulterous relationships out of the public domain.

An accomplished guitarist, he'd formed various bands over the past twenty years. *A leader*, Jackson thought, *not a follower*. Success had been patchy, but Canto had managed to make a living, 'which says a lot about his determination as well as his talent', according to one starry-eyed source.

Back to the profile, and Jackson spiked with excitement: Canto was thirty-nine years old and shared British–American nationality, care of his father, who divorced from his mother when he was five. A direct quote from Canto himself had Jackson screeching to a halt.

'As a young man and music student,' the article began. 'I returned to the States to discover my roots and reconnect, which is where I fell in love with rock music all over again.'

Was this man, with the large nose, tanned face and playful blue eyes, not only the same man that had visited Jordan Boswell nights before he died, but also Neon?

He picked up the phone to Mick Cairns. When the call went to voicemail, Jackson left a message asking for an urgent call back. He guessed Cairns was busy with Davey Jelf.

Next, he put a call through to Gonzalez at LVPD. He wanted to talk to him about Phil Canto.

49

'I came by cab. Tana couldn't make it.'

From Phil's disconsolate expression, Gary deduced that Tana had no intention of showing her pretty little face outside the bedroom. No matter. 'I'll get your car keys.'

'Thanks. You around tomorrow night?'

'Could be. Why?'

'The band are playing a set at Hubbub. Be good if you could make it.'

Gary's immediate reaction was *not on your life*. He'd rather be in his den, although, since Naomi's sudden return, his . . . *other* life was less easy to negotiate. 'Sure thing, Phil. What time are they on?'

'Around 8 o'clock.'

'Works for me,' Gary said.

'Bring Naomi with you.'

'You can count on it.' Anything to take her mind off the kid thing, Gary thought. Since she'd dropped her baby bombshell, he'd made every effort to give the subject a wide berth.

'What's that?' Naomi sashayed down the stairs and into

the tennis-court-sized hall. She wore a simple sweater with a cowl neck over jeans that clung to her as if she'd been poured into them. Her feet were bare, toenails polished. Gary watched Phil follow her with his eyes as she walked towards him and dropped a chaste kiss on his cheek. His wife was a very tactile woman. Men loved it.

She turned back to Gary and snaked an arm around his waist. Gary drew her close, basking in the envy of his friend. *Yeah, I bet you would, given half the chance,* Gary thought.

'Phil invited us to watch his band tomorrow night,' he told Naomi.

'*So* fun,' she gushed. 'Gary said you're not doing as much with RocknRoller.'

'You've not forgotten the gig?' Phil looked to Gary.

He had. Must have been all the excitement.

Naomi ruffled Gary's hair. 'Unlike you to let something like that slip your mind.'

Gary jerked his head away. 'I didn't,' he said, expressionless.

'Hey, it's fine, man.' Phil patted the air with his palms in a 'keep it cool' fashion.

Right at that moment, Gary itched to heat up the temperature and rearrange Phil's smug features. The sudden tension in the hall reminded him of the previous night's steamy activities. Guess who was in control then?

'Better shift,' Phil said. 'I'm on TV tonight.'

'Wow,' Naomi said. 'What time?'

'Six thirty, *Midlands Today*. Doing a feature about the kids, the reason I chose them. Deprived backgrounds, and all that shit.'

'We'll be sure to watch, won't we, Gary?'

'Sure.' He affected interest.

The minute Phil was disappearing down the drive in his Mustang, Naomi turned on him.

'You didn't have to be like that.'

'Like what?'

'Mean.' At that precise moment Naomi looked pretty mean herself. Her brown eyes darkened and she cupped her elbows so tight, her nails dug straight through the weave of her sweater. 'He's your friend, Gary.'

Technically true, if knowing someone for a long time equated to friendship. 'He's a prick. *Deprived background, and all that shit,*' Gary said, mimicking Phil's semi-American accent with uncanny accuracy. He'd always had an ear for a good impression. Naomi usually loved his impersonations. But not today.

'You're jealous.'

Gary burst into laughter, a cover for the surge of anger distilling in his gut. 'You have to be joking. A complicated private life, delusions of grandeur, a drug habit?'

'Drugs?'

Gary bit his bottom lip. He shouldn't have said that, although he was pleased to see Naomi's bravado dissipate. Her arms slipped to her sides, her stance softening from attack to defence. 'Recreational cocaine,' he qualified, 'I'm probably being a little harsh. Look, can we not argue?'

Naomi glanced down, flexed a leg and touched the carpet with the tip of her toes, ballet-dancer style. 'I hate it when we fight.'

'Me, too.' He walked towards her and drew her close. She

hugged him tight, pressed her cheek to his, her mouth close to his ear.

'I thought we'd get the house valued,' she said.

'Uh-huh.' He fought every physical sensation to throttle her.

'I've found some fantastic properties online. Want to take a look?'

Be nice. Act normal. Go along to get along. 'Sure,' he beamed, feeling the hinges in his jaw crack with the effort.

Naomi skipped into the sitting room. He followed in the same way a man approaches a firing squad. Scooping up her iPad from the coffee table, she bounced onto the sofa and patted the seat next to her, where he sat compliant and outwardly subdued.

With a few dexterous clicks of her manicured nails, she was onto a property website in Cumbria and pointing to the virtues of an enormous house with cottages, outbuildings and land. 'See how cheap it is compared to here.'

Yeah, and there was a reason for that, Gary thought. Rain and more rain. And where there's water, there's mud. She might as well have suggested a swamp in a jungle.

'What do you think?' She twisted round and dropped a frisky kiss on the side of his mouth.

He thought that, however big it was, however remote, it had none of the essential advantages of living where they currently did. It didn't have a man cave at the bottom of the garden for a start.

'Interesting,' he lied.

'I knew you'd warm to the idea. I've jotted down some basic *must-haves* in our new home. Stay there, I'll fetch my notepad.' She practically skipped out of the room and upstairs.

While she was gone, Gary took a sneaky peek at her work phone. Scrolling through the texts, he saw something that made his jaw grind.

The night he played with Phil's band could not come soon enough.

50

After a chat with Linda at The Vaults and a visit to a One Stop shop, Iris went straight to Davey Jelf's rental, a one-bedroom flat over a takeaway pizza parlour near Brades Village. The parlour was closed, a metal grille pulled down over the frontage.

Iris walked through a short alley to the back of the property. Taking out a skeleton key, she pried the lock and entered through the back door.

The smell of dog shit masked other unpleasant odours as she walked up a staircase and forced her way into Jelf's lair. With a whimper, Orchid hung back, her bony body shivering with distress.

'It's OK,' Iris said in a soft voice. 'I won't hurt you.' She slipped her hand inside her pocket and pulled out a dog treat. 'See, what I've got for you.'

Hunger trumped fear and Orchid slinked over, shyly took the treat as Iris slipped a length of rope around her collar.

'Good girl.' Iris gave the dog another treat and stroked her withered flanks, her fingers tracing numerous dents and bumps and badly healed scars, where the hair refused to grow, that criss-crossed, like stretch marks, along the greyhound's body. A thought came into her mind. She reached for a long-ago memory, failed to quite grasp it. 'Nobody will ever beat you again, Orchid.'

The dog sniffed her hand, viewed her with big eyes. *She understands me*, Iris thought. Dogs were much more intelligent than people. She gave the greyhound another pat, found an old cereal bowl, filled it with water and watched as the dog drank greedily.

When she'd finished, Iris said, 'Let's go and meet your auntie Linda.'

Linda dropped down to her knees, at eye level with the dog. 'My word, she's thin.' She glanced up at Iris. 'I've got a nice bit of cooked chicken to tempt her. Nothing too much for her tummy,' Linda said, in full-on maternal mode. She straightened up. 'So it's true what everyone's saying about Pardoe?'

'What are they saying?'

'That Davey Jelf squealed on him.'

Iris shrugged.

'Never did much care for him,' Linda said. 'Mind you, I didn't much care for Norman Pardoe either. Nasty man.'

Iris didn't comment. Nasty he may have been, but, thanks to Jackson, she was out in the cold with the man who had given her a regular income. Her association with Pardoe meant she was viewed as spoilt goods and, temporarily, unemployable. That represented a significant cash-flow problem. Her bigger worry was that she remained a target. Since Jelf's botched attempt on her life, Pardoe had been ominously silent. Had he already lined up someone else to shut her up for good?

After the handover, she walked out into the half-dead day. She resented the way Jackson had manipulated her. Tracking her bike was one thing, but her failure to suspect he'd done so another. It was amateurish. Was she losing her edge? Had the stress of the illness affected her brain?

But there was no point in worrying or staying angry, she reasoned. Being upset wouldn't get her the money she needed. Right on cue, her body reacting to her mind, a shard of pain flared in her back and shoulder. She took a breath, briefly closed her eyes and ran her thumb along the inside of her thumb. *Hush.*

She had to stay practical. She could not let pride cloud her judgement. Her only choice now was to throw in her lot with the detective's – and hope to fuck she stayed ahead of both Malaj and Pardoe's associates.

Jackson didn't know whether he was sweating because of the lights, or the stress of talking in front of a live camera to a female broadcaster with a sympathetic expression.

'Even for a seasoned police officer, discovering your wife must have been traumatic.'

He gave a dramatic pause. If she thought he was going to fill in details, she was mistaken.

The interviewer smiled and reluctantly returned to her notes. 'For operational reasons, you say a decision was taken to conceal the fact that your wife was Neon's latest victim.'

'That's correct, yes.'

'What was the thinking behind that?'

'We didn't wish to fuel the killer's ego or give him oxygen, in terms of editorial and newsprint.'

'Yet later that decision was revised.'

'Yes.'

'Why was that?' She leant in close. Every muscle in his body wanted to lean away. Jackson mirrored her move.

'Because the killer made a number of mistakes.'

'Can you describe these mistakes?'

Jackson shook his head. 'I'm sure you appreciate that's not possible.'

'I see,' she said, although he very much doubted she did. 'Have these mistakes provided a lead?'

'Several.'

'I'm sure the people of Birmingham will be relieved to hear it, but forgive me for saying, the police do appear to have been on the back foot with the investigation from the start.'

'I'm not sure I agree.' Even to his own ears, his words rang hollow.

'Aren't the public entitled to know how a killer can get away with murder in such a brazen manner, and on such a spectacular scale?'

'The public are entitled to us getting the job done in what is proving to be a complex case.'

'Complex in what way precisely?'

'The reconstruction and redevelopment in the centre of the City—'

'The Paradise Development?'

'And Centenary Square,' Jackson confirmed, 'has resulted in significant disruption, enabling the killer to move around more freely than would otherwise be possible.'

'Then isn't it time to bring in other agencies?'

'I'm not certain I know what you mean.' His was a simple deflection to buy him more thinking time. Naturally, he knew what she meant.

'Other forces.'

'As you're probably aware, we have a crisis of funding and resources in this country. Everyone is stretched, not least the MET.'

'So you agree that support from the MET would be welcome.'

'That's not what I said.' Jackson tried to mask his irritation at having his words twisted. Then again, what did he expect?

She waited a beat, as if she'd scored a point and wanted to savour the moment. 'I understand you're no longer in charge of the investigation due to the personal nature of your loss.'

'That's right, although I am, of course, kept abreast of developments in my wife's murder case.' Which was strictly true although there'd been damn all to report.

Another lean-in accompanied by a penetrating look. 'Do you have every faith in the Senior Investigating Officer in charge.'

She'd done her homework. Jackson met her eye. 'Absolutely.'

'So what's your message to the killer?'

Jackson looked straight to camera. At last the moment he'd been waiting for had arrived. Time to shove it to Neon as hard as he could. 'We're onto you and we're closing in. Your reign of terror is about to end.'

'Thank you, Detective Chief Inspector Matt Jackson.'

As the camera panned away, Jackson got up and was

ushered towards the Green Room. His collar was rimed with perspiration and his cheeks flared hot. Foundation applied by the make-up artist slid down his face like wet paint down a wall. He wrestled a tissue from his jacket and did his best to scrub it off. Now that was over, he had two objectives: get the hell out and find the nearest pub.

'You did good in there, man. Took guts.'

Distracted, Jackson wiped his face and looked across to the owner of the mid-Atlantic accent. The man, a good six feet tall and with a solid build, was already on his feet, his right hand extended. 'Phil Canto,' he said.

The face was unmistakable. The hairstyle was very different. Had Canto cut off his dreads deliberately?

Jackson felt as if he'd been zapped with a Taser. He took the offered hand and shook. It felt rough and, glancing down, he noticed that the skin on the man's knuckles was red and raw. Knight's comment about burns to his hands flitted through his mind.

'I've followed the investigation from the very first day,' Canto said. 'It's important not to believe the crap you read. You guys are doing a fine job in very difficult circumstances, never mind what she said in there.' He angled his head in the direction of the studio.

'Thank you, it's appreciated.' Jackson spoke mechanically, too shocked to make sense of Canto's brazen approach. Was this really coincidence or was there something else in play?

'I've always found music to be a source of solace at difficult moments.'

Jackson felt the hairs on his arms prickle.

Canto took a card from his pocket and pressed it into

Jackson's hand. 'Come find me at my next gig and I'll buy you a beer.'

Before Jackson had a chance to respond, a floor manager beckoned. 'You're on next, Mr Canto.'

'I sincerely hope you catch the killer, Matt,' Canto said, patting him on the shoulder.

Jackson flinched and watched Canto stride through the door and into the white-bright studio lights.

51

'Hello, Matt.'

'Iris,' Jackson said in surprise, although he had to admit nobody generally phoned him from a payphone.

She'd caught him off guard. Since exiting the studio the night before, his phone had not stopped ringing in the wake of the interview, but he'd been consumed by one question only: Was Canto a fit for Neon?

'I saw you on the TV,' she said.

'Not my finest hour.'

She didn't agree or disagree. 'Did it work then? Did it flush him out?'

'I don't know, but I'm following a lead.'

'Right,' she said.

Jackson cleared his throat. He hadn't forgotten that she'd given him a fake number. He sensed that now was not the time to flag it up. To be fair, after the bust-up over Davey Jelf, he wasn't sure that he'd ever hear from her again. He'd hoped she'd come back, if only for the money, but you never knew with Iris. Her call to him clearly an olive branch, he decided to accept and carry on as if things were back on the same footing as before. 'Any developments your end?'

'Not really.'

'Might be an idea to check out lock-ups and potential workshops for Neon's work.'

'Again?'

The edge in her voice was unmistakable. 'I'm not trying to tell you what to do, Iris.'

Silence spooled out between them. If he didn't make more effort, he'd lose her again and, like it or not, he still needed her.

'Look, I'm sorry if you think I made the wrong call with Davey Jelf.'

She didn't comment.

'So you're still in one piece?' he said, wincing at how unnaturally upbeat he sounded.

'What do you mean?'

'There's been no bother?'

'I don't know what you're talking about,' she said, clearly put out.

'Fine, fine.' This really was a crap conversation.

Another silence widened the chasm between them.

'So . . . um . . . be good to meet up,' he said awkwardly.

'Now?'

It wasn't like Iris to be so quick off the mark, he thought. 'I was thinking more along the lines of tomorrow morning, at the flat?'

'All right.' She sounded immensely sullen. 'You'll be there?'

'I will.'

He was about to wish her goodbye when she hung up. Left staring at his mobile, he wished he'd handled her better.

That was the problem with Iris. She was so closed down and defensive, it was almost impossible to have a conversation with her that didn't get her back up.

Glad that they were at least on speaking terms again, his thoughts returned to Phil Canto, a man who had seemed sincere and charming. He was also unnervingly direct, as if it were important to him to make contact. Jackson thought about that and compared his observation of Canto's behaviour with the content of his last conversation with Gonzalez. The LVPD officer had talked about the psychology of a killer like Neon and the potential disconnect between the trappings of a life that might appear happy and settled and successful, and the grim reality of what lay beneath.

'Every time he kills, this is his true self, not the one he fakes to the outside world,' Gonzalez had said.

'Nothing imaginary about his skill as a musician.'

'No, and it's an extremely useful talent to have if you want to attract the opposite sex.'

Jackson had described Canto's romantic history.

'Attraction to married women suggests he enjoys the thrill of the illicit and is probably flaky about commitment. What kind of women does he date?' Gonzalez had asked.

'Professional,' Jackson had replied.

'Which fits the profile.'

'Then why not kill them too?'

Gonzalez had been unable to answer explicitly. 'As likely as not, he'll have a dysfunctional relationship with his mother,' he'd said, promising to look into Canto before signing off.

Jackson called Cairns, whose line tripped to voicemail. He

left a brief message, after which his mobile rang immediately: Browne.

Expecting a bollocking for exploiting his police officer status when he no longer had a warrant card, Jackson was surprised to hear that the SIO was not disappointed.

'Although it would have been nice if you'd informed me and the press office first,' Browne said, adding a cautionary note.

'There was no time,' Jackson lied. 'You know how news-hounds work. How's the investigation going? Any breaks?'

'Like you said, we're following a number of leads.'

'Care to share?'

'We're re-interviewing Vicky Wainwright and Vanessa Booth's friends.' The first two victims, Jackson registered. 'Specifically, those they were with on the nights they died. I'll be in touch the moment we have something tangible.'

Jackson thanked him for the call and tried Cairns again.

'Sorry, sorry, sorry,' Cairns said. 'I got your message but couldn't get away. Jelf is squawking like a crow on speed. Interestingly, he knew Jordan Boswell. Seems Boswell was a bigger fish than imagined, mixed up in the cocaine trade.'

'Adding weight to Browne's argument that Boswell was killed by someone from the criminal fraternity.'

'Speaking of which, we picked up Norman Pardoe at 4 a.m. this morning. Forensics are giving his premises the full treatment.'

'What about Malaj?'

'The National Crime Agency is going to get stuck in.'

Jackson offered a silent thank you to the deities. At the very least, Iris was safe from Pardoe and the Albanian's clutches – for the moment.

'You played a blinder last night, Matt. If that doesn't get Neon crawling out of the woodwork, God knows what will. Browne's given the order to flood the streets with police. It's his top priority to reduce Neon's wriggle room. If he pops up, we'll be ready.'

'Does he still intend to use female PCs as bait?'

''Fraid so.'

Jackson thought of Shah and grunted his disapproval.

'Anyway, what's up?'

Jackson told Cairns about Phil Canto. He didn't mention that their paths had crossed in the Green Room.

'I watched him on the TV,' Cairns chipped in. 'Interestingly, he also happens to be Wayne Gardner's contact.'

'Canto's recording studio organised the promotion?'

'Yup.'

'But his band won,' Jackson pointed out. 'Surely, that's not allowed?'

'Dunno. His rules. His band. I'm more intrigued by the fact you believe Canto visited Jordan Boswell.'

'Can you carry out all the necessary checks, Mick, run Canto through the system and check with DVLA which vehicles are registered to him?'

'On it.'

By the time Jackson had eaten a sandwich, Cairns was back on the line. 'Canto drives a Transit, owns a motorbike and a yellow, left-hand-drive Mustang.'

Jackson felt a surge of adrenaline. In truth, it was circumstantial but, sometimes, circumstantial led to evidential. 'Pick him up.'

'What do I tell Browne?'

'Anything that sounds plausible. And check out the plates on the van, see if it matches any Transits entering Birmingham on the nights of the murders.'

Jackson waited in all day. He paced the apartment, as nervous as a first-time father waiting in the maternity ward. Having spent so long figuring out what Neon was like, Phil Canto did not square with the killer in his imagination, yet thinking like that was stupid and dangerous. He, of all people, knew that killers came in all guises, personalities and occupations. There was no one-size-fits-all. The biggest mistake any detective could make was forcing the evidence to fit the crime. Against all he wanted to believe, he understood that Phil Canto could have had a perfectly legitimate reason for visiting Boswell. It did not mean that he'd murdered him.

As the hours ticked by, he spent the time keeping abreast of the news: the carjacking of an expensive Audi; a handbag snatch; the council blocked from closing a day centre; a steep rise in railway deaths. He expected news to filter through of an arrest for the Boswell murder and the gig that evening to be cancelled.

The phone call from Cairns eventually arrived as Jackson was debating whether or not to walk into town, or cab it. Cairns came straight to the point.

'No dice.'

'What?'

'Canto knew Boswell because of his music connections. It checks out.'

Fuck, Jackson thought. 'He admitted to visiting that evening?'

'He did.'

Cairns seemed careful in his replies, cautious even. Jackson wondered what it was Cairns wasn't telling him. 'And your take on him?'

Cairns paused to consider. 'Seems a regular guy. You know the type: relaxed, charismatic, polite and helpful.'

'But?'

'There's something he's not telling us. For a start, he changed his story.'

'Go on.'

'At first he denied knowing Boswell. When we explained that he was spotted entering Boswell's house, he came out with some bullshit about mental overload.'

'As in it slipped his mind?'

'Exactly. The second he knew the game was up, he co-operated fully and, I have to say, enthusiastically.'

Hang on, Jackson thought. 'Why would someone like Canto, a successful guy, visit Boswell in his dead-end home in Quinton? It doesn't stack.'

'I agree, and yet if he was putting on a show, he's a damn fine actor. We had to let him go.'

And Browne wouldn't explore whether or not Canto was a fit for Neon because, according to him, Neon didn't kill Boswell, Jackson knew.

'No follow-up then?' he asked.

Cairns's hesitation was minimal, but noticeable.

'Released under investigation,' Cairns confirmed.

It looked like he was going to a gig that evening.

52

Jackson's entire auditory system felt under threat from noise and the razzle-dazzle of a million coloured lights that aroused memories he'd rather forget. When a strobe effect kicked in, he shut his eyes. Horrific images flickered into his mind, his pulse quickening as the feeling of panic swelled. He wanted to go but needed to stay.

Placing a hand against his chest to offset a full-blown panic attack, he lurked at the back of the venue with the other adults, as far away from the stage as possible. Warm beer sloshed out of a plastic pint glass and dribbled down his free hand.

Before him, hundreds of shrieking and weeping teens, waved their hands and swayed in time to a pounding beat, aided and abetted by screaming guitar riffs and voices pushed to their vocal limits – and sometimes beyond.

Not yet forty, Jackson felt unutterably old.

His mind returned to the frustrating news Cairns had just given him. Canto had been cleared. He represented yet another blind alley. All Jackson had to show for days of questions and legwork was another crime boss on his way to court and, God willing, the dismantling of Enrik Malaj's criminal empire, for which he would never receive the credit. Nor did he want it.

Mercifully, the support group announced a break. Already wavering after this musical taster, Jackson was not looking forward to Spaghetti Junction.

'I didn't expect to see you here.'

Jackson turned and met Kiran Shah's eye. She looked less officious in civvies. Softer, more approachable somehow. The Neon investigation was taking its toll on many, yet she seemed remarkably unfazed by it. He felt peculiarly pleased that she'd not been selected for Browne's 'bait' duty.

'I could say the same about you,' Jackson said.

Shah tipped her chin towards the front of the auditorium where a group of youngsters were moving amps and equipment, and adjusting microphones. 'I'm here with my daughter. She's nuts about the headline band, the lead singer in particular.'

'How old is she?'

'Twelve going on twenty.' Her eyes gleamed, speaking of a mother's pride. 'Kaylee adores music.'

Jackson nodded amiably.

'So what's your excuse?' she said.

'Me? Ah, I'm providing moral support for a friend whose daughter's up there somewhere.' He shifted his gaze vaguely in the direction of the stage. 'Single mum,' he added, gilding the lie.

'Is she here?' Shah craned her head.

'Popped to the loo.'

'She'd better hurry or she might miss the main attraction.'

Shah laughed. It was nice to see her carefree, Jackson thought. Shame on him, he'd always regarded her as more cipher than human being. 'Fasten your safety belt,' she said, 'Teardown's over.'

Jackson cast her a quizzical look.

'It means tidying up one band's equipment before the next one plays.'

'Right,' Jackson said, scanning the audience for signs of Phil Canto. He'd be mad to venture out into the roaring and baying crowd. He was probably lurking backstage somewhere. Jackson touched Shah's arm, pointed to his ear and mouthed, 'I'm leaving.'

She nodded that she understood.

He walked out of the building, onto the street and around to a side entrance, where a thickset man with a shaved head stood like a boulder in front of a cave.

'Police.' Jackson slipped his hand inside his jacket as if he were pulling out a warrant card. With luck, news had travelled of Canto's brief visit to the police station. 'To see Mr Canto.'

The security guard stepped aside, pushed open the door into an area that smelt of cold and damp and faded glory. Jackson had no idea which way to go and plumped for a flight of stairs that would take him up to the same level as the stage. He followed the noise and found Canto backstage, surrounded by a large group of stagehands and assorted others milling around, like close protection officers around a client.

Canto was in animated conversation with a stunning-looking woman who Jackson assumed to be a model. Another guy had his arm protectively around her waist. Dark hair crowned an unassumingly handsome face, despite the man's wide, flat boxer's nose. Fine stubble covered his cheeks and jaw. Each held glasses of fizz. They certainly made a picture-postcard couple.

At Jackson's approach, Canto broke into a smile. The woman's eyes displayed recognition, as if she registered who he was but couldn't quite place him.

'Mr Detective, I hope this isn't a business call,' Canto said.

Jackson played dumb.

'You don't know?'

'Not a clue, I'm afraid.' But he wasn't in the dark about the strong whiff of weed coming off Canto's clothes or the stoned look in his eyes. Immediately, he remembered Mick Cairns's comment about Boswell's connection to the cocaine trade. Had he supplied Canto? The drug-addicted had little choice but to float in criminal circles. No wonder Canto had been cagey about his visit.

Canto gave a light, incredulous laugh. 'The police had it in their heads that I was connected to a recent murder.'

'Christ,' the other man exploded.

'It's OK, Gary,' Canto said, turning to his dark-haired friend. 'Fortunately, it was all a silly misunderstanding.'

'I'm glad to hear it,' Jackson said.

Canto, as if remembering his manners, introduced him to Gary and Naomi Fairweather. 'Matt Jackson is a police officer,' Canto added. A little needlessly, Jackson thought.

'Can I get you a drink?' Gary Fairweather asked. He had deep brown eyes and spoke with a London accent, not strong. Didn't sound Estuary or Cockney.

'No, I'm all right, thanks,' Jackson replied. 'I don't want to bust up the party.'

'I insist.' With an expansive gesture, Canto whispered to one of the stagehands, a young woman with gap teeth, a gold stud in her nose and a row of earrings in each ear. 'I'm flattered you took me up on my offer so soon.'

'I don't think a man like Matt is here for the music,' Fairweather said, with a light laugh. 'I mean no disrespect,' he added, looking from Canto to Jackson.

'None taken,' Jackson said, ignoring the barbed remark and relieved to see his drink arrive. 'Always happy to support local culture.' He took the glass, chinked it with the others, eyes homing in on Canto's sore hands. 'Although I admit pop isn't quite my thing.'

'What *is* your thing?' Naomi asked with a sweet smile.

Jackson took a large mouthful of champagne. 'I've got pretty catholic tastes.' Polly was the music girl. He'd no affinity to any particular genre. Unbidden, 'The Sound of Silence' echoed through his brain. Jackson loosened the collar of his shirt, which suddenly felt too tight.

'Come along to one of our grown-up gigs,' Canto said. 'We're playing at The Jam House tomorrow night.'

The Jam House was a venue a stone's throw away from Jackson's flat. Was this a set-up?

'Will the lighting display be as impressive?' Jackson said.

'The kids love it, but, I agree, it's a little gruesome,' Canto remarked with a wide grin. 'It's more subtle at The Jam House.'

'Better than at the German Market, that's for sure,' Fairweather said, to which Canto laughed.

Jackson felt sure he was missing something.

Naomi leant across and touched his arm. 'Are you OK? You look a little warm.'

'Not wise to drink champagne on top of beer.'

'Why didn't you say?' Canto remarked, looking around. Jackson half-expected him to snap his fingers. 'I'll get you a pint.'

'No, I'm fine.' The last thing Jackson needed was more drink. There was definitely an odd vibe and he struggled to find a way to insert the questions he really wanted to ask, without looking overly obvious. Was he losing his touch? Perhaps he was only ever any good at this when inside an interview room. Fortunately, Naomi provided a lead. The standard opener to thousands of conversations up and down the country, she asked where he was from originally. He told her.

'Naomi's the only pure-bred Brum amongst us,' Fairweather said. 'And Phil, well, he's a mongrel.'

'Proud to be half-Brit, half-American.'

'Do you go back much?' Jackson asked Canto.

'Once a year to see my pa.'

'Where's that?'

'Boulder City, Nevada.'

Jackson suppressed a strong physical reaction. 'Near Las Vegas?'

'Twenty-six miles south-east. You been there?'

Jackson shook his head, thinking he should let Gonzalez know.

'An amazing place,' Canto enthused. 'Gambling, girls and gondolas.'

Jackson pulled a face, uncomprehending. Fairweather helpfully explained that, in imitation of Venice, it was possible to float along the Grand Canal. 'It's a popular tourist attraction.'

'How romantic,' Naomi said, giving her husband a seductive sideways glance. A sudden pebble of grief lodged in Jackson's throat and he drained his glass.

'I should be making tracks,' he said. 'Nice meeting you all. Thanks for the drink, Phil.'

'Don't forget our date at The Jam.'

53

Game on.

Nice to see the detective, Gary thought, but what a total letdown. He had hoped Jackson would be a worthy adversary and now, after a single conversation, he realised he was not. Why the hell Polly married him, he'd never understand, not in a million light years. All that disgusting perspiration, all those pathetically transparent, stating-the-bloody-obvious, bleeding-heart questions. What was the man thinking? Truth was, DCI Jackson wasn't thinking at all, was he? He was as miserable as he was dumb.

It was hard to admit, but Gary *almost* felt sorry for him, which he guessed was a pisser. If ever a man disliked pity, it was Matt Jackson. That much was clear from the TV interview, which Gary had been pleased to come across whilst waiting on that stupid interview with Phil. Gary wasn't fooled by his feeble responses. Underneath that controlled exterior, Jackson was a mess. And Gary knew a thing or two about a life led in tandem. *Seemed that Jackson's dark side was catching up with the exterior me – we share so much in common,* Gary mused. Only, in Gary's case, he considered the better part of him, the real Gary, was a damn sight more appealing and interesting than the dull henpecked version he portrayed to the outside world.

If rocking up to a teeny gig was Jackson's way of smoking him out, he'd made a miscalculation of epic proportions, deserving of an epic response. A pity darling Polly was dead because he'd genuinely enjoy killing her all over again.

Gary sighed with contentment. Jackson genuinely had no idea just how easy it had been to walk into her life. Never mind, another part of the puzzle would be heading his way in the not too distant future. The work was already in hand. The design for his lighting display, this time, was a real cracker. He couldn't wait to fire up the burners. All he needed now was a victim and, bless the detective Jackson had given him a terrific idea for the perfect woman.

54

Iris had done the rounds. She'd visited the guys in the car wash and discovered that Jakub had returned to Poland, so no lead there. She'd checked out every lock-up and potential 'studio' for Neon's lighting activities. She'd spoken to Dougie The Homeless and Caleb The Creep and Linda The Clueless. They had nothing. She had nothing.

Everything was shit. She wasn't emoting. She was simply telling it the way it was. And that shitty phone call with Jackson only made things worse. Basically, she'd nothing to tell him and she *still* had nothing to tell him. As a result, Jackson had no reason to keep her in the loop. She was redundant. End of.

Glaring at her work phone, she willed the bloody thing to ring. It stared back, squat and accusing. Fucked off, she decided to go to The Vaults and take Orchid for a walk. Afterwards, she'd head to Matt's and . . .

Her 'Dial a Death' phone suddenly sparked into life. Amazed, she snatched it up, ensured the voice-changing app was set and went through her usual spiel. Yes, she thought, listening; it seemed straightforward enough. Then: *Oh crap.*

The menu selection was à la carte. She couldn't translate the French phrase, but she knew what it meant. Expensive, which was good. Off the scale, which was not. In plain English: timing was ludicrous, location was dangerous and, unusually, the victim was female.

'Anything I need to know that would help ensure a smooth delivery?'

There was, according to the client. Iris listened some more.

'How tall is the subject?'

It went against her usual code, but, critical for this particular job, she paid attention to the answer.

Satisfied, she said, 'Wire the money. It will be done tonight.'

The call cut, she stood and looked out of the window, could just about glimpse the canal. She gauged water temperature to be around ten degrees, maybe cooler, and did a quick calculation. The biggest threat was the public nature of the location. Potential noise might also pose a problem. The weather was on her side; it was foul and damp. Many people stayed in during the month, saving their pennies for the big splurge in December, which reduced the risk of being sighted.

She reached for her crash helmet. At least tonight's job did not require a gun. This was strictly wet work.

Iris went outside, collected her bike and drove along the main road. Skyscraper office blocks ahead and crap shops that used to be nice shops, and vice versa. She signalled near Five Ways and entered Broad Street via the underpass.

From the second she stepped out of the car park onto the

street, she paid special attention to the placement of CCTV cameras; there were many.

A flight of steps down to the towpath and water's edge and a narrowboat cafe straight ahead, serving breakfast, one question prickled the back of her mind. Was six feet of canal water enough to get the job done? As long as it covered the target's nose and mouth, and stayed that way, it should be fine, she reasoned.

Iris turned right, past a row of olive trees decorated with lights, and approached Broad Street Tunnel – a low bridge covered in graffiti. Impossible to stand up straight due to the curved headroom, she listed to the left, clutching hold of open railings that offered little protection from the dirty depths on the other side.

The path broadened out into Gas Street Basin, in which The Canal House stood on the other side. Iris walked past a bar dedicated to selling gin, half the premises boarded up. A little further on, the famous Tap and Spile pub.

Iris turned and retraced her steps. Back inside the tunnel, her superficial surveillance suggested that it wasn't a bad place for a hit. She wasn't into casual or slapdash – she was into thorough. Looking up at the brick ceiling revealed flood-lights, switched off now, but they'd be ablaze later. What interested her most: the client had already done the home-work for her. He'd warned her that it was a no-go. Normally, clients weren't so accommodating.

Iris returned to the bottom of the steps and continued walking in the opposite direction. She passed a narrowboat offering cruises and noted that offices overlooking this stretch of water were empty and to let.

On her left was a big alcove containing a lift for disabled access. Further on, Brewmasters Bridge and a door in the wall signed 'Security Control'. It had a number to phone in case of emergency. She chuckled at the thought.

Iris tucked herself inside and scanned the opposite aspect for cameras. There was one and it was pointing the wrong way. She dropped her gaze to the water a few feet beyond. It gleamed in the chilly sunshine like wet coal. And there were no safety railings.

'Phil Canto, yeah, thirty-nine years old . . . Father lives in Boulder City, Nevada . . . Sure, I appreciate it . . . Apologies for the early call.'

Jackson signed off from Gonzalez when the entry phone buzzed.

'Iris,' he said, making a special effort to be pleasant, 'come on up.'

Hand in pockets, she shambled in, sat down, hunched forward. Not exactly approachable, he thought. He didn't offer her a drink or an apology for tracking her whereabouts by GPS. How else could he keep tabs on her if she refused to give him her number? As far as he was concerned, they were even. He didn't say that he was pleased she was in one piece and hadn't run into trouble. He *did* tell her that Pardoe had been picked up and that Malaj and his crew were in the National Crime Agency's crosshairs.

'Good luck with that,' she said, without intonation.

'You should be pleased. It reduces the risk of reprisals.'

'Says who? If they find the person responsible for Prifti's death, there's nothing you lot can do about it. And they won't stop until they find out who did it. Blood feuds last for generations.'

'Just as well you have no family,' he said, trying to deflect and lighten the tone. Iris's response was to hurl him an excoriating look.

He cut straight to Phil Canto and his legitimate connection to Boswell. He also described the gig, how he'd hated every second and how he'd tracked down Canto the previous evening, that it had been a weird encounter, in which Jackson suspected he'd been played. Iris couldn't have looked more bored had he recited a passage from the Police and Criminal Evidence Codes of Practice.

'Something on your mind?' he said archly.

She yawned. 'You said that Cairns cleared Canto even though he thought he was hiding something, and you're suspicious because the bloke's dad lives in the States.'

'Near Las Vegas.'

'Coincidence.'

'I don't believe in them.'

'You should. Life is a series of coincidences.'

He listened in surprise. He didn't think she had it in her to make such grand statements.

'You've got your tamed Yank cop on the Canto trail,' Iris continued. 'Meanwhile, back in good old Birmingham, we have jack shit.' She met his eye, defying him to tell her it wasn't so.

'You've heard nothing?' he asked.

'Never expected to. Like I said, Neon is a one-man-band.' The faintest glimmer of amusement played across her lips.

It would be funny if it weren't so serious, Jackson thought.

He waited a beat. 'If we could find where Neon makes his signs, we'd be home and dry.'

'I've done what you said and checked out as many lock-ups and workshops as I can.'

'There's a fairly inexhaustible supply.'

'Then maybe he's knocking up stuff in his basement.'

'Might be a bit dangerous.'

'*Dangerous*?'

'Electricity, gas, flammable material, confined space.' Jackson ticked off the list on his fingers.

'Oh sure,' Iris said drily. 'Health and safety figures big time on this guy's radar.'

'You're particularly waspy today.'

'I don't like going round and round in circles. It makes me dizzy.'

The atmosphere twitched with frustration and silence. A call to Iris's phone broke the impasse. She took it out, saw the number, glanced up at Jackson.

'I have to get this,' she said.

Jackson gave a small shrug, moved over to the kitchen area. She answered with a straight 'Yes?' He didn't hear what was spoken, but it seemed to last for a long time.

'OK,' Iris said, 'I can't really talk now. I'll call you later. Don't worry,' she said, in a tone he'd never heard before. 'I'll get it sorted.' With Iris, 'sorted' had a multitude of meanings, none of them good. Peculiarly unnerved, he asked himself whether she was in some way pulling a fast one. Devious as hell, did Iris believe she could use him? It was an unsettling thought.

She finished the call, slipped her phone back into her

pocket, looked up and through him. He felt as if she were daring him to ask who was on the other end.

'What are you doing tonight?' he said.

'Washing my hair.'

'Iris, for God's sake.'

She let out an enormous sigh. 'What did you have planned?'

'A gig.'

'Another one? From what you said, you couldn't stick it.'

'I'm not going for the music. How about it?'

'Can't.'

The sensation that she was definitely up to no good settled on him like a toxic cloud. 'Why not?'

'Because I can't,' she said, a warning in her voice.

'Iris, if you're up—'

'I would if I could,' she said airily. 'It's not possible this evening.' She pitched forward, drummed her fingers on the coffee table. 'Going back to Canto.'

'I'm listening.' Absolutely no point in pushing her. Iris had made up her mind and nothing he said would make her budge.

'He told your lot that he knew Boswell because of the music connection. But that's not why he visited.'

'Drugs?' he chipped in.

'Gotta be.'

'Glad we're on the same page about something.' It struck him the minute he caught the smell of skunk on Canto's clothing. Why else would a man like him take time out of a busy agenda to visit a bloke who played so badly?

'And that means he didn't kill him.'

'Because he was too important,' Jackson agreed. 'Why kill the golden goose?'

'If I were Boswell's killer,' Iris said, with a chilling note of authority, 'I'd be laughing my socks off.'

'You're not the first to say so,' Jackson acknowledged.

'While the cops are chasing their tails, Neon's planning his next murder.'

'You think Boswell's death was a smokescreen?'

She hiked a shoulder. 'More likely tying up a loose end. Maybe Boswell confessed to Canto.'

'And told him about Neon?' Jackson shook his head. 'If Boswell talked, Canto would be dead by now.' He looked away, deep in thought, a wild idea beginning to take shape. 'That's it. Canto's a stooge.'

Iris frowned in confusion.

'Think about it. Canto has all the right credentials. In fact, they're almost too perfect. The US connection, the flashy car, the fact he's a musician. He makes the perfect fall guy. Even the van.'

'What van?'

'He owns a Transit, presumably for shifting musical equipment.'

'Or a body. Check the plate, match it with CCTV?'

Jackson had already run the idea past Cairns. He remembered that Cairns hadn't come back to him, perhaps because a killer of Neon's calibre would have changed the plates. 'Already on it,' he told Iris, 'but I'm not that hopeful. I think this is more a case of misdirection. The whole music thing is one massive red herring.'

Iris's eyes gleamed with unspoken truth. Jackson

remembered how she'd strained to set up Davey Jelf in order to cover her tracks. Hell, he hoped he was right about Neon. Inside, he groaned at the prospect of travelling along one road only to discover he'd missed a turning ten miles previously. And if that was so, what then? Without warning, his heart rate stuttered, his breath became shallow and thready. When he clenched his hands to get a grip, his fingers shook.

'How long has it been since his last victim?' Iris said, utterly oblivious to the panic racing through him. *He could not fail. He must not fail.*

'Too long.'

'After you pissed him off in that TV interview, he'll up the ante. Won't be long before there's another.'

55

Screened by trees, and with shutters on the windows, he couldn't see out and nobody could see in, including Naomi. It was the only place in the garden out of bounds, a fair trade for her ongoing emasculation.

Gary pushed his arms out in front of him, spread his hands wide and opened and shut his fingers. Warmth spread from the tips, right through the muscles in his forearms, loosening them up. Next, he picked up his sax, fingered a low B flat and, opening up his throat, took a big, bold breath straight from his diaphragm and directed it down the horn, holding the tone to a count of five. He repeated it several times, anchoring himself in the sound. When he was done, he launched into the solo in George Michael's 'Careless Whisper'.

A couple of numbers later, he packed up his sax, made sure he'd got spare reeds and locked up the 'shed', as Naomi liked to call it.

'Hey, babe,' he said, stepping through the back door and into the kitchen. They'd had dinner earlier and Naomi was washing up.

'Hey,' she said.

'Why not chuck everything into the dishwasher?'

'Waste of water and money.'

'It's never bothered you before.'

'I like washing up. It's novel.'

Playing the domestic goddess did not suit Naomi. 'If you want *novel*, I have a way better idea.'

Naomi glanced over her shoulder, obviously intrigued by the low tone in his voice. 'Oh yeah?'

He put the sax case down, slipped his arms around her and whispered in her ear. He described what she was to wear.

'Gary,' she laughed. 'Are you serious?'

Next, he described when she was to wear it and where. Her body stiffened.

'But—'

'No buts, I'll be right there waiting for you, babe. You trust me, don't you?'

She leant into him. Her hair smelt of sandalwood. Her body oozed certainty. He ground himself into her rear, a promise of what would happen later. 'You know I do.'

'Up for it then?'

'Always,' she said.

56

Canto was right. Different line-up, different feel. Big bluesy numbers fused with traditional rock in a medley of cover versions and original songs. Loud, occasionally raucous, always accomplished, these guys – and one woman – knew what they were about. And it was hard to resist Canto, a born showman with a big voice, belting out an Aerosmith number about coincidental murder. Was there a message in the lyrics? Jackson wondered.

The big surprise was Gary Fairweather. Jackson had had no inkling the night before that the guy was more than just a supportive friend. Playing with control and brilliance, he was generous; not one to steal the limelight, even though it was clear half the audience couldn't take their eyes off him. Jackson was among the captives, mesmerised by the dexterity of the guy's fingers, the rope-like muscles in his arms, and the mellow tone coaxed from the instrument. Jackson had to remind himself that he hadn't gone for the music; he was there to observe.

He craned his head. It was difficult to see clearly because of the man's movement, the way the light caught his hands.

Earlier, he'd expressed the view to Iris that the music industry connection was a blind alley, but the more he stood and watched, the more he felt beset by doubt.

As one number finished to a round of applause, Jackson noticed a man lift a double bass onto his hip and walk it onto the stage. Canto introduced the musician, Tony Felix, to the sound of more clapping.

'OK, guys,' he said, patting the air for quiet.

Half of Jackson's brain focused on one of the most iconic bass lines in rock history, the other half on the size of the double bass, which had to be six feet in height. You'd have to be damn careful to transport it, without damaging the body of the instrument.

And then the wildest thought triggered something in his brain.

Jackson scanned the faces of the crowd. Naomi Fairweather was not among them. Perhaps she was at home, minding a tribe of kids. He scoped the room again. With looks like hers, she'd be hard to miss. No, she definitely wasn't there. Did it mean anything, or nothing at all?

Iris fell into step behind her quarry. She didn't mask her movement, didn't walk with a silent tread on her crepe-soled shoes. A gaggle of others surrounded her, a group of students, judging by their clothing. To an outsider, she was one more woman, walking solo, a little bit drunk, with a phone clasped to her chest and a trapper-style hat on her head. What possible threat could she pose?

As far as codes of awareness were concerned, Iris was looking for Code White, not Code Red. 'White' denoted the most switched off and vulnerable a victim could be – 'Red', the reverse. From what she'd observed, this was as 'White' as it got.

Ahead, the target tottered on high heels – more like spikes – down the steps to the towpath. Her long, dark hair fell around the shoulders of a thick fur coat that reached her knees. Iris couldn't tell whether or not it was real. Beneath it, the woman's legs were slim, calves straining. To counter the effect of a body pitched forward, she leant backwards, giving her an uneven and lopsided gait. At this rate she'd topple over into the water and drown, or break her neck, Iris thought, her own role rendered unnecessary.

At the bottom of the steps, the woman wobbled, stuck out a hand to steady herself on the uneven towpath and teetered towards Brewmasters Bridge. Unable to swim, her target was clearly afraid and she wondered how the client had persuaded her to take ridiculous risks so late at night. Iris could swim, although, in these temperatures, she wasn't sure how anyone could survive for very long in the dark waters of the canal.

A light, chilly wind picked up, plunging the already freezing temperature several degrees south. Iris lurched along, humming a drunken tune. The woman paused, tucked herself into the recess in front of the security door that Iris had noted earlier. She shivered and pulled out her phone. Iris drew alongside, reached into her coat, as if for a cigarette and asked the woman for a light.

'Sorry, no.' She was brisk and rude and didn't glance up.

Iris thanked her and, as the woman pecked at a number on her phone's keypad, she struck. Grabbing hold of a length of hair in one hand, she clutched at a coat sleeve with the other, embedding her fingers tightly into the fabric. The woman let out a shriek of terror, which Iris ignored. Pivoting on her feet, she spun the target around so that the woman had her back to the water. Stupidly, the woman clung to the mobile, despite the sound of clicking anklebones. Glancing wildly right and left, she stumbled, and Iris followed up, sweeping her leg around and dumping the woman flat onto her back. With a cry of pain, the victim scrabbled back up to her feet, pitching and swaying like a skittle in a bowling alley. Iris advanced again.

Like badly matched dancers, they tussled near to the edge, where, patiently glinting with anticipation, the canal opened its jaws, a crocodile ready to swallow anyone foolish enough to fall in.

Iris felt the skin on her cheek tear from a stray nail. Pumped up, she shut her ears and eyes to the danger, ignored the threat of discovery. The target opened her mouth to scream, as Iris anticipated she would. About to shut her up for good, a blare of police sirens sounded across the city, drowning out all noise for miles around. Iris didn't wait for it to die down. She thrust forward and gave the woman a final shove.

Arms flailing, a scream choked off by a fresh blast of what sounded like emergency vehicles, the phone hit the surface with a splash and the woman followed, jack-knifing into the water.

Impassive and detached, Iris watched her victim's head disappear below the surface before briefly bobbing back up, spluttering and choking. Back down it went, emerging again with more desperation. As the struggling figure made a futile grab for the side, Iris loomed close, ready to make sure the woman stayed down.

Still, the noise from the city raged and Iris lifted her head, listened, thinking there had been a terrorist attack and wondering where in the city it might be. Or maybe Neon had been up to his old tricks.

When she looked back at the water, the figure had disappeared. She guessed the weight of the coat had helped to drag her down. Iris had never liked furs, fake or real, or the people that wore them.

The band had finished a hip-twisting version of an old Roxy Music number when everything fell apart.

Above the clamour of applause and people heading for the bar, Jackson had already tuned into the wail of police sirens, distant at first and then louder and louder. Next, a disturbance at the back of the room, followed by the appearance of uniformed police. Heads turned. Mouths slackened. Some music punters hurtled towards the exits. In among the melee of officers, one figure emerged: Marcus Browne. He stalked straight towards the stage where the band was packing up. At the sight of the police, all but the drummer stopped what they were doing, bemused expressions on their faces.

Jackson hung back, glanced over his shoulder and saw Cairns, followed by Shah bringing up the rear. He attempted to make eye contact with his friend and failed. Shah, back in her police mode, ignored him too.

Jackson watched Browne flanked by a couple of uniforms. He made a straight line for Canto. It was heavy, brutal and very public. No cosy chat down the station, this was a full-on arrest. Had Browne changed his mind about Canto's relationship to Jordan Boswell?

Jackson wondered what reasonable grounds Browne had to suspect that Canto had committed a crime. Thinking back to his phone call with Cairns, he realised now why his friend had been evasive and hesitant. They must have something on Canto that hadn't been disclosed.

Those left in the room fell silent. Some strained to hear, including Jackson. Wisely, Canto opted to go quietly. He didn't have a choice with a pair of handcuffs clamped to his wrists. To Jackson's eyes, he appeared like a man blindsided. As the police marched a grim-faced Canto through, the crowd opened up on both sides like the parting of the Red Sea.

'What's going on?' Jackson muttered to Cairns, falling into step with him as he went past.

'Canto's under arrest for murder.' He spoke out of the side of his mouth.

'Boswell's?'

Cairns shook his head, kept his eyes on the exit.

'Christ, this isn't what I think it is?' *Canto was Neon?* 'Why the fuck was I not informed? I had a right to know, as do the rest of the families.'

Cairns frowned an apology and quickened his stride. 'This is an arrest, Matt. Canto hasn't been charged. Yet.'

Jackson grasped hold of Cairns's arm. 'Where's your evidence?'

'He was in contact with Vicky Wainwright.'

'What? That can't be right. It would have come to light in the original investigation.'

Cairns didn't say, *Well, you missed it*. His sympathetic expression said it all.

Jackson paled at the implications. Had he been so strung out that he'd failed to do his job properly? How many times had he argued with Polly about the senseless hours he'd put into the investigation, his lack of sleep and his dogged determination to keep going, no matter the toll it was taking?

'Tell me where I went wrong.'

Cairns looked through him. 'Matt, mate, I'm sorry, but I have to go.'

'Why on earth didn't you say something when we spoke?'

'Because I couldn't.'

'Mick, this is me. I need to know.'

Cairns patted him awkwardly on his arm. 'I'll call you tomorrow.'

'But, Mick . . .'

'We're taking a lot of heat, Matt. That interview of yours stirred all kinds of shit. We've really had to bring our A game to it.'

Jackson's mouth tightened. This was straight out of the Browne school of vocabulary. He released his grip and watched the man who was his best friend walk away.

Whatever they believed, or had cooked up at HQ, they were wrong.

57

Gary let himself back into the house at stupid o'clock. Considering the night's events, it could not have gone better. The threat to rural tedium had been removed. No more domestic drudgery. The cops entangled in an investigation going nowhere. *Hah, that will teach you to challenge me on prime-time TV, Mr Detective. The mistakes are all yours.*

He'd stayed behind with the rest of the band, chewing over the arrest, making a pretence of anxiety and confusion. The bewildered expression on his face when the cops had arrested Phil, however, was entirely genuine. He'd been gobsmacked by their stupidity. It boded well for the future.

Too wired to sleep, he poured himself a healthy slug of brandy – wasn't that what you were supposed to drink in a crisis? – and trawled through every room in the house, all 3,000 square feet of it. And now it was his to do with as he pleased. If he wanted to leave dust to collect in every corner, if he decided to let the roses wither and rot, he could, and Naomi wouldn't be there to scream at him.

He lay spread-eagled across the bed. Drowning was the least painful way to go, he'd heard, and, coupled with exposure, she would have faded away quietly. Nobody could say he was a cruel man.

Following a dignified period of mourning and, after he'd finished his life's work, he'd quietly sell up, move on and find another way to satisfy the electrifying urges that had plagued him for what seemed like forever.

He swallowed some more brandy, revelling in the fire and heat; the deep satisfaction of a good night's work. No more than he deserved, he thought. This was the main difference between him and Phil Canto. While Phil let himself be shaped by events, Gary made sure he crafted them to his specifications. He hated to bang on, but the trick was to plan and prepare. You don't wake up one morning and decide to start killing people. You have to work hard at it. Like most great things in life, it was an evolving process. And to set someone up you make good use of what is already available to you. A tracking app on his mate's phone had been a good place to start. You can't steal a van one day and use it for a job the next, even if you switch plates. As Phil and Kirsty will tell you – one of Naomi's favourite fucking television programmes – location is key. It takes weeks of careful scouting to find the ideal spot, then a ton of planning to work out how to pull off the impossible. In this regard it was not dissimilar to giving birth to a fuck-you-in-the-eyes neon sculpture. He smiled. Maybe he should use that phrase in his next installation.

Pondering this, he took a slug of booze and considered his next move. Naomi's body would not be fished out of the canal any time soon, which bought him some wriggle room.

In the meantime, Canto would be released, pending further enquiries.

Give it a few hours, he thought, glancing at his watch, and he'd call the police to report that his darling wife was missing. R.I.P. Naomi.

58

Much to Jackson's amazement, Iris buzzed his entry phone at ten the following morning. More astonishingly, she'd picked up breakfast en route.

Jackson viewed her with suspicion. 'This is unexpected,' he said, watching as she plonked two cartons of tea on the table, alongside bacon sandwiches in wrappers. He'd been up since six, combing through files in a desperate effort to pick up on mistakes he might have made. But had made no progress. 'What happened to your cheek?' he said, sitting down.

'Cat scratched it.'

'Must have been a big cat.'

She ignored the remark. 'How did it go last night?'

'Canto was arrested.'

'No way.' This was not uttered with surprise, but with a conviction that there had been a police blunder.

'I cocked up. I missed something in the original investigation.'

'What?'

'Canto was in touch with Vicky Wainwright, the first victim.'

'I said the women might not be random ages ago,' she commented.

'Thanks for reminding me.'

She shrugged. 'How come you didn't notice?'

'I don't know. I'm hoping Cairns will phone me later and explain.'

'You put too much faith in that man.'

Iris did not put her faith in anyone, including him, it seemed.

Jackson described Canto's arrest. Iris sipped her tea, and didn't say anything while he told her about the scars on Fairweather's hands.

'Could be from anything. Look.' She splayed out the fingers on her left hand to better display the change in pigmentation. She didn't explain how she came by it and he didn't ask.

When he slipped in his wild idea about how a body could be transported in a double-bass case, he thought she'd react more strongly. Then again, he had to remind himself that this was Iris. Iris didn't do emotion. It was a trait most often found in psychopaths, he recalled, smothering the thought.

'What's the dirt they have on Canto?' She took a big bite out of a bacon sandwich. He'd never seen her so ravenous. Perhaps it was a good sign. Maybe she was in remission. Iris never mentioned her health and, consequently, it wasn't a subject he was comfortable with. Any questions might seem too intrusive, insensitive even.

'Can't answer that until I hear why he's been arrested.' In his heart, he believed Canto was in the clear. In his head, and despite his private theories, he could not argue against incontrovertible evidence. 'Browne mentioned that they were going to re-interview friends and relatives of Neon's first victims. Maybe a connection was discovered.'

Iris shrugged. 'Neon's not going to kill anyone while he's in police custody because it's the best way to frame Canto.'

Interestingly, Iris didn't buy that Canto was Neon either, Jackson registered.

'If, however, Canto isn't charged, he'll be released . . .'

'And the second he's released . . .'

'Neon will strike.' *And nobody will be ready*, Jackson thought.

'What are we going to do?' Iris asked, taking a drink of tea.

Jackson had already given it considerable thought. Canto knew Neon or, put another way, Neon knew Canto. 'Neon is the Trojan horse in Phil Canto's life.'

Iris's mouth tugged into a grimace. 'What the fuck does that mean?'

'Someone who wants to destroy someone else from within.'

'Yep, I'm familiar with that. Happens in gangs all the time. So Neon hates Canto.'

'Agreed, and to hate you have to care. You need to be close.'

Iris's face lit up in animation. 'Like a parasite. Did you know that there's this bug that infects mice and rats and makes them change their behaviour? Instead of the rodent watching out for cats, like normal, they start taking stupid risks and wind up as dinner. Next thing you know, the cats are infected.'

Iris still surprised him with her breadth of knowledge and often odd way of thinking.

'Then we go hunt parasites.'

'Canto's friends?'

'I'll start with Tony Felix.'

'The double-bass player and potential undertaker?'

Jackson ignored her obvious cynicism.

'Why not Gary Fairweather?' she said. 'He's way more obvious.'

'Because you're going to take him,' he replied, ripping out an address he'd scribbled on a pad.

'Me?'

'You,' Jackson said firmly. 'Fairweather has no idea who you are.'

59

Gary adopted his most concerned expression as he saw the two police officers to their car. The wind was a bitch that made him shiver. From the look on the female WPC's face – a sweet-faced if dull creature – she'd interpreted it as symptomatic of his genuine distress. Her colleague, a short-arsed male PC, whose name Gary had instantly forgotten, was a walking, talking platitude.

'Honestly,' the male officer said, 'while I appreciate your concern, most missing individuals return home within a couple of days. There's usually a perfectly reasonable explanation.'

Like shagging someone else, running home to Mummy and Daddy, or getting pissed and winding up in a skip, yeah, they'd been through all the yawning possibilities in his lounge. (He could call it that now because Naomi was no longer around to correct him.) Gary had sworn he'd seen the policeman's eyes pop out of his bulbous head when Gary showed him a photograph of his wife, the dirty little creep.

With a trembling bottom lip, Gary had explained that Naomi wasn't the cheating type – which was true – and that it was out of character for her to go walkabout solo. Finally, he confirmed that he'd already phoned local hospitals and various friends, including her parents. To tell a whopping great lie and make it stick, it's vital to insert it deeply into a seam of truth, and he was an expert at this, having spent a lifetime devoted to the art.

'You've done all the right things,' the male copper assured him, standing next to the police car. 'In cases like this, we usually give it forty-eight hours before we make serious enquiries.'

'But that's ridiculous,' Gary said. 'I'm sure I don't need to remind you that there's a serial killer on the loose in the city.'

'The chances of running into a serial killer are a thousand to one,' the officer said soothingly.

'Tell that to the victims' parents,' Gary sniped back. He enjoyed playing devil's advocate.

'I appreciate what you're saying.' A lot of the officer's oily charm suddenly dispersed. 'I'm sure it will turn out fine, Mr Fairweather,' he said curtly.

Sucker, Gary thought. They hadn't even connected him to Phil Canto and his arrest the night before. Gary had to stop himself from shaking his head. Boy, could he teach this lazy couple of duffers a thing or two about staying sharp (or 'on it', as Phil would say).

'You'll stay in touch?' Gary cupped his elbows in his hands, his stance designed to portray heartache.

'Of course,' the WPC confirmed. 'And let us know if Naomi comes home. You have your log number?'

Gary nodded, forced another tremble from his bottom lip

and stood on the drive long enough for any nosy neighbours to see that he was a deeply upset husband.

As soon as the officers disappeared from view, he relaxed and turned on his heel. Reaching the front door, his mobile rang. He listened briefly before interjecting. 'Sorry, Mrs Gilroy, I'm going to have to postpone Aidan's lesson today. Yes . . . I do understand that it's important . . . But . . . if you'd just let me explain,' he said, thinking *shut the fuck up*. 'Yes, I see, but, due to unforeseen personal circumstances . . . Yes, if you'd let me finish . . . MRS GILROY, MY WIFE HAS GONE MISSING.'

Shaking with rage, he cut the call and stormed into the house.

60

Iris swallowed hard.

She'd watched the whole scene from behind the relative obscurity of a bamboo tree in the garden of the house opposite. First, the cops, followed by Fairweather's phone call and announcement to whoever was on the other end that his wife was missing. Temporarily stumped, she stayed where she was despite the sky opening and discharging a torrent of ice-cold rain.

The house was impressive. Big gates screened the grounds from the road. Iris wondered what lay behind them, what they might conceal.

She viewed the house once more. Fairweather was clearly occupied by the mysterious disappearance of his wife. There was no better time to strike.

She slunk over the road. The gates were high, possibly eight feet tall. It would be a risk to attempt to scale them, yet one she was prepared to take. *Desperate times*, she thought, cursing as the soles of her shoes crackled against gravel.

To approach an obstacle this size in a half-hearted fashion would sink her. The trick was to commit. Estimating a distance of about ten to fifteen feet, she glanced from side to side and, seeing nobody about, kicked off with her back foot and sped towards the gates, full speed. Leaping forward, she pushed the toe of her right foot out and down against the surface, at the same time powering through with her arms and letting her hands reach up. Grabbing the top of the gates, she almost winded herself. It made her feel a bit sick.

Catching her breath, she walked her feet up, finally swinging her left leg over, drawing the rest of her body up and dropping down onto the other side, allowing her knees to bend and cushion the impact.

As she straightened up, she was horribly aware that she had company. Before her stood Gary Fairweather. He had a set of car keys in his hand and an expression on his face that told her he wanted to kill her.

'Matt, it's Mick.'

Thank God. Jackson was beside himself with worry at the thought of missing a connection between Vicky Wainwright and Canto. 'Good to hear from you.' Jackson pulled over not far from Tony Felix's house in Moseley. 'Has Canto been charged?'

Cairns laughed. 'Browne would like nothing else.'

'You don't need me to tell you that you can't do someone for murder without any evidence.'

'I was coming to that. I'm afraid I wasn't quite straight with you, Matt.'

Jackson had already drawn that conclusion.

'When we interviewed Canto, initially, about Boswell's

death, I asked him where he was on the night of Vicky's murder. He gave us an alibi that didn't stack.'

'So you had him in for questioning again?'

'Yesterday, before the gig.'

Jackson recognised that the police would have been a lot more assertive second time around. It escaped him why people bothered to lie about their whereabouts when it was simple enough to fact-check.

'And how did he react to being caught out?'

'He was slippery and evasive.'

'Last time I saw him he was stoned. Might explain his memory deficit.'

'Canto must be senile to forget replying to a text from Vicky Wainwright on the night she died.'

'A reply? You mean Vicky texted him from her phone? How in hell did I miss it?

'Vicky used her friend's, Lucy's.' Jackson pictured the girl: petite, with lively eyes and an excitable manner. 'Vicky's was out of battery,' Cairns explained.

'And the text only just came to light?'

'When we re-interviewed, yes.'

Jackson briefly closed his eyes. He'd made a mistake, but it wasn't as grave a cock-up as he'd originally thought. 'What did it say?'

'That she wanted to meet him.'

'Implying she already knew him.' It represented a big twist in direction.

'She met him at his last gig in Newcastle,' Cairns said.

Jackson remembered that Vicky lived in Durham, a mere thirty-five-minute drive away.

'How did you find out?'

'Canto had a selfie of Vicky on his phone,' Cairns said.

Canto probably had hundreds of selfies taken with fans, but Jackson didn't reckon many of them would be on *his* phone.

'The point is Canto agreed to meet her outside the Sunflower Lounge,' Cairns continued.

Not a million miles from The Mailbox. 'What was the tone of the text?'

'Flirty.'

'Elevating the relationship to something more?' Jackson suggested.

'Not according to Canto.'

'How so?'

'He didn't recall the selfie, or the text. Said he received hundreds of communications from random women.'

'Does he?'

'Unfortunately, yes.'

'What about the meet?' Jackson said.

'It never happened.'

'You checked CCTV?'

'Yes,' Cairns confirmed.

Jackson thought about it. Had Vicky gone to meet Canto and been intercepted along the way? He put the question to Cairns.

'Seems likely.'

'So either Canto abducted her, or someone else was in on the conversation?' A friend like Fairweather, Jackson thought, wondering how Iris was doing. 'Worth taking a shot at his mates?'

'Chimes with my thinking.'

Without mentioning Iris, Jackson told Cairns that he was already on the case.

'Be careful,' Cairns warned. 'I can only cover for you so far with Browne.'

'Appreciated. What about the other girls? Does Canto have an explanation for his whereabouts on the nights of their murders?'

'Oh, he has explanations, all right. Got alibis coming out of his ears.'

Jackson let out a knowing groan. 'Don't tell me – he lied again.'

'That's when Browne decided to go in all guns blazing.'

Bearing in mind the seriousness of the crimes, Jackson couldn't blame him. 'So now what's Canto's story?'

'He's heavily involved with a married woman and refuses to tell us who she is. Says it will ruin her marriage, and he wasn't looking for commitment anyway.'

'Nice.' Matt remembered Gonzalez's take on Neon. *Attraction to married women suggests he enjoys the thrill of the illicit and is probably flaky about commitment*. Did one romantic cover story conceal another more sinister one?

'The problem is I think he's telling the truth,' Cairns said. 'We have evidence that he was staying at a hotel with a mystery woman a hundred miles away on the night of Vanessa's death. In short, we don't have enough to charge him.'

Jackson sat up. 'You're going to release him?'

'We already have.'

*

'You have me bang to rights,' Iris said meekly. She hunched over, made herself look as small and non-threatening as possible. It was easy to feign misery with the rain sheeting and dripping off the end of her nose.

Fairweather advanced on her. 'Who the fuck are you?'

The car keys jangled as he pushed them into his pocket. There was no mistaking the power of the man, Iris thought. He had broad, powerful shoulders. His hands were fists as he squared up to her. Eyes narrowed, his generous mouth was one big snarl.

'I'll ask you one more time and you'd better be ready to answer,' he said, glaring down, boxing her in against the gates.

'I didn't mean any harm. I thought no one was home.' She adopted the demeanour of a rank amateur whose ambition exceeded her abilities.

'You're a liar. You were going to break in, trash *my* property and steal *my* belongings?' With each accusation, his voice rose in volume.

My *property and belongings*, Iris thought, *not* our.

'I only wanted enough money to feed my family and I'd never mess up a house.'

He tilted his head, chin down and deeply aggressive.

'It's the truth. Please, I don't want any trouble. Just let me go.' Unafraid, Iris cowered.

'I should call the police,' he said. Some of the rage had dissipated, replaced by something sly, opportunistic and unpredictable.

'Please,' she begged. 'I won't come back. I promise.' She cast her eyes down to better fake submission while she estimated his next move. He'd pounce and when he did she was ready to go with it. It was always the second move that counted most, not the first.

The breath knocked out of her as he reached forward, lifted her off the ground by the collar of her jacket and banged the back of her head against the wooden gate. Iris let out a little squeal of surprise. If those fucking hands of his moved to her throat, she'd headbutt him right in the middle of his flat boxer's nose and poke his eyes out with her thumbs.

They were eyeball-to-eyeball. He thought he had her pinned down, she was pleased to see, thought he had her just where he wanted her. *Well, fuck you,* Iris thought.

Locking on to his gaze, she didn't flinch. Iris would recognise the cold dead eyes of a seasoned killer anywhere; she saw it in the mirror every morning.

Fairweather stared back and he was breathing hard. The corner of his mouth twitched and she wondered whether he saw the same darkness in her as raged in him.

'We have ourselves a little situation,' he said, almost to himself. She stayed still, bided her time. Suddenly, his grasp loosened. 'Luckily for you, I'm a forgiving man.' He set her back down with a bump. 'But if you ever set foot here again, I'll have you killed. I know the right person and you won't even see it coming.'

Iris started in shock. No, he couldn't mean what she thought he meant. His was just a turn of phrase designed to scare the crap out of her. *Wasn't it?*

Without another word, he opened the gates and pushed her through.

61

In an agony of doubt, Iris made a noisy exit across the gravelled drive and stealthily resumed her place over the road. Shaken, she now had a very good reason to access Gary Fairweather's home: to find out whether her horrible hunch was correct.

A sound from over the road alerted her to activity. Gates into the garden from the drive swung open and, after a pause followed by the sound of an engine starting up, Fairweather drove out in an SUV, a Toyota RAV4 in metallic silver. The vehicle briefly stopped, engine running, while Fairweather closed the gates, climbed back inside, the RAV pulling away and vanishing speedily into the grey, dull wet day. Not exactly the behaviour you'd expect from a husband nervously waiting for news of his missing wife. She hadn't forgotten that dead-eyed look in his expression.

Unsure of how long she'd got, she carried out the same manoeuvre as before. This time there was no Fairweather to greet her on the other side of the gates. Before examining the grounds, she walked across the rear of the house and peered in through the downstairs windows. Kitchen, fancy-pants conservatory, dining room . . . it didn't take her long to be drawn up short. Through the lounge window, she had a clear view of a professionally taken photograph hanging on the wall. In a cheesy pose, Gary grinned next to the same woman she had been paid to bump off. Iris jolted inside. Gary Fairweather, friend of Canto, Matt's suspect, was also her client. *Fucking hell.*

There was any number of reasons why spouses had their other halves done away with. Money was a popular motive for murder and, judging by this swanky pile of bricks, Fairweather would inherit a tidy sum. Passion came a close second. Spite third.

However she sliced this recent twist of events, she could not tell Jackson about her involvement in the death of Fairweather's wife. That would risk his wrath, after which he'd pull the plug on their agreement and shop her to the police. *No money. No life.*

She went over events again. Fairweather had obviously called the cops himself and reported his wife missing. This wasn't something to which she was accustomed – she hadn't done that many domestics. Usually, when people got popped, she just kept her head down, and the person ordering the hit continued with life as if nothing had happened. Either Fairweather was very smart, getting to the police before they got to him, or he had another agenda altogether. From her observation, he'd played the role of concerned husband brilliantly. She had no doubt that he'd be able to keep it up when news broke that his wife had been fished out of the canal. For anyone else it could be an issue, but not for a man like him.

Iris estimated how long it might take before the body was

discovered. The woman had been properly submerged when Iris left. Given the temperature, it would take longer for bacteria to produce enough gas to float her to the surface, a week or maybe more. Theoretically, it bought her time in the long term. Short term, she needed to get a move on.

Turning her attention away from the house, the scene ahead could rival the Botanical Gardens down the road. Not as big but as impressive. To her left: a triple garage that could house several generations of one family. Mature and landscaped gardens, with terraces and seating areas and a rockery with a proper waterfall, stretched before her. Beyond: woodland of copper beech, blazing with reds and rusts and yellows.

She walked straight down the middle of a gravelled walkway, and underneath an arch of wild roses, past an outdoor swimming pool emptied of water and derelict. It looked as if it hadn't been used in years. On towards a wooded area from where she glimpsed the top of a structure. For those few moments as she entered a blizzard of green undergrowth, she felt in thrall, caught in a magical world of plants and weird trees and bushes she'd never seen before. Her feet travelled as if they belonged to someone else, working independently to the rest of her.

And she knew why.

Perfectly camouflaged, a log cabin. Iris walked around the circumference, noted the blackout blinds at the windows and at the glass front door that was locked. What was inside? Only one way to find out . . .

62

Jackson had only one thing to say about Tony Felix. He was too dumb to mastermind a series of killings across the city. His job as a stock-control clerk at an electrical wholesaler was taxing enough as it was.

With regard to the double-bass case, Felix favoured soft, padded versions over the original fibreglass.

'You've never had one stolen, or lost any?' Jackson had asked.

Which in Felix's case, Jackson thought unlikely. The man was a list of 'didn'ts'. Didn't drive. Didn't drink alcoholic beverages. Didn't ingest gluten or dairy. Didn't have a girlfriend. Jackson thought he might be on to something when Felix expressed that he didn't like Phil Canto, until he found out that he didn't like Gary Fairweather or, indeed, anyone else in the band. His final word, as Jackson hurried out into the cold, was that he didn't like politicians. On this, at least they could agree.

Jackson climbed back into the Mini, intending to head back to the flat. There, he had phone calls to make to the parents of the dead girls.

The worst part of his job involved dealing with the relatives of victims of violent crime. He hated witnessing the derailment of their lives, the shattering of any faith they had, the way they, too, were dismantled piece by piece from inside, out. Only now he was one of them.

'Polly,' he whispered, resting his head against the steering wheel, a surge of raw grief ambushing him. Unbidden, his shoulders shook, his stomach tightened and the ache in his chest was as potent as if his heart was shearing in two. He sobbed uncontrollably then: for his wife, for his loss and for failing to catch her killer.

But there was still time, Jackson thought, slowly gathering himself together. To date, Neon had never struck during the day. He favoured the early hours, the better to display his craft. Jackson didn't think he'd change course now.

Grief abating, he started up the engine and hoped that Browne's strategy to flood the streets with police worked. He no longer cared who got to Neon first. It wasn't a matter of pride or honour or revenge, as long as the murdering bastard was caught and made to face what he had done. This was what he told himself as he swung back into traffic. Only Jackson knew that he was lying to himself.

Iris narrowed her gaze and gaped in bewilderment. She'd pictured bright blazing lights. She'd dreamt of every colour in the spectrum. She'd imagined sharp implements, glass and gas and heat and fire.

She'd been so sure, would have put money on it. And she was so wrong.

She stood in a house of musical worship.

Sound-recording equipment ran along one wall, an electronic piano along another. A table housed professional decks, like you see in nightclubs. There were speakers, amps and something labelled a subwoofer. Studying the knobs and dials surrounding her was like trying to read a foreign language.

A floor-to-ceiling shelving unit contained books and vinyls and sheet music and assorted musical accessories. Iris sifted through the titles and album sleeves, all of them way over her head. She read a few out aloud: Muddy Waters, Billie Holliday, Stan Getz, *The Dark Side of the Moon, Aqualung, In the Court of the Crimson King*. She'd never heard of any of them.

At the centre of the room, two clarinets and three saxophones, all on stands, flanked a microphone. Iris reached out her gloved hand, pressed down the keys and rods, listening to the click of steel against wood, brass on brass. The skill required to produce a note, a tune, a melody, to her mind, was awesome.

Taking a step back, she thought about the man who'd hired her to kill his wife. Wealthy, creative, doing something he really loved, with a beautiful woman beside him, he had it all, it seemed. Then why risk losing everything? In the event of any divorce or break-up, he'd still get half – and half of a place like this was more than most people she knew earned in a lifetime. But this was no ordinary domestic. Gary Fairweather was a stone-cold killer. Before today, she hadn't been sure whether this same man was Neon. After examining his face and looking closely into his eyes, she knew he was. But, to quote Jackson, she needed evidence.

She ought to leave, Iris realised, and quickly. It wasn't safe to stay, to push her luck. One last look, she thought, raising her head and scanning the room.

One of the compartments in the unit was transparent. She approached it. Inside, were lengths of black leather cord. Iris's blood suddenly ran hot. She plunged her hand inside and drew out what she now identified as a leather sling worn by saxophonists to support the instrument when they played. This one was double-stitched, with a cotton pad to absorb perspiration, and a thinner cord that hooked onto the sax itself. It looked strong.

In the right hands, strong enough to strangle.

63

Iris was in one of the most deprived areas of the city, where the rate of child poverty was at an all-time high and adult employment an historic low. Consequently, stabbings and shootings were common. Violence and sexual offences were off the scale. Iris paid attention to these things because it meant new business opportunities for her. And where there was new business, there was 'Little Red Riding Hood' or Red, as Iris called her, a baby-faced, mixed-race teenager who zipped around on a bicycle. Rain or shine, hot or cold, she wore a red hoodie and was generally known as a facilitator. She ran errands. She ran drugs. She was an encyclopaedia of knowledge, and the person you went to if you needed to know who not to piss off. She also acted as a dating agency for 'Dial A Death', matching punter to contract killer. Iris gave her a kickback with every job she got. Theirs was a relationship built on trust through shared experience – Iris had taken Red (once known as Jodie) under her wing at her last kids' home, before she was kicked out into the big, wide world.

Drawing level with a cafe that sold the best baklava in

the city, Iris heard a familiar screech of brakes behind her. She half-turned, watched as her mate stuck the tips of her trainers to the pavement, narrowly missing a pile of dog shit. Red broke into a grin.

They didn't embrace because neither of them cared for it. Iris stuck her hands in her jacket pocket, her fingers grazing the leather saxophone strap she'd stolen, and nodded in the direction of a quieter spot on the opposite side of the road, a doorway between a boarded-up phone shop and a barbers with a closed sign. Red pedalled silently beside her.

Once they were clear of the elements and tucked safely inside and away from listening ears, Red pushed away her hoodie to reveal almond-shaped eyes, which were the colour of weak tea, a scar on the bridge of her nose from a childhood beating and her tiny, undersized front overlapping teeth.

'How are you doing, Iris?'

'Same old.'

Red was one of the few people who knew about Iris's past and what she was facing. Red caught her eye and her tone. 'How's—'

'I didn't come to talk about that.'

'Fair do's. Any time you change your mind, you know . . .' she petered out, looked at the ground, rolled a dead cigarette butt underneath her foot.

'Did you give my number to a man recently?'

'Yep.'

Iris reached into her jacket. 'In the last forty-eight hours?'

'Uh-huh.'

Iris pulled out a wad of notes and thrust it into her mate's hands. Red hid it with the speed of a seasoned low-rung drug dealer exchanging a wrap for cash.

'I need information on him,' Iris said.

'You don't normally want to know.' A light flickered in Red's eyes, lightening them a shade.

'This one isn't exactly normal.'

Red clicked her tongue.

'Where did he approach you?'

'Outside on the street, close to Hubbub.'

'What were you doing there?'

'I'd been to a gig,' Red said. 'Spaghetti Junction.'

Iris suppressed her surprise. 'I didn't know you were a fan.'

Red shrugged.

'He came alone?' Iris asked.

'Yep.'

'What did he look like?'

'White, powerful build, six foot, maybe.'

'What colour was his hair?'

'Dunno. He wore a beanie.'

'How did he know to approach you?'

Red pushed out her shallow chest. 'My rep, sister.'

'Yeah, but this guy isn't exactly our usual clientele.'

Red rolled her eyes. 'He had money, and rich people like blow, and they know who to call when they want it.'

Phil Canto, according to Matt, was a drug user and also a mate of Gary Fairweather, Iris recalled.

'He wanted drugs *and* a course from the set menu?'

'That's right.'

'What was he like?'

'Cool, friendly and businesslike. Not like some punters, frightened of their own shadows.' Red looked off. There was a 'but' in there somewhere, Iris thought. She waited for Red to explain. 'I caught a vibe off him.'

'As in you wouldn't like to be down a dark alley in his company?'

Red shook her head slowly. 'Worse than that. Got the feeling he had a vicious streak. Know what I mean?'

Iris did.

'He was like one of them sick psycho killers that talk to you all nice while they stick a knife in your belly and give it a twist.' Red glanced around, waited for a police car to drive slowly past. 'Iris,' she said, dropping her voice, 'I know it sounds soft, but I wondered if he was that bloke who kills them girls. Dumb I know, because if he was that much of a lunatic, he'd do his own dirty work, wouldn't he? He wouldn't need someone like you.'

Iris nodded as if she agreed. 'Anything else?'

'He rode a motorbike.'

'You saw it?'

Red shook her head. 'He had a black crash helmet in his hand. Didn't think it was a style statement.'

64

'Thank you very much, Sheila,' Jackson said. 'I'm sorry to have troubled you. Thank you, yes . . . you take care too.' He put down the phone to Gina Jenks's mother with a heavy heart. He didn't enjoy lying about his quick return to work and, if Browne found out, he'd surely be kicked out of the force altogether, but he needed to act, to do something.

Both Vicky and Vanessa's parents confirmed that their daughters had seen RocknRoller in the past eighteen months, by accident rather than design. They'd gone along because someone else had organised it. Neither girl had mentioned Canto, Fairweather, Felix or any other band members.

Iris had not been in touch. A woman who lived by different rules in an alternative time zone, in which night was day and day was night, he had no guarantee when she would show up, or if she would have anything useful on Gary Fairweather. For that, he'd need Google. It wouldn't give him a complete picture. Whatever was available to public view would be a sanitised, glossy version, but it was still a good place to start. He turned to his computer screen and discovered that Fairweather was thirty-seven years of age, born in Barking, had lost his mother when he was fifteen and had enrolled in the London College of Music, where he'd studied classical piano. A preference for woodwind instruments apparently came later.

Jackson sat back. Gonzalez had spoken of a likely dysfunctional relationship between Neon and his mother. Didn't seem relevant in this case.

He stood up, rolled his shoulders and stretched. At a loss, unable to settle, he flicked on the TV and slumped in front of the screen. A local news bulletin reported that some poor woman had been removed from the water at the Gas Basin. Cameras panned to the area and then to the narrowboat owner who'd had the misfortune to find the body.

'I was casting off when I stupidly let my downstream rope trail in the water,' the man explained. 'It got stuck and I thought it was caught in the propeller. When I took a closer look, I had the shock of my life, I can tell you. I didn't think she'd been that long in the water, but there was nothing anyone could do . . .'

Jackson switched it off. Canal deaths were not uncommon in the Midlands, but he'd never heard of a drowning in such a populated area in all the years he'd been a serving officer. He'd bet good money booze was an issue and, if not, then suicide. He understood that depth of despair. At least, Neon hadn't got his hands on her.

Iris had a rule: Never go back.

The second she saw the police out in force near Brindleyplace, she realised what a fool she was to break it. She should have gone straight to Matt's, not taken a detour.

A crowd gathered, slow at first and then more swiftly, around the cafes and restaurants as police cordoned off the area. An old lady muttered to another that a woman had drowned and police were recovering the body.

'Do they know who she is?'

'They won't say yet, will they? They'll have to tell the family first, I'd have thought.'

'Dreadful,' she said. 'Not the kind of news anyone wants to receive, especially in the run-up to Christmas.'

Death was dreadful any time of year, Iris wanted to chip in, particularly when it might lead back to her.

She rolled her collar up and her beanie down, and strode away, her mind in freefall. She pulled out her phone and called a number she knew by heart.

'It's me,' she said. 'Yes . . . not long now . . . not long. I promise.'

65

Gary studied his latest installation, a fitting tribute to his next victim. Not as audacious as the tableau he'd crafted for *Not So Pretty Polly*, not as sensational as the set piece he'd been working on for the past twelve months in town, but from the point of view of location, it would send a bolt of electricity through those who viewed it. Yes, it would excite. This time, he'd wired the transformer individually into the sign. It would make a lovely sounding board.

He could now devote himself entirely to his next and final project: 'Something for all the family'. The culmination of his life's work so far. Who knew what other possibilities awaited him? *Naomi, babes, you really were missing a trick with me.*

A tingle of pleasure travelled up the base of Gary's spine at the anticipation of converting his next drawing to sculpted glass, then flame to light, and art to death.

Early in his career, he discovered that music was only as great as the musician creating the symphony or composition. Based on years of training, a gifted composer understands rhythm, range, tone and sound. He has imagination. Unafraid to break rules, he is bold. Each of his masterpieces begins with a pencil in his hand. So, too, the Neon artist who must master sculpting, glass blowing, understand the dynamism of colour and grasp the necessary technical scientific knowledge if he isn't to electrocute or gas himself, literally dying for his art.

The tip of Gary's tongue poked out between his whitened teeth as he manipulated a length of glass tubing over an 800 degrees centigrade naked flame, as fragile and dangerous as any woman. With each twist of his dexterous fingertips, a pushover for his musician's hands, he risked burns, which added an extra frisson. You couldn't play a woodwind instrument in gloves, no more than he could tease out a shape from glass or, for that matter, pleasure his wife. *Rest in watery peace, Naomi.* Blowing into the tube to prevent it from cracking was carried out at precisely the right moment. Timing was everything. Afterwards, you could pretty much do what you liked with the material in terms of bending and melting and creating those wonderfully memorable images.

After fusing the ends with electrodes, he'd take the tubing to the 'Mother Ship' or electron bombarder and pump 20,000 volts through to clean it up, rid it of impurities and dirt, and ready it for the insertion of gas to create colour. Later, he'd carefully wipe the lot with an ammonia solution to remove traces of his DNA.

Working with cold cathode lighting, as it used to be called, was the next best thing to well . . . you know.

Things were getting interesting when a noise echoed from the doorbell in the house to his lair below. Screw it, he thought, wondering who the hell that could be. Whoever it was, they'd have to wait until he was good and ready.

66

Jackson tamped down a surge of excitement.

For the past half-hour he'd listened to Iris recount her findings. When she showed him the saxophone strap, he determined to get it sent to forensics straight away to see if it was a match for the type of ligature used on Neon's victims.

'No evidence of a workshop, I suppose?'

She shook her head.

'Pity. If we're right about Fairweather, he won't stay quiet for long. He won't be able to help himself.'

Keen to phone Cairns and convey his findings, he pulled out his phone and put a call through. The second he mentioned Fairweather, Cairns stopped him.

'Police are with him now.'

'That was—'

'Not what you think. A woman resembling Gary Fairweather's wife was pulled out of the canal at Brindleyplace this morning.'

Jackson clasped the back of his neck. 'Naomi Fairweather? Christ, when did it happen?'

'Last night.'

Same time as Gary Fairweather was on stage. Same time as Phil Canto's spectacular arrest. Same time as . . .

'You still there, Matt?'

'Yes.' He ignored the feeling of unease that stretched over him like a shroud and turned away from Iris's curious gaze. 'Is there evidence of foul play?'

'She took some knocks entering the water. From what we can gather, she slipped and hit her face on the side of the canal on the way down. We found a shoe. Heel was at least six inches. We think she stumbled and fell.'

'Was she unconscious when she hit the water?'

'Too early to say,' Cairns said. 'She hasn't yet been formally identified. I'll be able to tell you more after the post-mortem.'

'Be good to know. How did you make the connection to Fairweather?'

'He reported her missing first thing. Uniforms thought it would go the way of most cases. Spouses often go walkabout, as you know.'

'What time was this?' Jackson said.

'CCTV picked her up on the approach to the towpath around 10.40 p.m.'

'Was she alone?'

'She wasn't with anyone,' Cairns confirmed, 'although there were plenty of others milling around.'

'What sort of others?'

'Noisy students, drunks, the usual.'

'Nobody stuck out from the crowd?'

'No.'

'So what was Naomi Fairweather doing there?' Jackson said. Why wasn't she at home as he'd expected, or at the gig?

'Meeting someone is my best guess.'

While Fairweather was out, Jackson realised.

'Beneath her fur coat,' Cairns continued, 'she was stark naked.'

67

How the fuck had Naomi's body been found so soon? This could screw his plans royally.

Vulnerability was an unfamiliar emotion to Gary. Sitting in front of WPC Latimer and PC Lane, the same police officers that had visited him earlier, made him feel exposed in a way he'd not banked on. He loathed it. The moral of the tale: if you want something done, do it yourself. When he thought of the money he'd transferred on his burner phone from Naomi's account, it made his eyes water. Naomi was very good at earning loot but hopeless at keeping track of it. Keeping a tight rein on outgoings was another of his duties.

Jesus, he realised with a thud, his carefully plotted financial plan had just capsized as surely as his wife's body had floated upside down in the drink. Maddeningly, he'd have no chance to reap the full rewards of her death. So consumed, he barely heard Lane droning on about the need for formal identification as though it was some massive deal.

Gary turned dead eyes on him. *If you knew how many stiffs I've had a good look at you wouldn't be so coy, officer.*

'So if you could come with us.'

Gary adopted his most helpless look. 'I need to get my coat.'

'Before you do, there's something you should know.'

That you're sorry for telling me not to worry, you thick moron? Gary drew his eyebrows together in what he hoped was a pained, questioning expression.

Lane looked at Latimer who swallowed and looked at Gary. 'Mrs Fairweather was found wearing a fur coat.'

Gary pressed a hand to his mouth. 'Oh my God. Not the Burberry. She so loved it.' *So?* Was Naomi's ghost fucking with him?

Unable to make eye contact, Latimer spoke while looking at her shoes. 'That's all she was wearing.'

Wow, that's my girl. Really going for it. What fun they could have had. Too, too bad.

He waited several beats. Let them think he was absorbing the implications. 'You mean,' his voice sharpened, 'she was going to meet someone when my back was turned? Christ, I can't believe it, not my Naomi.' Aware that he was probably overdoing the melodrama, he added, 'I suppose that's why she resigned from her job. She planned to leave me.'

'When did she hand in her notice?' Latimer said.

'A few days ago,' Gary replied, remembering the texts he'd read on her phone, the scheming, duplicitous cow. He slumped forward, clasped the side of his head with his hands. 'Oh my God, did some sick monster do this to her?'

Latimer looked to Lane. 'We're not treating the death as suspicious, sir. She was seen walking towards the towpath quite purposefully right before she disappeared from view.'

'Would you like some water?' Latimer said.

Booze was what he needed, lots of it and soon. 'Thank you,' he said, his voice pegged to a whisper.

'I realise that this has come as an almighty shock,' Lane said, as Latimer trotted off to the kitchen.

Gary didn't think the almighty had much to do with it. He drew his hands away from his eyes, sat up straight. Time to man up and look stoic.

Latimer handed him a glass.

Gary took a deep draught, inhaled a big breath and turned to both of them. 'I'd like to see my wife now,' he said feebly. He couldn't frigging wait.

68

'When were you going to tell me?'

'Tell you what?' Iris sat up straighter, alert and wary.

'About Naomi Fairweather.'

Iris looked at him blankly. 'Is she related to Gary Fairweather?'

'His wife.' Jackson silently cursed.

'What about her?'

'You know nothing about her death?'

'Why would I?' Her voice expressed confusion. She seemed to be telling the truth. *Seemed,* Jackson thought.

'Because you were at his house. You spoke to him. Remember?'

'We didn't discuss his wife. I was too busy trying to do what you asked and then I had to fend him off.'

Bristling with frustration, Jackson sat down, took a breath, rubbed his hands through his hair. 'That scratch on your face.'

'I already told you. My cat did it.'

'You like dogs.'

She glared at him. 'I like all animals, as long as they aren't human.'

Silence clung to him. Couldn't move. Couldn't think. Maybe they'd got it all wrong about Fairweather. Maybe there was someone from left field, someone they'd missed. Fairweather's wife had given him a dose of clarity. He likened it to getting carried away when a clue in a crossword puzzle apparently fits and then you find it doesn't. Put the wrong word in and it messes up the rest.

'More importantly, what did Cairns say about Fairweather?' she asked.

'I hardly got going before I was headed off at the pass.'

'Just because Fairweather's wife is dead doesn't mean he's innocent of other crimes. I know what I saw in him.'

'*I* don't know,' Jackson said, shaking his head. 'Where's the proof?'

'I thought I'd handed it to you,' she snapped.

'Unless a victim's DNA is all over that particular sax strap, it's only theory. We need more than that.'

'I'll go back to his house, get inside.'

'You can't, Iris. Police will be there.'

'So?'

'No,' he said sharply.

Iris glowered. 'Fairweather *is* Neon and he's hardly going to kill while the heat's turned up.'

'Then we use the time to check out other possibilities. We run through everything again.'

Iris's yawn told him to count her out.

'Much depends on the post-mortem report and whether or

not Naomi Fairweather fell, or was pushed.' Jackson angled his gaze. 'How come you never asked about Naomi?'

'Asked what?'

'How she died?'

Iris shrugged her shoulders.

'I thought death was your game?' he said.

'Only when it's me doing the killing.'

69

'Is there someone who can come and stay with you?'

Gary assured PC Latimer there was.

They were back home now. He wished they'd piss off and leave him alone. At the mortuary he'd wanted to savour the moment, bathe in it. Embarrassed by the effect of seeing Naomi dead, he'd forced himself to think of Aidan Gilroy, the talentless little prick, in an effort to prevent an erection. He'd only been half-successful. Thank God, for the overcoat he wore.

'You understand the need for a post-mortem, Gary?'

Having first created a fuss about it, he nodded his assent.

'Once we have a clearer idea of what happened, we'll talk to you again. A family liaison officer will be in touch.'

Over my very dead body. He offered a muted smile.

'Is there anything else we can do for you?' Lane said.

Go the fuck away would be good. Don't you understand I have things to do, stuff to get on with, creations to create? 'No, you've been most kind. I appreciate it. I'd like to be alone now. It's been the worst day of my life.'

Latimer threw him one last concerned look before leaving.

Gary closed the front door, rested his back against it and briefly shut his eyes. He silently ran through a mental list.

Start with the easy bits, he thought, glancing at his watch.

70

'Gary,' she said. 'I never expected to see you so soon.'

'All right if I come in?'

She stepped back, made way, although not before she checked he wasn't seen, he noticed. He doubted anyone spotted anything untoward in this dead-end cul-de-sac of appalling seventies link-detached houses. He'd nearly fainted when she announced she was moving closer following her divorce. Had she not heard the phrase 'Never shit on your own doorstep?' More to the point, on his. The good news was that she hadn't had the chance to sort out a security system. Every cloud, and all that.

He drew her close, felt her arms snake around his neck. 'Oh Gary,' she said, 'I don't know what to say. Such a terrible accident. You must be in pieces.'

'That's why I had to come.' He nuzzled her neck, felt her go loose. He imagined Naomi on the slab, white as cold porridge, as he kissed her.

She gasped for breath, held him away a little with trembling arms. 'This is a little weird, isn't it?'

'It's surreal,' he agreed. 'I guess I shouldn't really be here. I had nowhere else to go, nobody else to turn to.'

Her eyebrows drew together, expressing warmth and compassion. 'I'm glad you came. Who else can you turn to if not me?'

'Oh, hun, that's exactly what I thought.'

'You shouldn't be alone at a time like this. Although,' she said furtively, 'it's best you don't mention my name to anyone official.'

'God, no. Wouldn't dream of it.'

Relief flooded her face. He was amazed she didn't feel more guilt, if only by association.

'Drink? Kaylee's with her dad.'

He already knew this. During his last visit he'd studied the calendar hanging in the kitchen. He knew what Shah wanted and tonight she wasn't getting it.

'I can't stay long. I simply needed to see your lovely face.'

'Aw, Gary,' she said, squeezing him tight.

'I don't know how to feel. Does that sound odd?' It wasn't, as it happened. It's exactly what he'd expected.

'Not at all. Things weren't right between you and Naomi, but you'd loved her once.' She let out a little sigh and tiptoed up to the question he knew she'd ask. 'Any idea what she was doing out at that time of night?'

'Is this the police officer talking, or my lover?'

'What do you think?' She kissed him full on, open-mouthed. It wasn't unpleasant, Gary thought.

'Police appear to think she went to meet someone,' he said.

'So the rumours of an affair are true?'

He'd no idea that news travelled that speedily at the police station. Didn't they have better things to think about, like catching serial killers?

He stiffly disengaged from her.

'I'm sorry,' she said in dismay. 'It was insensitive of me.'

'It doesn't make it any easier, but, for what it's worth, I think Naomi *was* seeing someone. I can hardly complain,' he said with a level look.

She sheepishly shifted from one foot to the other. 'Is there anything I can do, Gary. To make things easier?'

'I'd appreciate it if we cooled things for a while.'

He watched in glee as her face folded in disappointment.

'It's for the best, hun.'

'I understand,' she said bravely. 'You will look after yourself, won't you?'

'I'm not the type to reach for a bottle, if that's what you're thinking.' He had way more inventive ways to relieve frustration and boredom.

'Are the police dealing with it appropriately?'

'Your colleagues are keeping me well informed.'

She reached out, rested her hand on his arm. 'Cup of coffee?'

Exactly what he was praying for. 'Go on. You've persuaded me.'

He followed her into a kitchen the same size as the utility room in his house. It had a harlequin black and white pattern on the floor. Grim little photographs plastered tastelessly over the fridge. Glad to see he wasn't pictured in the family hall of fame, he thought. Mercifully, the windows were closed and the blinds drawn.

'It's really important you talk things through,' she said, reaching for the mugs on the drainer. 'Don't bottle—'

He struck with speed, looping the cord tight around her neck, pulling her back in one elegant motion. Surprise had always been his best ally.

She let out a scream, bucked and arched her back in a similar way to how she made love. Arms flailing, her hands shot out, trying to grab onto anything that would supply purchase.

Oh no you don't. He clung on tight, keeping her close, restricting her movement. Body thrashing, her hands reached up to the cord around her throat, scrabbling to relieve the pressure and break his hold.

'Sshh,' he said. 'Don't fight it.' His breath was hot on her ear and he knew that she couldn't speak, or shout, or yell. He gave a final yank back. The fight went out of her as surely as her spirit would shortly leave her body (if you believed in that sort of garbage). At last, she sagged and buckled.

In seconds, she'd be unconscious. Ten seconds later her brain would start to die. Every beat using this technique was another step towards fatal. To finish the job, he made sure the larynx or windpipe was severely damaged, or broken. The former closed off the airway, meaning curtains if it wasn't treated quickly, and this baby was going nowhere. Closing off the trachea and main thoroughfare of oxygen to the lungs had a similarly devastating effect. And nobody, he thought, looking down into her bloodshot eyes, was going to come to the rescue any time soon.

71

Iris loped up and down the classy end of the road, knowing that she stuck out like a down-and-out on a catwalk. The bamboo tree, her chosen observation post, was off limits. Firstly, the owners of the house were in. Secondly, they'd only gone and decorated their porch in Christmas lights.

Gary Fairweather's house, opposite, was in darkness. Nobody home. So much for cops besieging the place, as Jackson had led her to believe.

She wondered how long before Jackson pulled the plug on their arrangement. He was smart. He didn't believe her. She couldn't blame him. It's why she had to deliver the goods quickly – the goods being Gary Fairweather. She hadn't needed Red to tell her he was a wrong'un. Jackson could spin his wheels looking at other likely killers, if he wanted to. Once she'd nailed Neon, Jackson would forget all about the murder down the cut. Do that, and her money problems would be over and . . .

Movement at the end of the road and a man walking towards her, head down, carrying a bloody big instrument case. Immediately, she recalled Jackson's theory about a body transported in a double-bass bag.

Iris stayed put and silent. She could tell from the man's build and the way he moved that it was Fairweather. His left hand clutched a strap in the middle of the bag, the scroll end over his left shoulder. He carried the case effortlessly. What if there was a body inside?

Sound echoed through the darkness. Drawing almost level, Fairweather hummed a tune, too engrossed in what he was doing to notice her. He didn't break stride as he approached the gravelled drive. She remembered his eyes, remembered the guy in the club too.

Iris bent down as if she were picking up something she'd dropped, reached for the blade she wore in an ankle sheath and straightened up. Preparing to cross the road and rush him as he set the bag down to take out his door key, she took deep slow breaths in and out of her nose, drawing air up from her tummy. Slow and calm and . . . Her personal phone rang.

She snatched it up and turned away. 'Yes?'

It was Mr Gudgeon, the consultant. There had been a setback, he explained. Iris listened, swallowed and tipped her face to the night.

'OK,' she said sombrely. 'Yes, I understand,' she replied, listening hard. 'I'll come straight away.'

By the time she turned back, she saw that the lights were on in Fairweather's palatial house, the door closed.

She slipped the blade back in the sheath and, with the heaviest of treads, walked away.

72

Jackson started from sleep the second his phone rang.

Muzzy, he fumbled for it and registered the time. It was coming up to four a.m. 'Yes,' he said, rubbing his eyes.

'I want a meet.'

Jackson sat bolt upright at the sound of Phil Canto's voice at the other end of the line. 'How the hell did you get my number?'

The voice on the other end gave a deep chuckle. 'I spent quite a long time with Polly in her home after I killed her.'

What? How could he have got it so wrong? 'You piece of shit, Canto.'

'Shut up. You need to stay very calm. It's important you listen.'

'Oh, I'm listening all right, and then I'm coming for you.'

'As expected, but I should warn that, if you bring backup, the woman I have right now will die.'

A shard of fear cut through Jackson. He climbed out of bed, was already reaching for his clothes.

'Do I have your attention?'

'Where do you want me to be?' Jackson crooked the phone

under his chin and swept up a pair of socks from off the floor where he'd dropped them.

'A place you know well. Home ground.'

Jackson listened and silently cursed.

'You have one hour. Don't be late. One other thing.'

'What's that?'

'Don't disappoint me.'

The line went dead.

Jackson raced into the bathroom, unscrewed the panel and removed the loaded Glock. Out of the flat, he raced down the stairs, through the entrance and headed to the car park below.

Normally, it would take him forty minutes to cover the twelve and a half mile journey. At this time he could shift it in thirty. He didn't think of misdirection, false theories or mistakes. At the front of his mind, another woman's life hung in the balance with Phil Canto's feet planted firmly on either side of the scales.

He drove out of town in the direction of Smethwick and Dudley, towards Sedgley. From there, he headed to Penn Common, via Gospel End. Having grown up in the area, he knew it intimately. In those heart-charged moments, it was a stranger. Fog had smudged its phony dirty face over the dawn, shifting boundaries, obscuring the light and distorting the landscape. He could barely see more than a few feet in front of him, and every second lost represented failure and death. He could not forsake another victim.

Knuckles gripping the steering wheel until he thought bone would burst through skin, he drove at an insane speed for the weather and thought about Canto. With his bravado and lies, his cool deception, he'd evaded them all.

On he drove. He was two miles from Wolverhampton. Urban gave way to semi-rural and then rural, with heathland and gorse and copses and watercourses. Jackson passed hedgerow and trees looming out of the mist, like skeletons. Memory reminded him of his father playing golf on the manicured green and lush fairways beyond. A seasoned killer, Canto had done his homework.

Jackson stared at the dash. Thirty minutes had passed. Another thirty and he'd either make it or a woman would die.

The road narrowed. He stepped on the gas, prayed that nobody was driving from the opposite direction. As he spun around a corner too quickly, a wall of light and heat blocked the road. The Mini's brakes locked hard and he flew forward, the seat belt painfully restraining him. Ahead, bold purple and yellow flame slashed through the damp air and shot up into the sky.

Winded, Jackson climbed out and, beaten back by the wall of heat, approached as far as he dared. The size of the vehicle alight indicated a van or an SUV, the inferno too intense for him to make a distinction. Unable to proceed, he glanced off to the right. The mist had thinned and, where the trees parted, he could see bright lights in the distance.

Jackson returned to the car, took out a torch, locked the Mini and stepped off the road and headed across a green with bunkers on either side. Before too long, he'd stumbled down a slope and into the rough. Cursing, he retraced his steps, taking a different route, ploughing uphill and, checking the lights, which shone brighter through the gloom. He took a dog-leg across the fairway, towards a green guarded by trees.

A flag drooping in the non-existent breeze acted sentry to a wood that he feared would take him nowhere. Despite the cloying cold, sweat gathered above his top lip. He was running out of time. So far, he'd seen no sight of another human being, dead or otherwise. Small comfort.

Squelching into ankle-deep water before finding his way across a ditch, a long stretch of land lay before him, flat enough to land a helicopter on. Up ahead, he could make out the blocky outline of a building, from where dazzling coloured lights penetrated the murk. Christmas decorations or . . .

Jackson sped up, the earth soft and springy beneath the soles of his boots. All of him wanted to reach his goal, part of him wanted to run hard in the other direction and never return. Instinctively, Jackson knew that Neon had been at work. This was no meeting. This was a demonstration of Neon's power and skill, and he wanted Jackson to witness it.

Springing off his left heel, Jackson hurried across the green. The building he'd spied grew in shape and form. Brick-built with blue signage, Christmas lights shone out of the display windows. Was this what he'd glimpsed from a distance?

Nearing a tiled forecourt, he narrowed his gaze to the ground. Telltale wires writhed from inside the Pro Shop towards a row of golf buggies, sitting squat, like all-in wrestlers before a bout.

Slipping out the gun, Jackson walked past each and around a corner, where he pulled up short, eyes blinded by the sight of a crime against colour and a naked Kiran Shah in the middle of it. Lit up in purple and blue, she was tied to a tree with wire. Her head was canted to one side. It looked as if her neck was broken. Above: a massive pair of handcuffs in blazing blue and yellow, shot through with the words 'MURDER HE WROTE'. Against her bare feet, a sign in fluorescent green and orange read 'SNITCH'.

73

All Jackson's nightmares attacked him at once.

Instead of Shah's face, he saw Polly's. Instead of the silence of the night, he heard the sound of a man's deep voice smashing out a tune that he could no longer abide. He thought of a child without her mother, of a mother without a daughter. It took everything he had not to scream out in shock and horror.

Blasted, Jackson staggered back, dragging his eyes away from one more life destroyed. He swept round to the front of the building and scanned as far as his eye could see, which wasn't far at all. Scrabbling for his phone to call it in, a roaring sound punished his ears. Angling his head, a single beam shone out of the gloom. Another throaty roar of engine, followed by another and another, each gunning for him, each a taunt. Jackson swung the Glock round and fired. A screech of tyres on wet tarmac signalled Neon's exit, his macabre showtime over.

Or was it?

A short way off, Jackson heard the engine idling. Why wasn't Neon driving away? *Because he wants to engage,*

Jackson realised. *He wants to play. All part of the sport, the game, the story. 'Don't disappoint me.'* This was personal and with that awareness came another thought that he dared not entertain. Not now. Not yet.

Jackson held his breath and tried to get his bearings. The shortest route back to the car was straight down a track flanking the road; one side of a triangle with Neon and his machine positioned on the main drive to the clubhouse on the other. Neon had a clear advantage. At any time he could outrun and outgun Jackson, but Jackson believed that Neon's desire to grandstand was greater than his need to avoid capture, or a bullet.

In a split-second decision, Jackson took to his heels and ran until his lungs shrank and withered inside his chest and his heart threatened to give up the ghost. Hitting the road, the muscles in his calves juddered with exertion.

The vehicle fire had reduced enough to allow him secure passage. He climbed inside the Mini, started up and drove at speed towards the entrance of the golf club. With a scream of power, a motorbike gunned its engine and swerved out right in front of him. Jackson caught a flash of a hunched figure in his driving lights. Not content with showing Jackson his most recent work, Neon wanted to draw him out.

It was a trap, Jackson thought, flooring the pedal as he sped towards the church and took a left-hand bend at suicidal speed. The whine of gears as the motorbike changed down and then back up was audible.

Past quaint cottages and houses in Vicarage Road, they hurtled towards The Holly Bush Pub on the opposite side of a dual carriageway. Fog had cleared with the impending dawn, another bleak day in progress. *Easier to see*, Jackson thought, a mixed blessing as he held his breath and careered out of the junction behind the motorbike. A blare of car horns boxed his ears as he tucked in behind, a finger's width from the bike's bumper.

On they flew. Jackson attempted to pull out, get ahead and cut Neon off, but the Mini was no match for the powerful bike. Flooring it, Jackson pulled out to the right, his aim to clip the rear wheel and send Neon into God knew where. The helmeted figure glanced over his right shoulder. Before Jackson stole a chance to make his move, the bike sped up and veered across, into the opposite carriageway, lights and bike facing a slew of oncoming traffic. Jackson smacked on the hazards. Laying rubber, he followed in pursuit.

The bike zipped in and out, Jackson weaving behind with his nerves flayed. It could only be a matter of time before he hit a motorist head-on. He watched in terror as Neon's brake lights flashed on and off, as effectively as a neon sign.

Tyres screeched. Brakes screamed. Vehicles swerved and darted, cars bumping up onto pavements and drives, others plunging wide and clipping the opposite lane.

'You're fucking insane,' Jackson yelled aloud as the motorbike crossed a junction and darted around an approaching haulage lorry. With no place to go, Jackson, in desperation, dragged on the handbrake with his left hand and pulled the steering wheel down hard to the right. The Mini spun sideways, juddered, missing the lorry by a coat of paint, and landed, by a miracle, facing the right way on Goldthorn Hill. A glance in his rear view revealed the vehicular carnage behind him.

Gulping in air, Jackson drove a short distance slowly and pulled over near a newsagent's. Shaking, he climbed out of the car, staggered to the pavement and pitched over. Hands clamped against his thighs, he threw up.

By the time Jackson returned to the golf club, Browne and Cairns were already there with Scenes of Crime officers and uniforms, the area around the scene cordoned off.

Cairns raised his eyebrows at Jackson's approach. 'This is no place for anyone, least of all you.'

Jackson glanced sideways to where Browne stood mute and broken like a man told that his entire family had been wiped out in a multiple pile-up on the motorway.

'Too late,' Jackson said. 'Neon called me in the early hours. I was here half an hour ago.'

'What?'

Before he could answer, Browne jolted out of his catatonia and stormed over. He resembled a boxer in the seconds before delivering a knockout blow.

'Why didn't you report it?'

Jackson explained about the threat, the lure, the trap and the rider's escape. 'Shah's life was never in the balance because she was already dead. She never stood a chance. It was Neon's way to get me here alone, without backup,' he said. 'The vehicle fire was purely designed to catch my attention and point me in the right direction.'

'Christ Almighty.' Cairns scrubbed at the top of his head with his hands. 'Did you recognise the voice?'

'It sounded like Phil Canto.' Which was true. The man had also stated his name.

'We should put out an APB.'

'Send officers to his house right away,' Browne barked, any pretence at cool composure vanishing into the surrounding mist.

'You're wasting your time,' Jackson said.

Startled, Cairns and Browne looked at each and then at Jackson. 'It was dark and foggy,' Jackson explained. 'I could hardly make out my own hand in front of my face. Anyone could have been a riding that bike.'

'But you said it was Canto's voice on the phone,' Cairns chipped in.

'It sounded like him, but it wasn't.'

'Now you've lost me.'

'For fuck's sake.' Browne's curse and rare lapse of anger took everyone by surprise. He turned his ire on Jackson. 'Will you stop trying to tank my investigation?'

'Marcus, I'm genuinely not. I want this guy as much as you do.' *Even more so*, Jackson thought, desperate to dial down the emotional temperature. He needed Browne onside. 'We've all suffered a devastating blow,' Jackson said softly.

Browne held his palms up, seemingly regretting his unusual loss of temper. 'Agreed. Then if you know something I don't, will you, please, spit it out?'

'Musicians have an ear for sound,' Jackson said. 'They're tuned in, literally. It's a talent shared with good impressionists.'

'You mean Neon was impersonating Canto?'

'Yes.' He'd cottoned on not long after he'd thrown up and was driving back to the golf club.

'I don't buy it.' Browne stepped away, pulled out his phone and gave the order for uniforms to put Canto under arrest.

'He won't be there,' Jackson said mildly.

'No, he's probably halfway to an airport.' Browne punched in another number on his phone.

Cairns scratched his chin, indicated to Jackson that they walk off a little. 'What's going down, Matt?'

'Neon is close enough to Canto to set him up. He knew that Canto had contact with Vicky. He knows Canto can't explain his movements. Canto has a bike, a van, but it's not *the* bike and van.'

'Then whose are they?'

Jackson had never felt such calm and composure, not since Polly's death. If he told Cairns the whole truth, would his certainty be dashed and ground into the gravel on which they stood?

He shrugged a *don't know.*

Cairns rolled his eyes. 'Oh, I get it, we're back to Fairweather the poor sod whose wife drowned.'

Jackson stood tall and resolute.

Cairns shifted his stance, raising himself to eye level. 'I took another look at the CCTV on the night Naomi Fairweather met her death. A random unidentified woman was there.'

Jackson thought immediately of Iris and her ability to insert herself chameleon-like into any situation. A cord of fear wound itself around his throat. 'You must be mistaken.' His accompanying laugh was as manufactured as the man who'd imitated Canto.

The noise of approaching footsteps crunching towards them made them spring apart.

Browne had his eyes to the dirt and his hands were fists. 'Canto's not at his house. I'm going to scour the country until I find that bastard.'

Jackson nodded as if he were in agreement. While Cairns and Browne chased Canto, he had a date to set up. Neon wanted a meet. He was going to get one.

74

Back in his car, Jackson put a call through to an operator at Lloyd House. 'DC Tonks, please.'

A brief silence followed by, 'She's on a rest day.'

'Mander then.'

Jackson waited. Shah's death would be headline news. He'd have no alternative but to lie about his suspension.

'Mander speaking.'

'Detective Chief Inspector Jackson.'

'Yes, sir.'

'Can you grab DS Shah's address from the system?'

'Um . . . well . . . not sure—'

'DCI Browne has authorised it,' Jackson lied.

'Oh, right, I'll text it through.'

'Make sure you do.'

Five minutes later, he started the engine and drove away.

Shah's house was a secondary crime scene. No way could Jackson enter without contaminating evidence. And he had no desire to.

A single uniform stood before the front door, Scenes of Crime not yet in evidence.

'Any sign of forced entry?' Jackson asked.

'None, sir.'

Which fitted. Shah had let the killer in because she knew him. Jackson thought back to the gig and the music connection. Kaylee, Shah's daughter, liked music. Maybe Shah liked Gary.

'I want a quick look in the front garden,' he told the officer.

'Fine, sir.'

Jackson walked back down the path to the edge of the boundary. A thick and overgrown privet hedge divided the lawn from the pavement and road. He stepped onto the grass and, keeping close to the border, slowly walked the length to the corner, his eyes fixed on the earth. At the apex, where the hedge ran back to the house, he squatted down, ran a gloved hand lightly over the area. Indentations in the soil suggested that something had recently rested there. He measured the distance with his eyes, around six feet. Jackson pictured the killer parking the instrument case here in the dark. He then goes inside, makes nice with Shah, strangles her, comes back out, picks up the case, stuffs her body inside and walks away. Jackson would put money on there being evidence of a fight. Shah would not have died easily. A part of him tore inside at the thought.

Straightening up, he caught a glimpse of what looked like a piece of wood lodged in the privet. Reaching forward, he plucked it out. Chewed to hell at one end, it was a pencil. Holding it in the palm of one hand, he slipped off a glove, wrapping the pencil inside and into his jacket.

Thanking the officer, he returned to the car and drove to the end of the close and parked. Walking back past Shah's house, he spotted police activity at the entrance of the cul-de-sac. He kept his head down and, taking out his phone to map his route, proceeded with a measured step, as if carrying a body. He wagered Fairweather's arms were stronger than his.

It took him twenty-five minutes to reach Gary Fairweather's house, a monster pile of bricks and mortar that, valued on the current market, had to be worth a million quid and the rest.

Retracing his steps, a call came through from Browne, who made a noise that was both greeting and apology. He'd looked broken when Jackson saw him last. Now he sounded it.

'Canto's staying at a hotel over a hundred and sixty miles away in Devon. You were right about him.'

'Do you know the cafe on the corner of St Paul's?' Jackson said.

'Yes.'

'Meet me there.'

'I failed her.' Browne stared blindly at the cup of coffee cooling in front of him. 'I should have seen it coming. I should have done more. This is my fault.'

'Nobody is to blame but Neon.' Jackson had had his issues with Browne, but he wouldn't see him bear a burden that wasn't his to carry.

'And I doubted you,' Browne said squarely.

'It's all in the past. The point is, I need your trust now. I want you to arrest Fairweather.'

Browne's eyes widened. 'You're surely not suggesting—'

'That he's Neon. Yes, I am.'

Browne loosened the collar of his shirt. He looked like a man who'd expected his winning lottery figures to yield millions and discovered he'd won a tenner. 'Does he have the necessary skills? Those displays weren't knocked up by an amateur.'

'I believe he's been honing his craft over many years.' Jackson told Browne about the book, the link to Las Vegas, the possible use of a sax strap as a ligature.

'And where does Canto fit?'

'Fairweather has been hiding behind him in a classic piece of misdirection. I suggest you check Canto's phone for spyware.' Jackson continued by revealing his theory about how Fairweather had managed to kill his way around the city. 'Massive redevelopment and the resulting chaos clearly helped, but I find it hard to believe that every piece of CCTV footage was out of action, obscured or faulty.'

Browne eyed him warily. 'Are you suggesting that DS Shah knew her killer and helped assist an offender?'

'I wouldn't put it that bluntly, but it might explain why Neon called her a snitch.'

'It's pure speculation,' Browne blustered.

'Yes, it is, but this isn't.' He produced the evidence bag containing the pencil he'd taken from Shah's garden. 'Get it analysed for DNA. Like Jordan Boswell, she had to die.' He described his theory about how Shah's body was transported.

Browne listened. Afterwards he glanced out of the steamed-up windows, deep in contemplation.

'In return for allowing me to continue to work off the grid,'

Jackson said, 'I'll share my findings and allow you to take the credit.'

Browne pushed the bridge of his glasses up his nose. 'Why would you do that?'

'Because I don't care about rank, ratings or clear-up figures.'

Browne fell silent.

'Do we have a deal?' Jackson asked.

'I'd prefer not to go in all guns blazing until I've had time to check the evidence.'

'Fair enough,' Jackson said. 'You'll also need to get a search warrant.'

'Which could take time.'

And time was something they were all short of.

75

Iris had parked herself outside Jackson's flat. She sat on the floor cross-legged, her back against the wall.

She looked up at him full of reproach. 'I've been here hours.'

Jackson didn't speak. He took his key out, plunged it into the lock and pushed open the front door. Iris scrambled up and followed him inside.

'Cat got your tongue?' she said.

He turned and faced her. 'Would this be the same cat that gouged a hole out of your face?'

Iris scowled. 'Do you want to hear about Fairweather, or what?'

'Would this be the news that he ordered a hit on his wife and paid you to do it?'

Iris's skin was so translucently pale it was impossible to see it leach colour. Jackson had spent enough time in the company of liars to understand the more subtle non-verbal signals. Her hands clenched and she stood a little straighter. On guard. Wary. 'So I have one night off and suddenly I killed her?'

'That's what you do, Iris.'

'We had a deal.'

'Which you broke the second you shot Valon Prifti dead.'

She met his eye with a stolid, uncompromising stare.

'You were seen, Iris.'

'By who?'

'Not who, but what: CCTV.'

Iris pushed her hands into her pockets. 'All right, then. So I was walking through Brindley, but I didn't kill her. Why would I?'

'Because you need the money, because you can't help yourself, because you're dying, Iris.'

She didn't look stricken. He shoulders didn't slump. Her bottom lip didn't tremble. Certainly, there were no tears in her eyes. She drew herself up and stared at him, defiant. At that moment he doubted the Grim Reaper could defeat her.

'I'm not going to turn you in,' he said with a level look. 'There's no point, but we can't work together anymore.'

'You need me. I can deliver Fairweather to you.'

'It's over, Iris.'

'Bullshit.'

'Go home. You need to rest and sleep and eat.'

Iris looked him dead in the eye. He wondered what it would take to break through the carapace she'd built to shield her from feeling any emotion.

'Where were you just now?' she asked.

He'd noticed that when she didn't want to answer a question or address a remark, she pretended it had never been uttered and layered it with a question of her own. 'Neon struck again,' he said plainly. 'He killed a female police officer, someone I knew.'

'Fairweather,' she said. 'I saw him last night.'

Jackson sharpened. 'Where?'

'Walking back to his house, carrying a big instrument case, like you said. The woman's body could have been inside.'

'What time was this?'

'Around eight o'clock.'

Time enough for Fairweather, aka Neon, to carry out the rest of his plan. 'You didn't engage?'

'Didn't have the chance. I got a phone call.' She looked away.

'What kind of call?' Jackson said suspiciously.

'Not the one you're thinking.'

'Right,' he replied in a disbelieving tone. 'So all the texts and calls you've been fielding have nothing to do with your night job?'

'If you must know, it was my doctor to tell me that a planned treatment plan was no longer available.' When she spoke, her voice was a dull monotone.

He was genuinely sorry and said so.

'My life is over if I don't find the money for alternative treatment abroad.'

'Like I said, I'm very sorry, Iris.'

'Don't be. Be smart. This is good for both of us.'

He knew it, but he could no longer trust her and he couldn't have another innocent woman's blood on his hands, even if it were by association. 'You take care.'

Her eyes narrowed. 'You're not serious?'

'I am.'

'What about our arrangement?'

'I'll let you know when I'm done.'

She crossed her arms. Her bottom lip curled in distaste. 'You don't have it in you to catch Fairweather, never mind kill him.'

'The door's that way,' Jackson said.

A shadow passed behind her eyes. In furious silence, she turned on her heel and banged out of the apartment, leaving a burst of chill air in her wake. He listened to her angry footsteps forging fresh holes in the carpet down the stairs.

Hollowed out, he peeled off his clothes, took a brisk shower. Heavy with fatigue, his eyes had the royal cold-water treatment. He needed more caffeine before he got started. Sleep could wait. Soon, he'd be having the big one, the one from which there was no return.

He forced down a cup of coffee and, taking out his phone, noticed he'd received a missed call then text from Gonzalez. It had come through at 9.20 a.m. which meant the US officer had phoned at 1.20 a.m. Las Vegas time, indicating it was urgent. Jackson phoned him straight back and hoped he wasn't asleep.

Gonzalez greeted him with a cheery, 'Hi'.

'You keep late hours.'

'I'm a terminal insomniac.'

Jackson flinched at the word 'terminal' and thought of Iris. 'What have you got?'

'Seventeen years ago, Canto spent eighteen months in the US with his father. During that time there were two separate reports of attacks on women in Nevada that match Neon's MO.'

'I'm listening.'

'On both occasions the perp attempted to strangle his victim. The attacks were out in the open, late at night, near diners, with significant neon signage. The first was thwarted by a passer-by. The second female survived by a miracle. The perp left her for dead when she fell unconscious. Unfortunately, that lady still has a tube inserted into her throat as a result of her injuries.'

'Did she see him?'

'No. He attacked from behind and wore a motorcycle helmet, visor down.'

'He didn't speak?'

'He did, but she couldn't identify the accent. She thought he was foreign, like a guy attempting to sound American.'

'Could the man have been British?'

'She wasn't that specific.'

In the circumstances, he could hardly blame her. Jackson thought it a fairly tenuous connection. 'Did she have any idea of the guy's size and height?'

'Around six feet, maybe 190 pounds.'

'Did she have any idea what he used as a ligature?'

'She said it felt like leather.'

'Did he wear gloves?

'Yep.'

Jackson got the impression that Gonzalez was saving his punchline. 'Am I missing something?'

'Canto didn't come alone. He had a friend with him, a guy called Gary Ancona.'

Jackson's blood stiffened in his veins.

'Seventeen years ago, you say?'

'Yeah. Ancona was a music student at college in Nevada,' Gonzalez continued. 'When Canto returned, Ancona stayed to complete his course.'

Gary Fairweather, as he was now known, would have been twenty-one and, Jackson thought, still at Music College in London. Had Gary finished one course in the UK to start another in the States? Jackson supposed it wasn't impossible.

'Did attacks increase during that period?'

'If they did, he was successful and we never found the bodies.'

'What was your unsolved list like back then?'

'You really wanna know?'

The tone suggested it was nothing more than a rhetorical question and Jackson thought better than to push it. He thanked Gonzalez for his time and input. 'If this breaks, I'll be sure to keep you informed.'

'Appreciate it.'

He clicked off and contacted the London School of Music, explaining that he was calling on a 'police matter'.

'I'd like to speak to the Director.' A few clicks later, he was speaking to a pleasant-sounding woman about former music pupil Gary Ancona.

'I wasn't working at the College seventeen years ago,' she said. 'Just trying to think who would have taught at that time.' She fell briefly silent. 'Getting my bearings,' she said slowly, 'it must have been around a decade after our move.'

'To central London?' Great Marlborough Street, Jackson believed.

'No, we moved *from* central London to merge with the Polytechnic of West London in Ealing.'

Jackson gasped, as if someone had shot him at point-blank range in the middle of his chest. He caught his breath, felt his limbs go numb, followed by his mind. *Polly, oh my God*, he screamed inside. And in that moment of weakness, what seemed impossible changed into possible, and suddenly things became perfectly and horribly clear.

'I'll put you through to our Head of . . .'

Jackson had already hung up.

76

It was two o'clock in the afternoon by the time Jackson sped across the pavement and gravelled drive to Fairweather's home, a vast property with a sizable frontage and a pair of large wooden gates to the left-hand side of the main entrance. Stepping up onto a wide-stepped stone entrance porch, he gripped hold of the bell pull and gave it a yank. Nobody answered. He gave it another go. Still nothing. Had Fairweather cleared out?

Tormented with frustration, Jackson crunched over gravel to the gates. The place was like a fortified castle. He wondered if the bike used that morning was cooling down on the other side.

Noise. Jackson turned and saw Gary Fairweather stride out onto the steps. He was barefoot, wore a hoodie and a bewildered look on his face. Hair sticking out at angles, his face dark with several days' growth of stubble, he looked like he hadn't slept in a month.

'Oh,' he said vacantly. 'It's you. I thought it might be the police.'

Jackson covered his aggression with a smile and walked over. 'I am the police.'

'Yeah, course. Sorry. Naomi said you were . . .' he trailed off, the mention of his wife's name, apparently, too much to bear.

Jackson didn't bother with condolences. Didn't see the point. Fairweather looked vague and out of it. Correction. Fairweather was bloody good at appearing out of it, Jackson thought. Beneath the fake sadness, his eyes gleamed with guile. Why hadn't he noticed how green they were before?

'I don't quite understand,' Fairweather said, intent, it seemed, on maintaining the role of bereaved spouse. 'Is your visit official?'

Jackson's answer was brisk. 'There's reason to believe that Naomi's death was not accidental.'

'God, you mean someone pushed her?'

He looked over Fairweather's shoulder. 'All right if I come in? We don't want to do this on the doorstep, do we?'

Fairweather gave a fair impression of an apologetic expression. 'Yeah. Sorry. Step inside.'

Jackson followed him into a sterile-looking kitchen, the only random item a large armchair in the corner. Fairweather pulled up a high stool that sat beneath a central island. A stack of paperwork littered the surface, which Fairweather smoothly stacked and cleared away. Jackson glanced at it and took a seat on the other side. They faced each other, no more than a couple of feet apart. Jackson had sat opposite killers before in the comfort and security of an interview room. This was different. He touched the pocket of his overcoat, felt the comforting outline of the Glock.

'Outside, you said that Naomi's death wasn't an accident,' Fairweather began.

'Correct,' Jackson replied.

Fairweather's fist flew to his mouth. 'You mean she was deliberately targeted?'

Jackson didn't answer. Let him run. Let him lie.

'But who would do something like that?' Fairweather said, seemingly aghast. 'She didn't have an enemy in the world.' He glanced at the walls as if someone was eavesdropping on the other side. 'You're aware she wasn't wearing any clothes beneath her coat? It tears at me to say it but . . .' He petered out.

'But what?'

Fairweather shook his head mournfully. 'Naomi took a shine to Phil. I'd always had my suspicions.'

'Aren't you forgetting something? Phil Canto was with you on stage on the night of her death.'

Fairweather checked a verbal response. The green eyes gleamed in the dead light.

'I gather you two go way back,' Jackson said.

'I've known Phil for the best part of twenty years.'

'When you were Gary Ancona.'

Fairweather didn't miss a beat. 'It's not a crime to change your name. It was all done legally, by deed poll. I mean, who'd want a name like that? Makes me sound like a Mafia hood.'

Jackson ignored Fairweather's effort to lighten the tone. He needed to get him off balance. 'Did you decide to change your name after you met Phil, or before?'

'Maybe after,' Fairweather said vaguely. 'I guess you can check if you think it's important.'

'Why Fairweather?'

Jackson saw the hesitation. Something unreadable travelled behind Fairweather's eyes.

'It was my mother's maiden name.'

Jackson nodded in understanding. 'Close to your mother, were you?'

Fairweather didn't answer. He looked ready to throw a punch.

Jackson found it deeply satisfying to observe how his question pressed a nerve. Keen to keep him off balance, he said, 'Did you fall out with Canto, musician's tiff, or what?'

'Why do you say that?'

'You just put him in the frame for murder.'

'Did I? I thought I put him in the frame for having an affair. Phil would be the first to tell you he's a dog where women are concerned. Had an eye for the girlies as far back as I can remember.'

'Even when you were in Vegas with him?'

'You *have* done your homework.'

Jackson noted a tiny crack in Fairweather's otherwise composed façade. 'Standard police procedure to look at the spouses of the deceased when there's a question mark over the nature of their deaths.'

'I understand,' Fairweather said, his tone wintry.

Good, Jackson thought, watching the crack widen a little. 'So what's the story with Las Vegas?'

'There is no story. I studied music at college in Nevada. Went out with Phil and came back with Naomi.' His face fell into a picture of contained distress once more at the mention of his dead wife's name.

'And before that,' Jackson reminded him, 'you were at the London School of Music.'

'For a brief time, yes.'

'Why brief?'

'I bailed on the course.'

'Is that usual?'

Fairweather met his eye. 'I wanted a more rounded and meaningful experience. I thought the States would offer that.'

'And did it?' Jackson eyeballed him back.

'Definitely.' Fairweather tapped a finger on the worktop, exposing the white scar on the back of his hand. Following Jackson's gaze, he explained, 'Childhood accident. My fault.'

Jackson nodded as if he believed him. 'Was there another reason you packed in your studies in London?'

'Like what?'

'Because of a girl?'

'Got the wrong guy, buddy.'

The conviction in Fairweather's tone rocked Jackson. Had he got it wrong? Had obsession and grief turned him into a fantasist? 'You weren't fleeing the pain of a broken love affair?'

Gary expressed confusion. His eyes, however, remained unnaturally bright and luminous.

'You don't remember Polly Fleet?' Jackson said.

'Her name means nothing to me.'

'Your paths didn't cross at college?'

'Should they have done?' Fairweather shook his head innocently. 'What instrument did she play?'

'She didn't. She was studying to be a primary school teacher.'

'Ah, well, that explains it. In a different department, mate. I only hung out with musos. And if that's all,' he said, leaning across with menace, 'I'd really like you to leave.'

'No problem,' Jackson said with a smile. 'I'll be in touch.'

77

Iris was in hell.

The ghost pain in her shoulder was as nothing to the real pain in her heart. When her time came, she'd imagined a bullet in her head, maybe her chest, maybe several. Not this. A slow eating up from inside out.

After leaving Jackson, she'd gone to Solihull to ensure that there were no loose ends, no danger of misunderstanding. She'd spoken to Mr Gudgeon for ages and, after a lot of argy-bargy, her normal cool temperament heating up like a dinner in a microwave, she'd threatened him in the only way she knew how. For the good of his health and the security of his wife and kids, he'd do what she asked. Luckily, he'd seen sense and immediately promised to sort out a flight and organise the medics at the other end. Hunting down Fairweather, or whatever he wanted to call himself, was now her priority.

Her best shot was to corner him in his lair, with his bloody horrible signs and lights. Job done, she'd deliver him dead to Jackson. He'd think differently about her then, wouldn't he? He'd have to pay her big time. She wasn't looking for an award, or absolution or forgiveness. She needed hard cash and was hell-bent on getting it.

With good reason, Jackson believed Fairweather and Polly had known each other.

Early in their relationship, she'd briefly mentioned a boyfriend that she'd dumped, although she'd never said his name. Pressed on the subject, she'd admitted to feeling ashamed and guilty for letting the guy down because he'd taken the break-up so badly. Devastated enough to jack in his music course and flee, she'd confessed.

A coil of pain tightening deep inside Jackson's gut told him that however convincing Fairweather had been, he was lying. With all his being, he believed that Fairweather was their man and regretted not forcing a confession from him. He should have pulled the damn trigger while he'd had the chance.

Recalling their conversation, Fairweather had performed well until Jackson questioned him about his mother. But what of the father?

Jackson put a call through to Barking and Dagenham Council and asked for the council tax department. Once connected, Jackson gave his credentials and asked for confirmation that a Mr Ancona still resided in Barking.

A few minutes later, and to his amazement, he was speaking to Sam Ancona, Gary's father, a man with a gravelly voice honed from a serious cigarette habit, Jackson surmised. Living in the UK had done little to tame the inflexion of Sam Ancona's Italian accent.

'My son? I haven't seen him in decades. What's he done?'

Jackson sidestepped. 'He's assisting us with enquiries. I'm afraid I can't discuss the nature of the investigation at this point.'

'Let me guess,' the old man said. 'He's robbed a bank.'

'Nothing like that,' Jackson assured him.

'Always a dreamer, my Gary,' the old man continued, keen, it seemed, to have a listening ear. 'Wanted the finer things in life. I kept telling him he needed to get a proper job, steady work with a decent wage, not this silly idea of chasing rainbows. Doesn't matter how good a musician you are, there is always someone better, I told him. But what can you do? Kids, huh?'

Jackson pictured Sam Ancona rolling his eyes.

'God rest her soul, but I blame his mother for encouraging him. Gary adored her. They were *molto simpatico*,' he said. 'Not always a good thing.'

'How do you mean?'

'They were too alike.'

'They sparked off each other?'

'Often,' the old man said with a chuckle. 'Always they made it up. It was a long time ago,' he added, as if wanting to temper any observation that put his son in a bad light.

'Forgive me for asking,' Jackson said softly, 'but how did Mrs Ancona die?'

'She suffered from epilepsy, had a fit in the bath and drowned. Unfortunately, Gary found her. He was only fifteen. A terrible thing to happen to him.'

Jackson clenched his jaw. He was no psychologist, but it

didn't escape him that flickering neon lights could induce a fit in an epileptic. 'I'm very sorry to hear it,' Jackson said.

'If my son has done something wrong, go easy on him, detective. He hasn't had the best life.'

Who has? Jackson thought. It didn't turn us all into serial killers. Jackson phoned Browne and described the content of his call with Sam Ancona. More painfully, he revealed a potential prior connection between Fairweather and Polly.

Browne listened and didn't blow him out. 'If you're right, it could be a game changer.'

'Worthy of an arrest.'

'Agreed,' Browne said. 'You were right about Shah, Matt, she was in a relationship with Fairweather, and techs have traced the origin of the spyware on Canto's phone.'

'Too soon for the results on the DNA sample, I guess.'

'I've marked it as urgent,' Browne confirmed. 'Cairns is pulling the other strands together. Are you OK for me to push the button?'

'I wouldn't have it any other way. But be careful. He's a dangerous and manipulative individual.'

Jackson should have felt some sense of satisfaction that the circle of events was reaching its natural conclusion. Instead, he was haunted by the thought that Polly had let Gary back into her life during the long, lonely hours when he'd been too consumed to pay her the attention she deserved.

Shame was the only reason he'd not drawn the gun and shot Fairweather in the head when he'd had the chance.

78

There were no signs of life at Fairweather's house. Iris reckoned he was in the wind.

The front door, with its mortice lock, a no-go; around the back was a different tale. She touched the pocket of her jeans, felt the skeleton keys inside, her talisman, and the torch she'd need to light her way.

Carrying out the same up-and-over-the-gates manoeuvre as before, she dropped down onto the garden path. To her left, a shed and triple garage. She peered through the windows of both. The RAV4 she'd seen Fairweather drive was inside next to a motorbike. No van, only a big enough space for one.

She let herself into the main house through a French window. Shining her torch around, she saw that she was in one of those posh kitchens you see in TV cookery shows.

From there, she fanned out and journeyed through every room. She didn't clock the expensive furnishings, or admire the chandeliers or marvel at the modern bathroom fittings or the art tat on the walls. She had one objective in mind: find Fairweather's workshop, find a lead to the man and, for fuck's sake, do it quickly.

Moving with the stealth of a cheetah, she combed every wall and large cupboard, the flats of her gloved hands checking for false doors that might lead to a basement. Gliding upstairs, she examined each fitted wardrobe in case an interior sliding door opened out onto another previously unknown level. Hers was not a hopeful shot in the dark. She'd worked with enough druggies and crime bosses to recognise that, however addled their brains, they retained an animal cunning for hiding the tools of their trade. So far, she'd not struck lucky.

One foot poised to creep downstairs; she was beaten back by noise and commotion. A glance out of the window revealed police in cop cars with sirens blazing. Others arrived in unmarked vehicles. A bloke wearing spectacles climbed out of one of the Beamers and strode across the drive. Flanked by uniforms, he banged on the door and pulled on the bell. Another bloke joined Mr Spectacles, followed by an army of policeman surging over the premises like maggots in a decomposing body. When a copper produced a battering ram, Iris got a shift on. She hammered down the stairs, across the hall and flew out through the back and scampered across the garden. Her only option: hide in the bushes and lay low until the police worked out that Fairweather had long gone.

Speeding along one of the paths, she fought her way blindly through darkness and tangled trees. Branches and twigs snapped at her face and caught in her hair. Silently cursing, she bumped up against a building familiar to her, the music room. Unfamiliarly, the door to the entrance was ajar. Touching it open with one hand, she slipped out her blade with the other.

79

Gary raved.

A soundtrack blasted through his head of wrongs, slights and rejections. How fucking dare that cunt suggest he'd legged it. Polly hadn't dumped him. *She* hadn't broken his heart. *She* hadn't. Why else would *she* smile when he'd turned up unannounced, you tosser? Why else did she confide in him after all those years spent apart? He wasn't lying about that. Sure, she assured him that she was happy. Yes, she said she enjoyed her job and told him she loved her husband. *But Polly, darling, loyalty is such a wasted virtue.*

She didn't love Jackson the way she loved him, Gary railed. She *said* she loved her husband, of course she did. Quite strongly, as he recalled. The prick had brainwashed her. But *he* knew the truth. Gary had seen it in her lovely eyes.

And she wasn't like the rest, not like those thrusting bloody bitches that set themselves up to compete in a dog-eat-dog world by acting like a man: drinking as much, fucking as much, and shafting anyone who got in their way. She wasn't like the Vickys and Vanessas and the Ginas. Polly wasn't a Naomi, with her mean streak, ruthless ambition and her desire to emasculate and control. Oh no. So why had Polly rejected him all over again? Why had she given him that funny look when he'd slipped his arms around her and suggested that they picked up right where they left off? Didn't she realise that all he'd ever done was for her, that he'd always loved her? That he'd *killed* for her?

She'd been turned. That's what it was. He could see that now. Living with a copper had rotted her brain. And now he, Neon, the illusionist, artist, performer and entertainer, was going to make him pay.

Oblivious to the pulse in his jaw, he recalled how she'd gone mad at him. Told him to leave. Screamed at him to get out. *Shouldn't have done that, Polly. Didn't suit you to be unkind.*

What choice had she left him?

If he was honest with himself – and he was one hell of a self-aware guy – he'd understood how it would roll long before he took one step over the threshold. It's why he'd gone prepared. Only a fruit loop would have trusted a woman who'd run out on him. Women were all the same; they never changed. He'd understood that when his mother abandoned him forever.

If only Polly had taken him in her arms, he'd have driven away happy, dismantled his creations and they could have lived a cosmic existence together, happy ever after. For Polly, he was prepared to say goodbye to his art and . . .

A dark frown tugged at the corners of his mouth. Who was he kidding? No, he would definitely have kept his hand in, adapted his more extreme creations and held on to his favourite pieces for old time's sake. For the memories.

But that was all in the past and he had the future to consider. That jackass copper wasn't going to screw his plans, or fuck with his story. He was going to be part of them. He was going to be his leading man.

80

A beam of light snapping through the trees and the sound of a large dog barking quickly made Iris modify her plans. Shit, she was trapped in Fairweather's man-cave-cum-music-room.

Backing up, she cast around for somewhere to break up her profile and hide. Pulling her hoodie over her head, she bobbed down behind a beast of an amplifier. Resting her hand against the wall behind, her fingers traced the outline of a metal lever running flush with the skirting board. Surprised, she gave it a tug. Immediately, there was the sound of ratchets and turning machinery as a section of floorboards against the opposite wall tilted downwards, disclosing a flight of brick steps.

A place of refuge or last resting place?

Iris looked to the door of the shed. It remained closed. Beyond, the collective noise of coppers smashing through the undergrowth grew in intensity. The dogs had changed pitch. More snarl, less bark. They were onto her. Be caught now, or take a risk?

Iris tipped up on her heels and scurried across to the opening and skittered down the steps to the level below.

Fumbling around, she found another lever at the bottom and hoped to buggery it did the business and covered her tracks. More clunking and clicking and the false floor closed back over.

She took out her phone and checked for a signal. There wasn't one. She was entombed.

Eyes sliding right and left, hand against the brick walls, she stood in the entrance to what she believed was an old air-raid shelter. The West Midlands were peppered with them. Most had been demolished at the end of the war as a civil defence measure, although some remained forgotten, and unsuspecting homeowners still made discoveries. Some were big enough to house two families. For someone like Fairweather it would be a gift.

Iris looked down at the floor to where a bright beam of light spooled across. Tightening her grip on the blade, she followed, turned a corner and walked straight into an eye-shattering wall of colour that battered her optic nerves. No area was left between one blitz of rainbow bling and blare and the next. The walls pulsated, writhed and breathed with a macabre and sinister beat.

She edged forward. To her mind, it was no different to the average enforcer's playground. Implements and blowtorches, even the kit was the same. She pictured Neon standing, stripped to the waist, the musculature in his torso indicating a strong and powerful man, a match for any woman. His arms held high, he'd do all that glass-blowing stuff over two gas burners, like a priest at an altar. Nothing religious about the sexually deviant stuff on the walls, she thought, pursing her lips. Who wanted to see oversized tits and vaginas, or a giant cock lit up in purple, yellow and pink, or a sign that said *Fuck Me, Fuck my Cat*? Where was the switch to turn this crap off, she silently ranted, half expecting to see Jackson planted in the middle, dead as a dinosaur. And the arty-farty crowd had the cheek to call this shitty stuff art?

Disorientated, she sniffed the air and caught a strong smell of burning wood and charred remains, like you sometimes find where there's industrial machinery.

Iris gave herself a shake. The place was creeping her out. Bedazzled, it was difficult to make out where one wall started and joined another. Maybe that was the point. Maybe the lights were deliberately designed to throw you off, like a sleight of hand in a magic trick. How to find the open spaces in between?

Noise above signalled the cops had found the music den. She didn't think they'd locate the hidden lever any time soon. They weren't that bright. More worrying, how long would she be stuck down here while they were thundering about up there? Was there another way out? And if she found an exit, what then? She had no idea where Fairweather was.

She inched forward and the toe of her boot bumped up against something hard. She crouched down, saw what it was – a gas mask – and remembered the night she'd gone to the club. If she'd known then what she knew now, she'd have gone for good old Gary in a heartbeat, and put him down like the vermin he was.

She scoped the room and noticed a roll of paper parked in the middle of a long trestle table. Iris unfurled it, spreading it out, the torch in her mouth, tilting her head to make out the design and read the location. Eyes widening, pulse racing, she had to get out of this place and fast.

A heavy tread of coppers' boots thundered above her head. Iris stood in the middle of the space. She centred her breathing the way she did before a kill. Neon, the planner, visual and escape artist; *I know where you are.*

Narrowing her eyes, she tried to zone out all the other colours and focus on her favourite, which happened to be blue.

A rectangular light, same as the tropical fish she'd seen in the Sea Life Centre, shone out of from the farthest wall. Mesmerised, she walked as if drawn by unseen hands, the framed space the gateway to another world and a steep flight of steps that led up to a door that was solid. Slipping the Ruger from her bra holster, she aimed it at the lock. Two shots fired and it was open. Iris careered out and into the night.

81

Jackson watched the sky fade from mercury to indigo and waited for the call to say it was over; not only for Fairweather, but for him too.

Accepting of his death, deserving of it too, it was obvious that Iris was too sick to play her part and he had no idea where he went from here.

His mobile rang. He expected Browne and got Cairns.

'Fairweather's cleared out.'

Jackson cursed for not foreseeing that his visit would spook him. He should have stuck around. Should have killed him. Should have . . . 'You're absolutely certain he's not lurking in a basement?'

'Uniforms have covered every inch. We had the dogs out too.'

'No evidence of his crimes?'

'If you mean a workshop or a place where he knocks up his works of art,' Cairns said, with sarcasm, 'nada.'

Jackson ran a hand across his scalp. 'What's Browne's response?'

'He's gone for the works, alerts on airports, ports and

he's flagged it up to Europol. Sorry, mate,' Cairns said sympathetically.

'Not your fault.' It was his.

'I'd best go,' Cairns said. 'There's a ton of stuff to process with the Shah murder. You'll be OK?'

Jackson told him he would, clicked off the call and slumped onto the sofa. Neon, the planner, the long game player, the muso and . . .

If he were Neon what would he do next?

An answer came back straight and true: Neon couldn't resist one last *Screw You.*

And where would that be?

Somewhere public. Somewhere that would make the most visual impact.

Jackson stood up, paced the room. Fairweather had let it slip when he was with Canto at the teeny gig. He'd said it deliberately. Misdirection or lure? Jackson wondered, suddenly feeling unsure.

It had to be somewhere close. Somewhere that drew the crowds. Somewhere he could set up, without fear of discovery.

Jackson remembered Fairweather's house, how sterile the kitchen had seemed, no sign of clutter, unwashed pots and pans, dirty mugs and the chaos that usually follows a sudden death, even if orchestrated by a spouse. The only oddity had been the stack of paperwork.

What had Fairweather been sorting through? Why did he make a show of sweeping it aside?

Jackson closed his eyes, pictured the scene, dragging the

image on the top sheet of paper from the deep recesses of his memory.

Yes, Jackson thought darkly. *Gotcha.*

Extending from New Street right up to the offices of Birmingham City Council, the German Christmas Market was home to dozens of stalls selling steins of beer, frankfurters and glühwein, china and chocolate and all the other shit associated with the festive period. Believing one a front for Neon's work, Iris stopped by each, looking for the unusual, the stall that was not yet trading, the one with false walls and trailing wires. So far, she had found nothing.

Undeterred, Iris pushed, shoved and clubbed her way through the seething crowd of revellers against a tidal wave of noise care of an oompah band and a middle-aged bloke murdering a cover version of 'Driving Home for Christmas'. Iris didn't believe in hell – dead was dead – but if she did, this was it. There were too many people, too many crowd-control officers in orange jackets doing sod-all, too much noise and food and booze. She'd always preferred the early hours when it was quiet and now she knew why.

A coarse-featured kid of about seventeen smacked straight into her. A pint of lager shot all over her shoes.

'Watch my fucking drink,' he said, amped on alcohol.

It took everything she had not to pull out her blade and stick it in his fat gut. Better still: put a bullet in his brain.

Elbowing past, a torrent of abuse boxing her ears, she made for higher ground, up the wide stone steps, past the fountain towards the council offices.

Standing at the top, sixth sense told her that someone was

watching. She glanced around. The feeling left her as quickly as it had come. Not like her to be jumpy, she thought, training her gaze back on the scene below.

What was she missing, she thought, peering through the sea of heads and faces, every route obscured by families and folk standing around, blocking her view. Merry sodding Christmas.

82

God Bless America.

Bewitched by a carousel of colour, hypnotised by the thrum of lights, Gary marvelled at the magnificence of his work and homage to Las Vegas. What better theme to choose than the good old U.S. of A? The Yanks did everything bigger and better, full on and full throttle – no pun intended. He laughed at his own joke. Shame Naomi wasn't around to enjoy it.

For years he'd bought up old stock from manufacturing companies during the downturn. Served them right if they lacked the patience, the wit and the *vision* – ha ha – for neon's glorious comeback as an art form. Their loss his gain.

Fizzing with adrenaline, he charted a path from the entrance, the display deliberately designed as a trick of the light, to draw punters into a maze of shifting walls of colour, through a journey of visual references to speakeasy and baseball, Elvis and cowboys. A Cadillac suspended from the ceiling hung like a sword of Damocles.

His eyes scrolled across a farrago of vintage signs depicting hot dogs and milkshakes, palm trees and motels. Setting the noble face of a savage – native red Indian to the PC – next to the chick cheerleader with the cute knickers was, to his eyes, the perfect blend of old and new. And he simply *loved* the retro cinema and movie signs; so classy and kitsch. The folks outside would go mad for it. Naturally, he'd added a few touches of his own, the 'Cops Can Whistle Dixie' sign and the AK47s. A paean to the States wouldn't be complete without guns and bullets. *No, siree.*

At the beating heart of his exhibition, tableau, the big finish, showstopper, call it what you will, suckers, a full-sized replica of an electric chair. And the biggest dopamine rush of all, he'd surrounded it with enough neon flashing lights to send an epileptic into a fit. *Yee-hah*. Temporarily, he'd inserted a mannequin. He couldn't wait to replace it with the star of the show. *How's that for light in your darkness, detective?* Jackson would look so cool with a flashing Stetson above his head and a bullet hole through his brain.

83

Jackson barrelled through a sea of shoppers, past banks and building societies, and hurtled towards the pop-up shop embedded at the corner of New Street. Men sprang apart. Women grabbed kids. Despite a slew of hostile looks, nobody stood in his way. He knew what they were thinking: trouble. Crowds had an ugly, febrile energy. One shot fired. One false voice raised and, fearing a terrorist attack, the whole lot could stampede.

Outside the shop, every capillary in his brain constricted. Metal shutters at the double-fronted windows and a blackout blind at the door prevented entry. The only other entrance was via the side street. And Neon would be waiting.

But a ligature was no match for a man with a gun.

Jackson slipped round, found the door and tried it. Unlocked. He was meant to enter, he thought, recognising that it was a deliberate invitation prior to an ambush. Prepared, he reached for the Glock.

His heart beating a tattoo against his chest, he pushed open the door, stepped inside into semi-darkness. Some kind of storeroom, he thought, arm outstretched, inching along, weapon at the ready.

Breath on his skin, followed by a ring of cold steel pressed to his temple.

'Creating works of art wasn't the only skill I picked up in the States,' Fairweather said. 'Don't move, or I'll blast your head off.'

Jackson gauged his chances. Near enough to mount a defence, he might land one solid punch, but if he was going down he had to take Fairweather with him. Any fool could see that the odds weren't great.

Jackson winced as Fairweather drove the muzzle of the gun deeper into his skin. 'You think I care? Pull the trigger.'

'Aw, but then you'll never know the truth about me and Polly.'

Jackson exhaled. Was this the truth he'd always known, deep down? As much as it sickened him, he ached to know for certain about the nature of the relationship between his wife and the man they called Neon. He couldn't die without knowing, however awful the truth might be.

'Hand me your weapon,' Fairweather ordered.

Stonily, Jackson complied.

Fairweather tucked the Glock into the waistband of his trousers and, with the revolver trained on Jackson's head, walked around to face him.

'Better.' Fairweather's eyes glittered malice.

Jackson had no doubt about what awaited him in the next-door room. 'You and Polly,' Jackson prompted.

Fairweather cracked his neck from side to side as if

limbering up for a fight. 'I met Polly in the students' union. Maybe she told you about me.'

'She didn't.'

Fairweather stared. Jackson caught a trace of disappointment in his expression.

'No matter,' Fairweather said tritely. 'Brown-eyed and blonde, she wasn't as pretty then. A little too bland, if I'm honest. Not enough character in her features, still a work in progress. Anyways, she was such a sweetheart, I fell for her. We had quite the love affair.'

'No,' Jackson burst out. 'You had sex. That was all. Nothing more memorable than two kids fucking.'

Fairweather snickered. 'What is it with you guys? You think because I get a kick out of killing women, I know nothing about love? It's because I loved her that I do what I do.'

'Don't you dare blame her rejection for your monstrous actions,' Jackson snarled.

'I'm not *blaming* her,' Fairweather said, wide-eyed. 'I'm *grateful* to her. Polly was the start of my journey. It was inevitable that I'd track her down one day and show her what she was missing. And I was right about her. Her exterior beauty definitely caught up with her interior. She was quite welcoming when I knocked on your door.'

Bile flooded Jackson's throat. He swallowed, told himself that Fairweather was playing him, yet deep down knew it wasn't so. 'Don't kid yourself. She felt sorry for you.'

'I understand you wanting to believe that. The truth is she was glad of the company, pleased to hook up with an old friend. Oh, she told me about the long hours you worked, how you left her for days and weeks all alone. Who knows what might have happened if things had been different.'

Fairweather's voice was a blade carving deep into his soul.

'Doesn't matter how many women you kill,' Jackson said, 'how many police officers you seduce, you're one sad fuck-up who couldn't take no for an answer.' *Kill me, you bastard. Get it over with.* The sight of blood on the floor and the smell of gunshot hanging in the air when Browne and the team finally burst in would provide the S.I.O with the incontrovertible evidence he craved.

Fairweather's face darkened. Jackson locked on to his furious gaze, refusing to turn away. It was like being sucked into a deep pond of green slime.

'You're just like Canto,' Fairweather said. 'You think you're better than me.'

'I don't think. I know.' Jackson shot forward. Pain, white-hot and blinding, tore into the side of his face. His right eye felt as if it had been pushed out of its socket.

Stunned, he hardly noticed when Fairweather threw a hood over his head and plunged him into sudden suffocating darkness. Dense fabric encased his nose and mouth, threatening to cut off his air supply. He fought not to panic.

'Walk,' Fairweather said.

Finding it difficult to breathe, Jackson's hesitation cost him. Another river of pain pulsated through his temples, releasing a warm flow of blood, matting his hair.

'I said WALK.'

Any decision to fight or run was tempered by the gun in Fairweather's hand that now rested against the small of his back. Jackson could not imagine the agony he'd encounter should Fairweather decide his time was up.

Walking awkwardly in tandem, Jackson edged forward. Cold, he sweated neat hot fear that turned to rage. He did not want to die here and now by this maniac's hand.

The sound of a door opening, followed by a shove between the shoulder blades and he stumbled from one room into another. Fairweather, his breath like a flame on his back, seemed anxious to guide him to exactly the right spot for reasons Jackson dared not think about.

At last they stopped and the hood was whipped from his head. Peering through his one good eye, nausea attacked him in waves. Vision blurred, Jackson scrabbled for a mental foothold under a visual onslaught of light and dazzle from dozens of neon signs winking and blinking and mocking his helplessness. A crazy distillation of glare and colour, Jackson felt trapped in an illuminated inferno, nuclear in intensity. The effect was as if he'd dropped acid. Robbed of coherent thought, all he could do was gape blindly at an orgy of images. It was like staring at the sun before it explodes and destroys the earth.

'Glorious, isn't it? And, see, I've marked a spot just for you, right there in the middle.'

Jackson squinted, narrowed his gaze. Terror should have bitten chunks out of him. It did not; he felt inspired.

84

Iris had blagged her way into the live music stand. Not that difficult to infiltrate in between acts. If you looked like you belonged, people generally thought you did.

From the elevated height of the stage, she'd spotted Jackson looking like a man about to collect. Alarmed, she watched as he took an interest in the frontage of a pop-up shop and then shot around the corner into the neighbouring street. After that, she lost him.

Jumping down, she squirrelled her way through the crowds. There were more people than ever and, if the emotional temperature was measured in units of alcohol consumed, it had reached meltdown.

Finally, she reached the shop, which was closed. Rather than following Jackson's lead, she released her conceal and carry, blasted the lock on the door and burst in.

She'd anticipated glare and poster-paint bright colour. She'd expected to be punched in the head with it. Switched off, every sign and image was stripped of life and energy, reduced to bare bones, like the bodies of dozens of corpses drained of blood.

In the centre, Matt Jackson stood with a gun to his head. Fairweather had his free arm manacled around Jackson's throat in a stranglehold.

'Let him go,' Iris growled.

'I will if you drop your weapon.'

'Take the shot,' Jackson commanded.

He wants me to kill them both, Iris thought. One shot straight through the pair of them.

Iris got into the zone. In all her days, she'd never heard anyone welcome death the way Jackson did. Most men screamed. Some wet themselves, and worse. Jackson didn't look scared. He didn't look sad. He was calm. *Not normal*, she thought.

'Come on, Iris.' Jackson shouted. 'You kill me. You kill him. What are you waiting for?'

'Fucking shut it,' Fairweather raged.

Iris looked deeply into Jackson's eyes. He met hers with a steady, accepting gaze.

Trust me, she whispered under her breath and, without bottling the shot, she squeezed her finger and fired.

85

A shot rang out, high and wide. Glass from a thousand neon tubes showered down on Jackson, slicing his face and hands. Fairweather let out a scream and Jackson, blood streaming down his face, lurched backwards. Whiplashing the top of his skull into Fairweather's face, the pressure on his throat released. Fairweather's gun went spinning. More shards tumbled from the ceiling and Jackson ducked, covering his head with his lacerated hands.

Glancing over his shoulder, he saw Fairweather down and bleeding. He'd fallen backwards into the middle of the display, glass shredding his skin to pieces.

Death in her eyes, Iris started forward to finish him off at close range.

'Get back,' Jackson yelled, arm extended, palm flat up, like a man hopelessly trying to halt a speeding rhino.

Iris skidded down onto one knee.

Arcing his body, Jackson dived for the electrics. Hand hitting the switch, 240 volts detonated through Fairweather's nervous system.

Jackson watched in horror, saw it all in slow motion: spark, explosion, flame and fire.

Fairweather's bloodied body shook, limbs dancing as if he'd been raked with heavy machine gun fire. The smell of flesh frying and organs burning clawed at the back of Jackson's throat.

Counting to ten, Jackson switched off the current, ripped an extinguisher off the wall and doused the small fire that had erupted.

Iris stood mute and stunned.

'You didn't take the shot,' he said.

An approximation of a proper smile flashed across her face. It quickly changed. 'I suppose that means I won't get my money.'

'You will, Iris. I promise.'

'How quick can you let me have it?'

'I'll wire it as soon as I'm done here.' What a crazy conversation to be having in the circumstances, he thought. Jackson tipped his head in Fairweather's direction.

'What about him?' she asked.

'Leave him to me. I'll call it in, but you need to leave.' Shots fired could only elicit one response: the area in lockdown and flooded with armed police.

She stayed where she was.

'There's a way out of the back,' he told her.

'I know.'

'So go.'

'But what happens afterwards?'

'Afterwards?'

'You. Me.'

'I'll contact you when I'm ready, if you're OK.' They exchanged glances. She knew what he meant.

'Bye then,' she said.

'Goodbye, Iris.'

86

People ran. No more Christmas music. Warnings, issued from loudhailers, blasted across the square. *Stay back and walk slowly.*

Sliding in and out of the fleeing crowd with a sure fast tread, Iris obeyed. She wasn't like the rest: frightened and scared. She couldn't be happier. Matt Jackson's money was her last shot at a future and she'd secured it. Everything would be OK. Hope rising, she bounced along, slipped out her phone to call Mr Gudgeon and tell him the good news. After that, one last call to make.

A hard punch to her stomach almost took her breath away. Some twat had knocked into her. She didn't curse. She didn't care. Kept walking, clicking in numbers, despite a stitch in her side, like a bitch. Waiting for the call to connect, she moved up the steps towards the big Christmas tree to get a better signal. It felt like ascending Everest. She felt a bit strange and giddy, thoughts scattering. Must be the excitement, the satisfaction of a difficult job done.

A woman screamed. Stupid bitch. Why was she gawping like that? Feeling a little woozy, Iris staggered. People peeled away, pointing. Iris looked down. Blood. Blood everywhere. Alarmed, trying to make sense of it, she glanced over her shoulder and glimpsed the broad shoulders of a man in retreat. He had a full head of grey hair and wore a full-length leather coat. *Malaj.*

Clutching her stomach, trying to hold the wound together with one hand, she hobbled across the road, the sound of screeching brakes and a man shouting at the top of his voice punching her ears.

Desperate, Iris fumbled a text, sent it and retched. Her legs were chunks of concrete. She could see the bike, but it seemed a very long way away. Tired and weak, she tried to take a breath in, but it wouldn't come. Just a little bit further, she thought, until, falling to her knees, she heard someone say, 'Are you all right, love?'

She shook her head, helpless, blood staining her teeth. She could taste the wire in it. Tilting her head to a starlit sky, she saw how beautiful it was, brighter and more luminous than any neon light. She reached up to touch it and heard Jackson's voice and was glad that she'd spared him. Then she heard the sound of a child, followed by a tinkle of laughter. It wasn't hers.

As the stars began to fade, including her own, and the ground accelerated towards her, she thought: *What a fucking stupid way to die.*

87

Jackson had spent the night at Lloyd House, answering questions.

As soon as Cairns told him that a young woman had been stabbed, not two hundred yards from the shop, Jackson knew it was Iris.

'She had a blade and a gun on her, so obviously not your average law-abiding citizen,' Cairns said.

Jackson guessed any number of people could have been gunning for her. Hours later, when her death was established, he discovered that Enrik Malaj had evaded capture by the NCA.

Jackson emerged into a cold, grey morning and studied the text from Iris for the millionth time. Would this last communication reveal the mystery behind her life? Exhausted and sad, he got Cairns to drop him off next to his car.

'You did good,' he said. 'Polly would be proud of you, mate.'

Jackson's response was wan.

He chucked the address from Iris's text into his satnav and

drove slowly. He didn't know what to think, let alone expect, only that it was important to do as she asked.

Leaving the inner-city landscape behind, he found himself in the glossy suburbs of Solihull and, specifically, a leafy street in which a modest thirties-style detached house sat well back from the road.

He drew up outside and pressed the button on an entry intercom. A woman's voice, with a distinctive Midlands accent, answered. As soon as he revealed his name, the woman stalled, gave a little gasp and the gates swung open.

The front door was of solid wood with stained-glass panels on either side. He didn't knock. He waited. Jackson had carried out many visits to break the dismal news to relatives of the recently deceased and, deep inside, or by sixth sense, they always appeared to know before the words that would change their lives forever were uttered. It never lessened the shock or the pain, and the woman standing before him now was no exception.

She was as dark-skinned as Iris was pale. Neatly dressed in a blouse buttoned up to her neck and a skirt that clung to her generous hips, she wore flat shoes and stood tall. Tears pooled in her eyes and, despite projecting a picture of restrained grief, one escaped and slid down a cheek. 'You'd best come in,' she said simply.

Jackson followed her through a generous entrance hall and into a sitting room, tastefully furnished with drapes at the French windows and antique light fittings on the walls. He felt ashamed for contemplating that this kind of house with its quiet style and sophistication was outside the reach of someone like Iris.

'Please sit down, Mr Jackson.' She told him her name was Norma and indicated a sofa nearest the doors to the garden. He did. She sat down opposite, feet positioned just so, precision in her movements. 'Iris knew this day might come,' she began sadly. 'You can't work in that type of business without running a risk. Iris was always honest about that. Did she suffer?'

Norma clearly thought that Iris had died the way she lived, which was true, yet she'd made no mention of her illness, which Jackson found odd, although perhaps no more strange than referring to Iris's occupation as a contract killer as if it were like any other job. 'I don't believe so,' Jackson said, realising Norma's complicity. 'You two were close?'

'Like sisters. We were in care together. I left before her, but she looked me up later. She was in a fix, but the truth is she rescued me.' Her eyes drifted into the distance, the set of her mouth suggesting an unpleasant experience best not remembered.

'She lived here with you?' Jackson said, looking around.

'She visited. She thought it better that way. It was important to keep us separate. She didn't want to lead the enemy home, she used to say.'

'I understand.'

Norma smiled sadly. 'Except you don't.'

Jackson caught her level expression and leant back against the cushions, mind whirring. For a woman who was on her last legs, Iris had seemed fit enough to kill when it counted. She rarely appeared to be in physical pain. He should have worked it out before. 'It's you, isn't it? Iris needed the money for your treatment.'

Norma stood up. 'Come with me,' she said.

Perplexed, Jackson followed Norma out into the hall and up a wide staircase. She paused outside one of the bedroom doors and tapped lightly. There was no reply.

Norma looked meaningfully at Jackson and pressed an index finger to her lips. He nodded back that he understood the need for silence.

Lightly turning the knob, she pushed and let the door swish across the carpet. Inside: an array of medical equipment. In the middle of the room, a double bed in which a girl, around fifteen years of age, lay asleep. Her hair was chemo-short and blonde, the paleness of her skin due to illness, Jackson thought.

'Meet Edie,' Norma whispered. 'Iris's daughter and the centre of her universe.'

88

Murderous and secretive, fearless and protective, just some of the descriptions Jackson used to sum up Iris and yet she remained as elusive in death as she had in life. For Norma, to whom Iris had fled after she'd been raped, she was a saviour. For Edie, she was simply Mum, who had a weird job that often took her away from home. Jackson couldn't condone Iris's actions and never would, but, months on from his visit to the little house in the suburbs, he thought he had a better understanding.

Since Edie's admission to a hospital in Heidelberg for experimental treatment, for which Jackson had paid, he had sold his house and set up a temporary home there. He and Norma had talked most days, mostly about Edie, who seemed to accept the death of her mother with the same silent stoicism she displayed towards her illness. 'It will be difficult for her later when she has time to think, when she feels she has a future once more, but one without her mum,' Norma had said perceptively. 'That's when we need to watch out, and when she'll need the greatest care.'

Edie's physical progress was good. The word 'remission'

was used and it was hoped that, if things continued, she would recover enough to go back to her studies. 'Iris was adamant about that,' Norma told him one warm day in April. They were sitting outside a cafe close to the hospital. 'She swore by education. It was one of her regrets that she hadn't had a proper crack at it.'

Jackson nodded in wonder. God knew what kind of life Iris would have carved if she had.

He sipped his coffee, thinking how far he'd come since those early dark days. The cost of treatment formidably high, he wasn't sure what he'd do when the money ran out. Suicide no longer featured so heavily in his thoughts. With Edie and Norma in his life, he had found a reason to carry on. Ironically, his gratitude for this slow change of heart went to a woman who'd once been prepared to kill him.

Acknowledgements

All writers write in isolation but a fleet of important others carries out the real 'hard stuff'. Firstly, my deepest thanks go to Broo Doherty, my agent, for her advice, diplomacy and determination – not necessarily in that order! Secondly, a huge thank you to Ben Willis for believing in me, championing the work (and some) and for pushing me to exceed what I thought were my limits. What genuine fun it's been and here's to the next time.

On the Orion team, thanks to superb copy editor, Jade Craddock, for polishing the script and weeding out my mistakes. Many thanks, too, to all those involved in selling the rights and spreading the word.

Graham Bartlett, former Chief Superintendent, who advised on some of the procedural aspects of the police investigation, deserves special recognition. Thanks, Graham, for your approachability, patience and humour – any errors made are mine alone. Finally, my thanks to David Canter, the UK's leading criminologist, for his excellent piece on 'Las Vegas' in 'Mapping Murder'. It sparked a fair number of ideas.